"You'd laugh at me!" Nicholas seemed to choke on his rage.

"No, by God!" he shout

The laughter froze dangerous glitter in his e reached out for her and the soft flesh of her arm.

She fought him but in his remorseless grip she found herself helpless as a baby. He reached upward with his free hand and snatched a riding crop from a wall bracket.

"Don't!" Angel's voice came whisperingly from a suddenly dry throat. "Don't whip me! Please! No! No!"

Unheeding, he spun her round, his hand tearing the fragile fabric of her gown. He did not see the pale, seamed back thus exposed; he saw nothing through the mist of rage before his eyes. "Damn you, you whore! You guttersnipe!"

The hand holding the riding crop lifted, descended; but Angel, with a strength born of terror, twisted in his grasp and took the blow full upon her face.

"My darling!" The words were torn from him as madness receded and Nicholas stared at the great gash the lash's weighted tip had opened on her cheek. "Oh, my little one, my darling. Forgive me!"

NOVELS BY
CONSTANCE GLUYAS

King's Brat
My Lady Benbrook

PUBLISHED BY
WARNER BOOKS

THE
KING'S
BRAT

by

Constance Gluyas

WARNER BOOKS

A Warner Communications Company

For Alice's "Jim"—
Leonard Henry Arthur Dixon

THE KING'S BRAT

A LIGHT RAIN, THE AFTERMATH OF THE storm, fell from the sullen April sky and then, as if a tap had been abruptly turned off, it ceased; the clouds, emptied of their burden, scudded in limp dingy puffs before a briskly pursuing wind, leaving in their wake thin streamers of clear, cold blue.

Angel Dawson, lying on the dirty malodorous straw covering the rough wooden planked floor of the lumbering prison cart, felt the first weak rays of the sun touching her bruised face. She moved cautiously and stole a quick look at the two men seated on a wooden bench above her. They sprawled at their ease, their feet resting heavily upon her body.

The smaller of the two men noticed the movement. "Ah," he said, grinning down at her. "You've woke up, me dear, eh? 'Bout bloody time 'n' all." He turned, nudging his heftier companion. "Ain't she somethin', Tom? I always been partial ter red hair. An' as for them eyes o' hers! Color o' viol'ts, they are, I'll take me bloody oath on it." He cleared his throat noisily. "Let's you 'n' me have a bit o' sport 'fore we hand her over. It'd be a reward for our trouble, eh?"

The other man studied the girl with cold expressionless eyes. "Gutter rat, she is," he pronounced. "Whore 'n' all, I shouldn't wonder." He shook his head warningly. "It jus' ain't healthy ter fool with the likes o' her, not 'less you're a-wantin' a dose o' the pox. Mos' o' these whores're lousy with it, take me word."

Angel listened, dully uncaring, shivering convulsively as the bleak wind penetrated the rents in her thin brown cotton gown. The rain-soaked cloth clung to her immature figure like an icy second skin; and the skirt, weighting her legs with its sodden folds, set her teeth to chattering. Pain stabbed through her jaw, and she raised a tentative hand, her exploring fingers touching the sore place cautiously. Blood from her split lip had dribbled down her chin and had dried there in a brittle crust. Her jawbone was bruised but not, she decided, broken.

Another gust of wind blew her long, tangled red-gold hair across her face. Brushing it to one side, she turned her head and for the first time looked directly at the men seated above her. The small man, meeting her furious hating eyes, chuckled hoarsely. "Look at the way she's a-glarin'," he said, prodding her lightly with his foot. "Like ter get at us, wouldn' you, darlin'? What'd you do, use them long claws o' yours on us?"

She stared into the narrow pocked face bent above her. "Bastard!" she spat out the word bitterly. "If I c'd get me han's on you, I'd—I'd show you! I'd rip out your stinkin' guts 'n' choke you with 'em! I'd—" she broke off with a gasping sob, as his heavily booted foot kicked savagely into her stomach.

"Oh, would you!" His foot drove into her stomach again, his laughter rising above her shrill scream of agony. "Respec's what you got ter learn," he shouted. "Respec' for your betters." He waved his foot menacingly before her flinching face. "Ain't that right, girl?"

She turned her head away, closing her eyes against the welling tears. "Yes," she whispered. "Yes! Yes! Yes!"

The cart lurched, and the man turned his head,

scowling at the small urchin who was inexpertly manipulating the reins of the tired horse. With a curse, he brought his attention back to the girl. "You lef' out somethin', ain't you?" he snapped. "Seems ter me like you still ain't got no proper respec'. You says 'Sir' when you speaks ter me. Un'erstan'?"

"Sir!" she brought the word out unsteadily as she tried to control her strangling sobs. "Y—yes, sir."

Satisfied, he settled back on the bench. "That's better, wench." Ignoring the other man, he folded his arms and relapsed into a brooding silence.

She forced herself to lie still, biting hard on her lip to stifle her cries. Pain raged through her body, and already the manacles cutting into her wrists had rubbed her flesh raw. But greater by far than her pain was the black, bitter tide of terror engulfing her.

Never before in her sixteen years of life had she felt herself to be so utterly, so completely alone. Yet, she reminded herself, she had always been alone, had always fended for herself. But it had been different; it was being alone but not lonely—it was being free, not chained up like an animal as she was now. Without a home or parents to care for her, she had begged her food or stolen it; she had slept wherever she chanced to be—in the shadow of a doorway; in a livery stable, snuggled in the warm straw, if she happened to be lucky; or curled warily, alert as a cat sensing danger, on the uneven cobbles of the streets.

She had feared nothing then. She was one of the band of homeless waifs who called the London streets their home, and it held a certain distinction to belong to this fraternity. Even the hawkers gave the waifs a grudging respect; it was based mainly on fear of reprisals if they did not, but it was nevertheless respect. More devils than angels, the street urchins held themselves apart; they ran in gangs, and an outsider was never, under any circumstances, admitted to their ranks.

Bitterly, Angel thought of the act of bravado that had got her thrown into the prison cart. Dared by her companions and knowing that to refuse that dare meant certain ostracism, she had attempted to rob a drunken passerby. He was old and fat, his wig awry, the pale satin of his breeches stained with wine. His heavy purse had actually been in her hands, but Angel's usual caution had deserted her. Contemptuously, she had turned her back on him. One hand on her hip, the other hand insolently swinging the purse, she had swaggered triumphantly toward her waiting friends.

But the man was neither as old as she had supposed him to be nor as drunk, and she was unprepared for the swiftness of his reaction. His heavy hand clamped down bruisingly on her shoulder. The waifs saw and promptly scattered. Deserted, Angel tried to fight him. His pudgy fingers bit into her flesh. For all the attention he paid to her frantic pleas for mercy, he might have been deaf. He dragged her along, his small truculent eyes as hard as stones in his heavy face. Finding the authorities, he had handed her over. Retribution had been swift; she was manacled and flung into the stinking prison cart. Her captor, a smile of satisfaction on his thick lips, had turned away and resumed his deceptively stumbling progress.

God! God! They were taking her to Newgate Prison! *Newgate!* The nightmare place where, after a long, agonizing time, her mother had mercifully succumbed to a jail fever; the place where her sister, Jane, jailed with their mother, had finally been driven insane by the horror about her. Jane had been sent to Bedlam Asylum, and Angel thought that if she still lived she must have become one of the poor lunatics who were daily exhibited in their swinging cages for the edification of the crowds of visitors.

It was one of the sights of London, the Bedlam lunatics in their cramped wooden cages, and a favorite sport to poke at them with sticks or to shower them with stones, rotting vegetables, or any other refuse available. Tormented beyond endurance, the mindless creatures, screaming and tearing frantically at the bars of their cages, provided the staring crowd with a full measure of enjoyment. Sometimes, though, the visitors, perhaps remembering their own loved ones, would be moved to a shamefaced compassion and instead of stones, they would toss in their leftover scraps of food. Laughing, their shame miraculously fled, they would crowd closer about the cages, watching with fascinated interest and soothed conscience as the lunatics snatched with avid hands at the bounty. Cramming it into their mouths, they gulped it down like the starving animals they so closely resembled.

In the hope of recognizing her sister, Angel had sometimes visited Bedlam Asylum. She had stared intently at each gaunt yellow face, had looked deeply into burning eyes that peered at her through wildly matted hair. She had found in them all a terrible similarity. That similarity was not to be borne, so, little by little, she had convinced herself that Jane was dead.

Her memory of Jane was vague; she had been very young at the time of her sister's imprisonment—her mother she did not remember at all—but sometimes that vague memory would show her somebody whom she thought of as Jane; a somebody with soft white skin, soothing hands, and big, gentle blue eyes. No! Jane could not be one of those caged creatures! She could not! She must be dead!

And now she, too, like Jane, was on her way to Newgate! What if she ended as Jane had done! What if she became one of those pitiful creatures! "No!" The word echoed inside her, a silent, fierce protest that welled from a source of courage she had not known she possessed. "Damn 'em! I ain't goin' ter let 'em do it ter me! Them swine won' crush Angel Dawson! Never! Never! I'll show 'em, I will. I'll show 'em all!"

The straw rustled beneath her as she moved her position. Stealing a quick fearful look at the two men, she was relieved to see them sleeping; their heads nodding and their feet, clear of her body now, swaying with the motion of the cart.

As quietly as possible, she began edging away. Reaching the side of the cart, she managed to pull herself into a sitting position. The familiar streets of London! A choking lump rose in Angel's throat. Would she ever roam those familiar streets again—or would she, like other poor wretches had been known to do—rot in Newgate for the rest of her life? The chill wind blew through her hair and dried the tears on her cheeks; it brought in its train a thick, overpowering stench of overflowing gutters. Angel scarcely noticed it. The odor was for her, as for most Londoners, an integral part of the city—the dreadful stench of the streets.

The horse, obeying the urchin's tug on his reins, turned a corner, his great hooves striking sparks from the cobbles. Head bent, the horse dragged the cart past a row of dingy-looking houses. Now that she was in danger of losing her freedom forever, Angel stared with yearning eyes at the ancient dwellings of chipped timber and scaling plaster. The houses leaned closely together—so closely that they shut out the sunlight and left the street in perpetual shadow—giving, too, the impression that they might at any moment topple and crash into the street. To Angel, who had never known a home, the houses spelled warmth, friendship—the love of a family. Perhaps one day she'd live in a house like that, Angel thought, her mouth wistful, but it wasn't likely. Newgate, it seemed, was to be her home from now on.

Her brooding thoughts were scattered by a shriek. Angel turned her head quickly and saw a child come darting from a side alley, closely pursued by an older girl. Recognizing them, Angel sat up straighter. The little girl with the bobbing, honey-colored curls was her friend, Nell Gwynne; the older girl was Nell's sister, Rose.

"I ain't comin' home," Nell shouted in her clear, carrying voice. Paying no attention to the oncoming cart, she stopped running and swung round to face her sister. "' 'N' you can' make me, Rose!" she added belligerently.

Rose stopped a short distance from the child. "Do like I say," she said rather wearily. She pushed her wind-blown hair away from her face with thin, nervous fingers. "Come on now, Nell. This bloody win's perishin' me. I don' wan' ter stan' about in the cold arguin' with you, you nasty little cow! 'Sides, if you don' get on home, Ma'll skin you alive."

"Ma!" Nell tossed her head scornfully. "I ain't afraid o' that ol' flea bag. You c'n tell Ma as Nell Gwynee'll come when it bloody well suits her ter come."

Laughing derisively, Nell sprang into an agile somersault, showing, as she did so, a pair of thin but well-shaped legs, bare buttocks, and a grimy petticoat—once white—with a torn lace frill. "There," Nell said, coming upright. "Now let's see you do it, ol' Rosie."

"You—you—" Rose broke off. "Why, you bloody little hussy!" she went on, her voice scandalized. "You ain't even dressed decen'! I'm goin' ter tell Ma on you, an' don' you go thinkin'—" Again she broke off. "Nell!" she shrieked. "Get out the way o' that cart! Come on, it's nigh on top o' you!"

The small driver glared at them. "Get out o' me way, trollop!" he shouted at Nell. Self-importantly, he spat into the street. "Go on, you, get a-hoppin' there!"

Nell returned the glare. "Who you callin' a trollop?" she screamed at him, her face flushing scarlet with fury. "Don' you go callin' me no names, you bleedin' little snot-nosed sod! You ain't nothin' but a bandy little bugger what thinks as he's ever'body jus' 'cause—" She stopped, her blue eyes widening in amazement. *"Angel!"*

"You ain't a-dreamin' it, Nell," Angel shouted above the squeaking of the slow-turning wheels. "I forked a purse off o' a fat toff an' the bastard had me nobbled." The men behind her woke suddenly. Angel closed her lips firmly, shaking her head in warning to Nell.

Rose Gwynne, her face blank with shock, came to stand beside Nell. "That ain't Angel Dawson, is it?" she said. "Nell! Surely that ain't Angel Dawson in the prison cart?"

Coming out of her temporary paralysis, Nell cast her an impatient look. "O' course it's her, you daft bitch!" Nell, her eyes blazing with excitement, pushed Rose to one side. "Hi!" she shouted, running after the cart. "Hi!"

"Nell!" Rose began running, too. "Come back!"

Catching up with the cart, Nell grasped at the back and swung herself upward. "You let her out o' this bleedin' cart, see!" Nell demanded of the two scowling men.

"Get off!" The big man, his face menacing, tried to pry her fingers loose.

"I won't!" Defiantly, Nell clung tenaciously. "You let Angel go! She ain't never done nothin' bad, you damned ol' cods' heads!"

The big man shoved at her again. "Askin' for a good bashin', you are, an' I'm the one ter give it ter you!"

"You jus' try it, you bastard!" Infuriated, Nell raked at his hand with her sharp nails.

"Ow!" He withdrew his bleeding hand hastily and examined it with anxious eyes. "Look, Jim," he said, holding the hand out for the other man's inspection. "See what the bloody cow's done ter me hand!"

The small man shrugged unsympathetically. His eyes were on Rose.

"Do like what they tol' you, Nell," Rose panted, pulling entreatingly at her sister's flying, skimpy skirt.

The small man glared at Rose balefully. "You'd better make her min' you," he snapped. " 'Less you wan' us to

16

take her an' clap her in Newgate along with the other 'un?"

"Don't do that, sir!" Rose cried, shrinking before his glare. "I'll see as she behaves!" Exerting all the strength in her skinny arms, she pulled Nell, still wildly resisting, from the cart. "Shut up!" Rose said desperately, struggling to hold on to her. "You lis'en ter me for once in your life, Nelly Gwynne, an' jus' bloody shut up!"

"Don' you min' 'bout them swine, Angel!" Nell shouted, ignoring Rose's efforts to silence her. "We'll get you out, somehow, so's you can see our bonny King come home!"

Angel watched as Rose dragged the struggling Nell away. Yes, the King was coming, Angel thought. Fightin against tears, she looked away. But she wouldn't be there to see him; she'd be locked away, forgotten.

She looked warily at the two men. They had lapsed back into conversation and appeared, for the moment at least, to have forgotten her. Fighting fear, Angel thought over all she had heard about Charles Stuart. If she thought hard enough about him, she decided, perhaps she could forget she was on her way to Newgate. Concentrating fiercely, she remembered that Charles Stuart's father had lost his head on the block. The martyred Charles had been a good king, some said; and it was generally agreed that whatever the late king's sins or graces, he had been preferable to the hated Cromwell. And now, at long last, his son, exiled for so long, was coming home. Charles Stuart would be Charles II of England. Under his rule England would begin to live again, and the dark shadow Cromwell had thrown over the land would vanish.

"Country's ruled by fools," the smaller of the two men said, the loudness of his voice capturing Angel's attention. "Aye," he went on belligerently, "an' it's them fools what expec' the like o' you 'n' me ter respec' 'em."

"Country ain't ruled at all, is it?" the other man answered gloomily. He shook his head portentously. "There's ol' Cromwell a-lyin' in his grave, an' it do seem as we had 'nough with him. We don' need this other'n a-comin' here ter mess thin's up again. Foreigner 'n' all, he is," he added darkly. "It jus' don' seem right."

The little man, taking exception to these remarks, said heatedly, "That's bloody well 'nough out o' you! Our Charlie ain't no foreigner, an' don't you think it!"

" 'Course he is. His mother's French, ain't she?"

"That ain't got nothin' ter do with it." The little man looked at him contemptuously. "Frenchie blood's weak, see? It don't count none. It's only the good English blood what's goin' ter count. Make a right lovely king, will our Charlie, 'n' he'll be the savin' of England 'n' all, you jus' mark me words."

The big man sniffed disparagingly. "Him 'n' his women!" he said broodingly. "I heard as he always has 'em. What I say is as it's a proper ol' scandal ter have the likes o' him for a king!"

"Shut your mouth!" the little man snapped. He waved a clenched fist under the other's nose. "I don' wan' ter hear nothin' more from you!"

Bored, the big man thrust his fist away. "So long's he don' bring his Frenchie ways here, him 'n' me won' fall out. But I don' min' tellin' you it fair—" he broke off as the cart lurched to a stop before the gray bulk of New-gate Prison.

Angel's mouth went dry. For a long moment she sat perfectly still, then as her terror mounted to frenzy, she struck out at the men with her manacled hands. "No! No!" she screamed. "I won' go in there!" Tears streamed down her face. "Please!" she began to beg them. "Oh, please! I won' never do nothin' bad no more! Let me go! Please let me go!"

"Shut your mouth, wench!" The little man seized her hair and twisted it brutally. It needed the two of them to control her, for Angel, half out of her mind, was imbued with an unexpected strength. She was a snarling, fighting animal, and when finally they dragged her from the cart, her body was as rigid as wood. Mercifully, her mind went blank; her eyes unseeing, she sagged brokenly between them. Only the smallest of whimpers escaped her lips as she was half-carried toward the great scarred doors of Newgate Prison.

THE PRISON GUARD'S HAND WAS BROAD AND freckled, the back tufted with sandy hair. Angel, aware once more but numbed with despair, watched as the guard recorded her name in the tattered prison book with a quill clutched between spatulate fingers. *Angel Dawson,* he wrote laboriously. *April 30th 1660.* Finished, he flung the quill down with a grunt of satisfaction and looked up at the two men.

"Well, what now?" he demanded. "Been paid, ain't you?" He jerked his thumb in the direction of the door. "Get out!"

The men nodded. Without another glance at the girl, they departed.

"Well, now," the guard said softly. "So you're Angel, eh?" His hard blue eyes ran over her appraisingly. "Funny name, that. You don' look like no Angel, not with that red hair 'n' all." His grin widened. "You'd be bad off in this place if you was 'n angel, an' that's a fac'." He waited for her to speak; then, as she remained silent, he went on. "Ain't no need ter be 'fraid o' me, you know. Jim Gibbons, that's me name," he said, tapping his chest for emphasis. "You'll fin' ol' Jim c'n be a good frien' to them what has the money ter pay for me good will." He stared into her white face. "You lis'nin' ter me?" She nodded, and he went on suggestively. "I bet you got lots'er money hid away—'nough o' it ter make Jim real frien'ly."

"I got no money," she said, staring at him with hopeless eyes.

His eyes narrowed. "Now, now," he said, a hard note creeping into his voice. "It won' pay you none ter try foolin' ol' Jim." His evil grin returned, and he began rubbing his hands together briskly. "Whore, ain't you? Ah, but whores is sly bitches! Always got money hid, they have."

Her dulled eyes flashed into life. "Don' you go callin' me that! I ain't a whore! I ain't!"

"Soon will be, then," he prophesied. "Won' take you no time 'tall." He scratched his stubbled chin thoughtfully. "C'n get money, though, can' you? Garnish, that's what we calls it. You got ter have garnish if you wants ter live nice in Newgate, see? I expec' you got frien's, ain't you? There must be them as'd be willin' ter pay so's you wouldn' have ter go without your comforts, eh?"

Friends? She looked away from him. None of her friends had money. There was blind Betty, of course, the old woman who sold herrings on the corner of Field Street. She had money—but she hated the waifs who made almost daily raids on the hawkers. Unlike the others, blind Betty was not in the least afraid of the gutter gang and would curse them venomously in her shrill, quavering voice. Perhaps Ben? There were some who swore that Ben had a fortune hidden away in his rat-infested home, but Angel had never been able to bring herself to believe it. Ben, dour and unsmiling to neighbors and customers alike, sold fruit and vegetables. Perhaps it was because he kept himself to himself and had never indulged, as did the others, in drunken carousal, and furthermore had never been known to buy the friendly pint of ale, that the gossip about his fortune had started. Angel's heart sank. It was useless to think of Ben. There was Meg, of course; she was always ready to help. Still, big, good-natured Meg, however willing she might be, made a very meager living hawking fresh milk and custards. Without a man—and having five children to support—she was unlikely to have money to spare. No, Angel thought. There was no one she could turn to.

"Well?" the guard said sharply. "You thought o' someone what'd help you?"

She looked at him, hating his pale, sly face, the untidy thatch of hair, and the twitching muscle at the side of his mouth. "No," she said, shaking her head. "I tol' you I can' get nothin', an' I don' know no one as'd len' me any."

His mouth tightened in anger. "In that case," he growled, his face flushing to a mottled red, "you can' blame Jim none for what'll happen ter you." He pointed to a bench nearby. "Sit there," he ordered her curtly. "I got ter shackle you."

Trembling, she sank down on the bench. Watching him make his leisurely selection from the shackles festooning the walls, her heart felt as if it would burst with terror. "Y—you ain't goin' ter put th—them thin's on m—me, are you?" she faltered as he came toward her, the heavy iron fetters dangling from his hand.

He bent, lifting her foot. "That I am," he said, stroking her ankle with his rough fingers. "Seems a proper crime ter do it ter you 'n' all. Them pretty ankles did ought ter be showed off, not hid."

"Then don' do it ter me. Please!" she begged. "I won' never be able ter walk in 'em!" He chuckled, shaking his head as if in mock reproof. Angel started, gasping uncontrollably as the iron cuffs snapped shut. Cruelly tight, they held her ankles as if in a vise, bruising the bone and gouging deeply into her flesh.

"No!" she screamed wildly, her heart thundering with panic. "I can' bear no more! Take 'em off! Please! Please!"

"I'll take 'em off when you comes to me with money in your han'," he assured her, smiling blandly. "Fit you with lighter shackles, then. Why, love you! You won' even know as you've got 'em on." He winked at her. "You're goin' ter fin' that ol' Jim's got a big heart. But Jim's poor, see? He's got ter have a bit o' money ter jingle, ain't he?"

Her hatred of him welled up. "Swine!" she shouted, lost to all reason. "Rotten dirty bastard!"

He looked at her for a long moment, his eyes expressionless. Almost casually, he lifted his hand and brought it crashing against her cheek. "That there," he said softly, "is jus' a little bit o' a lesson so's you'll 'member that Jim don' like ter be called names. It don' never pay to go hurtin' Jim's feelin's, an' 's long as you keeps it in min' you'll be all right, see?"

A blackness seemed to have descended upon her. Her ears were ringing and there was a brassy taste of blood in her mouth. Words that were soothing, pacifying, formed in her mind, but even as she thought of them she rejected them. Let him kill her—she wanted him to! Why not? She'd be better off dead! "A pox on you, you bloody scum!" she brought the words out hoarsely. "Damn you! Damn you! I hopes you bleedin' well rot in hell!"

"Ah! You done it now, you have!" His hard hands jerked her to her feet, his fingers biting into her shoulders. Spinning her round and, with one hand in the small of her back, he shoved her violently toward a great locked door. Unable to keep her balance, she fell heavily. "Clumsy," he said. "I do hopes you ain't hurt yourself, dear."

She felt the iron biting into her ankles, sending burning arrows of pain along her legs; she looked up at him.

He stood over her, legs apart, his hands on his hips. She tried to speak, fumbling for words of defiance, but her tongue felt too heavy, too thick.

He smiled down at her. "Spirited, ain't you?" he said, seeing the hatred blazing in her eyes. "I likes that, I do. There ain't no fun in breakin' 'em tame 'uns."

Abruptly, she recovered the use of her tongue. "You ain't goin' ter break me!" she shouted.

" 'Course I am," he said matter-of-factly. "Jus' take a bit longer with you, that's all." Bending, he grasped her shoulders and dragged her to her feet. "Pity you ain't got sense ter go along with all o' that spirit," he said, his face close to hers. "Now Jim's goin' ter have ter do somethin' about all o' them mean thin's what you called him, ain't he? You knows what I'm goin' ter have ter do, don' you?"

"No." She shook her head. "No, I don' know, an' I don' bloody care!"

"You will, darlin'," he said, his voice silky. "I promises as you'll care. There ain't a bit o' fun in bein' lashed —especial' when you're boun' ter a post an' ain't got no clothes on. Hurts, it do, hurts cruel bad, an' it'll grieve me ter do it ter you. I tol' you 'bout me tender heart, eh? Still 'n' all, got ter be done, an' never min' 'bout me heart." He thrust her away, remarking almost amiably as he fitted a key in the lock and threw open the door, "Floggin'll come later; I wan' you ter meet your little playmates now." He pushed her through the door into a dark corridor. "Pretty lot, they are," he went on. "You're goin' ter be ever so fond o' 'em."

He went past her, striding easily; she shuffled painfully after him, the length of chain between the anklets dragging noisily behind her. The incredible reek of Newgate rushed upon her, assaulting her senses. Instinctively she stopped short. It swirled about her in a thick, nauseating wave, pressing upon her like a smothering blanket,

24

driving the color from her face, and bringing a rush of bile to her throat.

The guard, stopping too, watched her intently. "What's up, dearie?" he drawled. "Ain't you feelin' well, then?"

She turned her white horrified face to him. "What's that smell?" she whispered. "What's that bloody awful stink?"

"Don' you like it, dearie?" he said, amused.

She retched. "I never smelt nothin' like that before!" She pressed a trembling hand to her mouth.

"You mus' be hard ter please if you don' like it. That's special, that is." He inhaled deeply, his malicious eyes on her face. "That there smell is Newgate perfume. Good 'n' strong today. Always is especial' sweet on Fridays, though," he chuckled, " 'cause that's when the hangman cuts down them bodies what he's had a-swingin' all week. The bugger don't half enjoy hisself 'n' all—a-cuttin' the heads off 'em 'n' a-boilin' of 'em up."

"Shut up!" Angel looked at him with loathing. "I don' want to be tol' no more 'bout it."

"Gallows meat stew, we calls it," he continued, ignoring her distress. "Ain't half tasty 'n' all." His mood suddenly changing, he shoved her roughly. "Come on, you. I got me job ter do. If I was ter let you stan' 'bout a-sniffin' an' enjoyin' o' yourself, I'd have all them others a-beggin' o' me ter let 'em do the same."

She said nothing and after a moment he went on. She followed him, hobbling along a bewildering maze of dark corridors, descending innumerable steeply twisting staircases that led into the very bowels of the prison.

Finally, when she felt she could drag herself no further, he came to a halt before a rusted iron door. "This here's your new home," he said, detaching a key from the ring at his belt. "Opens up on heaven that door do. It's cozy 'n' all—what with all o' them nice ladies jus' a-dyin' ter welcome you." He held up the key, his narrowed eyes mocking her. "Can' wait, can you, ter see for yourself how eager them ladies is ter greet you?" He chuckled low in his throat. "You're goin' ter be very happy here." He waved the key before her eyes. "But you're a-wantin' me ter let you in, ain't you?"

"Yes," she said, making a pathetic attempt at defiance. "Go on, then, whyn't you open up? Dyin' for a peep at me little nest, I am."

"Right." He slid the key into the lock. "Me ol' ma was always a-tellin' me as it ain't p'lite ter keep a lady waitin'. But 'fore I turns this key I'll give you 'nother chance ter think o' someone what'd be willin' ter pay for your comforts. Down here's what's known as the Common Side." He made a sweeping gesture with his hand. "Scum o' the gutters is in this here cell an' in them others. Don' seem right, do it," he drawled, "ter go puttin' a gran' lady like yourself in with 'em? But there, I'm always gettin' took advantage of. Ol' Jim's soft heart'll get him into trouble some day."

"That'd be a bloody shame," Angel said thickly. "Better open up 'fore that heart o' yours gets to bleedin'. It's like I tol' you before, I ain't got money—can' get none."

"You sure o' that?" he persisted. "Money's what'll get you better quarters. A room o' your own an' food what's sent in from the outside. Cooked good, it is—it ain't like them pig slops what we serves ter the paupers."

Her mouth trembled. "Leave me be!" she shouted, her voice shrill with despair. "I tol' you an' tol' you I can' do nothin'! Maybe you gone an' mistook me for a bleedin' duchess or somethin'."

"Jim give you a chance," he said curtly. "You don' get 'nother." He turned the key with a vicious twist. There was a choking sensation in Angel's throat as a thrust of his shoulder set the door creaking slowly open. Almost instantly, an uproar came from within; a screaming babble of voices and, rising high above the babble, a demented howling akin to that of an animal in pain.

"Here's a new 'un for you, me pretty dears," Gibbons shouted. His hand clamped hard on Angel's shoulder. "Give me a lot o' nasty talk, did this 'un. Know what that means, ladies, don' you?"

"Floggin'! Floggin'!" a voice screamed above the rest. "The new bait's goin' ter get a skin-strippin'!" Then, like a shrill chant, they all joined in: "Floggin'! Floggin'! Floggin'!"

"That's right," Gibbons shouted back. He turned his head and looked at Angel. "This bait'll get a skin-strippin' she won' never forget," his soft voice was for Angel's ears alone. "And that," he added, "I promises." His taunting smile vanished. "Here she comes, ladies!" he roared. He gave her a hard shove. "Get in there, you bleedin' little cow!" Grinning, he watched for a moment her frantic efforts to keep her feet. Then, stepping back quickly, he slammed the door shut behind her.

Angel's weighted ankles were too weak to support her. They gave beneath her, and she flung out her hands in a vain attempt to save herself. She crashed heavily to her knees, and fiery pain shot through them. Beneath her flattened hands she felt the cold sliminess of the floor; she jerked them quickly away, and the dim light showed her the sticky gray mass adhering to her fingers. Shuddering with loathing, she wiped them clean on the edge of her gown. Then painfully, clawing at the wall for aid, she hauled herself to her feet.

Ominous silence surrounded her. In renewed terror Angel swung round, her chains clanking. What seemed like a hundred women crouched before her. Their humped forms were shapeless wild-haired blobs; only their eyes glimmered in the half light, watching her intently. The flickering flame of candles set in iron brackets high up on the walls played over these creatures with a weirdly distorting effect.

Most of the women were naked, others clad in a few rags. Open running sores showed on faces and breasts. All were crammed into a cell that was perhaps twenty feet square. Much later, when the first keen edge of Angel's terror had dulled, she found that she had only thirty companions.

It was an effort to look away from her silent audience. There was something hypnotic about their fixed regard, and her flesh crawled with a sense of her own danger.

She stared about her with burning hopeless eyes. Dark walls rose high about her, so high that the ceiling seemed lost in the gloom; they gleamed with the moisture that, first collecting in little pools, constantly trickled downward. Windows that were little more than barred slits were propped open with wooden wedges. The thin drift of air they admitted made scarcely an impact on the breath-catching stench. It seemed to rise in thick waves. Her stomach turned over, but she controlled it with a deep, steadying breath. She looked up at the windows again. They were placed above the iron brackets that held the candles. There would be no chance for clutching hands to reach upward to grab at the bars, no relief from this dark hole in a view of the dim courtyard.

There was a shuddering all through her, and she wanted to scream in despair. She was one of these creatures now. She'd never be free again! Never feel the rain on her face, the sun warming her body! She was no longer Angel Dawson. Oh God! Was she to be locked away forever with these diseased and terrible women?

She looked down at the floor. Through a shifting haze of tears she saw the great blobs of spittle streaking its rough surface. Near to her feet was a greenish-yellow pool of vomit; it must have been there for many weeks, for it look solidified, and it was crusted over with a shiny skin.

In the corner, something that Angel had taken to be a pile of rags stirred suddenly. A woman with white stringy hair and a wizened pockmarked face stared malevolently at the girl. Cackling, she shouted in a shrill voice, "The new bait don' like it 'ere, I c'n tell. What's up then? Ain't none o' you goin' ter make the bas'ard comft'ble?"

A low growl from the women answered her. With a look of fear, the old woman's tense fingers clutched the rags to her. She looked across at the crouching women, then, reassured, she grinned, exposing toothless gums. "I don' mean no 'arm," she muttered, settling down again.

Near to the old woman's head was a bucket overflowing with excrement. The woman turned suddenly and jolted the rusted side with her elbow. It swayed perilously, and some of its disgusting contents slopped over and spattered the woman's hair.

"Oh!" Angel put a shaking hand to lips that felt tight and swollen. "Oh, no!" she wailed. "I can' stay here. I can'! I can'!"

As though her words had released them, the closely packed women stirred. "Garnish!" The cry was like a stone tossed into that pool of silence. They rose from their crouching positions and rushed upon her with hands extended. In the renewed uproar, Angel's wild, terrified scream was lost.

"Pick her over!" a small, shrew-faced woman, filthy matted hair streaming over skinny shoulders, commanded. "Lis'en, you," she said menacingly, thrusting her yellowed, pockmarked face close to Angel's. "New bait ain't welcome here—not 'less they's willin' ter share."

"Get away!" Angel struck out wildly at the screaming, jostling women. "No! No! Get away from me!" Gag-

ging on the acrid unwashed odor of them, she was helpless against the hands that tugged at her gown, the fingers
fumbling over her hair, her ears, her face and throat,
the crevice between her breasts; questing, knowing fingers
that, used to strange hiding places, sought avidly for any
valuables she might have hidden on her person.

"I got nothin'!" Angel panted. "Lis'en ter me, can'
you! I got nothin'! Nothin'!"

"She's right. The bloody bitch ain't got nothin' 'tall!"
It was the shrew-faced woman again. "Strip her!" she
yelled.

"Don' touch me, you filthy scum!" Angel shrieked.
"You let go o' me! Let go!"

Crowding closer, they tore the gown from her body,
and the skimpy shift beneath it, but they were not yet
done with her. Disappointed at the meager pickings, they
attacked with renewed savagery, backing her shivering
naked body against the wall. Jagged fingernails stabbed at
her face, her breasts; other hands jerked her hair, banged
her head viciously against the wall, and pinched at her
flesh.

"Bastards!" Angel saw their malevolent faces through
a swirling red mist of pain, and madness seized her. With
a strength born of terror and desperation, she raised her
manacled hands and clubbed at them—hard, punishing
blows that brought screams and curses. She struck at them
again and again. "Don' you touch me no more!" she
panted. "I'll kill you, you hear me? I'll kill you, you lousy, scabby bitches!"

Amazingly, they fell back. Trembling violently, on
the edge of screaming hysteria, Angel was scarcely able
to believe in such an easy victory. Her body tensed and
made ready to spring into action again. She watched them
warily as they huddled down on the floor. Some of them
were clutching at pieces of her gown, and she realized
then that she had not so much triumphed over them but

they, with their easily distracted minds, had—for the moment—forgotten her.

A sudden snarling quarrel broke out over the ownership of the few poor pieces of material, and Angel, not wanting to draw their attention again, turned quickly away and limped back painfully to her former position. The wall grazed her back as she sank down onto the puddled floor. She scarcely noticed it; her body was one burning, throbbing ache. From the corner of her eye she caught a flicker of movement. She turned her head sharply and saw a rat advancing boldly over the floor, the dingy gray body quivering, the long snout questing. The creature seemed indifferent to the huddled group of women, but at Angel's indrawn breath of horror he stopped short, sensing danger. Crouched low, gray fur bristling, yellow teeth bared, his narrow, glowing eyes darting first this way and then that—he was, Angel thought, just another part of the nightmare into which she had been plunged. She stiffened, bracing her limbs for the rat's expected spring, but even as she waited, the tense moment passed. Turning, he ran off.

Shuddering, Angel looked across at the women. The quarreling voices had risen to a fresh screaming pitch, and she found herself wondering if they were ever quiet—if they ever slept. Despite the miserable conditions in which they lived, they seemed possessed of a boiling feverish energy. She studied them intently, her heartbeat quickening again. Would she begin to resemble them after a while? . . . Her hair hanging in long greasy hanks, open sores on her face, her body gaunt, afflicted with disease, and scarred from constant lashings?

Most of the women had been flogged—some quite recently, judging from the puckered, angry lines—and still others had the thin, red ridgings of long-healed wounds. She gripped her cold, trembling hands together. Jim Gibbons had promised her a flogging, and he would keep his word. He would enjoy hearing her screams. She clenched her teeth.

But I ain't goin' ter scream, she thought. *You ain't goin' ter hear nothin' from me, Jim Gibbons! You c'n flog me till you bloody nigh kills me, 'n' still you won' hear nothin'!* She drew up her knees, resting her manacled hands upon them. *'Course you'll scream,* her thoughts ran on. *You ain't brave, you stupid bitch! You'll scream like ol' Cromwell was a-comin' after you his bloody self!* She closed her eyes. *I know I ain't brave,* she answered that inner, accusing voice, *but I c'n bleedin' try ter be, can' I?*

The voices of the women faded away into the hazy distance. Worn out with pain and terror, Angel slept. The rat came back from its foraging and, indifferent now to the motionless figure, it crawled over her bare feet. Angel did not stir; she was sunk fathoms deep in blissful darkness.

It WAS MAY 24, 1660. A DAY OF DESTINY. MELlow sunshine lay golden upon the white cliffs of Dover; it radiated from the brass-trimmed helmets of the soldiers who, drawn up in attitudes of stiff attention, stood beside the huge cannons that guarded Dover's coast; it played over the calm blue swell of the sea and sparked the lazily rolling waves with dancing diamonds of light. The people massed upon the lower cliffs and the shore felt that the sunshine was a good omen; they were grateful, too, for the warmth. They had waited many hours for the coming of their king, and now the moment was almost upon them. Cromwell—that joyless tyrant—was dead, and a new page in England's history was about to unfurl before them.

It was exactly three o'clock when the brigantine *The Royal Charles* was sighted. As it drew close an order was shouted; the soldiers fired the cannons twenty-one times in a salute that reverberated over the waters and temporarily deafened the bystanders. The quivering silence that followed was broken, after a stunned moment, by the indignant screaming of the gulls. Motionless, the people waited, the laughter and good-natured banter which had sustained them through the long hours stilled; even the children fell silent, awed by something they sensed but did not understand. The brigantine, the Royal Standard flying from the masthead, cut steadily through the waters until at last its thrusting prow was nudging the shore.

Sailors sprang into activity, some securing the brigantine, others furling the sails, and lowering the long gangplank down which Charles Stuart would shortly descend. Still the curious hush that had fallen over the people persisted. *We can wait,* their silence said. *Have we not waited, endlessly patient, for the return of our beloved exile? We have fought, too; aye, and we've schemed against the mighty forces of Cromwell—we've bled— that we might see this day.*

A bugle sounded. As if pulled by a single thread, their heads turned; eyes were fixed unblinkingly upon the deck. The bugle was followed by the staccato rattling of drums and the thin wavering notes of a pipe. And suddenly he was there—Charles Stuart—rightful heir to the throne of England. He came into their sight almost casually, walking with a lazy stride past the orderly row of sailors now lining the deck.

A freshening breeze, blowing his black, crimson-lined cloak away from his shoulders, stirred the crimson plumes curling about the broad-brimmed black hat. With that innate sense of drama which was so much a part of Charles' nature, he had chosen to wear black. But his costume was robbed of any suggestion of somberness by a foam of white lace at his throat and wrists.

Following a few paces behind Charles were his two brothers: solemn-faced staunchly Catholic James, and Henry, his face glowing with excitement.

"Welcome, Your Majesty!" a woman's voice screamed. "God bless our bonny Charlie!"

That lone voice shattering the silence brought from every throat a great swelling roar of welcome. The tumult echoed over the cliffs, drowning out the frenzied screeching of the seabirds; it rebounded and echoed yet again.

Charles, looking out at the sea of upturned faces, wondered if he did but dream this moment. His narrow, fine-boned hands gripped the deck rail tensely, and his dark-complexioned, rather melancholy face was solemn. Soon he would awaken, he thought, as he had awakened so often before, and he would find that he was that same home-hungry exile. Charles Stuart, the king without a crown.

Another roar from the crowd, more fervent than all that had gone before, broke through the dream. Nay, it was true. They called to him, his people. Their noisy generous welcome was for him! His hands loosened on the rail; beneath the narrow line of his moustache his lips parted in a smile of such warmth and charm that the bitter lines beside his mouth were temporarily erased. He lifted his arms in response. His deeply tanned, attractively ugly face was blazing with emotion. He looked much younger than his thirty years. Tears filled his dark eyes, and the scene before him shifted and wavered; to cover his emotion, he snatched off his plumed hat and waved it enthusiastically.

Watching his beloved brother, Henry felt his own eyes fill. He swallowed against the painful lump in his throat. "God bless you, Charles!" he thought.

Henry was the youngest of the three brothers. Their sister, Henrietta Anne—Minette, as Charles affectionately called her—was the one who prayed for peace and harmony in the family and was herself so driven and bedeviled by their fanatical mother.

Henrietta Anne loved all her brothers, but Charles she adored. Charles was her favorite topic of conversation, and she spoke of him perhaps more frequently to Henry, who had been separated from his family for such a long and weary time.

It was a compensation to Henry for the coldness of

his mother, who had found him staunch in his refusal to enter the Catholic faith and therefore refused to acknowledge his existence; and he listened eagerly to Henrietta Anne.

Through Henrietta Anne's eyes, Charles, the brother he barely knew, came alive for him. Complex Charles Stuart in all his cynicism, his wisdom, and his tenderness. Lazy Charles, who did not often put his inherent wisdom to good use if, by doing so, it would bring about discord, which he abhorred. Tenderhearted Charles, who could not bear to see suffering and whose heart was instantly melted by a woman's tears.

Henry, coming to know Charles for himself, adored his lazy good humored brother. With him he found the peace denied to him by their mother. Although believing in God, Charles was not of any particular religion and was therefore tolerant of the beliefs of others. There were so many things to love about this brother, Henry found: his hatred of all forms of malice and cruelty, his generosity—often foolish—and above all, the zest he had for the mundane business of living.

That there was another side to Charles—the side that so shocked their mother—Henry knew. His pronounced sensuality, his many mistresses; his open and unashamed affection for his bastard son, James, born of Lucy Water. His refusal to either confirm or deny the rumor that he had gone through a form of marriage with Lucy; and his indifference—though only in their mother's opinion—to his family obligations.

Henry, however, was not shocked by this other side of his brother; he was, if anything, wistfully admiring. It did not seem strange to Henry that Charles—while definitely not handsome—should prove irresistible to women. He had seen that white smile flash in the dark face, and he had known that to feminine eyes dazzled by the Stuart magic he appeared handsome, larger than life, and twice as fascinating. So Henry, as he loved Charles for his virtues, loved him also for his faults.

The cheering was loud in Henry's ears. "We're home, Charles," he whispered, as the King stepped back. "Oh, Charles, we're home at last! Thanks be to God!"

The trumpets blared again, and Charles, followed closely by his brothers, walked past the line of sailors. At the head of the gangplank, Charles stopped. It was as if he had need to draw on his strength to face this moment, so longed for in the days and nights of his exile, the moment of glory. He looked from Henry to James, and their solemn faces brought out his wry grin.

"Come, brothers," he said, beginning his slow descent. "The people await."

The crowd jostled and pushed against each other in their eagerness to get near to him, but they fell back as the soldiers snapped smartly to attention. They stared admiringly at the tall, elegant figure of this man who was their king. Eyes, long wearied of the puritanical garb decreed by Oliver Cromwell, admired the rich black velvet sheen of his costume, the lace falling over his jewel-laden hands. For them, too, in that moment, he seemed not quite real—the familiar well-loved figure of a favorite dream who might vanish at any moment.

Charles felt a rush of emotion as his feet touched earth. He smiled upon his people, touching eagerly held-out hands, caressing with his fingertips the face of a baby thrust forward for his inspection. But behind the smiling eyes, his thoughts were busy. *This is English earth beneath my feet,* his inner voice said. He swept off his hat again and waved it, enjoying the wind that blew his long dark hair away from his face. *And an English wind,* his thoughts ran on, *that blows through my hair. These are English faces that smile now upon me. Can man—be he king or commoner—ask more?*

Though reluctant to let him go, the people allowed themselves to be herded into order by the soldiers, whose duty it was to clear a path to General Monk. The latter waited some distance back to greet the King with due ceremony. It was General Monk, who had won the day and brought about the victorious return of Charles Stuart.

Monk held his plumed hat over his heart and kept his stout figure at rigid attention. Nonetheless, he felt a trembling afflict him as Charles came to a stop before him.

"General," Charles said, his eyes warm with affection, "it did but need your presence to make my happiness complete."

"Sire!" Monk said huskily, his broad red face flushing to a deeper shade. Sinking on one knee, he lifted pale-blue eyes, tear-suffused, to the King's face. "I welcome Your Majesty in the name of all England."

Charles took the General's hand in a firm grasp. "I thank you, General," he said clearly. "Pray rise. I would have you by my side."

"You honor me, sire," Monk said. He rose quickly. "If I be guilty of presumption, Your Majesty," he went on, a faint smile touching his lips, "then I trust you will pardon me. But I felt that your welcome would not be complete without the presence of one who fought by your side in so many campaigns. He waits now to render you his oath of loyalty and devotion."

"One who fought by—" Charles' puzzled face suddenly cleared. "Tavington!" he exclaimed. "Tayington here?" His smile flashed out. "He is fully recovered, then?"

"Aye, Sire."

"Od's Fish!" Charles said. " 'Tis many long months since last I saw him."

The crowd cheered, loving the quick eager note in Charles' voice. It made him human, even as they: his emotions showed in his expressive face. He did not trouble to hide his deeper feelings, it seemed, and because of this they felt as one with him. He was their own bonny Charlie.

It had been different with Cromwell. Cromwell had hidden a devious brain behind a blank unsmiling face; and the more he had tried to woo the people to his cause, the more sullen and obstinate they had grown. He could not win them, could not force one grain of loyalty from them; they eluded him always, and it maddened him. Tactfully reminded by his closest advisers that the stiff-necked, tenaciously loyal English would never bow the knee to a conqueror, he had refused to believe it. Even when he lay dying, the sorely disappointed and frustrated man still would not believe it. "They will bow to me," he had whispered. "They will bow freely and willingly. They will! They must! I'll break them yet! I vow it!"

The grim ghost of Cromwell was not even a memory on this happy day. The people watched with fond eyes as Charles Stuart, breaking with stiff royal tradition— as he was to do all of his long life—went forward with outstretched hand to greet his greatest friend, Nicholas Tavington, ardent supporter of the Royalist cause and one of the country's most admired heroes.

"This is a happy day for England, sire," Nicholas Tavington said. Kneeling, he took the King's extended hand and raised it to his lips.

"Rise, my lord," the King commanded. "You, who have risked your life so many times in my cause, should not kneel to me."

"Should I not, sire?" Nicholas Tavington, fourth Earl of Benbrook replied, rising. His darkly handsome features, somewhat severe in repose, were softened by his smile. "Surely," he added, the smile lingering in his dark eyes, "Your Majesty would not for the sake of our friendship deny me the privilege of kneeling?"

Charles laughed. "Nay, you rogue, not if such be your desire." He touched Nicholas lightly on the shoulder.

"You will take your place beside my brothers, old friend. 'Tis fitting, since you have ever been to me as a brother."

"Your Majesty is gracious," Nicholas said, the expression in his eyes softening the formal words. Bowing low, he stepped back. James, by whose side he took his place, acknowledged him with a small, tight smile. But Henry, who greatly admired Nicholas and placed him second only to his brother Charles, gave him a wide, friendly grin.

Charles turned to the excited crowd. Raising his hands for silence, he said, "I thank you all for your welcome. God, in his infinite mercy and justice, has brought me forth to stand vindicated before you, and with his help I shall not fail you." His vivid smile flashed out, embracing them, drawing them close. "I am come home to my green and gracious England. Here shall I live and die, for I vow to you, my people, that Charles Stuart will go no more a-wandering."

They were dazzled by the potent Stuart charm, that same charm that had been Mary Stuart's and had driven the Earl of Bothwell in his lonely foreign cell mad with longing.

"God save the King!" The cry was taken up, becoming a swelling roar of sound. "Health and long life to His Majesty!"

Before them all, Charles sank to his knees. With his head bowed over his clasped hands, he rendered his thanks to God. It was a short prayer, and touching in its very simplicity. Charles was not by nature a humble man, but Nicholas Tavington, watching him, knew that his prayer was sincere. There was something about the kneeling figure of the King, a touch of exultant glory in the absorbed dark face, that made the artist in Nicholas ache for his brushes and canvas. He had painted princes and dukes and the leading beauties of the day, recording their features for posterity—but he had never been inspired as he was at this moment. *I will remember that look,* he vowed silently. *I'll get it on canvas for all to see. I'll call it—I'll call it—"A Stuart for England."*

Charles rose to his feet. Above his head gulls screamed, flying in wildly wheeling circles. A blue-gray feather drifted downward, coming to rest at the King's feet. Stooping, he picked it up. " 'Tis a gift from above," he cried, putting the little feather into his pocket. "It shall be my good-luck piece."

The Mayor of Dover, though slightly shocked by Charles' apparent indifference to ceremony, was himself very conscious of the importance of the moment. Moving with slow dignity, he now approached. The laughing people fell back, and Charles turned to greet him with a smile. Bowing, the Mayor extended his white staff—the symbol of his office. "I tender unto Your Majesty my staff," he said in a low solemn voice. "Know you now, sire, that it represents the badge of my service."

Charles took the staff and held it in his hands for a brief moment. "This staff do I place once more into your keeping, good Mayor. You have ever been honest and vigilant. I pray you to continue so in our service." Charles smiled again into the earnest face. "We thank you," he said softly, "for the loyalty of the years."

Not quite able to hide his pleasure, the Mayor bowed once more. "I thank Your Majesty." Straightening, he drew forth from the recesses of his flowing scarlet cloak, a Bible, stamped and clasped in gold. "Receive into your keeping, sire, this sacred gift." Reverently, the Mayor placed the Bible upon the King's outstretched hands. "I pray that the blessing of Our Lord be ever with you." He bowed stiffly once more and stepped back.

The King's eyes glowed, and he clasped the book to his breast. "The sacred words contained in this Bible," he said, "shall be my guide before all other things in this world. So do I swear, in the presence of God, my judge, who looketh into the hearts of all men."

The echoes of his vow seemed to linger on the air as Charles moved toward the ceremonial canopy. His brothers and the Earl of Benbrook walked behind him, the Mayor on his left hand and General Monk on his right.

Beneath its shade he stood tall and erect, smiling out at his people, lifting his hands in response to their cheers. The boom of cannons thundered forth again shaking the earth beneath. Bells rang out, their deep tolling carrying the glorious news that Charles, by the grace of God—King of England—Defender of the Faith—was home at last.

FROM EVERY PART OF LONDON THE BELLS rang forth, their joyous clamor penetrating the dim fastness of Newgate, carrying the message that the King was coming. Tomorrow, the twenty-ninth of May, he would enter his capital.

Angel Dawson's dull indifference to the message of the bells was pierced through with a sudden stab of bitter longing.

She pictured the gray streets—brightly decked in honor of the King—water-carrying conduits would for this special day flow with wine. The houses would be decorated, too. The shops, the gin parlors, even the whorehouses would be heaped with streamers and flowers. There would be dancing in the streets and people laughing, singing, cheering.

Angel shrugged her longing aside, then cursed softly to herself as the movement brought a reminder of the oozing wounds across her back and shoulders. She touched the hot puffy flesh with careful fingers. She'd been in Newgate almost a month now, and in that period she'd been flogged four times.

She'd been lucky so far, Angel thought. Luckier than the new girl, Marianne. At least she hadn't been in a flogging fight. Most of her other cell mates had, and after the fight they were carried back to the cell moaning, more dead than alive.

Angel looked across at an old woman, who sat in the far corner of the cell, mumbling to herself. Old Flo had been the victim of a flogging fight; her upper lip had been torn away, exposing her toothless, perpetually mumbling gums. "Our Alf," was the subject of the old woman's conversation, and she talked to him night and day. Mary Bates, another victim, was just nineteen years old—though she looked years older. She'd been lashed across the eyes and was permanently blinded.

Shutting her ears to Flo's mumble, Angel groped behind her for the piece of bread she'd saved from last night's frugal meal. The bread was green with mold and pulpy from contact with the damp floor; but Angel, cramming it hurriedly into her mouth, ate it almost with enjoyment. Where once she had vomited at the mere sight of such food, she now endured. "Bread's bread," she told herself philosophically. It was surprising how good it tasted when you were hungry.

Finishing the bread regretfully, Angel sat back against the wall, her arms hugged about her shivering naked body. Perhaps she wouldn't live long, she thought hopefully. The rigors of winter had been known to kill many of the women off, and perhaps she'd be one of them. It would be better than going on and on in this place. Anything—even dying—would be better than that! Perhaps if she prayed hard enough, God would listen to her prayers. When she first came to Newgate, she'd asked Him every night, begged Him to strike her down, to release her. She hadn't prayed just lately, but God was always ready to listen, even if, Angel thought guiltily, she did sometimes question His existence. She did wonder how He could look down, seemingly unmoved, on the misery borne by His creatures.

A low, quivering moan broke in on her thoughts.

Angel leaned forward; her eyes softened as she looked at the girl who was lying a short distance away. It was rare in Newgate to feel pity for another, and Angel, full of bitterness at her own lot, had fought it, but the plight of this girl was such that compassion had won out.

Marianne—for that, she had confided in Angel—was her name, had no other memory of her past. If she had a family, their identity was hidden from her. She had awakened one morning and found herself a prisoner in Newgate. Of the events that had led to that imprisonment she knew nothing, and if her jailers knew, they did not choose to tell her. One thing only had her clouded memory given to her—a name—Marianne, and to this she clung.

Before being brought to the Common Side, Angel knew, Marianne had been lodged for some months in the better quarters of Newgate. But now that the money found on her person was exhausted, her rapid demotion to the Common Side had been inevitable.

Marianne's voice was soft and cultured, her manner and bearing quietly dignified, and perhaps it was these very qualities that had aroused the cruelty of the guards, for her money had not saved her from frequent floggings while living in the better quarters. Now, thrust into the Common Side penniless, the floggings had become a daily routine.

They were all scarred from the whip, of course, Angel thought, but not one of them had been called upon to endure a daily flogging.

Angel rose to her feet. Shrieks and obscenities were hurled after her as she made her way to Marianne's side, but no one attempted to interfere. She had earned the grudging respect of these women. Their earlier attacks upon her person had—after that first day—been met with a savagery that was equal if not greater than their own; and they would not willingly brave her sharp, stabbing nails, her butting head, or her hard feet that, kicking out ferociously, seemed to find at once their most vulnerable places.

Angel was no stranger to death, and she knew, even as she crouched down beside the girl, that Marianne was dying. Against the grayish tinge of her skin, the shadows beneath her closed eyes stood out like great purple bruises.

"Marianne." Angel touched the burning hand gently.

Marianne's colorless lips moved, "A—Angel. I—I hoped you would c—come to me." With a great effort, she opened her eyes. "Stay with me, Angel, I p—pray you. It has grown so dark! I'm afraid! Oh, Angel, I'm so afraid!"

Resentful of the tears forming in her eyes, Angel blinked fiercely. "We're all 'fraid, ain't we?" she muttered. "Ain't no use for you ter go a-talkin' like you was the only one, is it?"

She scowled, and Marianne smiled faintly. "There is n—no need for pre—pretense between us, Angel. You have a—a very kind heart, and I am most gra—grateful for your friendship."

"I ain't no one's bleedin' friend." Angel's scowl deepened. "No one don' care nothin' 'bout me, see? An' I don' care nothin' 'bout you! Go on an' bleedin' die, see if I care!"

"Am I dying, Angel?" Marianne's frail fingers touched Angel's wrist, tightening about it with surprising strength. "Tell me!"

"How'd I know?" Angel said belligerently. "Ain't God, am I?"

"Angel, I have heard that pr—prisoners who are without money are buried in the l—lime pit." Horror stared from her eyes. "I cannot bear the thought! Indeed I cannot!"

Angel stared at her. "I'll try 'n' stop 'em from doin' that ter you," she blurted. "I will! I'll do me bes', I will, but you can' expec' me ter make no prom—" she broke off, her head turning alertly at the sound of a key grating in the lock.

Every eye turned to the door. It creaked ponderously open, and a burly guard entered. He was followed by two other guards obviously new to their job. They stood awkwardly, not looking at the prisoners, and each man's hands, poised above the whip carried in a loop of his belt, were unsteady.

The burly guard, apparently deriving a malicious amusement from their nervousness, grinned broadly at the sullen women and closed one eye in a wink. "You nice ladies is goin' ter make these men feel welcome, ain't you," he said lightly.

His remark was greeted with screams of derision. "Shut up!" he bellowed after a moment, flourishing his whip threateningly. "Hold your bleedin' row."

He peered about him and turned back to the two men. "Tha's the one what I want," he said, pointing a thick finger at Marianne. "Her over there. Bring her."

Angel crouched over Marianne. "Leave her be!" she screamed, as they stopped before her. "She's dyin', she is! Ain't that 'nough for you, you swine?"

"Heath," the guard at the door instructed loudly, "drag that wench over here. An' you, Turner, I wan' you ter give that big-mouthed cow a good bootin'."

Heath dragged Marianne to her feet. His face paled as she began to scream wildly. Recovering, he hauled her across the rough floor and flung her down by the door.

"Go on," Angel said defiantly, glaring at the man, looming over her. "Boot me an' get it over with. Go on, I ain't 'fraid o' you."

She curled herself into a ball. "Go on! Enjoy your bleedin' self!"

The guard dropped his whip. Bending to pick it up,

he whispered urgently, "I ain't goin' ter hurt you, you stupid bitch. What you take me for? But you scream when I touches you, un'erstan'?"

Dazed, Angel answered with a barely perceptible movement of her head.

The guard straightened up. From the corner of her eye Angel saw his foot draw back. "Here it comes, you bitch!" he roared.

His foot lunged forward with such savage intent that Angel winced despite herself. The foot stopped short at the base of her spine, and she felt his urgent prod. Her mouth opened wide, and she screamed lustily.

"Tha's the way ter learn 'em," the guard at the door called approvingly. "Now get yoursel' over here, Turner."

"Yes, sir." Turner grinned down at Angel, and she answered him with a tremulous smile. Then he turned and went back to the door.

"What you wan' us ter do now, Mr. Barker?" Turner asked.

"Wait for 'structions, tha's what you do," Barker answered ungraciously.

He turned to the women. "You ladies is in for a treat," he said loudly. "Ter help us cel'brate our gracious King's homecomin', we're goin' ter let you see a floggin' fight. How's that for gen'rosity, eh?"

A babble of voices arose. A woman pushed herself forward, her flabby breasts swaying. "Which o' us is ter be flogged?" she demanded.

"You ain't got nothin' ter worry 'bout," Barker said, grinning. He prodded Marianne with his foot. "This 'un here's the flog bait."

"No!" Angel screamed, fighting to make herself heard above the uproar. "She won' be able ter stan' it! She's dyin'! Can' you see she's dyin'?"

"All right, Turner," Barker yelled. "You 'n' Heath start formin' 'em in ter two lines, then march 'em straight

48

to Upper Court. Use them whips if you have ter." He glanced down at Marianne's crumpled figure. "I'll bring her 'long."

Herded along with the rest, Angel found herself once more traversing the endless corridors. Mounting the steeply winding staircases, she stumbled several times, and felt the sting of Heath's whip across her back.

Tears blurred Angel's vision. *Marianne! Marianne! I wish I could've helped you. Don' die, Marianne! Oh, God! Dear, merciful God, don' let her die!*

THE UPPER COURTYARD WAS A CHILL GRAY
place. Shut in as it was, it seemed to be shrouded in perpetual winter, even the advent of spring and summer making little difference to the bleak atmosphere. Tall leaning
buildings shut out the sunlight; trees encircled the prison
closely, resting heavy leaf-burdened branches on the high
wall and trailing their fountains of greenery into the
courtyard itself. The fluttering leaves, though providing
a touch of beauty, emphasized the unrelieved gloom of
the place.

To Angel Dawson, emerging for the first time in
many weeks from the depths of the prison, the courtyard
seemed full of light. She filled her lungs with cold air and
felt a new vigor, a renewed stirring of hope.

"Look," the woman standing next to Angel said,
poking her sharply in the ribs. "Look at them sods."

Angel followed her pointing finger and saw a group
of chattering, laughing men and women seated about a
table in a large, cleared space.

"You wouldn' never think as they was pris'ners like
you an' me, eh?" the woman said. She spat disgustedly.
"The diff'rence is that they got money." She spat again.
"Money! Buy you anythin', it will."

Halted by the guard, Angel stared in unabashed

curiosity at the group of apparently carefree prisoners who were, by virtue of money, the aristocrats of Newgate.

One man dressed in frayed satin held a quizzing glass to his eyes; so haughty was his mien as he surveyed the assembly that he might indeed have been an aristocrat who, forced to mingle with the plebeian, found himself coldly offended.

Some of the women were naked. One such wore a long string of amber-colored beads looped twice about her throat, the rest of the necklace trailing down between her breasts. Another woman had a wreath of withered flowers resting at a coquettish angle on her mop of dark hair. She had painted her plump nude body with vivid streaks and whorls of color.

But most of the women were clothed, some in neat, dark garments which gave them the odd look of respectable housewives who had strayed into Newgate through no fault of their own. There were women arrayed in bright cottons, striped calicoes, and dark silks. Others, apparently having known better days, were garbed in jewel-toned satins, often frayed, the colors fading, but lavishly frilled and flounced with quantities of yellowing lace.

The women, even the plain and elderly ones, did not lack for male companionship. Even the haughty aristocrat in the frayed satin, Angel noted, had his arm about a small, giggling girl clad in a red silk dress. For all the attention he paid to her she might not have been there, but the girl seemed to be content with his company.

Angel's eyes widened, and her mouth watered with longing as she saw the food. There was an amazing quantity and variety of it. The elite of Newgate were chewing on hunks of meat, bulging pastries, chicken legs, crisply roasted and beaded with golden juices. A woman was carving a huge meat pie and handing round generous slices oozing with a thick, rich, brown gravy. They all ate voraciously, washing the food down with copious drafts of wine.

One couple, uninterested for the moment in food and wine or perhaps sated with both, were making violent love on the floor. The man, cheered on by his ribald and interested audience, thrust savagely into the woman. Her legs writhed with each thrust, and she gave little whimpering, ecstatic cries.

An elderly woman with a pleasant motherly face and neatly banded white hair stared fixedly at the couple; her eyes were glassy and her mouth slack. Coming out of her trance, the woman turned to the young man who lounged lazily at ease beside her. A jerk of her head toward the couple indicated to him her desire. Grinning, he watched her begin to unbotton the bodice of her prim, dove-gray gown. A button eluded her groping fingers, and she swore vilely; in sudden trembling frenzy she began tearing at the bodice. Disrobed at last, she stood up and bending over the young man she helped him pull off his tight breeches.

Angel turned her head away. She was not interested in their love play; she had seen it all before. The gutter gang to which she had belonged had coupled hungrily and often, but Angel had held herself inviolate. Stoically she had endured jeers and laughter, but had remained an aloof spectator. There were times when she had wondered if there might be something lacking in herself, but finding no satisfactory answer, she had dismissed the notion. She was aware of vague longings, of a need to love and to be loved, but it must be with a special person, and there must be a special moment. Angel, though she did not realize it and despite her street-brat toughness, was an incurable romantic.

Turner's voice startled her out of her thoughts. She looked round at him and saw that he was telling them where to sit. Obediently Angel moved forward, but a slight shake of Turner's head stopped her.

"Go further along," Turner said, coming up to her. "Ain't no room for you there, as you'd see if you was ter use your perishin' eyes." He prodded her roughly in the back with the butt of his whip. "Go on, get a move on!"

Out of earshot of the other women, Turner whispered hoarsely, "I'm a bleedin' fool, tha's what I am, but that frien' o' yours has been askin' for you. I c'd lose me perishin' job for doin' this, but—well, it don' look ter me as she's got much longer. You'd better go an' see what she wants. She's over there." He pointed with his whip. "See her?"

Angel nodded. "Thanks," she said hoarsely. "Thanks kin'ly."

"Ain't no need o' thanks. If Barker comes back an' catches you with her, I don' know nothin' 'bout it, see?"

"I'll 'member that," Angel answered. "You're decen', you are. You don' belong in Newgate. Why 'n' you get out 'fore they makes you like what they are?"

"Need money," he answered briefly. "Got an' ol' woman an' little 'uns. I'll leave when I can." He poked her with the whip. "Go on." Deliberately, he turned his back on her. "I never see you go," he muttered.

Marianne was lying at the foot of the flogging post. Her eyes were closed, and the looming shadow of the post had marked a dark cross over her face and body.

Impeded by the ankle fetters, Angel dropped clumsily down beside her. "Marianne," she said urgently. "I's me."

"Johnnie!" Marianne whispered. "We'll be married, my darling. We will, I promise you. No, no, you needn't fear Nicholas! He can't hurt us anymore."

"It ain't Johnnie," Angel's voice was rough-edged with fear. "I's Angel."

Marianne's head turned restlessly, her breathing grew agitated. "My Johnnie dead!" she cried. "You're lying, Nicholas! Oh, God! Make it a lie!"

"Shut up!" Angel placed her hand lightly across the girl's mouth. "I's Angel, Marianne, do you hear me? I's Angel."

Marianne's lashes fluttered. "Angel," she repeated in a faint voice. "Angel?" Her heavy lids lifted slowly. "It —it is you. But I th—thought—" her voice trailed away.

"I's me all right." Angel glanced about her swiftly. No sign of Barker yet. Turner, his back still turned, was standing a little distance away. Heath was indulging in rough play with the nude woman wearing the long string of amber beads, and as most of the guards were similarly occupied, Angel felt herself to be reasonably safe. True, some of the Common Side prisoners were glancing her way, but they were too stirred up to pay her much attention. Later, when the excitement was over, they would remember what they had seen and report it. That would mean a flogging for her but an extra slice of bread to the first who reported.

Angel bent nearer to Marianne. She was relieved to see that the dazed expression had left Marianne's eyes.

"The guard said you wan'ed ter speak ter me, Marianne."

"Angel!" Marianne's hot fingers groped for Angel's hand; finding it, she clung tightly. "I've—I've rem— remembered everything. There was an accident—c— coach overturned—men! Men robbing us!" She stared up at Angel, her eyes dilated. "Ellen! They k—killed her! Blood! Ellen's b—blood everywhere!"

"Wha's your name?" Angel hissed.

"Marianne T—Tavington. My brother is—is Nicholas T—Tav—" her voice faded away for a moment, then resumed with an effort. "Lives in S—St. Bernard's Square. He—he—Earl of Benbrook's home—ask for it—ask—" She took a deep shuddering breath. "Go to N—Nicholas when you're free. He'll—he'll h—help you."

Angel paid little attention to the last. She was not

likely to be free, so why worry about it. She was, however, impressed with the location of the house. "Fancy that!" she said, awed. "Wish I had a brother a-workin' in a gran' house like that, an' workin' for the Earl 'n' all. Frien' o' the King, the Earl is, ain't he? Do your brother drive the Earl's coach, or is he maybe one o' them stuck-up footmen?"

Marianne's eyes were clouding again. "Promise!" she gasped. "Go to—to Nicholas. Promise, Angel!"

"All right," Angel said soothingly. "Ain't no need ter get upset. O' course I'll go."

"T—tell him—coach robbed—Ellen killed. I—I was robbed of papers—mistakenly con—convicted. Say that —th—that I'm sorry—didn't understand. Tell him I—I love him."

"I'll tell him," Angel assured her, striving to keep her voice steady. "Don' you worry no more."

"Never again." Marianne's fingers loosened, fell limply away from Angel's hand. "Thank you, dear Angel."

"Here, you!" the bellowing of Barker's voice shattered the moment.

Angel turned her head. Barker was running toward her. Behind him, striding lazily, but appearing for all that to cover the ground as fast as Barker, came a tall, grotesquely fat woman. She was naked, and her breasts jounced as she walked; in her right hand she clutched a heavy, black-handled whip.

Reaching Angel, Barker grabbed her shoulder roughly.

"What you doin' here, eh? Bloody Turner!" he said contemptuously. He gave her a push, sending her sprawling. "I knew the sod wasn' no good."

"Turner don' know 'bout me slippin' off," Angel said fiercely. "I done it when he wasn' lookin'."

"Good for you, dearie," the naked woman said, stopping before them. She turned to Barker. "It ain't her

55

I'm fightin', is it?" She flashed a smile at Angel. "Don' mean ter offen' you, dear, but you ain't got more 'n' a happorth o' meat on them bones o' yours."

Barker looked uncomfortable. "No," he snapped irritably, "it ain't her." He nodded toward Marianne. "That 'un there, she's who you got ter fight."

The woman began to laugh; the loose flesh of her belly wobbled. "Tha's a good joke," she wheezed, slapping Barker on the back. "Me? Fight her!" She went into another paroxysm.

Barker glared at her. "Laugh all you wan' ter," he said loudly. "But tha's the one."

The woman's laughter died abruptly. Her coarse-featured face hardening into a mask of fury, she swung round on Barker.

"You ain' makin' a fool out o' Mary Johnson, an' don' you think it!" She waved a clenched fist menacingly. "I ain't fightin' no bleedin' plucked chick'n! What you take me for?"

"Gibbons give the order," Barker said almost desperately. "He ain't goin' ter like it if you make a fuss."

"That so?" Mary Johnson tossed her mane of black hair. "I's my money what keeps that bastard in comfort. My money what keeps you 'n' all, an' i's me what's a-goin' ter call the tune. You go 'n' tell him I says so."

"Can't." Barker's face flushed to an angry red. "Some dressed-up whelp came a-demandin' ter see Gibbons, an' he's a-seein' him now. Got one o' them parchmen's in his hand, had this whelp. Got seals a-danglin' from it. You'd think as it was from the King himsel'."

Mary Johnson, her good humor restored, remarked jovially, "I don' know nothin' 'bout no dressed-up whelp, but I do know I ain't fightin' *her!*" She gave Barker a little push. "Off wi' you. Fin' Lucy Bagget for me. Tell the cow I'm goin'er give her her wish. She's been wan'in' ter fight me for long 'nough."

Barker flung her a fuming look, but he turned away with unexpected meekness. "If I got ter, I got ter."

Mary Johnson waited until the guard was out of sight, then she turned to Angel. Her small light eyes, set like gooseberries in the immense, doughy round of her face, were soft as they rested on Marianne's white face. "She remin's me o' me own little wench," she said, pointing at Marianne. "Emmie, tha's what her name was. Loved her, I did, but the fever took her off. I ain't never stopped missin' her." She looked at Angel. "Maybe I c'd do somethin' to help that little 'un, eh?"

"You can' do nothin' for Marianne," Angel answered sullenly. "I's too late. She's dyin'."

"Maybe it ain't too late," Mary said eagerly. "I c'd have you 'n' her moved ter better quarters, an' I c'd see as you're fed good."

"I don' wan' nothin' from you," Angel muttered. "Don' wan' nothin' from nobody." She touched Marianne gently. "I don' min' you doin' somethin' for her. You c'd maybe ease her las' moments."

"I will," Mary promised. "You has me word on it. I wish the little 'un didn' remin' me o' Emmie, though. It hurts bad, that do."

Mary turned her head as a voice hailed her. "There's Lucy Bagget," Mary said, her hand clenching over the whip. "I allus hated that cow," she muttered. "I'm goin' ter ribbon her up proper." Mary's eyes dwelt once more on Marianne, then, nodding to Angel, she strode swiftly away.

Lucy Bagget looked up at Mary's approach. She greeted her with a self-assured grin, but her light-blue eyes were hostile. She was shorter than her opponent and slighter of build, but she was tough and well muscled. She had escaped the prison pallor; her skin had a healthy glow and her eyes were bright.

"You don' look well, Mary love," Lucy said. She

57

wriggled out of her gown and threw it to one side. "Don' you worry none," she went on, her eyes glinting maliciously, "I ain't goin' ter cut you up too bad."

"You ain't goin' ter cut me none at all, you bitch!" Mary hissed, her gray eyes blazing. "I'm the one what's goin' ter be cuttin' meat, an' i's goin' ter be yours, see!"

"Ain't nothin' ter stop you from dreamin', is there?"

Smiling, Lucy began walking away, her bare rump twitching with every step.

"I'll ribbon you, you little bastard!" Mary shouted after her.

In the space reserved for the fight, the two women faced toward the guard who was to give the signal. They were indifferent to the screaming of the prisoners; their eyes were fixed on the handkerchief in the guard's hand.

There was a slight delay, occasioned by the two hysterical exuberance of the prisoners from the Common Side. Guards moved among them, quelling the disturbance with ruthlessly flailing whips. Order finally restored, the guard with the handkerchief held up his arm again. There was a breathless pause, then his fingers opened and the handkerchief fluttered to the ground.

The two women began to circle each other warily. With their stiff-legged gait and the forward thrust of their heads, they looked like a pair of fighting cocks.

The audience was silent for a moment, then, growing impatient, they began to hoot their disapproval.

Mary's pride in her reputation as a champion fighter was stung, and her scorn of her opponent goaded her into instant action. Her whip, its heavy, leaded tip dully gleaming, whined through the air with a sound resembling a swarm of angry hornets; expertly wielded, it exploded against Lucy's back with searing, savage violence.

Lucy screamed wildly. Her back was ripped apart from shoulder to waist. She jumped about frantically in her agony, and the blood bubbling from the gaping wound speckled the faces of the onlookers.

Breathing in great gasps, Lucy fought for control. Her eyes murderous, her lips skinned back in a snarl, she slashed out viciously, and the whip went straight to its target. The thong wrapped itself about Mary's left breast, cutting as it tightened. Lucy wrenched it free, uttering a scream of triumph as blood poured from Mary's half-severed breast.

A groan went up from those prisoners who from long experience knew that the fight must now be necessarily a short one. They glared malevolently at Lucy, shouting insulting remarks. She should have kept the fight going, she should have remembered that the big slash, the killing slash, was always reserved for the last few minutes. It was no fight at all with that bloody great ox of a Mary bleeding to death before their eyes.

Lucy screamed back at them, defending herself. Grumbling, they settled back again to await future events, if any.

Mary stood there. She stared about her but saw nothing except a swimming mist. She felt dazed; she remembered that she was there to finish off Lucy Bagget, but although the whip was still clutched tightly in her hand, she felt strangely disinclined to fight. Her body felt stiff and damp; she looked down, and the mist cleared sufficiently to show her the bright coating of blood on her body, the little pool of it about her feet, widening even as she stared.

Mary frowned. Her head felt light, she couldn't seem to think. Somebody—she'd forgotten who it was—had mentioned Emmie. Her Emmie! Her little girl! The breath rattled harshly in Mary's lungs. She wouldn't let them bring Emmie to this place! She wouldn't let them hurt her! No, no! Her little Emmie was good, she was sweet and pure. But somebody wanted to hurt her little girl! That was why she'd been fighting, wasn't it? Fighting to protect her Emmie! Mary glared about her, forcing her dimming eyes to focus; she saw the posturing Lucy, and standing beside her was another little figure.

Emmie! Big, shy, wistful looking eyes in a little, pale, pointed face. Emmie, standing in the way so well remembered, one tiny foot pointed outward as though about to dance.

Mary lunged forward on her weighted legs. Emmie was back! Oh glory, she was back! She'd just been hiding from her old Ma, that was all! But that Lucy Bagget, she'd hurt Emmie!

"Don' you touch my girl, you cow! You bastard!" All of the fury and pain, the bitterness and grief of Mary's life was in that hoarse, primitive bellow, and it sent a false strength surging through her.

Lucy whirled round, her eyes widened in terror as she saw that the huge bloodied figure was almost upon her . . . recovering herself quickly, she drew back her arm and lashed out at the staggering woman.

"Emmie!" Mary said, coming on with a terrible persistence. "Emmie, my baby! Ma's own dear little lass!"

She did not feel the frenzy of Lucy's blows, she knew only that Emmie waited for her, depended upon her for protection. Her bloodied hands outstretched and twitching, Mary reached for Lucy Bagget.

Lucy, her appalled eyes on her nemesis, fell back one step at a time, wanting to run but finding herself unable to. Again she lashed out, and again. One of her frantically aimed blows opened a cut beneath Mary's eye, but still the grim figure came on.

"Give the big cow a proper lick," somebody yelled. "Go on, Bagget, don' tickle her!"

"Ain' nothin' c'n stop her!" Lucy screamed. She fell back a few more paces. "Oh Christ! Somebody stop her!"

Lucy's white face and her starting eyes seemed to swim menacingly toward Mary. Her face grew large—larger. That evil face belonged to the woman who had dared threaten her Emmie! She would smash it! She would grind the face to powder!

"I won' let you touch my baby!" Mary snarled. "I'll kill you, you bitch! I will!"

Mary's arm had become a huge block of stone; she lifted it with an effort. The whip, she thought, it was so big, so heavy! It was the trunk of a tree she held in her hand! She forced her hand to move and the mighty trunk obeyed her will. Faint, far off, she heard the high whine of the whip—surely the world itself had been slowed down? The lash moved slowly, so slowly. She saw the graceful arcing, its outward, reaching curl; it touched Lucy's face gently, so gently, reducing it to a shattered red ruin.

Just for a moment Lucy's face felt numb, then the pain came—white-hot! Searing! God! Oh God! Screaming madly, she fell to her knees. There was an explosion in her head, something tore itself loose with a loud, explosive popping sound; a wet, glutinous mass touched her cheek and hung suspended there.

"My eye!" Lucy shrilled, feeling with frantic fingers the rounded spongy thing. "My God! She's cut out my eye!"

Her screams dying to anguished moans, Lucy huddled there, and she did not notice the heavy thud of a body falling beside her, or the sound of grunting, laboring breathing.

Lucy touched the wet dangling thing again, and the horror of it drove reason from her mind. Her mouth opened and she began to scream like a trapped animal.

Sprawled beside her, Mary said quite clearly, "Ma's comin', Emmie love. Ma ain't goin' ter let you get hurt."

With painful slowness Mary straddled Lucy's screaming, writhing body. Her trembling hands crawled upward and touched Lucy's uninjured eye. Triumphantly, she ground her thumbs into the socket; squeezing, pressing, until the eye popped free and dangled beside its fellow.

Lucy made no attempt at fighting, she seemed to feel nothing. She lay very still, her crazed face turned skyward, the empty sockets oozing, but from her throat there still issued those piercing, mindless screams.

Mary's thumbs trailed downward through the blood and slime covering Lucy's face and came to rest against the tortured straining throat. The thumbs pressed hard, choking off the screams, leaving behind a heavy, throbbing silence.

Shrieks broke out again almost immediately. Scraps of food, bones, and empty wine bottles were hurled at the two women lying so still on the red-spattered ground.

"Shut your row," a guard shouted, running over to the still forms. He bent over them. "Dead," he said, straightening again. "They ain't never goin' ter fight for you no more. The perishin' pair o' 'em are dead."

The crowd shifted uneasily, but their laughter soon broke out again. They were better off dead, weren't they?

Sickened, Angel looked away. Barker had forced her to return to her seat among the other prisoners. She looked up again and saw that Turner was watching her. At his almost imperceptible nod, she rose as quickly as she was able and hobbled back to Marianne's side.

Marianne was lying in the same position. "Marianne," Angel sank down beside her. "Fight's over," she said, touching the girl's hand.

Marianne made no answer. She lay there unmoving, her thin body relaxed. There was a faint smile on her lips.

"Marianne!" Angel touched the cold hand again. "Marianne! You ain't dead, are you?"

Angel's burning eyes looked at the stilled breast, the opened hands, palms uppermost. "No! Marianne, no!"

She seized Marianne's shoulders and dragged her upward. The girl's head lolled helplessly, and the wind blew a strand of her hair against Angel's mouth. Hot tears welled into Angel's eyes. "Damn 'em!" she said. "Damn the filthy swine!"

She eased Marianne down gently. "If I ever get a chance, Marianne," she said, "I'll pay them sods out! I'll do it for you 'n' for me!"

"What you doin' here again?" Barker's loud voice broke in on Angel's brooding thoughts. "Askin' for it, ain't you?" he bellowed. "Get on over with them other bait." He pointed to Marianne. "An' while you're 'bout it, drag that bitch along too."

"She's dead," Angel said dully.

"Eh?" Barker's eyes narrowed. "Dead, eh? Leave her lie, then. Get on back to them others."

"No," Angel said, her eyes defying him. "I'm stayin' with her."

"That so?" Barker raised his whip threateningly. "Maybe you're a-wan'in' me to lash you ter the post an' ribbon up your hide?"

Angel controlled her instinctive fear. "Do what you bleedin' like," she said in a choked voice. "I don' care no more! I jus' don' care!"

"You'll care," Barker snapped. "I promises you that! You'll bleedin' care so much, you'll—" He broke off, turning his head at the sound of running footsteps. "Here comes Mr. Gibbons," he said to Angel. "We'll jus' see what he's got ter say 'bout this."

"Barker." Gibbons came to a panting halt beside them. "Where you been, you bloody fool? I been lookin' all over for you."

"Sorry, sir," Barker said placatingly, "but this bitch here's been givin' me trouble. Won' 'bey the rules, she won' an' if you was ter ask me, I'd—"

"Shut your stupid mouth," Gibbons cut him off

brusquely. "See this," he said bitterly, holding out a tightly rolled parchment scroll. "You ain't never goin' ter guess what's writ on it."

Barker looked curiously at the scroll. "That the one what the scented fop brung?"

"This is the one." Gibbons swallowed hard. "This here's a royal proc'mation, an' owin' to His Bloody Majesty's gen'rous heart, we got ter let all o' them what's first offenders go free. It's writ down like that, says somethin' 'bout it bein' in cel'bration of his return."

Barker stared at him, his jaw drooping. "But you ain't a-goin' ter do it, are you? You ain't a-goin' ter let them scum go free?"

Gibbons glowered at him. "I ain't got no perishin' choice," he answered sullenly. "That bloody mincin' swine what brung it ter me, he jus' kep' on a-tellin' me 'bout the trouble I'd be in if I never 'beyed it."

Angel sat very still. She had heard, yet she could not believe she had heard correctly. Could it be true? She was a first offender, and that meant—that meant that she was to go free! Impossible! It couldn't be! Nevertheless, as the reluctant Barker ran forward and began bawling for silence her eyes took on a shine. She felt joy trembling through her. It was true, then! Their new King had done this wonderful thing! He had thought of the wretched ones in his kingdom. Angel felt a passionate gratitude.

"Oh, bless you!" she whispered. "May heaven bless you, Your Majesty! And thank You, God! Thank You!"

"God bless him!" a woman shrieked out suddenly, echoing Angel's thoughts. "Long life ter the Stuart, an' a bloody good health!"

Angel looked down at Marianne, and some of her glowing joy faded. "Marianne! Marianne! Why couldn' you have lived to hear them words?"

A shadow fell across her face. She looked up and saw Gibbons staring at her. "Dead, ain't she?"

A shadow fell across her face. She looked up and saw Gibbons staring at her. "Dead, ain't she?" he said. "Barker jus' tol' me."

She could see no regret in his face. "Yes," she said curtly. "He tol' you right."

Gibbons' eyes narrowed. "You fin' out the bait's name, did you?"

Angel hesitated. "Tavington," she said at last. "Marianne Tavington. Ain't no won'er she's dead, is it?" she went on, a tremble in her voice. "She was beat to death, an' you give the orders to have it done!"

"You thinkin'er makin' trouble for ol' Jim?" Gibbons drawled. "If you are, me dearie, I might jus' keep you here with me."

"But—but—" Angel stared at him, her heart beating suffocatingly. "But you can' keep me here," she blurted desperately, "you got ter do like what the King tol' you. I hear you say so ter Barker."

"Wha's one bait more or less?" Gibbons taunted her. "Who's goin' ter notice if I was ter keep one back? You don' think as the King's goin' ter be waitin' outside ter count the bait, do you?"

Feverish color flamed into Angel's pale cheeks. She'd beg him if she had to! Yes, she'd even do that. She'd beg the swine to let her go free!

"Lis'en," she said, nodding at Marianne. "I ain't goin' ter say nothin' 'bout her. I ain't, honest! Marianne—she—she tol' me as her brother works for a gran' gent in a rich house. He's boun' ter have money, ain't he? I c'd maybe spin him some yarn 'bout how good you allus was ter us, eh?"

She stopped, looking at him appealingly. There was a sly amusement in his eyes, but no sign of softening.

Hating herself, she rushed on breathlessly. "He'd wan' ter pay you, see, for bein' good ter his sister. M—Marianne says as he'd pay you g—good if you was—was ter bury her decen' 'n' all."

"You goin' ter tell him 'bout how good I was ter her, are you?"

"Yes," she whispered. "I—I don' min' tellin' him that."

Gibbons chuckled softly. "I thought as you said that I had her beat ter death. Ain't that what you said?"

He was playing with her. "Yes," Angel said, staring boldly in his eyes. "But I ain't no fool, not me! What'd I wan' ter go an' tell him that for?"

"I won'er?" Gibbons' grin broadened, but there was a thoughtful look in his eyes. "S'pose I did let you go," he said slowly, "it wouldn' be no use you thinkin' ter go back on me, you know. Ol' Jim'd fin' you no matter where you hid. You wouldn' never see the outside no more, not once I brung you back."

"I won' go back on you."

"Le's see." Gibbons' fingers rasped against his stubbly chin. "What gent's her brother work for?"

Angel took a deep, shuddering breath. "I ain't goin' to tell you that." There was a dryness in her throat, and her nails were biting into her palms, but she forced a confident note into her voice. "I tol' you I wasn' no fool, didn' I? But I'd be one, all right, if I was ter tell you 'bout where he works. Wha's ter stop you goin' ter him an' givin' him the tale, an' maybe keepin' me in Newgate 'n' all?"

"I c'd flog it out o' you," he threatened.

She took a gamble on his greed. "You c'd if you was of a min' ter," she agreed, "but then we'd both be out. I wouldn' never tell you! Never! An' I'd be dead, an' you wouldn' have nothin' for your trouble."

"You mean that, don' you, you bitch?" He shook his head in a baffled way. "You'd let me kill you 'fore you'd tell, that it?"

She nodded. "Yes, 'cause I'd rather be dead than ter stay here."

"I b'lieve you." Gibbons stared at her for a long, silent moment. "How'd I know I c'n trust you?"

" 'Cause I don' never wan' ter see this place no more," she answered quickly. "An' 'cause I b'lieves you when you say as you c'n fin' me any time you wan's ter. An' 'cause I give you me word."

"Your word!" Gibbons gave a harsh bark of laughter. "Fat lot o' bloody good that is!"

He seized her wrist and dragged her roughly to her feet. "I's fear what'll keep you quiet, not your bleedin' word!" He twisted her arm up the back, laughing as she gave a shriek of agony. "Jim don' like gettin' done, see? He don' like it one little bit. Makes him angry, that do!"

He gave her arm another wrench. "So if you was thinkin' 'bout goin' off an' forgettin' 'bout Jim, you c'n bloody well have another think!"

"I tol' you," she shrieked, tears of agony spraying from her eyes. "I don' know what else I c'n do!"

"I get paid off reg'lar, 'member that?" His grip tightened excruciatingly. " 'Cause if I don', sweetheart— if I don', then I comes a-huntin' of you. Fin' you an' all, I will."

She nodded, her lips white with pain.

He released her arm. "Get 'long," he said, giving her a push. "I'm goin' ter let you out with them others. But you 'member what I tol' you."

She stumbled hurriedly away from him. At the door she paused and looked back at him.

You wait! she thought. *Jus' you wait, you bastard! I'll pay you out, an' it'll be more ways 'n' one!*

67

Seeing him take a step toward her, she forced her trembling legs to move. Once out of his sight, a fever possessed her. Free! Free! Her joy made light of the heavy anklets. She walked, head high, past the line of eagerly shuffling prisoners.

ANGEL WALKED PROUDLY, HER FINGERS CAressingly brushing her billowing skirt. The gown she wore had obviously been made for an older and much larger woman, for it hung baggily on her slender frame. It was shabby, and it smelled faintly musty; the original black of the material had faded to a rusty brown; the skirt, patched in many places, was puckered as a result of these inexpert repairs and it hung unevenly. It was the best, however, that the Gray Sisters of St. Luke's Convent had been able to provide on such short notice.

To Angel, moving like a wondering child through streets she had thought never to see again, the gown was beautiful. She was free! Nothing could daunt her now, not even the blisters on her heels caused by shoes too wide and heavy for her narrow feet.

It was early yet; the sonorous notes of Big Ben striking the hour of six still vibrated in her ears. Her steps slowed a little as she gazed her fill upon a transformed city.

The narrow streets, their gray cobbles hidden beneath blankets of flowers, filled her with delight. The houses, huddling cheek-by-jowl and made beautiful by great swags of bunting, dazzled her. Thickly strewn flowers floated upon the open gutters, camouflaging with indifferent success their ugliness. People early abroad, their faces bright with anticipation, rivaled the hanging decorations in the brilliance of their attire.

Angel's bedraggled appearance drew from them many curious and disgusted glances. Their nostrils caught the odor of her long unbathed body. The newly laundered crisply fresh skirts were drawn hastily aside to allow her a clear passage. Nobody called a "good morn" to her, but Angel, heady with freedom, scarcely noticed this lack of civility.

She would mingle with the crowd this afternoon, she was thinking, and catch a glimpse of the wonderful King who had decreed that she go free. Her stride faltered a little as thoughts of Marianne intruded. If only Marianne could have lived to see this day! But she'd keep her promise, Angel determined; she'd seek out this Nicholas Tavington. Jim Gibbons' mustn't bury Marianne's little body in the lime pit, as he would surely do if she didn't reach the brother soon. Gibbons' mean vengeful face seemed to rise up before her. Shuddering, Angel thrust the thought of him away. She wouldn't think of him now; first she would think of the Royal Parade.

Idly, she wondered if the Earl of Benbrook would be riding with the King. She would like a glimpse of this almost legendary man. All London knew that the Earl was a hero. He had been twice seriously wounded in the service of his King; he had been the quarry in a prolonged and ruthless manhunt by Cromwell's men. Imprisoned several times, tortured for information, yet always as elusive as a wisp of fog, he had managed each time to escape his captors.

Now that the hostilities were over and Charles Stuart restored to his rightful place, the Earl had given up his military life in favor of his career. He was not only a hero, he was also a great artist. All this information had been culled by Angel after overhearing a conversation between two of the prison guards.

Angel glanced down at her gown again, and for the first time doubt struck her. Her appearance was not all it should be. Angel's brows drew together. Perhaps she could do something to improve herself; she would need to look at least clean when she paid her visit to the grand house in St. Bernard's Square.

Nell! Angel's frown lifted. Why hadn't she thought of her before? Nell Gwynne, though only ten years old, had been a good friend to her, the only friend, in fact, that she'd ever had. Somehow you didn't think of Nell as being only a little girl; she was more assured than her older sister, the dark, quiet Rose. There was another difference between the sisters, and it concerned their mother, Madam Gwynne, as the woman insisted upon being addressed. Nell frankly loathed the fat, gin-soaked old woman, but Rose adored her and was blind to her selfishness; she slaved willingly for the woman, obeying her in all things. Madam Gwynne took the girl's adoration for granted. Her eldest daughter was a source of income, too, for even when she sold the girl's body to the highest bidder, Rose still made no protest. She hadn't been able to turn Nell into a whore, though, and Angel doubted if the strong-willed Nell would allow herself to be so used, not at least to profit Madam Gwynne.

Angel began to hurry. It was still early. Nell was a slugabed, and she was bound to find her at home. She'd get Nell to heat some water for her; she wouldn't be happy until she'd washed the prison stink from her hair and her body. Her hair? Angel shrugged. She couldn't do anything about the lice that infested it, but at least it would be clean.

Her unwashed gang had often teased her, she remembered, about her passion for cleanliness. It was more than a passion with her now; it had become an obsession.

Angel turned a sharp corner and entered the Hop Garden; it was here that the Gwynnes had their dank little house.

The mingled odors of decaying refuse and animal and human excrement rose to her nostrils. The stench, by virtue of the crisp, cool morning, was slightly subdued; but later, with the rising of the sun, it would become overpowering. As usual, the gutter running the length of the street overflowed with rubbish; the green scum that floated over the accumulated filth was alive with fat sluggish white maggots, and hovering above were swarms of black flies.

No one, it seemed, had thought to cover this gutter with flowers. Angel felt almost childishly disappointed, though she knew the Hop Garden to be one of the meaner streets in a district that abounded with them. Still, they might have bought a few flowers to mark this very special occasion, she thought, and a few strings of bunting, however meager, would have made quite a difference to the gray houses.

A man came lurching from a narrow doorway, startling her. She stopped, staring at him with open curiosity. He was very drunk, and he did not appear to notice his interested audience.

Angel's experienced eyes ran over his person. A swell, she thought, noting the richness of the plum-colored satin jacket and breeches. The jacket was torn at the lapels, the front stained with vomit. His lace-trimmed waterfall cravat had been wrenched open, exposing his thick flushed neck, and his tilted black wig showed an expanse of shaven skull.

"You dirty old bawd!" the man suddenly screamed out. He shook a clenched fist in the direction of the doorway. "Damn your impudence! You'll pay for robbing

Harry Killigrew. I'll have you clapped in Newgate! Plague take you and your diseased whore of a daughter! Why, even the dogs would scorn to snuffle at such a vile wench!"

Angel suddenly realized that she stood before Nell's house. She heard Madam Gwynne's unctuous voice replying, and her interest deepened.

"A decen' womin's what I am, sir, as well you know," Madam Gwynne said. "You gone an' struck me clean to me heart! Yes, sir, woun'ed me ten'er mother's heart, tha's what you done, with you a-sayin' them things 'bout me sweet Rose. Don' see how you c'n bring yourself, sir, 'deed I don'! You know me Rose were a virgin when you bedded her."

The man snorted disgustedly. "Why, you damned lying old bag of offal! Virgin! Huh!"

"That ain't nice o' you, sir," Madame Gwynne said plaintively. "If I had a man ter defen' me, you wouldn' be a-sayin' them things to a poor lone womin." There was a pause, and she added cajolingly, "Come now, sir, I'll make all right with you. I'll give you—" Here there was another pause, and Angel could hear the woman's loud, wheezy breathing—"I'll give you me little tre'sure, her what's as del'cate as a bleedin' bubble atop a glass o' wine."

"Nell?" the man said, an eager interest in his voice.

"The very same, sir. Ain't she a sweet little bud, then? Temp' a perishin' saint, would me darlin' Nell."

The man seemed to lose interest. Angel saw his florid color recede rapidly, leaving his face a grayish-white. A white ring appeared about his mouth; his wide nostrils flared, bubbles of saliva formed at the corners of his slack mouth and, breaking, dribbled down his chin. He made a guttural sound, then, spinning round on his high, red heels, he broke into a stumbling run. Avoiding a pile of rotting fish-guts, he reached the gutter just in time. Coughing, belching, retching painfully, he vomited into the seething scum.

Angel laughed aloud, and Madam Gwynne said sharply, "Who's that?"

"Me," Angel said, stepping forward to confront the woman in the doorway. "I's Angel Dawson."

For a moment the tall, monstrously fat woman stared at the girl in astounded silence; then her round blue eyes, embedded in pouched flesh, began to fill with indignation. Her triple chins quivered, and the pursed pale button of her mouth hardened.

"Bleedin' hussy!" she said harshly. "You keep away from me gels, Angel Dawson. I don' wan' no trollops in me decen' house, so be off with you!"

Angel smiled. "Maybe you'd like me ter tell Nell what you jus' tol' the gent?" she said silkily. "Nell ain't goin' ter like that, is she? Make ever such a row 'bout it, will Nell."

Madam Gwynne closed her sagging jaw. "Oh!" she explained, giving an exaggerated start. "So you're that Angel Dawson. I ought ter have knowed it, 'cept that me ol' eyes ain't what they uster be."

"What a shame," Angel said pleasantly. "But how many Angel Dawsons do you know, then?"

"Come in, come in," the woman said hastily, ignoring the question. She stepped back from the door and as Angel entered, slammed it against any further incursions from the swell. "How'd you get out o' Newgate, eh? But there—" she broke off, her vast bosom heaving emotionally, "you'd better not tell me! I can feel me blood startin' to run col' when I think on what you mus've been through, you poor little perisher!"

"You sure you wan' me in here?" Angel said. "What 'bout me bein' a trollop?"

Madam Gwynne seemed to be having difficulty with

her voice. She swallowed twice, then said, "Now, now, I tol' you 'bout that, eh? I thought as you was some other little bleeder. 'Sides," she went on, "ain't you allus been welcome in me home?"

"No," Angel answered, "I ain't. You tol' me, las' time I was here as you'd beat on me arse if I didn' get out your house."

"Me!" Madam Gwynne looked pained. "Cut out me tongue, I would, afore I'd say such a thing! Why, you allus been like one o' me own bleedin' gels!"

Angel gave her a long look as she went through the open door to her left and entered the dingy, furniture-cramped front room. Choosing a stool, Angel sat down.

"C'n I see Nell?" she said to Madam Gwynne, who had waddled quickly after her.

The woman's small, suspicious eyes darted quickly round the room, as if mentally assessing its contents, then reluctantly she turned back to the door. "I'll go'n call the lazy little bleeder," she mumbled. "Cow should've been up long since."

Seeing her hesitate, Angel remarked coldly, "You don' have ter worry. I ain't goin' ter pinch nothin'."

Madam Gwynne turned as fast as her bulk would allow.

"Why, Angel gel," she said, putting her hand to her bosom, "I wouldn' never think nothin' nasty the like o' that 'bout you! Treasure, tha's what you are. Jus' like one o' me own gels."

"You said that a'ready. C'n I see Nell now?"

"O' course, love." The woman's eyes, hard with dis-like, rested briefly on Angel. "You sit an' res', dear," she cooed, turning once more to the door. " 'Bout that little joke what you heared," she went on, her back to Angel, "ain't no need ter mention it ter Nell, is there? The cow wouldn' un'erstan' as it was jus' a joke. Nell ain't never had no un'erstan'ing 'bout them kin' o' thin's. Why, she might go 'n' think as I meant it."

"I won'er why?" Angel said. "But there ain't no need for you to as' me that. You trus' me, don' you?"

"No I bleedin' well d——" Madam Gwynne broke off. "Oh me head!" she moaned. "Hurts me so crool bad that I don' know what I'm sayin' half me time. 'Course I trus' you, sweetheart. Bless your dear, kin', gen'rous heart." She turned her head to bestow a beaming smile on Angel, then she went quickly from the room.

"Nell!" Angel started a little at the penetrating scream. "Get out o' that bleedin' bed," Madam Gwynne shouted, "or I'll take me whip to your skinny arse!"

"Shut your mouth, ol' fat buttocks!" came Nell's answering scream.

"You hear her, Angel gel?" Madam Gwynne lamented. "Ain't nat'ral her a-talkin' to her ol' ma that a-way."

"Wha's that?" Nell shouted. "You talkin' to yourself 'gain, you daft ol' bowl o' jelly?"

Angel got up and went to the door. "I's me, Nell," she called. "Angel Dawson. I come ter see you."

"What!" Nell appeared on the landing. "Angel!" Nell's piquantly pretty face split into a grin of delight. She ran down the stairs. "I can' hardly b'lieve it!" she said, gripping Angel's arm. "Look, Ma, i's Angel!"

"I seen her," Madam Gwynne answered sourly.

Nell's delight was genuine, and Angel was touched by the glow in her big dark-blue eyes. "I's me right 'nough, Nell," she said huskily. "Seems that the King writ out a proc'mation what said me 'n' some others was ter go free. I still can' hardly b'lieve it."

Nell swung round to her mother. "Ain't it won'erful, me ol' gin pot?" she said gleefully.

Madam Gwynne uttered an outraged scream. "Don' you call me that! Ain't you got no respec' for your ma, you perishin' little sod?"

76

"Respec'?" Nell's eyes widened in surprise. "What'd I wan' ter go havin' respec' for? Sell me for fourpence you would, you bleedin' ol' faggot, an' you knows it."

Madam Gwynne darted a quick look at Angel. The girl looked back at her, her expression blank.

"Oh!" Madam Gwynne's bosom began to heave so violently, that Angel stared, fascinated. "How c'n you talk to your ol' ma so crool?" she cried in a trembling voice. "Ain't I work me bloody fingers to the perishin' bone for you? Ma loves her two little buds, she do. You 'n' Rosie posie is the joy o' me bleedin' heart!" She clutched herself somewhere in the region of her heart, adding ominously, "Me heart, what ain't got much longer ter go on a-beatin'."

"Don' blame it," Nell retorted cheerfully. "I wouldn' wan' ter go on beatin' neither, not if I had ter carry roun' all that load'er jelly. I bet it's a-lyin' under all them pillers er fat jus' a-cryin' its bloody eyes out."

Nell grabbed Angel's hand. "Come on," she cried. "We don' have ter stay here with ol' guzzle-guts. Le's get a good place so's we c'n see the King ride by."

Angel hung back. "I ain't goin' nowhere till I got me hair 'n' body clean," she stated flatly.

Nell frowned impatiently. "Oh, all right." She smiled suddenly. "You always was pertic'lar 'bout bein' clean."

"Was I?" Angel smiled back at her. "It's been so long that I don' 'member."

"Hmm!" Nell's eyes swept critically over Angel's gown. "That don' look nice," she pronounced. "It don' suit you. Don' matter, though. I c'n len' you one o' Rose's gowns. She won' min'."

Rose, entering the house at that moment, started in surprise at the sight of Angel; and Angel, forestalling her questions, launched once more into explanation. After a while she noticed that Rose, though nodding now and

77

again, was only half-listening; her loving, anxious eyes were inspecting her moaning mother.

"Tha's nice, Angel," Rose said absently, at the conclusion. "I'm glad as you're out." She took a step away, then turned back to Angel. "I's Ma, see?" she said apologetically. "I got ter see ter her. She's—well, Ma's del'cate like."

Hiding her smile, Angel said reassuringly, "I un'erstan', Rose. You go 'n' look after her, then."

Rose looked at her gratefully. "Let me jus' get Ma settled, then you 'n' me c'n have a nice talk."

Nell gave a smothered laugh. Rose rounded on her.

"Now then, Nellie Gwynne," Rose said sharply. "Don' you go upsettin' Ma. You know she ain't feelin' good."

At this, Madam Gwynne began to moan piteously. "Huh!" Nell said contemptuously. "But the ol' bag'll be well 'nough ter go out 'n' guzzle the King's wine. You jus' see if she ain't."

"That's 'nough out o' you, Nell!" Rose's face was stern and set. "I's you 'n' your rotten selfish ways what gives poor Ma these bad turns."

"Wha's the use?" Nell said, shrugging. "You got somethin' loose in your head, you have, Rose. Don' you go stayin' in 'cause o' ol' gin tonsil. She'll on'y slip off when you ain't lookin'. Me 'n' Angel's goin' upstairs ter get ready for the parade. I'm goin' ter len' her one o' your gowns, Rose."

Rose nodded vaguely. "Tha's right, Nell. See if you c'n fin' her one what ain't too patched."

"Nell!" Madam Gwynne shrieked. "Nell, gel, don' say as you're goin' off an' leavin' your ma ter die all 'lone?"

" 'Course I am," Nell said. She mounted the stairs firmly, pushing Angel before her. "You ain't goin' ter die for years, you ol' faggot," she called back. "I ain't daft like Rose, you know. You c'n save it up if you like, then I'll be here when you go." Laughing, she disappeared.

"Why'd you say that, Ma?" Rose turned wounded eyes on her mother. "You ain't 'lone. I'm here, ain't I? Don' I count?"

Madam Gwynne threw her an impatient look. "Stop your whinin', Rose, do! That bleedin' long face o' yours gets on me nerves!" She chuckled and nodded her massive head. "Cow, that Nell is. Don' know why you can' be more like her, Rose. Bleedin' little sod, she is, an' got plen'y of spirit too, the same like I had when I was her age. Remin's me a lot o' meself, she do."

Rose's dark head drooped meekly. "I'll try 'n' be more like Nell, Ma, if—if tha's what you wan'."

Madam Gwynne gave a scornful laugh. "You! You ain't got it in your ter be like her. Fit for a perishin' king is my pretty Nell!"

Even the weather seemed determined to give of its best on this significant royal occasion, for it was unusually temperate for May. The sun, riding high in the cloudless blue canopy of the sky, bathed the people lining the Royal Way in a gentle warmth; giving the lie to those pessimistic souls who had predicted rain.

All over London the bells chimed forth together, the deep tolling of some and the high, silvery chimes of others competing with the enthusiastic roar of the crowd and the ground-shaking booming of cannon from Park Green.

The soldiers ranged in front of the people, immaculate in their red and white uniforms, looked like toy soldiers, stiffly unmoving. Nevertheless they managed to resist all efforts to scramble past them. Wooden-faced, ignoring the insults flung at them, they kept the Royal Way clear. Only their eyes could be observed to move very slightly as the King rode slowly past.

Charles Stuart did not disappoint his subjects. Seated astride his great white horse, the reins held loosely in thin, jeweled hands, he was a striking figure. One could not have mistaken him for other than he was—the King of England!

The crimson velvet of his jacket and breeches was heavily embroidered in a design of gold butterflies and silver bees; a double flounce of silver lace decorated the knees of the breeches, the edge of each flounce sewn with small emeralds.

Charles, smiling and waving at his people, had the feeling that the horse beneath him did but carry him forward through a familiar dream. Was it really happening, or would he shortly awaken in his bed at the Hoogstraeten in Holland? Fifteen years of exile he had endured—fifteen aching years; and not a day had passed that he did not pray for the vindication of his beloved father and for the news of his own restoration.

"God save the King!" The roar of sound lanced into his consciousness, bringing him back to the reality of the moment. His swarthy face in the shadow of his plume-laden hat glowed with emotion.

His people! His! He would not let them down! Long after he was dead, let it be recorded that Charles Stuart's homecoming was a joyous occasion, and a glorious turning point in England's history! Fervently he prayed that it would be so.

He looked upward. There were faces at every window. The curving balconies, draped with the flag of England, were crowded with men and women in bright garments. One balcony bore a bevy of young ladies. Charles could not help a stir of sensuous pleasure as his eyes lingered on them. They were lovely in their swaying, rainbow-hued silks. Their wide-brimmed hats, dripping with plumes, cast intriguing shadows over smiling, painted faces. Aware of his interest, they curtsied as he passed.

Charles lifted his arm in response to another thunderous ovation. The fine laces at his wrists fluttered in a slight breeze. The trumpets blared forth; the drums boomed out in loud triumph. Flowers rained down from the balconies, and behind the soldiers the people surged forward like a cresting wave. The soldiers linked arms with stiff, precise movements, effectively resisting but showing the strain in their eyes and in the grimly set line of their mouths.

Nicholas, Earl of Benbrook, riding to the King's left, slightly behind, felt the deep exaltation of this moment. The long and bitter fighting they had endured—the poverty of their king and of themselves; the unrelenting pursuit of their enemies, and the ever present danger that Charles might be captured and beheaded, as his father before him—it had all been worth it, for it had led to this moment. Their king rode triumphantly before them, and there was not a man in the long retinue who would not lay down his life for him. Not a man, Nicholas amended, except one. George Villiers, Duke of Buckingham, traitorous turncoat!

The Duke, riding to the King's right, had successfully reestablished himself; just as once before, deserting Charles and his cause, he had ingratiated himself with Cromwell.

Nicholas' lips tightened. The King was too forgiving. Had he also forgotten the Duke's marriage to Mary Fairfax, the daughter of the Roundhead General, who was then the King's most tenacious enemy?

Nicholas did not believe, as the King apparently did, in the seeming warmth and sincerity of the Duke's repentance. Buckingham and his cousin, Barbara Palmer—the King's favorite mistress—were, in Nicholas' opinion, cut from the same cloth. Both of them were greedy and ambitious; both were treacherous.

Barbara was a shrew—an impossibly demanding, violent-tempered and selfish woman. But she was also exquisitely beautiful and the King at the moment was enslaved by that beauty.

As though Charles had become aware of Nicholas' sober thoughts, he turned his head. The jeweled hand lifted, beckoning him forward. "Attend me, my lord," he called lightly.

"Sire?" Nicholas said, bringing his horse alongside.

Charles smiled at him warmly. "Grave faces are not permitted on this day of days. Come," he said, his voice deepening. "What troubles you, friend Nicholas?"

"I, sire?" Nicholas returned the smile. "Not a thing in this world, I do assure you. But you, sire? Is all well with you?"

Charles hesitated. "All is well," he said slowly. "I would indeed be ungrateful were I to say otherwise. But—"

Charles broke off to acknowledge his people. He turned from side to side, waving his hand, smiling his brilliant, charming smile.

"But," Nicholas pursued, when he once more had the King's attention. "It is not quite perfect without the presence of your sister."

"Ah, Nicholas, how well you know me," Charles said. " 'Tis selfish of me to want more and yet more, I know it. But I would give much to have my little Minette at my side."

There was always that tenderness in the King's voice when he spoke of his sister. Nicholas had heard it many times before. But there was also the underlying note of sadness. Fate, it seemed, with the able assistance of their dominating mother, conspired to keep the brother and sister apart.

"Depend upon it, sire," Nicholas said encouragingly. "The Princess will not tolerate another delay in her sailing."

He smiled at Charles. "We know, do we not, sire, that Her Highness has quite a will of her own?"

Charles laughed. "Aye, and a temper, too. We sampled it, remember? Poor helpless devils that we were! If you are right, Nicholas, then France's loss will be my gain."

"I trust so," Nicholas replied.

Smiling, Nicholas watched as Charles deftly caught a thrown flower; he raised it to his lips, and the women, intrigued by this gesture, screamed their pleasure.

Yes, Charles knew how to please, Nicholas mused. He would be a popular king. A good king, too, for Nicholas was aware of his ardent desire to be all in all to his people.

The women, competing now for the King's attention, began pelting him with flowers. Smiling, king and earl rode slowly through the scented barrage.

"Your pardon, sire," Nicholas said. "Should I not drop back into position?"

"Nay," Charles said quickly. "Stay by me. I would have you share in these moments."

"Sire," Nicholas began. "I have no right. I—"

"No right?" Charles looked at him in astonishment. "We were together through the lean bad years, were we not? It is fitting therefore that you share in the honors my people accord me."

He raised a hand, stemming further words. "You have also the right of my express command. Is it enough for you, Nicholas?"

"It is enough, sire," Nicholas answered, bowing his head.

A man in the forefront of the crowd, recognizing Nicholas, yelled excitedly, "Look! 'Tis the 'vanishing Earl' who rides beside the King!"

It was a popular nickname, for thus, in the light of his many miraculous escapes, they had dubbed him.

The crowd, bent on honoring him, too, began to chant, "The vanishing Earl is Cromwell's curse—is Cromwell's curse—"

A great cheer went up as Nicholas lifted his hand in response.

"You see?" Charles said, raising his voice to compete with the uproar. "Where else should the vanishing Earl be, if not at his King's side?"

There was no jealousy in Charles, and he smiled on his friend, well pleased. "I pray you, though," he went on, a laugh in his voice, "do not vanish now. I fear that it would greatly discomfit your admirers."

Nicholas answered in the same light vein, "You have my word, sire. But when you command that it be so, I will vanish in a cloud of smoke."

Now the crowd's attention turned to the old Emir of Banderpur—loyal friend of Charles I now paying honor to his son. The Emir rode slowly by, and behind him, mounted on black horses, were his sixteen veiled wives. They rode demurely sidesaddle, and the jeweled reins of their horses were held by small black pages clad in coats of peacock-blue silk, the backs embroidered with a large silver tiger, emblem of the House of Banderpur. Baggy trousers of emerald-green were tucked into boots of silver kid; green turbans decorated with silver plumes sat low on their heads. The eyes of the women smiled above veils of golden mesh edged with precious stones; their limbs showed faintly rosy through tissue-thin silk trousers. Little black jackets, banded with jewels, were parted to show high breasts straining against flimsy silk; henna-tinted nipples thrust arrogantly through heart-shaped embroidered holes. Their headdresses rose like golden minarets, tinkling with small bells.

The crowd cheered them, but there was much laughter and many ribald comments. The Emir himself was almost somber in a black silk coat, the high collar edged with emeralds, and plain black silk trousers. He had been a good friend to their past king and was prepared to befriend Charles Stuart, so for him their cheers were loud and prolonged.

Behind the Emir's procession came his strutting

House Guard, in tight-fitting uniforms of purple and gold. Beneath tassled gold caps their bearded faces were set and stern. They marched, staring straight ahead, right hands resting on the hilts of scimitars thrust through wide golden cummerbunds.

Surfeited, the fickle crowd deserted the Emir. Pushing and jostling behind the line of soldiers, they fought to reach the head of the procession again.

At Hill Mount the procession stopped on cue, and the exciting boom of drums and the blare of trumpets were heard.

From all sides hysterical screams of delight arose as the Stuart Battalion, rounding the mount, hove into view.

The battalion, formed in the time of the ill-fated Charles I, had been disbanded with the advent of Oliver Cromwell. Now, re-formed by General Monk, they marched proudly in their immaculate uniforms of red and white, wide sashes of Stuart Tartan, and tall black hats pinned with the emblem of a crouching lion within a circlet of Scottish thistles. They drew their swords as they approached the King, and the sun flashed on the naked blades held high in salute.

Tears stood in Charles' eyes as he acknowledged them with uplifted hand. As a little boy he had stood beside his father and watched them parade. He had sensed his father's pride in the battalion; and this salute, though not unexpected, he found very touching.

The long parade was almost over, and the people made a concerted effort to get nearer to their king. The soldiers, perspiring in their thick uniforms, stood firm, and once again came the shouted order to link arms. The people surged against the reinforced line; finding it unyielding, their efforts gradually ceased. They dropped back a little, contenting themselves with shouting insults at the soldiers.

Relieved, the soldiers allowed themselves to relax

slightly, and it was then that it happened. One of the soldiers, caught off guard, felt a mighty push against his legs; his knees buckled, and before he could stiffen them again, two girls had wriggled through and darted straight into the path of the King's advancing horse.

"What the devil!" Charles exclaimed. His hands tightened on the reins, drawing the nervously curvetting horse to a standstill.

Nicholas had dropped behind a little. He spurred forward quickly. "What is it, sire?" he shouted.

With a clatter of feet, the Royal Guard appeared on the scene. They had received their orders earlier. "At the first sign of trouble, protect the King's person." Instantly they ranged themselves about the King in a tight ring, weapons drawn and ready.

But the girls were within the ring. They turned frightened faces to the King, looking up at him appealingly.

Charles smiled at them reassuringly. "No cause for alarm," he said, addressing the Captain of the Royal Guard. At a sign from the Captain, the Guard fell back. They were not dismissed, however. They stood at alert attention awaiting further orders. The Captain, red-faced and distinctly at a loss, stared into the middle distance and hoped quite fervently that he would not have to render an accounting to his superior.

Charles' eyes were kind as he looked into the two upturned faces. Their action, he decided, had done no real harm. It was unheard of to hold up a Royal Parade, but Charles dismissed this thought easily. With the shrewder part of his brain he knew that his indulgence had been noted and admired by the startled onlookers. As was usual with him, his weakness for the feminine sex, young or old, far outweighed his shrewdness; and with easy facility he had already assessed the charms of the two young creatures.

One was but a child, but a most attractive child, he

noted approvingly. Her honey-gold curls and large, gold-en-lashed blue eyes, her piquant, fair complected face, now dimpling with smiles, was pleasing to him.

The older girl, though atrociously clad in a green gown, overburdened with cheap lace trimming, was truly lovely. She would be lovelier still, Charles added a mental note, when she filled out a little. At the moment she was painfully thin. Red-gold hair framed a face that was slight-ly yellowed, as if from the lingering results of a long ill-ness, and the violet-blue eyes looking into his had an oddly haunted look.

Charles held out his hand to the older girl. Blushing scarlet, she dropped a quick curtsy, then, taking his hand gingerly, she pressed a kiss upon his jeweled fingers.

"Thank you, Your Majesty," she said, releasing his hand. "I thank you more'n you c'n ever know!"

Somehow Charles knew that she did not refer to his gesture. Intrigued by the fervent note in her voice, he would have liked to question her. Instead, he said gently, "Permit me the honor of knowing your name, mistress."

"Me name's Angel Dawson, Your Majesty," she answered, and her voice trembled a little.

"A pretty name for a pretty girl," Charles said, with the gallantry that was second nature to him.

He turned to the child and held out his hand. Nothing loath, she grabbed it eagerly and planted a loud, enthusiastic kiss upon his fingers.

"Me name's Nell Gwynne, Your Majesty," she informed him in a high excited voice.

Angel eyed the man mounted on the big, chestnut horse who had for some time ridden in the place of honor beside the King. She knew that he could be none other than the Earl of Benbrook.

Almost as if he felt her stare, the Earl turned his head and looked down at her. The dark, arrogant face was cold and unsmiling, and there was something in his eyes that made her shiver involuntarily. He looked away again, and she felt that he had dismissed her as unimportant.

Perhaps she was unimportant. But anger rose in her that he had made her feel so with the merest glance of those black, bitter eyes. She didn't like him, she decided. He was hateful!

Neither did she admire the plain cut of his emerald-green satin jacket. It was unadorned, as were the matching breeches. Unlike the King and the other gentlemen in the retinue, the Earl wore no wig. His dark hair was brushed smoothly back from his face and fastened at the nape of the neck with a narrow, black ribbon.

A laugh from the crowd drew Angel's attention to Nell. She felt ashamed and embarrassed when Nell said boldly, "Don' forget Nell Gwynne, Your Majesty! Don' forget 'bout me!"

"Shut up," Angel said in a low urgent voice. "Who'd you think you are ter go a-sayin' that?"

The King was raising his arm in the signal of departure. "Farewell, ladies," he said pleasantly. " 'Twas a most enjoyable meeting."

The soldiers dropped back into position, and the parade went on. Nell looked after the King wistfully. "Ain't he gran', Angel?" She tugged at Angel's sleeve. "Come on," she cried. "Le's see if we c'n catch up 'gain."

Angel ignored her. "Did you see the Earl, Nell?" she asked.

" 'Course I did. Han'some, ain't he?"

"I never thought he was," Angel answered coldly. "I didn' like him."

Nell stared at her. "Ain't nothin' ter like or not ter like. How c'n you tell if he never talked ter you?"

"I c'd tell."

"Well," Nell said indifferently, "it don' matter, do it? Anyway, i's the King what I like." She sighed. "He is nice, ain't he, Angel?"

"Yes," Angel said. "But I didn' like the other 'un."

"Never min' 'bout him," Nell said impatiently. "Lis-'en, Angel, I jus' made up me min' ter somethin'. I'm a-goin ter be the King's mistress, tha's what."

Angel laughed. "Some hopes!" she jeered. "The King wouldn' never look at you, you silly cow!"

"He will! He will!" Nell shouted, glaring at Angel. "I made up me min', see? Jealous, tha's what you are, Angel Dawson!"

"I ain't."

"Yes you are, an' why? 'Cause you know that once Nell Gwynne's got her min' made up, she gets what she bleedin' wants, tha's why."

Nicholas Tavington studied the finished portrait of the Countess of Barchester. It was good, he decided, but he was glad to be finished with it at last. The Countess was always an irritating woman. Lately she had been more than usually trying, and his temper, never equable, had been rubbed raw by her petulant demands.

Picking up a cloth, he draped the portrait. The brush he had been using he thrust in with several others that he had been meaning for some time to clean. At a loss, as he invariably was at the conclusion of one work, he began moodily pacing the cluttered room, his mind already racing ahead to his next subject.

The big, bright, curtainless room was Nicholas' private sanctum, and the paint-stained floor, the dusty confusion about him, did not disturb him, normally fastidious though he was. He had forbidden the servants to enter; he allowed nothing in the room to be disturbed.

Only Mrs. Sampson, the housekeeper, dared to break this rule; but, as the servants well knew, the housekeeper was a privileged person. She had been with the master from the day of his birth; she respected him, even loved him, but she did not go in awe of him as they did.

The servants found Mrs. Sampson's partiality for the Earl hard to understand. The general consensus was that the Earl, though undoubtedly handsome, was simply not human—so cold, so rigidly unbending was he. He was invariably polite, thanking them for the smallest service they performed for him; but he did not smile, his eyes did not warm to life, and he might just as well have been speaking to the wall.

Mrs. Mott, the cook, always ready to give an opinion, stated that the woman capable of thawing out the Earl didn't exist. The newest scullery maid, however, being inclined to a more romantic turn of mind, had been heard to wonder just what it would be like to be loved by —as she put it—"a gent like that."

Mrs. Mott, who believed it to be her duty in life to correct the natural stupidity of the lower domestics, had answered the scullery maid quite sharply. "A body might jus' as well be loved by a winter's wind as ter be loved by him. An' tha's enough o' your foolish talk!"

It would have surprised them to know that the Earl's grimly unapproachable outer covering hid every human if inarticulate yearnings; for the shell he had built about him with the years was far too thick to show him the true nature of those yearnings. He was a man that, not knowing himself, was often intensely and achingly lonely.

When the people had affectionately nicknamed him the "vanishing Earl," they had no idea that the name was suited not only to his daring escapes, but to that deep reserve in his nature that caused him to retreat more and more into himself. He would allow no one to probe too deeply into his personal life, not even the King, to whom he gave his loyalty and who was his dearest friend.

Sometimes, wandering restlessly about his great echoing house in St. Bernard's Square, Nicholas would become aware of a certain lack in his life. But he had no idea what that lack might be, and so he disciplined himself against these vague longings until they disappeared.

He was an artist of quite astonishing genius, and he

was entirely absorbed in his career. Posterity would be enriched by his glowing canvases and the air of radiant breathing life he gave to all his subjects. But there were times—though he was not consciously aware of it—when bitter cynicism guided his brush to a somewhat cruel portrayal of his subject.

He could not be said to be a recluse, for the women in his life were numerous and remarkably varied in their attractions. Yet again there was that lack, for he brought no tenderness to these associations. To him, women were merely a means to assuage his sexual appetite; he asked and expected nothing more of them, and in truth he entertained for them the deepest contempt.

The contempt had grown up in him very early in life, inspired by the example of his mother—Lady Catherine Tavington. Lady Catherine, though of good birth and breeding, had been hardly better than a prostitute. For Nicholas, her dark, grave son, and her tiny daughter, Marianne, she had only indifference to offer, and for her elderly husband, John Tavington, a sneering disregard. Nicholas had loved his father dearly, and he had seen him die little by little until, finally, broken by Lady Catherine's never-ending string of lovers and by the results of her horrifying excesses, he had closed his eyes one evening and surrendered willingly to death.

Ironically, it was very shortly after John Tavington's death that Lady Catherine had come to a violent end. She had been strangled by a jealous lover.

Nicholas, bereft of both parents, found himself the guardian of his sister, Marianne. There was love in him for his sister, but when he looked at her he remembered their mother. He was harsh with her but just, and always ready to ruthlessly suppress any inherited and undesirable traits. The gentle and biddable Marianne was not in the least like her mother; but Nicholas was not reassured, and he continued to watch her closely.

When circumstances turned his life into another course, Nicholas was compelled to relax his strict supervision. Uneasily he traveled to London; and he did not know that Marianne—despite everything—grieved for him. He did not expect her love, nor did he show his love for her. But to the young girl leading her lonely life at Benbrook Manor, the family estate in Worcestershire, Nicholas represented an ideal. Not until the advent of John Bannister did she realize that grimness could be replaced with what she took for love, and suspicion with tenderness. Held in John's arms, his kisses on her mouth, Marianne found that love was an important part of life, the most important part, and she sighed for the unhappiness she now knew must be her brother's.

It was on the occasion of one of Nicholas' rare visits to Benbrook Manor that he discovered the intrusion into his sister's life.

Only once had Nicholas met John Bannister, the youngest son of the Duke of Fernbury. John, though only twenty years old, had already acquired an unsavory reputation, and Nicholas had heard of the many scandals attached to the young man's name. When John presented himself at Benbrook Manor and requested permission to pay court to Marianne, Nicholas had been outraged. He had not heeded Marianne's tearful declaration of love for Bannister; instead, he curtly ordered the young man out of the house. If ever he attempted to see his sister again, Nicholas had promised grimly, he would have him soundly thrashed.

Bannister was unused to being thwarted, and he left the Manor in a towering rage. If Marianne had cherished the hope that he might rescue her from her miserable isolation, her hopes were in vain. Seeking a panacea for his blighted love, John was already well on his way to London. And it was there that the end of Marianne's love affair was to be written.

Filled with self-pity and fancying himself to be genuinely in love with Marianne, Bannister had confided his story to Peg Mallison, his current mistress. It proved to be his greatest mistake. Peg, fuddled with wine, filled with jealous rage, had stabbed him to death while he slept.

For once, Nicholas found himself at a loss. He did not know how to deal with the grieving Marianne. Shaken temporarily out of his reserve, he had confided the story to the King on his next visit to London.

Charles had a deep affection for Nicholas, and pitied him for his inability to conquer the dark demons that drove him. He decided to take a hand. He expressed a wish to Nicholas that the eighteen-year-old Marianne, whose pathetic little love story with its tragic ending had touched his tender heart, be brought to London and presented to him.

Nicholas had not answered at once. He was clearly struggling with himself. Charles' eyes lingered thoughtfully on that arrogant profile. More was required he realized. And so he had commanded Mistress Marianne's presence. Nicholas bowed stiffly in response. He had said nothing more. Charles had been well satisfied, for even the imperiously proud Nicholas would not disobey a direct command.

Nicholas wandered over to the window. Standing there, his unseeing eyes on the mud-splashed cobbles below, his thoughts turned to his sister. It would be as well to obey the King's command, he thought. Yes, Nicholas made up his mind abruptly. He would bring Marianne to London. Her presentation to the King might in some small measure console her for the death of John Bannister.

His brows drew together in a frown. But not even for the King's pleasure would he allow his sister to be exposed over long to the licentious atmosphere of the Court. The lords and ladies had assembled abroad during Cromwell's time. Now, with scarcely an interruption in the old pattern save that it was presently conducted in luxury, they congregated about Charles in London.

Nicholas moved uneasily. It had been his unpleasant duty to break the news of Bannister's death to Marianne. She had taken the news calmly enough. At first this had puzzled him; then he had realized that Marianne quite simply did not believe him. She had thought it another of his ploys to keep them apart.

Keeping his voice as gentle as possible, and feeling with an unaccustomed pity the pain that must soon be hers, he had tried to convince her that John Bannister was indeed dead.

Marianne had brushed all his words aside but suddenly she had cried out, "You're incapable of love, Nicholas! Yes, yes, it's true! You will die unloved!"

He had been unbearably stung by her words. "I do not need this so-called love," he had replied, "and certainly I have none to give, unless it be to you."

She had backed away from him. With her hands outflung to ward him off, she had reiterated her belief that John Bannister still lived. "I will find him for myself," she had said in a trembling voice. "Nothing you can say or do shall keep me from him!"

Nicholas had stayed at the Manor for a few days. Marianne's attitude, save for her stubborn belief, had been perfectly natural. Yet on his journey back to London, he had found himself remembering the hard, dry glitter of her eyes, the composure that upon reflection now seemed unnatural.

With every mile of his journey his uneasiness had increased, and almost he had turned back. Had it not been for Ellen, Marianne's personal maid, he would certainly have done so. Ellen had proved herself to be trustworthy, and she was devoted to Marianne. He could safely leave her in the woman's hands. If he should be needed, Ellen would send a servant posting to London. There were enough of them idling about the Manor, he had thought sourly; it would do them good to have some task.

No message, disturbing or otherwise, had come from the Manor, and with the preparations for the King's return, his odd uneasiness, almost a sense of foreboding, had been thrust into the background of his mind. Sometimes though—as now—it returned to plague him.

Three months, he thought, drumming his fingers on the window frame. Yes, it must be all of three months since he had seen Marianne. He had been harsh with the child—too harsh. But he would try to make it up to her. He did not believe in marriage for himself, but he would not put an objection in the way if Marianne would but present him with a decent and suitable candidate.

Disinterestedly, he watched a bright-haired wench picking a gingerly way over the slippery cobbles. Pausing before the house, the girl stood hesitantly as if not quite sure that she should approach the gate.

A new serving girl, Nicholas thought. They were always coming and going.

About to move away, Nicholas looked at the girl more intently. There was something familiar about her; he had the feeling he had seen her before, and quite recently. His eyes lingered on her hair. A most unusual color, he thought appreciatively; its rich brightness reminded him of a newly minted coin.

The girl moved out of his vision, and Nicholas' brief spurt of interest died. He would set out for Worcestershire tomorrow, he decided. He had been neglectful of Marianne, but perhaps it was not too late to establish a new relationship with her. He thought wryly that it would have to be one with a great deal more understanding on his part.

Unaware that she had been observed, Angel Dawson took several more halting steps. She stared wide-eyed at the imposing home before her.

Semicircular marble steps, their whiteness veined with gold, led to immense double oaken doors. Either side of the steps were two lions, their skilfully carved bodies looking so real that one almost had the feeling that the crouching beasts were readying to spring. They were an intimidating sight, the tawny yellow painted bodies and black bristling manes shining in the sunlight. There was a dazzle of sunlight, too, across the innumerable windows.

Except for the open carriage space that led to a sweeping drive, the house was circled by high ornamental railings. The front lawns stretching out on both sides of the drive were a cool green, pricked here and there with beds of brightly colored flowers. Beyond the house, looking to Angel's awed eyes as if it must surely reach for miles and miles, she caught a vista of rolling park grounds.

Reluctantly, but mindful of her promise to Marianne, Angel moved away from the great door. Walking slowly along the smoothly paved winding drive, she wondered if there might be another entrance. Still, she thought, if she went far enough, it must lead to the back premises.

The house was even larger than she had expected, and the drive curved faithfully about its many odd and unexpected angles. Eventually, just as she thought that it might be wiser to retrace her steps, the drive branched to the left, leading away from the house; the smooth paving ended and gave way to a roughly cobbled path that led her to the stables.

Two boys lounging on stools before a long wooden table were busily engaged in eating. They looked up at Angel's approach, staring at her curiously.

"What you doin' here?" one demanded, putting down a half-chewed bone.

"If i's any o' your business," Angel retorted sharply, annoyed at the grins spreading over both faces, "I come with a message."

"Who for?" the burlier one said.

She tossed her head indignantly. "It ain't none o' your bus'ness, an' I ain't goin' ter tell you."

"I c'd make you if I was of a min'," the boy said half threateningly. His grin returned. "But there, you're a pretty wench, so I won' give you the clout 'cross the head what you're a-askin' for. If it's the kitchen what you're wantin'," he went on, pointing with a grimy finger, "i's 'long that path."

"Thanks," Angel said, nodding.

She was about to move on, when a plaintive whinny from behind her followed by a nudge in her back caused her to swing around sharply.

A chestnut horse, his head thrust over the half door of his stall, was regarding her with mournful liquid brown eyes.

"Oh, ain't you a beauty, then!" Angel exclaimed in delight, patting the handsome head. The satiny nose sniffed at her inquisitively. "Sweet," she crooned, stroking the nose lovingly. "You're a darlin' sweet, ain't you!"

"Tha's 'nough," the burly boy said, coming forward. "His lordship don' like for no one ter touch his horse. Partic'lar strangers."

"Won' poison it, will I?" Angel said indignantly. With a final pat, she moved reluctantly away. "Wha's the horse's name?" she asked.

"Don' know much, do you?" the boy said, giving her a scornful look. "Tha's Victory, o' course. Famous, he is. I thought ev'body knew ol' Vic. He was with his lordship all through the fightin'. I's Vic what carried His Majesty to safety after Cromwell's lot'd taken his lordship pris'ner."

He patted the horse. "Victory's gettin' old now, but his lordship won' ride no other. He sees to it as we treats ol' Vic good 'n' all."

Remembering the arrogant dark face of the Earl, the hard, proud curl of his lips, Angel said heatedly, "An' so he should. Leas' he c'n do, ain't it?"

"You don' have ter worry 'bout Vic," the boy said, grinning. "Got a good life, he has. Which ain't su'prisin', seein' as his lordship likes an'mals better'n what he do humans."

Angel shrugged. "Well," she said, stepping onto the narrow path, "I'll be gettin' 'long then."

"Don' forget ter give me'n Jem a kiss when you comes back," the burly boy shouted after her. Ignoring them, she walked on. Around the next bend the delicious odor of roasting meat wafting toward her led her to the half-open kitchen door.

Cautiously Angel peeped in. A fat woman, her face red with heat, her gray hair skewered tightly on top of her large, round head, was standing before a table in the center of the room; her arms moved rhythmically as she rolled out pastry on a floured board. To the left of the room three girls seated on stools before a well-scrubbed wooden table chattered together in low tones as they sliced vegetables into big brown basins. To the right of the room a man seated at a smaller table was polishing a pile of silver, whistling tunelessly between his teeth as he worked.

Studying the back of the man's bald domelike head, Angel wondered if he could be Nicholas Tavington.

The man threw his polishing cloth aside. "Tha's that lot done," he announced. Standing up, he turned, stretching his arms above his head.

"Here!" he said, his eyes widening as they alighted on Angel. "What you doin' at that door? What you want, eh?"

Stopping their work, they all stared at her. Angel's face flamed. The fat woman's eyes hardened with suspicion. "Well?" she said sharply. "Speak up!"

"I got ter—" Angel began.

"You ain't beggin', are you?" the fat woman interrupted. "If you are, you c'n jus' get your bloody self out o' me kitchen."

"I ain't no beggar!" Angel answered her truculently. "I got a message."

The man's light-blue eyes were still boring Angel through. He sneered. "I heard that 'un afore."

He turned to the fat woman. "You'd bes' sen' her off, Mrs. Mott," he said warningly. "If you don', you'll rue it. Newgate bait, is that wench. I c'n tell by her skin. It's sort o' yellowy like, if you c'n see what I mean. Gives 'em away ev'ry time, do that skin, though it fades when they been out for a bit."

"How'd you know?" the fat woman inquired.

" 'Cause I was a guard at Newgate, tha's why. I'd know that kin' o' plexion anywhere, I would."

A guard! Angel gripped her trembling hands together. But she was free now! He couldn't hurt her! She stared back at him boldly, but there was hatred in her eyes. "Where I come from's me own business," she said, loudly defiant. Her eyes turned to the fat woman. "I jus' wan' ter give me message, tha's all."

A door at the other end of the kitchen swung open, and a thin woman clad in black entered the room. For a moment she stood there looking at them, then she said in a high, imperious voice, "What is it, Mrs. Mott? Why have you all stopped working?"

"Ain't nothin' ter worry 'bout, Mrs. Sampson, ma'am. Jus' a beggar girl, tha's all. I was tellin' her to get out o' me kitchen. I don' wan' her hangin' roun', special as Bill says as she's jus' out o' Newgate."

"I's a lie!" Angel shouted. "I keep a-tellin' 'em that I

come with a message, but they won' lis'en. I don' wan' nothin' from 'em. I wouldn' take nothin' if they was ter beg me!"

The thin woman ignored this outburst. Coming closer to Angel, she said quietly, "My name is Mrs. Sampson. Will you tell me for whom this message is intended, please?"

Swiftly Angel's eyes took in the woman's richly rustling black gown. A white lace cap, stiffly starched, was set primly upon iron-gray hair. The woman's blue eyes were sharp in her thin austere face, but they were not unkindly, and Angel decided that she must be the mistress of this great house. His lordship's mother, perhaps.

"Well?" Mrs. Sampson said, a faint edge of impatience in her voice. "What is your name, child?"

Angel hesitated, then she said quickly, "Me name's Angel Dawson, ma'am. I got a message for one o' your servants, ma'am."

"I see. What is this servant's name."

"Tavington, ma'am. Nicholas Tavington."

"I beg your pardon!" Mrs. Sampson's taut jaw sagged very slightly. "Is this some kind of a jest?" she said.

"I—I—" Angel swallowed. Why were they staring at her like that? "I don' know what you mean," she said miserably. "I tol' you who the message was for." She looked from one face to the other. "What you lookin' at?" she demanded. "I ain't done nothin'!"

A subtle change had taken place in Mrs. Sampson's blue eyes. "I believe you to be sincere," she said kindly. "However, you are mistaken in supposing that Nicholas Tavington is a servant employed here. Quite the contrary, in fact. I am the housekeeper here, and Nicholas Tavington is the master of this house."

"He's the—the—" Angel's brain was spinning confusedly. "But the—the Earl of Benbrook, ain't he the master?"

"He is," Mrs. Sampson answered calmly. "Nicholas Tavington, you see, is the Earl of Benbrook."

The man was staring at her again, his light eyes mocking, and again Angel felt the clutch of a terrible fear. She'd done nothing! But these people could send her back to Newgate. Marianne! Marianne! What shall I do?

"She—she never tol' me," Angel forced the words from her trembling lips. "She never tol' me as he was the Earl."

"She?" Mrs. Sampson said encouragingly. "Come now, child, there is no need to look at me like that. I'm not going to hurt you, you know."

"Marianne," Angel blurted out. "Marianne, tha's who I mean."

"Marianne?" Mrs. Sampson's firm mouth set in a stern line. "Do you, perhaps, refer to the Lady Marianne?"

Angel's hands clutched at the door. "I don' know nothin' 'bout that. Marianne, she tol' me her name was. She tol' me ter come here an' fin' her brother, this here Nicholas Tavington."

She turned blindly away, intent on escape. "Tha's all I know! Tha's all! I got ter go now, ma'am."

"Remain where you are," Mrs. Sampson said sharply. "I think," she added in a more kindly tone, "that I should hear your story from the beginning."

Ignoring the staring servants, Mrs. Sampson turned, beckoning for Angel to follow. "Come along," she added.

Angel clung tightly to the door latch. "No!" she said defiantly. "I don' wan' ter go with you. I ain't got nothin' more ter tell you!"

The man moved quietly, menacingly toward the girl.

"Do like what you're tol'," he said, his voice dangerously soft, his eyes relishing her terror. "You hear what I tell you, bitch?" His hard hand clamped on her arm. "You hear?" he repeated.

Angel saw not his face but Gibbons', ugly and cruel, and she screamed suddenly, piercingly. "No! No!" her voice rose, thin-edged with hysteria. "Don' you touch me, you bleedin' swine! Take your hand off me! Take it off!"

Mrs. Sampson's gown rustled as she came toward them.

"Jenkins!" her voice was a cold whiplash. It brought a flush to the man's face. With a muttered curse, he dropped his hand.

"On'y tryin' ter help, ma'am," he said ungraciously.

"When I need your help, you may be sure I shall ask for it." Mrs. Sampson waved an imperious hand. "Return to your duties, Jenkins. And have a care of the spoons, please. I noticed last night that several of them were smeared." To Angel, she said, "Come with me, please. I promise you that you have nothing to fear."

Angel moved blindly toward her. "You won' let him touch me no more, ma'am?" she begged. "I can' bear for him to touch me!"

The housekeeper inclined her head gravely. "I give you my word."

Angel looked into her eyes, sharply blue, intelligent, and she sensed the kindness in the woman, despite the stern, pale mask of her face.

"I'll come with you," Angel said, and the small sigh she gave was her surrender to the vagaries of fate. She was tired—so tired! Let them do with her what they would! But following after the stiffly erect woman, she felt a faint, warm stirring of hope. Hope? For what? But it didn't matter; it was there, and she had thought it long since dead.

The woman led her through the door at the end of

the kitchen and into a narrow, stone-flagged corridor. The corridor, winding to the left, brought them eventually to a heavy door that opened into the main part of the house.

"Oh!" Angel's fears fled as if they had never been, and she gazed wide-eyed at the somber richness of the great hall.

"Lov'ly!" she said of the ceiling that loomed high above her, gilded and domed.

"Ain't it beautiful!" she said of the walls that enclosed her in a dull gleam of dark wood panels, their darkness gradually shading to a lighter color at the center of each panel, and carved into the intricately wrought shapes of rearing horses.

Mrs. Sampson watched her understandingly, but now she said, a touch of impatience in her voice, "You may examine the hall later, if you wish." She indicated an open door. "In there, please."

Reluctantly, her eyes lingering admiringly on the mirrorlike glass of the floor, the great rugs that were islands of brilliant color on that surface, Angel followed the woman through the door.

The room, like the hall, was huge, and to Angel it seemed to be full of delicate light.

Walls hung with a tapestry of blue and gold reared upward to a lofty ceiling that, obviously painted by a master hand, represented a summer sky. At either end of the room were tall windows draped with lustrous heavy blue satin, and between them, like a fragile gold mist, a center panel of fine gold lace.

The glittering black marble floor, broken here and there with vivid rugs, threw Angel's reflection back to her, giving her the odd illusion that she was poised upon black trembling waters.

Under one window stood a couch; semicircular in design, it was upholstered in a brocade of varying shades of blue. Under the other window another couch, long and simple of line, was upholstered in a darker blue with a design of gold leaves.

There were three large easy chairs with high cushioned backs and broad cushioned arms, their upholstery carrying out the same blue and gold motif. But it was the piece of furniture in the center of the room that attracted Angel's close attention. It looked rather like a long, low, padded bed, but a bed with head and foot rails removed, upholstered in a soft, pale-blue velvet; it looked, she thought, very comfortable.

Mrs. Sampson noticed her interest. "Unusual, is it not?" she said with a disapproving sniff. "It is a French import, popularized by His Majesty. One expects the French to err against good taste, of course, so perhaps it is hardly surprising that they named it 'the love nest.' "

Angel laughed. "An' I c'n guess why."

"Indeed?" The housekeeper pointed to one of the cushioned chairs, near to which stood a round table of highly polished wood, bearing a silver bowl of sweetly scented early blooming roses.

"Sit down, please," the housekeeper said.

Gingerly, Angel obeyed, but she sat stiffly, afraid that she might spoil the soft perfection beneath her.

"You like this room?" A faint flush rose in Mrs. Sampson's cheeks as she asked the question.

"It's lov'ly," Angel answered. "Jus' like a palace."

"It was designed originally for Lady Catherine, his lordship's mother. She, however, disliked it."

Angel looked at her, her eyes faintly bewildered. What had any of this to do with her, she wondered. Why was the woman telling her this, and why did she look so uneasy?

"I don' wan' ter be no bother," Angel said slowly. "I'd better tell you me story, eh? Then I'll go."

Mrs. Sampson seemed not to have heard her. "The

room did not, in any case, suit Lady Catherine's particular coloring," she went on. But it would be perfect for his lordship's sister, that is, if he decides to bring her to London."

"Oh," Angel's brow was faintly wrinkled. Something was clamoring at the back of her mind. "His lordship's sister, you say?"

She had spoken vaguely. But there was nothing vague about Mrs. Sampson. Her eyes, steely bright, fixed themselves on the girl's face.

"Do you think it would suit her coloring?" the woman asked.

"Who?"

"His lordship's sister, naturally."

"How'd I know?" Angel spoke sullenly. Her uneasiness was back. She wished the woman would stop talking for a moment. There was something she had to work out in her mind. She hadn't thought of it before—she'd been too frightened. But it was coming to her now. If this Nicholas Tavington was the Earl of Benbrook, then Marianne must be—. Her thoughts scattered, then came scampering back like frightened mice. Marianne? The Earl's sister!

Angel half rose from her chair, then, hypnotized by the woman's eyes, she sank back again. The Earl's face swam into her mind. The bitter dark eyes, looking for a brief moment into hers. He'd blame her for Marianne's death! He would, of course he would! No use to explain —he'd hear only what he wanted to hear! He'd have to blame somebody, and it would be her! Her! He'd have her sent back to Newgate! He had a hard face! A bitter, unforgiving face!

"Would you care to?" Mrs. Sampson was saying.

Angel looked dumbly back at her. Trying to subdue the sick terrified beating of her heart, she said, "Care ter what?"

"You weren't listening," Mrs. Sampson said shortly. "I asked if you would care to see a portrait of my lady?"

Without waiting for an answer, Mrs. Sampson crossed briskly to the opposite wall. A silk curtain was hanging there—Angel had noticed it and wondered what it covered—now, as the woman drew it aside, she knew.

"My Lady Marianne," Mrs. Sampson said, and stood to one side.

Angel stared at the portrait, and felt thankfulness flooding into her being. That wasn't Marianne! It wasn't! It wasn't! How could it be?

The young girl in the portrait wore a white gown; the crisp folds of the flowing skirt were drawn back, carefully arranged to show just a glimpse of pale-blue shoes. Large dark eyes dominating the exquisite oval of her face looked shyly from the canvas. Lips, softly smiling, serene; flowers cradled in the curve of one slim arm; black, glossy ringlets spilling down, resting upon sloping white shoulders.

Oh God! Clearly now, Angel could see superimposed over those lovely features that other and familiar face. Marianne's face! White, haggard! Shy, doelike eyes, terrified. Ringlets, glossy no longer, but dulled, hanging lankly to shoulders that were raw and suppurating.

"Marianne!" the word burst from Angel's lips like a cry of despair.

She stared wildly into the housekeeper's blanching face. "I never done nothin'," she cried. "I tried to help her, I did! But I couldn' help her, nobody couldn'! They took her an' they beat her to death! Don' sen' me back ter Newgate! Don'!"

"What are you saying?" the housekeeper whispered. "Oh, my dear child! What are you saying?"

"I'll tell you all 'bout it." Angel held out imploring hands. "On'y don' sen' me back! I don' wan' her brother to help me, like what she says he would. I don' wan' nothin', I jus' wan' ter be free!"

"Tell me, child! Tell me!"

Sobbing, Angel poured out the story, interspersing it with pleas and protestations of innocence.

Mrs. Sampson listened. Frozen, her eyes burning like blue flames in her thin face, she listened, and disbelief gave way to belief. Marianne! Small, sweet Marianne! Her heart shook, began a labored, painful beating. Marianne! Horror took deep root inside her. Marianne! Oh, Marianne!

Angel's voice had ceased long since, but her stifled sobbing went on and on.

It will kill his lordship, Mrs. Sampson thought. "Poor lad!" she said aloud.

"Who?" Angel raised her tear-drenched face.

"His lordship." Mrs. Sampson turned stiffly to the door. "He must know, but how in the name of God am I to tell him!"

"Wait!" Angel leaped to her feet and faced the woman, a small, wary animal, her fists clenched at her sides. "You ain't sen'in' for the Watch, are you? You ain't goin' ter sen' me back to Newgate?"

"Oh, no, you poor child! Believe me, no!" She swallowed and said with difficulty. "Wait here, please. His lordship will want to see you."

"No! I don' wan' ter see him!"

"You must." Mrs. Sampson took a step toward Angel. But suddenly she changed to a new tactic. "Do you trust me?" she asked.

Angel hesitated, unwilling even now to place her trust in another. "Yes," she said after a moment, the word leaving her lips draggingly. "You—you ain't been bad ter me."

"Neither will his lordship be."

"Him!" Angel's eyes widened slightly. "I seen him, I did. On'y I never knew he was Nicholas Tavington." Her eyes pleaded with the woman. "He won' b'lieve me! He'll sen' me back!"

"Nonsense!" Mrs. Sampson thrust down the clamoring grief, forcing a coldness into her voice that effectively quelled the girl's, rising hysteria. "Naturally," she added, "his lordship will wish to question you. But you are not to blame in any way, and I do assure you that you have nothing to fear."

"I been blamed 'fore this for things which ain't been no fault o' mine," Angel muttered. Her eyes went to the door; she was conscious of a longing to be gone. She looked at the woman. "Whyn' you let me go?"

"You are not a prisoner here." Mrs. Sampson's lip curled slightly. "Go then." She stood away from the door. "If you are too cowardly to face his lordship, then I shall not detain you."

"I—" Angel took a quick step forward then stopped, looking uncertainly at the woman. "I ain't no coward!"

"No?" Mrs. Sampson waited, her hands folded in front of her.

"No!" Angel said. Something was happening inside her, but she did not recognize it as the reawakening of her pride.

"I don' have ter stay if I don' wan' ter," she blurted, taking a last stand.

"Quite true," Mrs. Sampson answered. "However, it would please me if you would do so."

"Oh," Angel said, shrugging. "I might as well stay then."

"Thank you." Without another word the housekeeper went to the door. "I'll return as soon as possible." She left the room, closing the door firmly behind her.

The click of the door brought back some of Angel's fear. To distract herself she began to wander around the room. She fingered the smooth satin of the drapes; touched with gentle fingers the curling scarlet petals of the roses and, stooping, examined her face in the silver bowl. She came at length, as she had known she would, to stand before Marianne's portrait.

"Marianne," she whispered, staring at this elegant stranger who was Marianne—and yet not Marianne. "Marianne," she said again, "I done like you tol' me an'—an' I hopes you know it."

Beneath the draped folds of the white bodice, Marianne's slight breasts seemed to rise and fall. Almost Angel felt that she could reach out and touching one of those narrow white hands, feel beneath her fingers the warmth of living flesh.

Firmly she shook the fantasy from her. Marianne was dead. It was she, Angel Dawson, who lived. It was she who must remember, terrified, Jim Gibbons and his threats.

The thought of him seemed to bring the man to fill the room with his presence, so that she trembled. The blue and gold of the room darkened, swirling about her. She wiped her damp forehead with the hem of her gown, and kept her wide-open eyes fixed on the portrait. Gradually Gibbons' menacing presence receded, but still she stood there, finding in her intense study of the painted features an antidote against thought.

She was still standing there when the door was jerked open behind her. A faint tremor went through her; she knew who would be standing there, but now that the moment was upon her, she felt curiously weak and she did not turn.

"Nicholas Tavington stood there watching her. "Calm," he told himself. "You must be calm. You must not allow the wench to sway your judgment with her lying tales."

He thought of Mrs. Sampson, the severe lines of her

face broken with grief, the tremble in her voice as she told him the fantastic tale of Marianne's tragic end. But he was not so easily gulled, not he! Marianne dead! Beaten to death! Marianne! Thrown into Newgate Prison like any common drab? No—impossible! Marianne was safe at the Manor. The wench lied!

Unnerved by the silence, Angel turned slowly to face him. He was staring at her, his eyes so darkly glittering that they seemed to burn from the expressionless mask on his face. He was wearing a loosely fitting brown jacket of some thin, smooth material and rough brown breeches, both liberally smeared with paint. His hair was unbound, curling in wisps over his forehead, but she found him no less intimidating.

"M'lord," she said, bobbing a clumsy curtsy.

Nicholas did not answer at once. He knew her now, he thought, his eyes narrowing. She was one of the girls who had held up the Royal Parade. Was it then that she had thought of coming to him with her lies! But the rest of her tale—Ellen—the mention of John Bannister's name—how could she have known of these things—how? Perhaps the girl had a sweetheart employed at Benbrook Manor. Perhaps together they had—his thoughts broke off. By God! She'd pay for her lies!

"You, girl," he snapped, striding toward her. "Why have you chosen to come here with your farrago of lies?" His hands clamped bruisingly on her shoulders, drawing her close to him.

"What did you hope to gain?" he said, shaking her. "Was it money? Tell me—was it?"

"Let go!" she shouted, trying to pull free.

His hands tightened, and he shook her again. Now her fear was swallowed up in rage, in a blazing hatred. He didn't care about Marianne. There was no grief in him.

"Call me a liar, will you, m'lord?" Angel's voice rose.

"Well, I ain't, you hear me? I ain't! An' I don' wan' nothin' from you, see? I wouldn' take nothin'—not if you was ter beg me!"

"You—you—" His hands dropped away so suddenly that she almost stumbled. "It cannot be true!" he seemed to be speaking to himself. He turned away from her as if he had already forgotten her, and she saw that his face had taken on a grayish tinge.

At the door he turned his head and looked at her again. "I will, of course, investigate your story," he said in a low voice. "In the meantime you will remain here."

"I ain't stayin' here!" she flared. "An' wha's more, you can' make me!"

"You are quite mistaken," he answered. "You will do as you are told, or it will be the worse for you."

He was gone before she had a chance to reply. Fuming, more shaken than she cared to admit, she listened to his firm footsteps crossing the wide hall. A door was opened, and she heard his voice issuing curt commands. Sometime later she heard the clatter of hooves; his voice again—then the hooves receding along the drive.

When Mrs. Sampson entered the room, Angel exclaimed in relief, "I was hopin' you'd come, ma'am. I was wantin' ter say g'bye ter you, see?"

"Sit down, please." The housekeeper seemed not to hear her words. Her face was composed now, but Angel saw that her eyes were red-rimmed and puffy, the corners of her mouth still trembling slightly.

"I can' sit down." Angel tried to edge past, but the woman stood between her and the door. "I wan' ter go now, please, ma'am."

"Hear me out, please. I have something to say to you."

Mrs. Sampson seated herself, and Angel, after a moment of hesitation, sat down reluctantly.

"What you wan' ter say?" Angel's voice was ungracious, and the eyes turned on the woman, suspicious.

"Angel—that is your name, is it not?" Receiving a nod, Mrs. Sampson went on quickly. "Will you tell me where your home is?"

"Why?" The doubt in Angel's eyes deepened. "What you wan' ter know that for?"

"I have a reason." Mrs. Sampson folded her hands in her lap, calmly waiting.

Angel averted her eyes from the steady gaze. "I ain't got one," she muttered.

"I beg your pardon?"

Angel flushed. "I said," she raised her voice slightly. "I said that I ain't got no home."

"I see." Mrs. Sampson nodded. "It's as I thought. Now listen to me, child. You were kind to Lady Marianne, and I would—"

"His lordship don' b'lieve me," Angel cried out. "Not as I cares what he thinks 'bout me. But he don' seem ter care nothin' for Marianne. He ain't got no heart, he ain't!"

Mrs. Sampson shook her head sadly. "He does believe you, Angel, but he is trying desperately not to. As for his heart, he very definitely has one. You may take my word for that."

"Don' seem like it ter me," Angel muttered.

"Perhaps not. But we are not discussing his lordship, are we?"

"All right," Angel said, stung by the reproof.

"I was about to say," Mrs. Sampson said in a milder voice, "that since you were kind to Lady Marianne, I would like to offer you a home here."

"Here?" Angel stared at her. "I don' know what you mean!"

"I have need of a sewing maid," Mrs. Sampson answered. "If the prospect of a comfortable home, a soft bed

114

to sleep in, and good nourishing food appeals to you, then the position is yours."

Angel struggled for words. She was sorely tempted by the offer and dazzled by a prospect that, to her, seemed like an invitation to enter heaven. But there was his lordship—that hard, hateful man. How could she live in his house? How could she eat the food of somebody she hated?

"What 'bout him?" Angel said at last. Seeing the housekeeper's raised eyebrows, she added hastily. "His lordship, I mean. He won' wan' ter have me in his house."

Mrs. Sampson smiled. "His lordship would approve my decision, I feel sure," she said calmly. "I must tell you, however, that in the course of your duties you will see little or nothing of him. He does not concern himself with household affairs, and I doubt, unless it is pointed out to him, that he will even be aware of your presence."

Angel felt suddenly and unreasonably annoyed at this last statement, but, as another consideration came to her, the annoyance faded. Maybe in this fine home she would be safe from Jim Gibbons. He wouldn't dare seek her out here. He'd said he'd find her wherever she went, but surely even Gibbons wouldn't think of looking for her here?

"Well?" Mrs. Sampson said.

Angel smiled. "I'd like ter work for you, ma'am, an' —an' thank you kin'ly."

"I'm glad." Mrs. Sampson rose to her feet with a crisp rustling of black silk. "I believe, too, that my—" she broke off, turning her head away quickly. "I believe," she went on, having regained her calm, "that m'lady would have wished you to be cared for."

"She was nice, was Marianne," Angel said slowly. "She wasn' like him."

"That will be enough, Angel," Mrs. Sampson said

sharply. "You will not discuss his lordship with me or with the other servants."

Again Angel was caught up in annoyance. "I ain't no gossip," she said stiffly. " 'Sides, I got better things ter do 'n' talk 'bout him."

"Angel!"

"Well, I have," Angel said, unrepentant. She smiled impishly. "Still, I won' say it no more," she promised.

Softened by the charm of a smile that had caused the girl's sullen face to blossom into vivid beauty, Mrs. Sampson said indulgently, "Very well, child. We will say no more about it."

"When'd you wan' me ter start me work?" Angel cried, leaping excitedly to her feet.

"Tomorrow or the next day," Mrs. Sampson shrugged the question aside. Stretching out her hand, she picked up a lock of Angel's vivid hair. "A very pretty color," she commented, "but not, I fear, very clean. The fault is not yours, I know," she added quickly, seeing the danger signals in the outraged eyes, "and I know you will understand when I tell you that it must be deloused."

She dropped the lock of hair. "One more thing. It is a rule in this house that everyone must bathe daily. It is the one thing on which the domestic staff find me quite inflexible."

"Ev'ry day?" Intrigued by this novel idea, Angel's anger ebbed slightly. "Go on! No one don' bathe ev'ry day. It'd wash their bleedin' skin away."

"Nevertheless," Mrs. Sampson assured her, "I insist upon it."

"I'm clean," Angel cried, her anger rushing back. "I like ter be clean, I do!"

"Then we are in agreement. As I have said, your hair will be deloused and, if it should prove to be necessary, cut close to the head."

"No!" Angel looked at her with stricken eyes. "I ain't

goin' ter let you cut me hair." She touched her hair with a trembling hand. "I'm—I'm proud o' me hair, I am."

"And rightly so," Mrs. Sampson answered understandingly. "But I promise you, Angel, that, if it must be cut, it will be in a very pretty style."

"I don' see what you got ter cut it for."

"There may be no need," Mrs. Sampson said bracingly. "We'll wait and see, shall we?" She moved resolutely to the door. "But we must not waste time. Come with me, child."

Mrs. Sampson's back was stiff and straight as she led the way. She was glad she had this strange child on which to concentrate. She would be kind to her, she determined, but not stupidly indulgent. It was what her ladyship would have wished, she felt.

Her eyes misted, and she stumbled slightly. Recovering herself, she marched on. Now was not the time to mourn; she must not let the domestics see her in a moment of weakness. Later, in the privacy of her room, she would remember her Lady Marianne.

She stared at the touch of a hand on her arm. Turning her head, she looked into Angel's eyes.

"I's all right, ma'am," Angel said softly. "I had a cry 'bout Marianne too."

"I am not crying!" Mrs. Sampson said irritably.

"No," Angel answered, nodding her head wisely. "But you ain't far off, ma'am."

"Nonsense!"

"Yes, ma'am," Angel said demurely.

Seated BEFORE THE WINDOW, HER SENSES succumbing to the somnolence of the golden summer day, Angel gazed out sleepy-eyed at the view before her. Encircling trees, their leaves rustling musically in a slight breeze, sent dark, lacy shadows swaying over the cool, green velvety sweep of lawn. Nearby a hummingbird hung poised above the scrolled blue petals of a flower, its vivid delicate wings in tremulous motion.

Angel, though all too guiltily conscious of hands that lay folded in her lap and a pile of pillowcases yet to be hemmed, continued in her idleness. A light, inconsequential stream of chatter from Bessie Harper, her companion sewing maid, came faintly to her ears; but since Bessie neither expected nor required an answer, she paid her scant attention.

Angel started a little as a bee, swooping down suddenly, bumped its dusty brown body against the windowpane. The bee's drone grew louder as, angrily insistent, it thrust at the pane again; after a moment, baffled, it flew heavily away.

Angel leaned forward, her eyes interestedly following the flight of the gossamer wings. The bee made a few aimless circlings, then settled itself on a clump of flowers. Angel watched as, its energy apparently spent, the bee remained motionless for some moments; after a while it began crawling drunkenly along a scarlet petal and disappeared finally into the yellow heart of the flower.

Bessie Harper's mouth moved on in full spate, her seemingly innocuous chatter hiding the barb of her spite.

Bessie disliked everything about Angel, and she bitterly resented what she considered to be the preferential treatment shown to the girl by the grim-faced housekeeper. But most of all Bessie, plain and stocky herself, resented Angel's vivid and now quite astonishing beauty. Her eyes lingered on Angel's short, gleaming halo of feathery red-gold curls; on the gracefully rounded curves of her body, the creamy transparency of skin, faintly rose-flushed at the high cheekbones, and she remembered a very different Angel.

Skinny as a starving cat, Angel Dawson had been; her skin bore the yellow cast of prison pallor, and the red-gold hair was full of lice. She'd been pretty even then, Bessie grudgingly admitted, but now, with plenty of good food, regular hours, and fresh air, she was dazzling. Looked like a highborn lady, did Angel Dawson, Bessie thought, her eyes narrowing enviously. Looked like it, but you knew different when she opened her mouth.

Bessie's thoughts turned to the master of the house, and she wondered, as she had so many times before, just what there was between the icy, stiffly unbending m'lord and Angel Dawson? There was gossip that Dawson had in some way been mixed up with his lordship's dead sister, but she had never been able to discover the truth of it.

Something terrible had happened, Bessie was quite sure of that, judging from the look on his lordship's face whenever he chanced to pass Dawson. It was a funny look, really, almost as if he couldn't bear the sight of her —as if just to see her brought him pain. And Dawson? Well, there was no mistaking her feelings. She hated his lordship—really hated him! Bessie, though seldom agreeing with Angel, could quite understand why. Crack his face if he smiled, would his lordship.

Him and his women! Bessie thought virtuously. She'd seen them come and she'd seen them go. Painted, scented trollops, they were—for you couldn't call them ladies—wearing their elaborate gowns, their hair piled high, and sparkling with jewels. And for all that their eyes were inviting, it was plain to see that they bored his lordship to death. After he'd bedded them, Bessie thought, like as not he was done with them.

Bessie went back to pondering on the strangeness between Dawson and his lordship, for you couldn't call it anything else, really. Why didn't he let Dawson go if just seeing her annoyed him? Why didn't—Bessie checked the thought. No use going over and over it. It'd go on being a mystery, for no one, least of all Dawson, was likely to explain it to her.

Bessie's eyes fell on the neatly folded sheets on her table. Mrs. Sampson had placed them there earlier, explaining that since the regular maid was ill, Bessie must make up the master's bed.

Why should she make up his bed? Bessie thought. It wasn't the job of the sewing maid to change bed linen, and anyway, why her? Why couldn't Dawson do it?

Bessie's eyes gleamed and a grin stretched her mouth. Dawson was good-natured enough if you caught her in the right mood. Yes, she'd put the job onto her, and serve her right if she ran into his lordship. Not much hope of that, though; he spent most of the daylight hours painting in that room of his. Still, you never know. Cheered, Bessie bent her head over her work.

As if some of Bessie's thoughts had communicated themselves to her, Angel, too, found herself thinking of the Earl; annoyed, she moved uneasily in her chair.

The Earl troubled her thoughts often—too often—

and though she seldom saw him, she was always conscious of his presence. She hated him! He had no heart! None of the softer emotions! How could anybody, except Mrs. Sampson of course, care anything for such a man? He repelled affection, and she knew, on those rare occasions when she would pass him in the corridor, that he had the greatest contempt for her. It was her hatred, she told herself, that made her flesh prickle in that odd manner. Hatred that caused the hard rapid pounding of her heart and the wave of scorching color to mantle her cheeks.

His lordship would give a stiffly polite inclination of his head when he saw her, but he had never deigned to speak to her again. All his words had been said on that first terrible meeting. Even his gratitude for her care of his sister had been conveyed to her through Mrs. Sampson. As far as he was concerned, it seemed, the matter was closed. All the same, Angel would sometimes wonder if he had as easily dismissed all thoughts of Marianne from his mind?

Angel's dreams were still haunted by memories of Newgate. Jim Gibbons' brutal face. Marianne, peaceful in death, the looming shadow of the flogging post striping her still body with the sign of the Cross. Sometimes it was gross Mary who invaded her dreams. She would see the great body swaying, the severed breast dangling, held to her only by a strip of flesh. Then there was Lucy Bagget. Lucy, blinded by blood, screaming like a tormented animal, her gouged eye bobbing against her cheek.

Angel would awaken, her body trembling violently. But in her daze it would gradually come back to her that Jim Gibbons and six of his confederates had been hung, paying the supreme penalty for the murder of Lady Marianne and their many brutal crimes against the other prisoners. Only then would her trembling cease—only then did she feel safe. For that, at least, she gave grateful thanks to the Earl.

She had heard from Mrs. Sampson that the Earl, once convinced, had ridden straight to Newgate and Gibbons had been fairly caught. Gibbons, the greedy one. She'd counted on his keeping Marianne's body until the last moment, hoping that the grieving brother would be grateful for the chance to give his sister a decent burial and would certainly reward him for his charity. Only it hadn't worked out that way. She'd liked to have seen Gibbons' face when the Earl walked in. One look at his lordship would have told him that here was no meek little man he could browbeat. Had Gibbons suffered when he had been confined to a cell and forced to await the King's pleasure? She hoped so!

"Serve the bleedin' swine right!" Angel said on the day they hung him.

Angel had stood at Mrs. Sampson's side with the other servants on the occasion of Marianne's funeral. The King had been present. Angel had had a clear view of his lean elegant figure clad in black velvet, his hat adorned with the purple plumes of royal mourning. The King had laid a wreath of white and scarlet flowers upon Marianne's grave.

Standing beside the King was the Duke of Buckingham, tall, blond-wigged, and arrogant of feature, and at the King's right, the reigning mistress, Barbara Palmer.

Even on that sad occasion, Barbara had been the cynosure of all eyes, so enchantingly beautiful was she in her gown of deep-blue velvet with her matching wide-brimmed, plume-laden hat. Beneath it the loosened auburn hair spilled over her shoulders like a cascade of flame.

In the three months she had spent thus far in this great rich house, Angel had come to understand Mrs. Sampson, and for this woman, whose bark was so much worse than her bite, Angel had a genuine respect and a growing liking.

Bessie was still talking, but it was a sudden noisy quarrel breaking out among the birds congregated on the lawn that finally recalled Angel's straying thoughts. She picked up her work reluctantly. A moment longer she watched the birds, but their quarrel ceased as abruptly as it had begun; with a flutter of brown and white feathers they disappeared, losing themselves among the glossy leaves of a tall oak tree.

"Angel," Bessie said plaintively. "I was wonderin' if you'd min' doin' somethin' for me?"

"Wha's that?" Angel said, looking at her vaguely.

Bessie put a hand to her forehead. "Me head's painin' cruel, an'—an' I was wonderin' if you'd min' doin' the master's bed for me?"

Angel rose slowly to her feet. "Have ter, then, won' I? Han' us them sheets."

Smiling, Bessie watched her go. Hope his bloody lordship's in his room, she thought. If he is, her face ought ter be a sight ter see when she gets back.

Her LOUD KNOCKING ON THE WHITE PAN-
eled door brought no response, and after listening carefully for sounds of movement from within, Angel turned the
carved doorknob and stepped into the Earl's room.

Closing the door behind her, she leaned against it,
the clean sheets clutched tightly in her arms. Looking
curiously about her, Angel saw ivory-colored walls that,
except for three framed paintings on the wall opposite to
her, were bare of ornamentation. Two large windows
hung with drapes of ice-green satin were open to the air;
a soft breeze fluttered the edges of the drapes, bringing
with it a flower-laden fragrance from the gardens below.

The furniture consisted of a large couch with a
carved wooden headrest, two large chairs, and a smaller
couch, all of them upholstered in tapestry the color of
ivory with a faint thread of silver running through it. A
large desk overflowing with papers stood in a corner. In
the center of the room a table of light wood held a pile
of stacked canvases and a silver tray with a decanter of
wine and four silver-rimmed goblets resting upon it.

This, then, must be his dressing room, Angel thought.
That other door, half hidden behind a green and silver
drapery, must lead into his bedroom.

Bolder now, Angel crossed the yielding silver-gray

carpet and went to stand before the paintings. The first painting, a hunting dog with wind-ruffled black and white fur, a lolling tongue, and a feathery tail held eagerly erect, brought a smile to her lips; so full of quivering life did he seem that he might have been about to leap from the frame.

She turned to the second painting, and her smile vanished. A deer, obviously at the end of the chase, was sprawled beneath a tree; leafy shadows dappled the brown flanks, and in the large, glazed eyes there was such panic that Angel felt a lump rising to her throat. Hunted! Trapped! How well she knew that feeling! The third painting was of a little girl. She was clad in an emerald-green riding habit; a tiny hat of the same color with a curling white plume decorating the crown and caressing the side of one cheek was perched upon her curls. The child's lips were smiling, but looking into the too solemn eyes, Angel instantly recognized Marianne.

Turning away sorrowfully, Angel went swiftly to the door behind the green and silver drapery. She must hurry she thought, opening the door. She'd lingered here too long.

The bedroom, much larger than the dressing room, was decorated in tones of blue and gold, but Angel, unaccountably nervous now, gave it scarcely a glance. Mounting the two wide steps that led to the bed, she pulled the shrouding blue silk curtains to one side.

"Oh!" Angel stared at the man who lay sprawled on top of the rumpled bedclothes.

In sleep the Earl looked much younger; the bitter lines about his mouth were temporarily erased, his hair was ruffled, the rigidly held lips, softened now, gave him a vulnerable look.

He'd been working, Angel thought, noticing the traces of blue paint on his fingers, and the long smear across the front of his black dressing robe. But what was he doing here? Was he ill?

The Earl moved, turned restlessly on his side, and muttered something in a low voice.

Cautiously Angel backed away, but in her agitation she had forgotten the steps. Losing her footing, she gave a little shriek as she fell heavily to the floor.

There was movement above her, the rustle of bed-clothes, then the Earl's voice curtly demanding, "What the devil are you doing here?"

She made no attempt to rise. The hot color of embarrassment flooded her cheeks, and she kept her head lowered.

"Well?" he said.

"Come ter do your bed, m'lord," Angel muttered, pointing a trembling finger at the scattered sheets.

"I beg your pardon. What was that you said?"

The drawl in his voice stung her suddenly, unbearably.

"I says," Angel half shouted, "that I come ter do your bed."

"Why are you shouting?" he said coldly. He descended the steps, and Angel, her eyes still lowered, saw his feet, shod in soft leather slippers, advance toward her.

"Are you perhaps under the impression that I am deaf?" he went on.

She stared fixedly at the floor, wondering if she had imagined the hint of laughter in his voice. She must have! He never laughed! Never!

"No—no," she stammered. "It—it ain't that I think you're deaf, m'lord. I's j—jus' that I'm upset, see? I come ter do your bed, an'—an' I never knew as you'd be a-sleepin' in it."

"I see," he said, his voice dry. "Pray accept my apologies for the inconvenience I have caused you."

She felt bewildered. There was no anger in him, she sensed that. Again she had the impression of suppressed laughter; it was as if he mocked her lightly, amusedly.

She said, blurting out the words, "I expec' you was tired, m'lord. Why—why don' you go back ter bed. I c'n come back ter do your bed later."

He did not answer at once, then he said slowly, "Thank you, but it will not be necessary. Come," he extended a hand toward her, "pray allow me to assist you to your feet."

"I—I—" Angel lifted her eyes slowly. "You don' have ter."

He did not withdraw his hand. "I am not an ogre, you know," he said softly.

"N—no, m'lord," Angel said, putting her hand in his.

His firm cool fingers closed about her hand, and again she felt that prickling of her flesh. Her heart choked her with its rapid beating. She scrambled so hastily to her feet that she stumbled. His arm came out, steadying her, and for a moment she was drawn close to him.

"Thank you," she said.

His arm seemed to be burning through her clothes, and her strange discomfort had increased. Why didn't he go away? It was like him to stand there making her feel uncomfortable and silly.

She groped after her hatred—remembering Marianne, remembering herself, frightened and desperate. He had shaken her, he had called her a "liar." He didn't grieve for Marianne! He didn't! He didn't! There was no love in him, no compassion. He was hard and cold and cruel, and she hated him!

She stepped hastily away. "I got me work ter do, m'lord," she said, her voice sullen.

He seemed not to have heard her, and he was staring at her so intently that once again she felt herself flushing. Why was he looking at her like that, she wondered, backing away another step. What was the matter with him?

"Stand still," he commanded.

It was the voice she remembered so well, the voice she sometimes heard in her dreams. Harsh, domineering, as it had been that first time.

He came closer to her, his hand outstretched. There was a violent trembling all through her body, and she half closed her eyes as his long, cool fingers touched her hair lightly. What was he going to do with her?

"Damn!" the Earl said. "I'm a blind fool! It's wrong. It's all wrong!"

Her eyes flew open. "W—what, m'lord? What's wrong?"

He frowned at her, his dark brows meeting in a straight line. "The hair, of course," he said curtly. "The color's wrong."

"Oh," she said blankly. Suddenly she wanted to hit him. He had no right to put his hands on her! Did he think, just because she was only a servant girl, that he could touch her whenever he pleased? Well, he couldn't! She'd run away. She'd not stay here and be insulted by him! Putting his hands on her! The idea! Telling her he didn't like the color of her hair! She had nice hair—everybody said so. She'd thought for a moment that he was going to kiss her. Not that she'd have liked it, of course! If he had kissed her, she'd have—she'd have scrubbed her mouth with boiling water! But she had thought, just for —well, she didn't want him to. She hated him! Really hated him! But—but he needn't have said that about her hair!

"I don' know what you mean, m'lord." She looked up at him, not realizing that there were tears in her eyes.

"What on earth are you crying about?" he said impatiently. Without waiting for her answer, he grabbed her hand. "Come with me, please," he said.

"I can't!" She tried to pull her hand free. "I got me work ter do, m'lord. I tol' you that."

"Damn the work!" He tugged at her hand. "You have two choices, wench. You may proceed on your own two feet, or I will damned well carry you. Which is it to be?"

Her eyes flashed angrily. "I'll come with you, m'lord. I—I don' know what you think you're a-goin' ter get up ter with me, but I ain't no w—whore, nor I ain't never done nothin' bad with no man."

Her mouth trembled, and she put up her free hand to hide it. "Speakin' ter you with all respec', m'lord, but I ain't goin' ter let you do nothin' with me."

"You think—" He broke off, staring at her in such utter astonishment that for some reason she was unable to define she felt that this was the greatest insult he had offered her thus far.

"Gentlemen is all the same," Angel mumbled stubbornly.

"Well! Upon my word!" The Earl laughed shortly. "Whatever you have heard of my moral character, you may rest assured that I do not rape children."

A child! She'd show him! "I ain't!" she shouted, losing her head completely. "I'm a full-growed woman, I am, m'lord!"

"I see." His eyes traveled over her slowly. "But your virtue, if indeed you have any, is in no danger. You have my word on it. Now come along, please."

She followed after him as slowly as she dared. Her mind was so busy with the things she would like to say to him that she scarcely realized that he had stopped before the door of his workroom.

The secret room! Angel drew in her breath excitedly. Nobody else except for Mrs. Sampson had ever been allowed to cross that mysterious threshold.

Nicholas was well aware of the many colorful activities he was purported to perform in this room, most of the them highly dramatic and criminal in nature, he felt sure; so he was not surprised, when he stepped aside for Angel to enter, to see her expression of disappointment.

Angel was indeed disappointed. Why, she thought, it's nothing but a big, dusty old place in need of a good cleaning. The round curtainless windows were smeared and the floor paint-splashed. Piles of canvases were stacked high against the walls; jars of paint stood on the floor. Beneath the window was a long bench. A palette knife, obviously thrown down in impatience stood upright, its sharp tip buried in the wood. Beside it were two more knives, and a jar of colorless liquid held several brushes. Half buried beneath a pile of paint-stained rags were more brushes, the fine hairs dry and stiff. Nearby on a table were two palettes smeared with paint. But it was the little piles of various colors that caught Angel's eyes. Ranged neatly along the front of the bench, the sun shining on them, they looked like heaped-up jewels.

"Ground pigment," the Earl said briefly when she turned inquiring eyes to him.

"Oh." What was pigment, she wondered. She shrugged and continued her inspection of the room.

A huge easel stood in the center. There was a long padded bench, two wooden stools, and an armless chair with a sagging red brocade seat. Behind the door was another easel, bearing a draped canvas.

"What did you expect to see?" Nicholas said softly.

She flushed. "I don' know, m'lord," she said hastily, avoiding his eyes. She nodded toward the canvases. "I bet them's all pict'res what you done o' the great ladies, ain't they, m'lord?"

"Great ladies?" Nicholas spoke the words acidly. "No, the canvases are empty." He looked at her curiously. "Tell me," he said, "what is it, in your opinion, that constitutes a great lady?"

"Don' you know?" Angel countered, playing for time. His question, the words he used, bewildered her.

"I know what a lady should be," he answered, "and so seldom is."

There was something about his faint smile and the tone of his voice that made Angel feel very uncomfortable. "Why—why ain't they, m'lord?"

"That," he said, "is a profound question, and it is one for which unfortunately I have no answer." He waved a hand toward the padded bench. "Sit down, please."

"I ought ter be gettin' on with me work," Angel said, seating herself reluctantly.

He frowned impatiently. "You have a morbid preoccupation with work. Let it wait."

Nicholas seated himself on the stool opposite to her.

"Now," he said, his dark eyes on her flushed face. "Your idea of a lady, please."

"Well—" she hesitated, biting at her lip. "A real lady's someone like what I always wan'ed ter be. S— someone what c'n talk good, an' c'n go roun' wearin' them silks an' sat'ns, an' smellin' nice 'n' everythin'."

She forgot that he was watching her. Her words tumbled out eagerly as for the first time she spoke aloud her secret yearning. "If I c'd be gran' like that, talkin' good 'n' all, I wouldn' never ask nothin' more!"

Strange, Nicholas thought, looking into her glowing face, that though he had recognized her beauty, he had not noticed how truly rare was its quality. But was it so strange? Just to look at her must always remind him of Marianne, of her tormented death, and his own load of grief and guilt.

He looked at Angel, frowning. His thoughts rambled on. He had painted this wench from memory not once but many times. Why? Had she, in some way, become his conscience? Were the paintings perhaps a mental hair shirt? He only knew that this girl was the living reminder of his harshness to Marianne, his lack of understanding.

He rose abruptly. Angel watched him uneasily, wondering how soon she might escape. But did she want to escape? It was funny, really, because she did, and then again she didn't. Just watching him made her feel very odd, she couldn't think why. He'd put a canvas on that easel thing. Now he was frowning at it. That frown of his! He was handsome, of course, the handsomest man she'd ever seen. But when he frowned like that, it made him look like that picture of the devil that Nell had shown her.

"Come here," Nicholas said, startling her out of her thoughts.

She jumped quickly to her feet and went to stand beside him.

"Oh!" she exclaimed, her widening eyes on the canvas. "Oh, m'lord! Tha's me, ain't it? You've gone 'n' painted me!"

"Yes, of course it's you."

His fingers were touching her hair again, but this time she did not flinch from him. "Tha's me!" she said again.

"It is indeed," Nicholas said half absently. He twisted a lock of her hair about his finger, inspecting it closely. "But the hair, as you can plainly see, is much too dark."

Angel was uncritical, even a little impatient with this trifle. "I don' min', m'lord," she assured him quickly. "It ain't that differen', is it?" She looked at him, her violet-blue eyes brilliant. "I's lov'ly, m'lord! Jus' lov'ly!"

Nicholas had painted her in the striped blue and white silks of a medieval page. The painted figure stood proudly, and behind her, sketched in indeterminate lines, rose a castle. She looked, standing with her long, slender legs slightly apart, her hands planted firmly on her hips, the short, red-gold curls feathering about her head, exactly like the proud, strutting boy Nicholas had intended to portray.

Nicholas, watching her, saw that some of her joy was fading. She leaned nearer to the canvas, frowning faintly.

"What is it?" he asked. "I thought the painting pleased you."

"It ain't that," Angel said slowly. "I's—i's jus' that me eyes look—well, they look like me eyes, an' yet they don', m'lord." She looked at him inquiringly.

Nicholas nodded. "You mean that the eyes look calculating. They were intended to be, you see. I have called the portrait Ambition, and the eyes of the boy are the eyes of a ruthless schemer."

"Oh." She looked at him rather blankly. "I see," she said, not seeing at all. "But how'd you get ter paint me so good?"

"How did I— Oh, I see what you mean. To paint you without a sitting is an exercise in memory. Many artists set themselves this test. Memory paintings, we call them."

Nicholas picked up another canvas and placed it over the first. "There," he said, stepping back. "Behold my Lady Angel."

Angel was so startled to hear her name on his lips that for a moment she did not look at the portrait. When she did so, she stared at it hungrily, almost like someone in a trance.

"M'lord," she said huskily. Tears welled into her eyes and ran down her cheeks. "You painted me like I c'd on'y dream o' bein'!"

The exquisite, poised young woman looking back at her was clad in a gown of pale-green satin. A tight bodice molded itself to the curve of her breasts, and a low, square neckline, bordered with diamonds and pearls, emphasized the whiteness of her neck and shoulders. The bodice flowed into an extravagant skirt, the front of which was divided by a narrow panel of silver lace, heavily embroidered with pearls. Silver lace frothed about the hemline, and the skirt had been slightly lifted in front to reveal small feet in green, diamond-buckled shoes. Nicholas had chosen to paint the red-gold hair long. It was swept up to form a shining, braided crown on top of her head, and from this braided crown there fell a shower of glossy ringlets. Painted lips smiled seductively, but once again, as in the other portrait, the eyes were wrong. They were hard, greedy, boldly inviting; the eyes of a woman who, demanding everything, would give nothing in return.

One could paint such eyes on all women, Nicholas thought bitterly. They were representative of the sex. Only in shape and color were they different.

Nicholas glanced at Angel. He saw that she was still overcome with the vision of herself as she might be—as she could have been, had fate been kinder.

He strolled over to the window. Staring at the lengthening shadows on the lawn below, he thought, the eyes are wrong for Angel Dawson now; but give her the opportunities of—well, of Barbara Palmer, for instance, and they will very soon acquire that hard, greedy expression.

He frowned, annoyed at the touch of sadness he felt. Angel Dawson, that little guttersnipe! Why should he waste a moment's thought on her? Angel Dawson, his conscience. Was she? Angel Dawson, his legacy from Marianne.

Marianne! Would he always be haunted by his last glimpse of her? The pitiful little body, cold in death; the unbelievable lacerations, the shredded flesh! Why, a full-grown man would have broken under such cruel punishment!

Nicholas' hands clenched. He could still see Gibbons' furtive face, the naked ugly fear in his eyes. At his hanging he had screamed with fear; he had gone down on his knees and pleaded for mercy. Mercy! He who had shown none! Gibbons had paid for his crime. *But I have not,* Nicholas thought in despair. *I shall go on remembering, regretting!*

Marianne had sent Angel Dawson to him. Mrs. Sampson, pouring the story into his stunned ears, had told him so.

My little Lady Marianne wanted you to help her, Master Nickey, Mrs. Sampson had said, her voice trembling.

Nicholas rubbed the smeared window. He had helped Angel Dawson, hadn't he? She had a home, a bed, food. Could Marianne have asked more?

Yes, the ruthlessly honest part of him answered. The effort had been on Mrs. Sampson's side, and it had cost him nothing. But what could he do? What would Marianne have wanted him to do?

"At leas', m'lord," Angel's voice said, "I got ter see what I c'd look like if I was a lady, an' there ain't many as c'n say that. I wan' ter thank you kin'ly for showin' me them beautiful pict'res."

Nicholas stood very still. That atrocious speech, coming from such an exquisitely shaped mouth! Incredible!

Suddenly, as if the idea had been lurking at the back of his mind all the time, he knew what he could do for Angel Dawson. After all, was she not his legacy?

He swung round to face her, and his usually bleak eyes were gleaming with excitement. "You shall not only see," he said loudly. "You shall experience. I will make you into a lady, Angel Dawson, the kind you aspire to be. I shall educate you, groom and clothe you. There! What do you say to that?"

Had he gone mad, she thought, staring at him with

135

wide, startled eyes. "Wh—whatever you—you say, m'lord," she stammered, backing toward the door.

"Come back here, you little fool!" He spoke in the curt, cold voice.

She came toward him slowly, her feet dragging. She looked warily up into his face. "A—ain't you feelin' well, m'lord?" Her fingers nervously twisted a corner of her apron, but she plunged on boldly. "It—it ain't that you're feelin' bad in your head, is it?"

His brows rose in haughty offense but, seeing her patent anxiety, he replied quietly, "Perhaps you are right, wench. Perhaps there is something wrong with a brain that can so easily accept the formidable task of turning a little guttersnipe into a lady."

"I ain't no guttersnipe!" she said fiercely. "I don' like ter be called that, m'lord."

Suddenly ashamed, he said abruptly, "I beg your pardon."

She did not answer him, but he saw the angry flash of her eyes, her tightly clenched hands. Good, he thought, pleased at this manifestation of spirit. Doubtless too, she had a temper to go with that spirit. He found himself hoping so, it would add zest to what might very well prove to be a thankless task.

She was standing so close to him that he could see the fine graining of her skin. The flare of her nostrils, the curve of her lovely mouth, both spoke of a suppressed arrogance, of a strong and dominant personality hidden under a guise of enforced meekness. He smiled inwardly. He thought himself to be a good judge of character. No, he told himself, she would not be easily molded, this child of the London gutters, and if driven too harshly, the smoldering defiance within her would erupt. He felt a sudden excitement at the thought. She would be a challenge, then? And faced with a challenge, he was at his best. He would incite her, madden her. He would prod her ruthlessly until, when she at last emerged from his tyranny over her mind and her thoughts, she would be exquisite—as colorful and as perfectly executed as any of his paintings; only this painting would live and move and breathe.

There must be no fault in her, he planned rapidly. When she made her debut into the fashionable world, she must meet every test, however searching. Jealous eyes would be upon her; there would be discreet though searching inquiries into the antecedents of this new and mysterious beauty who had so suddenly appeared on their horizon.

Her debut? Nicholas' mouth quirked wryly. It wasn't enough for him, then, to feed and clothe and educate her? No, fool that he was, he must needs sponsor her into society—perhaps introduce her into Court circles.

The flare of excitement within him grew. To bring this child to the attention of the King—to expose her to the jealous eyes of Barbara Palmer—ah, that would be the ultimate test!

Suddenly he wanted to laugh at himself. He was taking a great deal for granted, wasn't he? Suppose he had been mistaken in his estimate of her character? Suppose he dealt not with fire and defiance but with a meek, spiritless mouse of a girl?

He stared at her, his eyes inimical, his countenance coldly impassive; he noticed in her once again the flaring of angry resentment. No, he thought, feeling oddly relieved, he wasn't mistaken. Guttersnipe into lady? He could do it—he would do it!

Angel moved restively. His long, silent regard began to unnerve her, but she stared back at him, feeling a renewal of her hatred and a blazing indignation that he had dared to make fun of her secret dream. "I will make you into a lady, Angel Dawson," he had said. But he hadn't meant it; of course he hadn't. She said hoarsely, "C'n I go now, m'lord?"

"No," he said. He reached out and grasped both her wrists in his big hands. "I will help you attain this ambition of yours. I will make you as perfect as it is possible for a human creature to be. But understand me, Angel Dawson, when I tell you that I am not gentle by nature. I am often harsh and intolerant, and I have little patience with fools. There will be times when you will hate me; times when I will be so heartily sick of the sight of you, that I will wish I had never seen or heard of you. It is for the sake of my—of my sister that I do this thing, you understand? It will not be easy. You have a long hard road to travel. But if such be your wish, I will help you. What do you say? Is it a bargain?"

Her eyes were changing, softening. They glowed bright with incredulous joy. She tried to speak, but she could only nod and smile.

He saw the deepening pink of her cheeks, the long, fluttering dark lashes, golden at the roots, and he had the uncomfortable feeling that the wench possibly was expecting more than he was prepared to give. He looked into her sparkling eyes so seemingly without guile, and he remembered the eyes of the girl in the portrait.

He said coldly, "You will be the pupil, I the teacher. That is the only relationship that will exist between us."

She stared at him blankly for a moment; then he saw that she had understood. She did not move away from him, but he sensed her inner withdrawal.

"Do you understand?" he said harshly, irritated by the look of profound shock she now turned upon him. Angel found her voice and it was firm. "Tha's all I wan', m'lord, jus' ter be a lady. I wouldn' ask nothin' else from you. I wouldn' wan' nothin' else."

His annoyance deepened. Why did she look at him like that? Surely her words had been unnecessarily vehement?

He said softly, and wondered why he played so foolishly with words, "Such a relationship will not be difficult for you, wench, will it?" He smiled, but the smile did not touch his eyes. "Since you entertain a quite healthy hatred for me. Am I correct in this belief?"

Still afraid that the dream might yet be snatched from her, she hesitated over her answer. Instinctively, then, she knew the folly of lying to this man. "Askin' your pardon, m'lord," she said hoarsely, "but no, I don' like you. I don' like you at all. But—but I'm ever so grateful ter you."

"I am not interested in your gratitude." He dropped her wrists. "But if you are grateful," he said, turning away from her, "then it may best be shown in hard work and diligent study."

The wrists he had held felt cold and numb without the warm pulsing of his grasping fingers, and she rubbed at them abstractedly. She looked at his tall back and felt within her an urgent need to apologize. She did not fear the loss of her dream now; her need was to still the throbbing ache that his aloof and suddenly lonely figure had inspired.

"I—I—" she began. "M'lord, I—"

He turned swiftly. "Yes?" he said impatiently. He waited, his dark brows drawing together in a frowning line. When she said nothing, he said quickly, "You are wondering what to do next, is that it?" He turned away again. "You may go now," he said carelessly. "Oh, and send Mrs. Sampson to me, please."

She went swiftly to the door. "Yes, m'lord." She hesitated, her hand on the door latch. "Wh—when was you wantin' ter begin me lessons, m'lord?"

He turned his head, a faint smile on his lips. "You are impatient, I see. A very commendable attitude. I had intended Mrs. Sampson to convey my instructions to you. However, I will wish to see you tomorrow morning immediately after breakfast."

Her skin tingled with excitement. "Tomorrow! Yes, m'lord," she said breathlessly. "An'—an' thank you."

He nodded dismissingly. "Please be sure you are well bathed."

The newborn feeling of warmth vanished on a wave of indignation. "I'm clean, m'lord." She had wanted to answer him with some of his own haughty coldness, but to her dismay she heard her voice rise on the last word. Driven, she added defiantly, "An' wha's more, m'lord, I been clean ever since I come to this house!"

His faint smile deepened to one of genuine amusement. "I had not intended to lacerate your feelings," he said. "Pray accept my apologies, Mistress Dawson." His eyes gleamed mockingly. "But I must confess," he went on, "that I am vastly relieved to hear you say so."

Her fingers tightened on the latch. "I'll fin' Mrs. Sampson," she muttered, jerking the door open. She waited a moment, enduring his eyes. When he said nothing, she marched out stiffly, closing the door noisily behind her.

Walking along the corridor, her head held very high, she felt an overwhelming desire to confront him again; to rush upon him and strike out at his dark haughty face.

Angel SAT DOWN ON THE STOOL, FORGET-
ting, as she always did, to hold her back straight. Her
hands were quivering, and her heart was beginning that
now familiar heavy pounding. Soon, five minutes from
now exactly, she would hear m'lord's swift firm tread
along the corridor.

She looked about her with tear-swollen eyes, hating
the bare room originally used for storage, but now turned
into a schoolroom. Hating herself for the foolishness of
her ambition, but most of all hating the man who had
taken her pathetic dream of being a lady and turned it into
a nightmare.

She heard his harsh commanding voice in her
dreams. Back straight. Straight, I said! Are you deformed,
you little fool, that you cannot straighten your back? But
perhaps I have been misinformed as to the exact nature of
your ambition. Perhaps you are practicing to be a hunch-
back?"

His dark brows would rise, and he would stare at her
contemptuously.

"Shut up! Shut up!" she had screamed at him once.
"You're drivin' me off me bleedin' head, tha's what you're
doin'!"

"Very pretty!" he had said, his tone freezing. "We

have indeed made remarkable progress if after six months you still cannot remember that words have endings."

"I don't care!" she had retorted.

"Ah!" He had looked at her with that slight smile that always made her ache to strike him. "We must cherish our small gains, must we not? I do not care for the contraction of words as a general rule. However, in this particular contraction you had the grace to sound the *t*. Brilliant, my dear Mistress Dawson. Quite brilliant!"

Again she had lost her head. "I hate you! You're a swine! I don't wan' you to learn me no more."

"Be silent!" He strode toward her so rapidly that for a horrified moment she had thought he meant to strike her. He had not done so, but the look in his eyes had subdued her.

"You will never again," he had said, spacing his words evenly, "address me in such a manner. I will not now or at any time tolerate your insolence."

Her crushed spirit asserted itself again, and she said belligerently, "Who do you think you are, then? Bein' a perishin' lord don't make you God, do it?"

He had looked her up and down. "The matter is closed, Mistress Dawson."

"No it ain't. I—"

"I repeat," he had interrupted coldly. "The matter is closed. However, should you be foolish enough to pursue it, then I think that I may promise you that you will be quite unhappy."

Now sitting on the stool, she forgot to straighten her back. Remembering how she had begged him to release her and his calmly obstinate refusal to do so, she gritted her teeth. There had been those times she had run away; only, it seemed, she could not run fast enough nor far enough. His indomitable will, beating down her own, always forced her to return.

There was something quite terrible about his grim

refusal to deviate from the course of action he had set for himself. The knowledge that his dead sister in some measure dictated these actions made it nonetheless dreadful.

Angel thought of Mrs. Sampson. The housekeeper had pointed out that she had a freedom of choice—something Angel had been too miserable and harried to think out for herself—and strangely, now that she realized that he could not hold her against her will, she determined to master her lessons. She would be a lady and be damned to him!

She'd show him! And now she heard his approaching footsteps. Never again would he call her an imbecile. She would really be, as he so sarcastically remarked, quite, quite brilliant.

The door opened. "Good morning," Nicholas said. "Your back is hunched. Straighten it, please."

Angel rose from the stool. "Good morning, my lord," she answered, sweeping him a graceful curtsy. "It is a fine morning, ain't—is it not?"

His look of surprise was quickly controlled. He made her a slight bow. "It is indeed, Mistress Dawson."

The weeks passed swiftly, as swiftly as leaves blown in the wind. The weeks turned into months, and Nicholas was always beside her, directing her, guiding her. Sometimes—and she came to watch for it—he would give her his rare smile; she would feel absurdly triumphant. There were other times, though, when she would deliberately try to provoke him. She told herself, seeing the sudden flash in his eyes, the tightening of his lips, that some awareness of her as a person in her own right had pierced his chill reserve. But Nicholas, she found to her dismay, was a man of fire and ice. Should she provoke the fire—which she seemed to do increasingly—she was horrified by the violence of his rage.

Thanks to the hated board which he had insisted be

strapped to her back, her carriage grew gracefully erect. Her tongue, once stumbling and stuttering over difficult words, now brought them out delicately formed, richly golden of tone; and there would be warmth in Nicholas' eyes, a growing enthusiasm that carried her along. Instead of sleeping, she would find herself going over and over her lessons, planning to surprise him and bring that look to his eyes again. Why the approval of this man, whom she had vowed to hate forever and ever, should be important to her, she did not stop to ask herself.

Now she could converse with ease, and her life, if growing more burdensome, was also tinged with excitement. Nicholas introduced Monsieur Duval into the household, and under the little Frenchman's tearful, excitable tuition she grew amazingly proficient in that difficult tongue. There were dancing teachers, music teachers, and finally instruction in Court etiquette.

Materials were brought to the house, and Nicholas, ignoring her own choice, would turn the beautiful fabrics over thoughtfully. It was later, when she paraded before him in the completed gowns, that she realized the wisdom of his selection. The clear colors he chose were a perfect foil for her creamy skin and her bright hair, and the simplicity of line of the costumes showed her graceful figure to its best advantage.

Nicholas she could never like, Angel constantly told herself. She was therefore mystified and annoyed the more by her growing awareness of him. When he touched her or bent close to explain a point, her breath seemed to come with difficulty, and her skin, from that careless contact, would sting and glow.

Sometimes she would soften toward him, and she would find it difficult to remember her hatred. Such a time had been when, not thinking, she had called him Nicholas.

He had looked up quickly. "Repeat it, please," he'd said.

Her face scarlet, she'd stammered an apology. "I'm—I'm sorry. I—I did not mean to call you so."

He said, with his faint smile, "I pray you, Mistress Dawson, to repeat it."

"N—Nicholas." Growing bolder, she said defiantly. "Yes, I said Nicholas."

"It comes pleasantly from your lips." He regarded her for a moment. " 'Tis after all my name; therefore why not call me so?"

He had looked down at the papers before him, and she had found herself regarding his absorbed face almost lovingly. The folly of this was amply demonstrated when, a few moments later, she had given him a wrong answer to a question. His cold cutting comments had roused her quick anger.

He was hateful! Hateful!

Her life was in a state of flux. Divided between her hatred and that odd treacherous softening, she knew not from one minute to the next whether she would find herself laughing or crying.

Nicholas himself seemed more easily aroused to anger these days, she noticed. Where once he would have been contemptuous of her blunders—albeit they were growing increasingly rare—they ofttimes earned his fury.

There was a queer tension between them. Once, not noticing where she was going, Angel had stumbled. She would have fallen if Nicholas had not caught her. His hands had tightened on her arms. His dark eyes gazing intently into hers had been unreadable; and yet, at the faint forward inclination of his head, she had had the strongest impression that he meant to kiss her. Her breath had come faster. She had found herself swaying toward him.

He had put her from him quickly. "You are clumsy,

Mistress Dawson," he had said, and his voice was quite unlike his usual crisp, clear tones. "Sit down. We will proceed with the lesson, if you please."

Humiliated, though nothing in his manner gave her a reason to be so, she had sat through the lesson, and she had hated him more than ever before. When she found herself remembering his smile or the approving touch of his finger against her cheek, she would remind herself hastily of her true feelings toward this cold dominating man. It was annoying, quite infuriating, in fact, how little this reminder served to comfort and strengthen her.

THE LITTLE ORNAMENTAL POOL HAD AN air of enchantment about it, a timelessness. It lay quiet and neglected in a hollow of the estate, a forgotten place, for no gardener ever ventured near to disturb its dreaming peace.

Angel had found it quite by accident. Desperate to escape for a little while the demands made upon her by Nicholas, she had burst into the little clearing, her breath coming in gasps, her face stained with angry tears. She had stood very still, looking about her wonderingly, and she had fallen in love with the quiet, flower-perfumed, bee-haunted sanctuary.

Weeds grew high between chipped flagstones; iris, purple and white and yellow, fringed the pool, poking sword-shaped leaves through the strangling weeds and inclining long, sturdy stems to reflect their beauty in the still water. Doves mourned in the close-growing trees; plundering bees, working industriously in the scraggly flowering bushes, droned incessantly.

Angel managed to spend part of every day in her "secret place." In the winter, when the trees dripped pearls of moisture and raised dead skeletal arms toward a leaden sky, she would come to her sanctuary. Beneath the heavy cloak, her arms were hugged about her body for warmth. Nonetheless, walking beside the little pool, her eyes searching for the first stirrings in the frozen earth— the first frail green shoot—she would be happy.

Now, lying on her stomach beside the pool, the thickly foliaged trees screened her from the June sunshine, and the damp chill of the flagstones penetrated her white muslin gown. But Angel was conscious only of her anger.

Watching the dark, weaving shapes of plants just below the surface of the water, she momentarily forgot her rage, wondering, as she had many times before, whose hands had lovingly set the plants. Who had sat beside the dim, silver mirror of water, delighting in the beauty and the riot of color?

Had it been Nicholas' mother? Nicholas' mother, whose name was a scandalized whisper on the tongues of servants? Had it been she who had planned this place, that she might dream her afternoons away in this soothing atmosphere? Nicholas had never discussed his mother, but Angel knew that he had despised and hated her. Was it by m'lord's orders, then, that the place was untended, deliberately forgotten?

Angel moved restlessly. So even here Nicholas must penetrate. Her ears seemed still to be filled with his implacable commanding voice. How furious he would be, she thought, if he could see her now. The crisp white folds of her gown had wilted, and its draped front was slimed with moss; she had lost her hair ribbon, and her red-gold locks fell untidily about her shoulders.

She stared at her reflection in the water, smiling a little, pleased at the thought of Nicholas' anger. With a sudden movement, she shook her hair forward, watching the bright curling ends float on the water and darken. Almost two years of bondage to Nicholas—for so she still thought of it—and in that time her hair had grown well past her waist.

She sat up abruptly. Water dripped from her hair,

and dampened still further the front of her gown. Impatiently she tossed the wet ends over her shoulders. Two years, and Nicholas had not yet, as he had promised to do, presented her at Court.

She was almost nineteen now—and restless. Nicholas had taken her, raw and ignorant, and bullying her, commanding her, had shaken her violently. Nicholas was nothing if not tenacious. He had succeeded in bursting asunder the stultifying chrysalis of her ignorance.

She had become all that he desired her to be. In a moment of rare geniality, he had told her so. He had complimented her on her voice, admiring its now low, soft, exquisitely modulated tones. She herself knew that her walk was graceful, her general knowledge and her understanding of the arts extensive. Her French was somewhat more advanced that Nicholas'. Her poise now was unshaken except when she was angry at Nicholas, and she was capable of conducting herself with propriety under all circumstances. But still Nicholas avoided the subject of her debut. Why, when she spoke of it, did he become so angry? What more did he demand of her?

Angel folded her arms about her knees. Near to her a cloud of yellow butterflies hovered in fluttering dance. A willow tree, hanging over the bank, trailed a trembling fountain of green leaves to brush the water to an agitated life. The breeze sighing through the fluttering leaves sounded oddly like a grieving woman. Raising suddenly from a clump of pale-pink blossom, a bird skimmed low over the water, trailing its fragile shadow behind it.

She must go back to the house soon, Angel thought, resting her head upon her knees. He would be awaiting her, and he would be angry, for Nicholas hated unpunctuality.

Half asleep though she was, she could still feel an inner recoil at the thought of provoking another of those painful scenes.

Nicholas! He was a riddle. She still wondered why he refused to let her go. She had given him plenty of reasons to wash his hands of her, yet he had not. To Nicholas, a promise, even if made only to himself, was still a promise. That much, at least, she knew of him. In the beginning her trouble had been that she would not guard her tongue. But Nicholas had had a summary method of dealing with what he termed her "damned insolence," and this had taught her an unwilling respect. There had been times after that when she had felt a closeness to him. Nonetheless, there was always that something in him that kept her slightly at a distance; and even had she wished to—which she assured herself she did not—she felt that the barrier he had erected about himself was too strong to break through.

Sometimes when she would surprise his eyes upon her, there would be something in their expression that pained her. But the pain she felt was for him. Driven by a wish to console him, she would be gentle; her voice, her smile, sought to coax a response from him. Sometimes she succeeded; more often she did not. The lesson would resume, but when she looked into his eyes again, it was to find them shuttered against her. Now she welcomed his sarcasm, his sardonic smile, for it fed her hatred which, these days, needed a constant reminder.

What did he see when he looked at her, Angel wondered? Did those things about her which he had brought into being please him? Or did he look beyond her outer veneer and see her very clearly as that same little "guttersnipe"? She brooded on the question darkly. He had not said so, and nothing in his manner remotely implied it—but she knew! She knew!

Angel put her hands to her forehead, pressing her fingers deeply into her temples. Only yesterday she had been seized with a conviction that she was going insane; for how else could she explain the extraordinary melting sensation that had swept over her. Watching Nicholas' moving lips, she had wondered how it would feel to have those lips pressed passionately to her own. She who hated him, despised him! She'd die if he touched her! She would!

Bending over the pool, Angel splashed water over her flushed face. She sat there for a moment longer, slowly dabbing her face dry with her kerchief; then she rose to her feet. Walking reluctantly back to the house, she was acutely conscious of her rumpled hair and her ruined gown. The thought of Nicholas' anger no longer pleased her; she stopped, patting at her hair with anxious futile hands, and trying to smooth the worst of the creases from the front of her gown. There was nothing she could do about the long green smear. If anything, her efforts had merely resulted in spreading the stain. Cursing herself for her cowardice, Angel moved on.

"I am not afraid of him!" she said aloud. "I am not! Why should I be?"

Nearing the house, she was annoyed to find that she was trembling. Damn him! she thought. Oh, damn him!

Mrs. SAMPSON STOOD ON THE MARBLE STEPS, watching Angel's approach. She put down the basket of freshly cut flowers she had been carrying and waited, her hands folded in front of her. She did not smile, but her eyes were affectionate.

The child moved so gracefully, Mrs. Sampson thought. So gracefully that she seemed to float rather than walk. Who would have thought the little Angel with her pinched, sallow face and frightened defiant eyes would have developed into this lovely girl? Who would have thought that the harsh coarse voice would have gentled to such soft, melodious tones?

"Angel!" Mrs. Sampson said in dismay as the girl stopped before her. "What on earth have you been doing with yourself? Look at your gown! Your hair!"

"I know." Angel smiled apologetically. "I'm sorry."

Mrs. Sampson looked at the leaves and the small pieces of twigs caught in the girl's tumbled hair, the mud that streaked her left cheek. The double flounce at the hemline of her gown was torn; her white velvet shoes, darkened with moisture, had lost the little bows that decorated them.

"Angel," she said, "you must change at once. The

master will be very angry if he sees you in such a condition!"

The stiffening of Angel's slight figure told her that her words were ill-chosen. She sighed. "You will change your gown, won't you, Angel?"

"Later, perhaps," Angel answered. "But I am already late."

"I know. He has been asking for you. Nevertheless, Angel, I think—"

"I will go to him at once." Angel's smile, the pressure of her hand on the housekeeper's arm, robbed the interruption of rudeness.

The great door to the entrance hall stood open, and Angel went through boldly, her head high. Mrs. Sampson watched her cross the gleaming floor. The sun streaming through the latticed windows threw checkers of light and shadow over her moving figure and picked out fiery lights in her hair.

Angel stood hesitantly before the door of the library, her hand half-raised to knock. Shaking her head, Mrs. Sampson turned away. I must be getting old, she thought, as she went outside and picked up her basket of flowers. But I could swear those two silly young creatures love each other.

Her finger ruffled the petals of a flower. Young? Angel was young, yes. She was but nineteen. Master Nicholas was thirty-two years old. But what of that? Love took no account of a difference in ages. It was high time Master Nicholas learned to trust. High time he was married.

Through the still-open door Angel caught a glimpse of the housekeeper walking along the winding path that led into the orchard. Why, she wondered, was Mrs. Sampson going to the orchard?

Angel frowned. What did it matter? She was only playing for time, trying to delay the moment when she must face Nicholas. Quickly she raised her hand again and rapped sharply on the door. Hearing the rumble of Nicholas' deep voice bidding her enter, she turned the handle. Her hands clenched as she entered the room. She was prepared for battle. She wasn't a child that must be directed and guided; she was a woman. Or perhaps the ever honest Angel amended to herself, she no longer needed guiding or directing.

Nicholas was standing by the window, his back to her, absorbed apparently with the view. "Close the door, please," he said, without turning.

"Certainly, m'lord." Angel shut it with a loud slam. Leaning against the door, she waited for him to turn. She was behaving stupidly, childishly, she thought ashamed. She would apologize.

"I—" she began. His cold voice cut her off.

"You are late, Mistress Dawson."

Mistress Dawson, indeed! He must be very displeased, then. "I'm sorry," she said.

He made no answer. Why didn't he turn? How dare he ignore her!

She glared at his straight back. Nicholas, as always except when he was painting, was immaculate. His dark-red velvet jacket showed not the faintest of creases; his hand rested lightly on the window frame, and she caught a glimpse of the snowy ruffles at his wrist. But she, though she tried hard to preserve her appearance, was always ripping her skirt, losing her hair ribbon, or ruining her shoes.

Thoroughly incensed, Angel said sharply, "I regret, m'lord, this intrusion upon your dreams. Perhaps I should return when you are less preoccupied."

"Stay where you are, please." Nicholas answered.

What ailed him, Nicholas thought savagely. Why this reluctance to face a stupid chit of a child? He disliked her. She was an insolent guttersnipe! A damned thorn in his flesh! He had to get rid of her. She must leave this house, and soon. Her face came between him and his work. He was never free of her. Even her voice seemed to echo through his dreams.

Her voice! The hard lines of Nicholas' mouth softened. Her beautiful, melodious voice. He had not dreamed of the perfect pitch, the haunting quality that lay waiting beneath the strident ugliness. He had discovered that voice. If she should say to a man, "I love you," she would make the simple words into a strain of glorious music.

Nicholas stared at the bush outside his window. It was laden with scarlet blossoms, but he was blind to their beauty. If Angel said, "I love you!" Damn the baggage! She'd probably say it to a hundred different men, and each time she would mean it less. She was no different from any other woman! They were all whores or would-be whores.

He listened to the small fidgeting movements she made. There was nothing more he could do for her. It was time now for her to venture out into the world. His world—the world she had never known. He smiled grimly. Angel would very quickly find herself a protector. She was so beautiful, so glowing—men would be mad for her. If the King should set eyes upon her, he would desire her.

Nicholas stiffened. Well, why not? Above all else, Charles loved beautiful women. He pictured the lust in Charles' eyes; he saw the slender, jewel-laden fingers caressing Angel's white willing body, the full lips, beneath the narrow line of his mustache, fastening greedily on hers.

Nicholas found that he was trembling. Yes, the King should have her. Angel would have luxury, perhaps power; above all, she would have achieved the ultimate triumph; she would be mistress to the King of England. He did not doubt Charles' desire to possess her. Angel would be the favorite mistress—it was inevitable. Barbara Palmer, lovely though she was, paled in comparison to Angel.

"M'lord," Angel said softly, "your hand is trembling. Are you ill?"

"No," Nicholas answered, thrusting his hand out of sight. "Thank you for your concern."

She grimaced at his back. "I am happy to hear it," she answered demurely. "May I have your lordship's permission to retire? The view of your back, though interesting, has become somewhat tedious."

"Saucy wench!" He turned, smiling. "You may leave when I give you perm—" His smile faded. "You look deplorable!" he snapped. "How come you to be in such condition?"

"I'm sorry," she said, hoping to evade an explanation. "I will go to my room and change my gown."

"No." He shook his head. "You have wasted enough of my time."

"I!" she cried, stung by the unfairness of the charge. "Nay, m'lord. 'Tis you who have wasted time." She turned to the door. "I will return shortly."

"You will not leave this room." A pulse throbbed savagely in his temple. He reached her side, and his hands, as if acting independently of his will, grasped her hair and twisted it brutally.

"You will do as I say!" he shouted. "And never turn your back on me again! Do you understand?"

Her struggle ceased. "I hate you!" she whispered. "Hate you! Hate you! Why, you—you—"

"Yes, go on, tell me what I am!" he said hoarsely, thrusting his face close to hers. "Wait. I'll tell you. I am the fool who took a cheap gutter prostitute and turned her into a high-class whore!"

"You—you think that of me?" The anger had left

her eyes; they looked wounded. "So that is your opinion of me, m'lord!"

He looked down into her white face, her quivering lips, and he was suddenly appalled at his own words. "Forgive me," he stammered. "I did not mean—I had no right to say that to you."

Her anger leaped back, and she trembled with the force of it. "I'll never forgive you! Never! Never!" she cried. She struggled from his loosened grip, and struck at his face savagely with her long, pointed nails. "Never! Never!" she repeated.

Nicholas pushed her from him. "Damn you, you hell-born bitch!" He pulled a handkerchief from his sleeve and dabbed at his bleeding face.

Angel struggled to control her rising hysteria, but she could not force it down. Laughter, shrill and helpless, burst from her.

"You'd laugh at me!" Nicholas seemed to choke on his rage. "No, by God!" he shouted, striding toward her. "You'll not laugh at me!"

The laughter froze on her lips. Alarmed at the dangerous glitter in his eyes, she shrank back. His hands reached out for her and his fingers bit, iron-hard, into the soft flesh of her arm.

"You trollop!" he snarled, dragging her across the room.

She fought him, and her fear was such that she remembered and employed all of the cunning tricks of her one-time precarious existence. It availed her nothing. In his remorseless grip she found herself as helpless as a baby.

He reached upward with his free hand and snatched a riding crop from a wall bracket. He saw the naked terror welling into her eyes, and he began to laugh immoderately. All of his torturing self-doubt, his frustrations, his lifelong bitterness, and his refusal to face the truth—where this girl was concerned—converged in that laughter and swept him away on a tide of frenzy.

"Don't!" Angel's voice came whisperingly from a suddenly dry throat. "Don't whip me! Please don't! No! No! You mustn't!"

Unheeding, he spun her round, his hand tearing the fragile material of her gown. He did not see the pale, seamed back thus exposed; he saw nothing through the mist of rage before his eyes; he heard nothing through the drumming in his ears. "Damn you, you whore! You guttersnipe!"

The hand holding the riding crop lifted, descended; but Angel, with a strength born of terror, twisted in his grasp, and in so doing took the blow full on her face.

"Dear God!" The madness receded. Appalled, Nicholas stared at her mutilated face, at the great gash that the leather thong with its weighted tip had opened up on her cheek, the bright welling of blood that stained her neck.

"N—N—Nicholas!" Her voice was a faint, mournful thread of sound. She swayed between his suddenly nerveless hands. He heard the sighing of her breath as she crumpled at his feet.

"Angel!" Nicholas fell to his knees beside her. His name on her lips! How sweet it always sounded in his ears.

"My darling!" The words were torn from him. He saw clearly the ridges of long-healed scars on her back, and his throat tightened with almost unbearable pain. "Oh, my little one," he said softly. Turning her gently, he held her cradled in his arms. "My darling! Forgive me, my darling!"

Angel's scream was trying to force itself through her lips, but she could not bring the sound out. It seemed to be burying itself deeper within her, and now she could hear it echoing over and over again in her brain. She was back in Newgate then? She had been sent back to hell! She could hear the ugly chanting of the women—"Floggin'! Floggin'! Give her a skin strippin'!" The women! Oh God! They were all about her! She could see their gloating eyes; their faces, yellowed and diseased, were thrust close to hers.

A floggin! Jim Gibbons, who held her now, had ordered it. She struggled, knowing that she could not escape his hold. But she'd been flogged once today, and the pain of it! How could she bear another flogging? Would Gibbons order it to be done over and over again? Would nothing satisfy him but her death?

Feebly, desperately, Angel fought against his tight hold.

"No! Don' whip me no more!" she moaned, her careful new accent fled. "I won' tell on you, I swear ter God! Let me go! Let me go! I can' take no more floggin'!"

"Hush, my dear! My darling! You're safe!" Tenderly, Nicholas held her. "No one shall ever hurt you again. I I swear it, my little love!"

It was as if a stranger spoke through his lips, so unused was he to tenderness of speech, for never before had he spoken thus to any woman. For Angel, wandering in a labyrinth of pain and renewed fear, his voice was silent; she heard not one word.

Nicholas did not hear the door open, and he started when Mrs. Sampson's voice spoke sharply from behind him. "I heard Angel cry out, Master Nickey. Forgive the intrusion, but I was worried."

Nicholas did not answer. The housekeeper was silent for a moment; then she came swiftly toward him, her skirts rustling crisply. He heard her indrawn breath of horror, then her shaken, whispering voice, "Oh, Master Nickey! What has been happening here? What have you done, my boy? What have you done!"

He looked up slowly. He saw the worried blue eyes fixed on him, the mouth opening on speech, and he guessed what she would say.

"No, Sampson, it wasn't an accident, and there is no excuse you can find for me."

"But, Master Nickey," Mrs. Sampson said, her eyes widening in dismay, "it must have been an accident. Why, I know you! You wouldn't hurt—"

"I would! I did!" He would spare himself nothing. "I meant to hurt her, Sampson, God forgive me!" His face quivered. "But not like this! I didn't mean to touch her face—her lovely face!"

"I'm sure you didn't." Mrs. Sampson's hand touched his shoulder gently, reassuringly.

"For God's sake—don't soothe me!" He looked at her with burning eyes. "Can you help her?"

She knelt at Angel's side, her cool fingers gently examining the wound. "It looks much worse than it really is, I believe," she said thoughtfully. "There," she smiled at him, "don't you go fretting. Some of my special salve will work wonders, you'll see."

"Are you sure, Sampson? What if—what if she should be disfigured?"

"She won't be." A brisk, no-nonsense note entered the housekeeper's voice. "Come now, Master Nickey, lift her up and carry her to her room."

Angel felt arms lifting her, and she heard the murmur of voices, but her delirium had left her. She knew where she was, whose arms carried her. She moved her head slightly, fearful of the searing pain. None came; but how strange the side of her face felt—it was numb, and her cheek felt swollen, as though it was twice its size. She felt the hatred filling her. He had done this to her! The great m'lord! She'd have her revenge—someway—somehow! Damn him, the swine! She'd never forgive him! Never!

Nicholas, carrying her carefully to the stairs, saw

the flutter of her eyelashes. He ascended slowly, watching her face with anxious eyes. His thoughts were in turmoil; anguish and self-disgust swept over him. His words came back to him, the words he had used when she lay at his feet, so small, so helpless. "Darling!" he had said. "My darling! My little one!"

Nicholas felt heat flushing his face. Was he in love with the wench then? Impossible! He? He, who had sworn never to render himself vulnerable as his father had been. To love a woman was to invite misery, and over the years he had had no cause to change his opinion. If anything, his contempt for women had grown instead of softening. And now here was this chit of a girl, with her great violet-blue eyes and her bright hair, forcing words from his lips that surely only a dolt far gone in love would utter.

Outside her bedroom door, he stopped short; looking at the girl in his arms, his eyes were bemused. And if he had been such a fool as to fall in love—what then? His lip curled bitterly. In love with a child of nineteen, and he approaching his thirty-third year!

You fool! he thought wildly. One would think you to be in your dotage. Nicholas Tavington in love! Caught in a trap he had determined to avoid. And what of Angel? Could he hope that she might return his love? His cynicism surged back on the thought. It was so easy for a woman to say, "I love you," and so hard for a man to believe.

All these thoughts were tangled in his brain on that one short trip up the stairs. Mrs. Sampson was fussing behind him, but he scarcely heard her.

Mrs. Sampson opened the door, and he did not see her speculative eyes as he walked over to the bed. With infinite care he laid the girl down.

If Angel said, "I love you!" Looking down at her, Nicholas felt the leap of his heart. She would never say it of course, why should she? Did he want her to say it—

did he? And if she did, would he accept her words as truth? After what he had done, she never would.

"You can leave her with me now, Master Nickey," Mrs. Sampson said. "I'll take good care of her."

"Yes," he said absently, making no move to leave. "Thank you, Sampson."

Angel moaned faintly. Her eyes opened suddenly and looked straight into Nicholas'. The hatred rushed out, and though he had expected little else, the force of it struck him like a physical blow. He wanted to take her hands in his and beg her to forgive him. Instead he retreated into coldness.

"My behavior was unpardonable," he said stiffly. "I ask you to forgive me, Mistress Dawson."

Oh the icy formality of him! Why could he not smile at her? Why could he not say with some degree of warmth, "I'm sorry, Angel. Please forgive me." His eyes were bleak, his manner arrogant, and there was no repentance in him. But if he had smiled—the smallest of smiles would have done—perhaps then she might not have hated him quite so much.

Mrs. Sampson watched Nicholas with sympathetic eyes. My poor Master Nickey, she thought. You're in love for the first time in your life, and you don't know what to do about it.

"Go away, m'lord," Angel said.

She closed her eyes, turning her face to the pillow. The numbness had left her cheek and, after the respite from pain, the hot, throbbing agony was hard to bear. Tears slid from under her lashes.

"It hurts!" she sobbed. There was relief in tears, and it was comforting to feel Mrs. Sampson's ministering hands, but she was chagrined that Nicholas had seen her in her weakness.

She must be as hard as he, she told herself. She

must match coldness for coldness; and above all, she must never let him realize how rapidly her hatred would disappear if he would but give her a kind look or word. She could never like him; that would be quite impossible. But sometimes, when by chance her hand had brushed his, she had felt—had felt—

She turned restlessly on the bed, feeling a vague danger in the trend of her thoughts. "Go away," she said again, her voice trembling childishly.

"There's nothing to worry about, Angel," Mrs. Sampson soothed. "His lordship has gone."

"Oh!" Angel's eyes jerked open. Two minutes ago she had wished him to leave; and now that he had done so, she felt annoyed and neglected.

"Perhaps," Mrs. Sampson said, reading her thoughts with uncanny accuracy, "he would have stayed had he felt you wished him to do so."

Angel looked at her sullenly. "Why should I wish it?"

Mrs. Sampson's hands worked the salve gently into the injured cheek. "I can't imagine, child." She eyed Angel sharply, adding, "I am very disappointed in his lordship. He has faults, as who does not, but I have never until now thought him to be cruel."

With one of the lightning changes of mood that had just lately begun to characterize her thoughts of the Earl, Angel said quickly, almost defensively, "He didn't mean it. I struck him first. I—I provoked him."

"I see." Mrs. Sampson hid a smile. "Then you don't hate his lordship?"

Angel looked up quickly. "But I do, of course I do! It was just—just that I provoked him, but I can still hate him, can't I?"

"Of course." Mrs. Sampson finished her work. "There, Angel, that feels more comfortable, doesn't it?"

"Yes it does, thank you. Angel looked at her gratefully. She was silent for a moment, then she said in a subdued voice, "Mrs. Sampson, will I be scarred?"

"Gracious, child, no. Your face is very painful, I know, and quite possibly it will be bruised; but you will not be scarred, take my word for it."

"Perhaps if I had been," Angel said darkly, "he might then have been sorry."

"His lordship is very sorry." Mrs. Sampson settled the pillow comfortably beneath Angel's head. "But he sometimes finds it difficult to express his feelings."

She moved to the door. "Rest now, Angel."

Angel lay very still. The pain in her face had eased considerably, and she felt sleepy. Was he indeed sorry, she wondered. Her thoughts played happily with a humbly contrite Nicholas, and this idea, though patently absurd, was still in her mind when she drifted off to sleep.

ANGEL PEERED ANXIOUSLY AT HER FACE in the hand mirror. The pain had gone, but her cheek was still swollen and discolored. She was ugly! Damn, Nicholas to hell! He had disfigured her for life, and it was quite useless for Mrs. Sampson to tell her otherwise. Angry tears filled her eyes and she swung round to face the housekeeper, who was seated on the edge of the bed, watching her with sympathetic eyes.

"Look at me!" Angel cried. She glared at the roll of neatly folded linen, the basin of warm water and the small jar of salve Mrs. Sampson had placed on the table beside the bed. "Your salve won't help me—nothing will help!" her voice broke on a sob. "W—why do you keep 1—lying to me and pretending? I'll always be ugly, always, always! And he did it. Yes, your wonderful Master Nickey!"

"I was not aware that I had ever referred to him as wonderful."

Angel glowered at her. "But you think so, I know. How can you care for such a—a savage, such a beast!"

Mrs. Sampson smiled. "Don't be childish, Angel."

Angel refused to be diverted. "And another thing. Why hasn't he come near me?" She leaped to her feet.

"He's ashamed.'"

Angel blinked. Nicholas ashamed? Nonsense! She didn't believe it. Nicholas was never ashamed. He walked as though he owned the earth, and he was never wrong—or so he thought.

"I don't believe it," Angel said loudly. "And even if that were true, he might at least have inquired about me."

"But of course he inquires." She rose to her feet. "Sit down, Angel," she said, gesturing to a chair. "I'll bathe your face and rub in some fresh salve."

"Why do you trouble yourself?" Angel sat down slowly. "You know it's hopeless, don't you?"

"I know nothing of the sort." Mrs. Sampson worked in silence for a few moments, her hands gentle on the maltreated cheek.

"Well?" Angel said suspiciously. "Why don't you say something?"

Mrs. Sampson wiped her hands on a small linen towel, then she picked up the jar of salve. "Hold still," she commanded.

Fuming, Angel waited until the woman had completed the tedious and necessarily slow process. "You can't say anything, can you? You're afraid to tell me!"

"Oh, Angel, you really are a trying child." She placed the jar on the table and returned to her seat on the bed. "I have told you over and over again that you are healing beautifully, but you refuse to believe me. What else can I say?"

"You might have a little sympathy for me."

"I am not a demonstrative woman, but you may be assured of my sympathy."

"But—but you feel sorry for him, too."

"Yes." Mrs. Sampson folded her hands in her lap and surveyed Angel calmly. "It was an unpardonable thing for his lordship to do, but I do feel very sorry for him. The injury and pain you have suffered is equaled by the pains of his conscience."

"Conscience? He hasn't any!"

Mrs. Sampson's mouth tightened. "Nonsense!"

"Well," Angel mumbled. "If he has a conscience, I never noticed it."

"Haven't you?" Mrs. Sampson smiled faintly. "I think, child, that you are very much aware of his lordship. Much more so than you are prepared to admit."

Angel flushed. "What do you mean?"

"I mean that you don't hate him." Mrs. Sampson shook her head sadly. "Although I have no doubt that you will go on telling yourself you do."

"I do!" Angel stared at her with outraged eyes. "I do hate him, I tell you. I do!"

"No." Mrs. Sampson looked down at her clasped hands. "Angel, I have never betrayed a confidence in my life, but I am going to do so now. There are things in his lordship's life, things that have made him hard and bitter. I would like to tell you a little about his earlier life."

"Why?"

"I have my reasons." Again the faint smile touched her mouth. "I think it will help you to understand him. Will you listen?"

Angel wanted to refuse—then unwittingly she found herself remembering Nicholas' rare smile; the way his somber eyes would soften when she had managed to please him. "Very well, I'll listen." She had meant her words to sound casual and was annoyed when she realized that they came out eagerly.

Mrs. Sampson did not seem to notice. Relieved, Angel assumed an air of studied indifference. Then, touched by the tenderness in the woman's voice, she began to listen attentively.

Mrs. Sampson made her see the small Nicholas, so

lonely, so afraid, roaming the echoing corridors of Benbrook Manor. She could feel with him his anguish for the frail elderly man who was his father; and his bewilderment as his natural love for his mother turned to loathing and disgust. It was a disgust that was too big for him to understand, and it terrified him. There was another terror too. Shocked and trembling, the boy was forced to witness the act of sexual love—and for no other reason than that it gave to Lady Catherine, his mother, an added zest.

Lady Catherine cared nothing for her husband, and she brought her lovers openly to the house. With her bedroom door standing wide open, her small son crouched frozen on the floor watched her entertain a series of men. The men, because she was so beautiful and so skilled in the eroticism of the act, were lost to shame. It was doubtful if they noticed the suffering child. He was there at the command of his mother; it amused her, and after a while they forgot he was there. Only once had he broken his silence; he had suddenly and violently been sick. The sound of his miserable retching was disturbing, Lady Catherine told Mrs. Sampson, who had come hurrying in answer to the imperious ringing of her bell. Without comment, Mrs. Sampson had gathered the sobbing Nicholas into her arms and taken him away. Lady Catherine returned to the arms of her lover, and there was no thought in her mind for her son and certainly none for her gaunt-faced husband with his wasted frame and his tormented eyes.

All that night, the housekeeper told Angel, she had sat in a chair with the boy cradled in her arms; and he had clung to her and implored her never to leave him. So distracted was he, so fevered was his skin, that Mrs. Sampson had begun to fear for his sanity. It was then that she made up her mind that "Master Nickey," come what may, must be kept away from "that woman."

Nicholas was then Mrs. Sampson's only charge. Marianne, daughter of one of Lady Catherine's lovers, had not yet been born. The housekeeper found to her dismay that it was not always possible to guard the boy from his mother. She would come seeking him, laughing at the other woman's passionate plea for the child. So he would go with his mother, moving beside her like some small, hypnotized creature.

Mrs. Sampson had finally gone in desperation to Lord John, Nicholas' father, and had poured out her anxiety for the well-being and health of his son. Surprisingly, Lord John had not known of the boy's enforced witnessing of his mother's degradation. He was a weak man, as he well knew, but on this occasion he had been roused to quite terrible rage. Ineffectual, as it turned out. Lady Catherine had laughed at him; the only difference was that now she bolted her bedroom door, and Nicholas, barred from possible rescue by his nurse, was twice a prisoner.

The years passed. Nicholas grew hard and aloof, and the bleak bitterness of his expression deepened. He gradually freed himself from his mother's domination; and when forced to address her there was a biting and unmistakable contempt in his voice. Lady Catherine, usually the boldest of women, now saw in this implacable, icy-eyed, grim-faced man who was her son an unrelenting enemy who was to be feared. She mocked at herself and tried to deride her newborn fear, but she could not. Consequently, she grew careful in her speech and she treated him with a wary respect that was utterly foreign to her nature.

Nicholas watched his beloved father die, and those who were also in the room noticed how empty of expression was his face and mien, and they whispered among themselves, telling each other that he was "cruel and unfeeling." Only Mrs. Sampson, who understood him and loved him well, had known of his inconsolable grief.

With the death of Lord John, Lady Catherine's suppressed fear of her son finally overcame her and in a surprising way contributed to her death. Now that his father was dead, Nicholas refused to allow her to entertain her lovers in the Manor. Outwardly defiant, she removed herself to London and established herself in the house in St. Bernard's Square, where she continued to receive her lovers. In so doing, she revived old scandals and added further infamy to her name.

On a bright June morning, some three months after Lady Catherine's departure from Benbrook Manor, a child playing with a companion in a field had found her naked dead body lying half-hidden in the long grass. About her neck a silk handkerchief was knotted, biting deeply into her flesh. She had been dead for quite a few days. Lady Catherine was buried in the family vault. A week later Arthur Minter, an old lover of hers of whom she had long since tired, confessed to the crime of vengeance.

Nicholas appeared indifferent. He went about the estate as usual, his face imperturbable. But on the way to the funeral, which he had attended, he returned to the house and locked himself in his room for hours.

Marianne believed Nicholas' father to be her own—and he did not disillusion her. She adored her big brother and followed him everywhere. But Nicholas grew sterner and yet more unbending, for he viewed her growing likeness to Lady Catherine with suspicious dismay. He loved the child, but it was all but impossible for him to express it. Though she continued to love him, Marianne gradually became resentful of the strict puritanical rules Nicholas laid down for her. She was afraid of him but secretly rebellious, and so she lived from day to day—torn between her love and her natural wish to escape the awe-inspiring shadow he cast over her young life. When Nicholas rallied to the standard of his wandering prince and departed the Manor, Marianne for the first time knew freedom. So intoxicated had she been that she was inclined to behave recklessly.

"His lordship was never one to explain his attitude," Mrs. Sampson said, "and he never did tell her that he loved her, or that he was stern only because he feared she had inherited her mother's weaknesses. And so my little lady, believing that her brother hated her and would take away her freedom upon the moment of his return, grew increasingly reckless. I believe it was desperation that sent her into the arms of John Bannister. For I really cannot believe that she loved that young libertine."

While she waited for her face to heal—and she was optimistic now that the swelling had gone down—Angel thought over the story many times. It had given her a new insight into Nicholas' complex character. She felt for the lonely and betrayed little boy he had been. With each passing day her resentment and bitterness toward him softened. She still stubbornly refused to attend her lessons until her face had completely healed, and Nicholas, oddly enough, did not demand her presence, but Mrs. Sampson was able to report to Nicholas with a clear conscience that Angel had forgiven his assault upon her. What Nicholas' reaction had been—if indeed he had one—was not known, for after telling Angel that she had had a conversation with his lordship, Mrs. Sampson said no more, and Angel did not press her.

June slipped into July, and the only evidence of Nicholas' savage attack was a thin red line upon Angel's cheek. It was all but invisible, and Mrs. Sampson told her it would soon disappear completely.

On a morning when the sunshine lay golden across the lawns and her room was filled with the scent of full-blooming roses, Angel gave in to her growing restlessness. She refused to acknowledge the feeling for what it really was, a longing to see Nicholas. She told herself she was bored. When Mrs. Sampson entered the room to inquire after her health, as was her daily custom, Angel said casually, "If you should see his lordship, be so good as to inform him that I shall attend lessons this morning."

"It will be my pleasure to do so," Mrs. Sampson answered, her mouth twitching slightly.

"Why are you smiling?" Angel looked at her suspiciously.

"Was I smiling? I was not aware of it. But if I feel like smiling, then surely I am entitled to do so." The housekeeper turned to the door. "I will deliver your message," she added with a touch of irony.

Angel dressed rapidly. Brushing her hair, she was annoyed to find that her hands were trembling. But half an hour later when she entered the room set aside for the morning's lesson she was perfectly calm.

Nicholas was seated at his desk, his head bent over some papers. He had not heard her enter, and Angel studied his frowning brows and the straight line of his mouth. A shaft of sunlight from the window behind him touched his hair and brought out unexpected bronze tints. He was thinner, and there were faint shadows beneath his eyes. He looked, she thought, as though he had not been sleeping well.

"Good morning, Nicholas," she said. The softer feeling engendered by Mrs. Sampson's story was reflected in her tone.

Nicholas looked up quickly. "Good morning." There was no perceptible change of expression, but his eyes, lingering for a brief moment on her cheek, seemed warmer. "I hope I see you well?" he added.

"Yes, indeed." She smiled brilliantly.

He was silent for a moment. "In that case," he said dryly, "we will proceed."

She sat down, arranging her blue skirt about her. No apology? Well, she had not expected one. He would never apologize, not he. He was stiff-necked, arrogant, and hateful! But she was reluctant to let go of her new mood, and she would not let her indignation develop. Instead, she forced herself to remember Mrs. Sampson's words. "Master Nickey finds it hard to apologize," the housekeeper had said earnestly, "but he feels things inside, Angel, believe me. Because he is so stubborn and proud, he suffers more."

"Hold your head up," Nicholas said curtly, "and straighten your shoulders."

"Yes, Nicholas." She obeyed him without question, and again she gave him that brilliant smile.

Nicholas watched her closely. What was the matter with her? What new game was this? He had expected anger and defiance, perhaps hatred. Instead, her manner was gentle, her smiles radiant, and her voice positively cooing. Had he not known it to be impossible, he would have thought she was trying to charm him. But perhaps she was trying to wheedle him into granting her some favor. His brows drew together ominously. If she wanted something, let her ask for it. He hated wheedling women. He did not know this girl with her air of courteous attention. He preferred the old Angel with her fiery temper, her often insolent tongue, and her deliberately contrived air of stupidity—adopted, he well knew, in an effort to goad him and to force him into losing his self-control.

The morning wore on, and still Angel continued with her new kindness of manner. Nicholas' anger and bewilderment grew and he continued to repulse her. Her well-meant efforts he viewed with dark suspicion, and he glowered at the stranger who sat demurely in Angel's seat.

Once, when Angel was puzzled over a question and approached his desk, Nicholas, impatiently explaining, was taken aback when she gave him a tender look and laid her hand on his.

He jerked his hand away. "Return to your seat," he directed her coldly.

It was too much. She had tried to be nice and this was her reward. Outraged, insulted, she cried out, "Damn you, then! It's impossible to be nice to you, quite impossible! I hate you, do you hear me? I hate you!"

"Ah!" he said, relieved by this outburst. His glance lingered on her with mild amusement. "I have missed you, Mistress Dawson, and I bid you welcome. Nevertheless," he continued, "you will sit down, if you please. We have a great deal of work to do."

She knew the gesture to be childish; but she stamped her foot, her eyes defying him. "I won't sit down! We have been working for the past five hours. Surely, m'lord, you will have the courtesy to grant me a small respite?" She flung up her head. "Am I your slave?" she demanded. "If so, be good enough to tell me."

"Slave?" he said musingly. "No, I think not." His dark brows rose mockingly. "Very well, infant. Since it seems to mean so much to you, you have my permission to rest."

Infant! Angel's eyes blazed. How dare he. Oh, how dare he!

"Let me assure you, m'lord," she said, her voice dangerously soft, "I am no infant. As you would know, should you ever decide to really look at me."

"What! What the devil do you mean by that?" He shot the question at her so abruptly that she was startled and confused.

"Oh!" she shouted. "How do I know what I mean? I believe you deliberately try to provoke me." She turned on her heel. "And now, since I have your gracious

174

permission to rest, I will retire to my room. Providing, of course, that the arrangement meets with your lordship's approval."

"Quite," he said. He gathered up the papers from the desk before him. "On your way, perhaps you will be so kind as to place these in the library for me."

"Very well." She took the papers from him. Looking up, she saw his smile. The smile was mocking and the expression in his eyes so cynical that a wave of self-pity swept over her. Why should he look at her in such a way? He had injured her, not she him. Well, she had tried to be nice, but he would have none of it! So be it. She didn't care. After all, why should she care?

Her lips began to tremble. It was only an emotional reaction, she told herself—but if he noticed, he would undoubtedly call her "infant" again. She deliberately dropped the papers on the floor. "You take them," she said rudely. "I don't think I'll go to my room. I believe, instead, that I will take a walk in the fresh air."

Nicholas smiled. She had fled, expecting his anger. But he was not angry. His smiled deepened to one of genuine amusement as he stooped to pick up the scattered papers. "You baggage," he murmured. "There are times, little Mistress Dawson, when your insolence goes beyond all bounds. Strange that I should tolerate from you that which I would certainly never tolerate from anyone else."

He straightened up. "Mayhap the years have mellowed me." His smile turned wry. "And mayhap I have become a suitable candidate for Bedlam Asylum, for why else am I standing in this room and talking so busily to myself? I very much fear, Mistress Dawson, you have much to answer for."

He went back to his chair and sat down slowly. He should be more friendly to the child. He frowned, remembering the interlude in the library. Dear God! The blood on her face and her neck! When she had crumpled at his feet he had thought her dead. Killed by his hand, by his unreasoning savagery! He had wanted to die too. Had she forgiven him, really forgiven him? Resolutely, he turned his mind to other things; it did no good to dwell on it. Yes, he really should be more friendly. She tried very hard, and she had proved herself to be an amazingly brilliant pupil. Mayhap if he smiled more frequently or gave her an occasional cheerful word, it would achieve far more than his usual frown.

The absurdity of him! Nicholas began to laugh softly. A smile and a cheerful word! Nay. She would think him mad if he began suddenly to beam upon her. Indeed, how could he blame her when these days he was by no means sure of his stability.

First there had been his attack upon her. Now there was his inclination to smile at her, to take her hand and run with her in carefree abandon, to tell her of his dreams and hopes.

He thought of her as a child; yet uneasily he could well remember his emotions when he had carried her unconscious form to her room. Nonsense! He had been distraught. One felt and said many foolish things at a time like that. He frowned. Or could it be, he thought with a flash of honesty, that he was afraid to recognize her as a woman? He was gripped by a sudden deep fear. Or was it that, having recognized her as a woman, he feared that he might see in her eyes that certain look—that hard, greedy glitter. Castlemaine had it. His mother had had it. Would he see it in Angel's eyes? No! No!

Nicholas shook his head to clear it. He didn't understand himself. Why the devil was he sitting here thinking of Angel Dawson? Damn the cursed insolent wench! What was she to him? Nothing! No, nor ever could be. She could vanish from his life tomorrow—he cared not.

His sudden feeling of desolation shocked him, and

he hastened to cover it with his anger. He belonged to himself, only to himself! His hands clenched. He would no longer tolerate Angel's impudence, as she would very soon find out! Ah, but she had been so small, so broken, such an innocent victim of his violence!

"Stop it!" he said aloud. "Be silent, you babbling fool!" Angel Dawson should bend to his will, not he to hers. He put a hand to his forehead. The Honors Ball, he thought with a flash of inspiration. Perfect. At last he would present her to the King, and the devil take the hindmost!

Mrs. SAMPSON'S KEEN EYES SOFTENED AS she looked at the girl who waited eagerly for her judgment. Angel was always beautiful, but tonight in her gown of white French silk she was exceptionally so. The Honors Ball was the most glittering and important occasion of the year, and of the many beautiful women assembled there, she had no doubt that Angel would stand out. His lordship would be proud of her this night.

Angel revolved slowly, and the housekeeper gave her a nod of approval. The gown was high at the back and effectively concealed the puckered scars. The front of the bodice was cut fashionably low. The white silk clung to Angel's small shapely breasts and molded her tiny waist. The extravagant skirt stood out stiffly and looked not unlike the inverted petals of a flower. The hem, trimmed with blue and silver lace and sewn with tiny brilliants, glittered with her every movement. Jewels studded the heels of her blue silk slippers. Her bright hair was swept smoothly to one side in the new French fashion and held in place by a butterfly clasp, so that a cascade of soft ringlets descended to her shoulder. She held a fan of blue ostrich feathers, and her only other ornament was the single string of lustrous pearls about her long white neck.

"Well, will I do?" Angel said breathlessly.

"You'll do." Mrs. Sampson picked up the blue velvet cloak from the chair beside her. "You look lovely, child," she said, draping the cloak about Angel's shoulders. "Get along with you now. His lordship will be getting impatient."

Angel grimaced. "Is he ever anything else?"

Mrs. Sampson shook her head reprovingly, but a slight smile touched her mouth.

Halfway down the stairs Angel paused. Nicholas was standing in the hall, his black cloak over his arm. How like Nicholas, she thought, with a touch of amusement. Even for the Honors Ball he had not deviated one whit from his usual mode of dress; he despised the spectacular court costumes, the silks and satins and perfumes affected by the Court dandies. Tonight he was elegant in a severely cut jacket and breeches of black velvet. His one concession to fashion was the faint tracing of silver embroidery edging the collar and the wide cuffs of the jacket. His small cravat of lace was held in place by a plain silver bar, and a narrow frill of lace showed below his cuffs. He wore no other jewelry; and since he did not care for the long curling wigs popularized by the King, his hair was dressed in his familiar fashion, brushed back smoothly, and secured at the nape of his neck by a narrow black ribbon.

Nicholas looked up as Angel came slowly down the stairs. "M'lady," he said, making a small bow.

The small byplay seemed to augur well for the evening. Angel paused before him and, as she had done for Mrs. Sampson, she turned for his inspection. "Do I please you, Nicholas?"

He studied her carefully. "Yes," he said in a cool voice. "You look beautiful. Is that what you wanted me to say?"

She flushed. "You may say what you please, m'lord."

Nicholas was silent for a moment, then, "I'm sorry,"

he said abruptly. "That was a churlish thing to say." He smiled at her. "You really do look beautiful, Angel."

Following him to the carriage, Angel held her skirt away from contact with the dusty drive.

The coachman stood by the open door of the carriage, his face impassive. As he held out a gloved hand to assist Angel, Nicholas said impatiently, "We're a little late, Baxter. I'll aid Mistress Dawson."

"Yes, m'lord." Baxter turned away. He climbed up to his high perch and took the reins in his hands.

"In you go." Nicholas picked Angel up, ignoring her gasp of surprise, and deposited her on the seat. "It's a little high for a lady who is wearing a very special ball gown," he said by way of explanation. He nodded to Baxter and got in beside her.

Angel saw his faint smile. She settled back in her seat, feeling a sudden surge of exhilaration. She, Angel Dawson, was on her way to Whitehall Palace! She was to be presented to the King! Lovingly, she touched the soft silk of her gown. At last the time had come!

The carriage swayed round a corner and bowled unevenly over the rough cobbles of Chancery Lane. Angel drew aside the leather curtain and peered outside. It was not yet dark, and the narrow lane, edged on either side by huddled black buildings, was divided by the heaped-up piles of filth choking the central gutter. A group of children, their voices rising in shrill excitement, were jumping over the gutter and shouting each time they cleared it. They stopped their game for a moment to stare at the passing carriage; then the smallest urchin stooped and threw a handful of filth at the carriage.

"What is it?" Nicholas said, as Angel drew back with a gasp.

"Just some children playing," she said hastily. She drew the curtain aside again and was relieved to find that they had turned into The Strand. The carriage proceeded without difficulty along the wide thoroughfare. Here the cobbles were smoother, the leaning houses large and prosperous-looking; but the central gutter, though not quite as choked as the one in Chancery Lane, gave off a putrid stench. Fish bones, offal, and excrement bobbed sluggishly on the green scum, and, as the carriage turned left into King Street, Angel caught a fleeting glimpse of a dead cat. King Street was crowded with people. A man standing on a corner was exhibiting his performing dog to an admiring audience, while his partner collected coins in a battered hat. Still another man, a tray slung by a leather strap about his neck, was holding up carved wooden models of animals and wheedling the passersby. "Only look, my fair wench," he cried or, "Gallant sir!"

Angel let the curtain drop. Soon they would be turning into Palace Yard and the long-awaited moment would be upon her. Dismayed to find her hands were trembling, she clenched them together. Her mouth felt dry, and the beating of her heart seemed to shake her body. She couldn't do it! No, no, it was impossible!

She turned impulsively to Nicholas, her mouth opening to voice a wild plea to be taken home. He was watching her, and for once his dark eyes were almost gentle.

"You mustn't be afraid, Angel."

"But I am! Oh, Nicholas, I am! They'll know me for what I am. They'll—they'll laugh at me!"

"Nonsense." He took one of her cold hands and held it tightly. "People will speculate, but you must expect that." He hesitated, then went on firmly. "There have been rumors, of course, about the mysterious Mistress Dawson. But that's all they are, just rumors. Your past life is your own, Angel, and gossip though they may, they cannot prove anything."

"You think not?" Angel's brow wrinkled in thought. " 'Twould not be too difficult, would it."

He dropped her hand, patted it, and said with a trace of impatience. "You are to be introduced as my cousin. Why should they question your identity?" He smiled at her. "The King has but to look at you, and if the rumors have reached his ears, he will instantly dismiss them from his mine. Others will follow his example. I assure you."

She was warmed by the implication of his words. "The King has but to look at you," he had said. Her shoulders straightened and her courage returned. Nicholas was proud of her. He had no doubt of her ability to carry herself well; therefore would she strive to justify his faith. There were flaws in his argument, of course. Rumors were not easily crushed, and some there were who would be at great pains to ferret out her background and prove the Earl of Benbrook a liar. But she would not worry about that now. Let them gossip! Nicholas believed her to be in ignorance, but she had heard there was much curiosity in Court as to the reason for the Earl's reticence regarding this particular branch of his family. Was she perhaps born on the wrong side of the blanket? Benbrook, despite the stigma of his mother, was well known for his pride of family. Could it be that the girl, socially ambitious, had uncovered another secret from his past and was threatening to bruit it abroad unless he introduced her into Court circles? All this had come to her ears, but the real truth—doubtless started by the seamstress who had made many of her gowns—that she was a guttergirl, an ignorant impostor with whose presence the Earl intended to hoax them, this they were inclined to ignore. Even he would not dare to present such a girl to his king but it might well be that she was Benbrook's favorite whore. If this were so, the good-natured King would find it the lesser crime. How could he fail to do so when his own whores went openly about the Palace? One in particular, Lady Castlemaine, he had foisted on his reluctant and weeping Queen. As a Lady of the Bedchamber, Lady Castlemaine held a position of considerable importance, and she cared not a snap of her fingers for the little Queen's undisguised hostility. Some of the Court gossip always found its way to her through the servants. Despite her determination to ignore the stories, the thoughts kept slipping into her mind as the carriage moved toward the Palace.

Angel shot a sidelong look at Nicholas. Benbrook's favorite whore indeed! If they only knew how little she was to him. He had been kinder to her of late, but it was a disinterested kindness. It meant nothing, just as in his eyes she was nothing. The thought brought a quick flare of pain, and she smothered it with her anger. Her vanity was hurt, naturally, but she was fully as indifferent to him as he to her. He was cruel, too. Automatically she put a hand to her now flawless cheek. Had it not been for Mrs. Sampson's skill and patience, she might have been disfigured for life.

The carriage was slowing. Angel's heart beat a little faster; she swallowed hard and was relieved to find that she had recovered her calm. Nicholas might be indifferent, but he was proud of his creation. She would show him that he had reason to be. She would be just as gracious, just as witty and brilliant as a highborn lady.

The carriage rolled to a stop. Angel heard voices and the sound of running feet. She drew the leather curtain aside and peered out with eager curiosity. Green-liveried servants, holding flaring flambeaux high above their heads, approached the carriage. Over short powdered wigs they wore wide-brimmed hats, the sides turned up and decorated with white cockades. Nicholas leaped down from the carriage, and this time he allowed the grooms to help Angel to step into the flagstone courtyard.

Eventually they were handed over to the care of a tall footman wearing plum-red livery and an immaculate powdered wig. He bowed and escorted them into the Palace. A long corridor stretched before them, deeply carpeted and illuminated by hundreds of candles set in glittering chandeliers. The walls were banked on both sides by masses of sweetly scented flowers. At regular intervals stood other footmen, who bowed as the couple passed.

Bewildered by the vast silence, Angel pressed Nicholas' arm. "Where are the people?" she whispered. "Are we late?"

"No," he answered, amused. "We are not conducted in crowds; it would not be proper. There is another couple following behind us, and they too are being led by the personal footman assigned to them." Angel looked quickly over her shoulder, and Nicholas added sharply, "Don't gape!"

"I'm sorry," she said, not sounding sorry at all. She had caught a fleeting glimpse of a short stout gentleman in blue velvet, and a tall woman with diamonds in her hair, wearing a floating green gown. "Who are they, Nicholas, do you know?"

"The Duke and Duchess of Havenhurst."

About to ask another question, Angel refrained as she caught the faint sound of music.

The footman paused at the end of the corridor and waited for them to draw near. With an inclination of his head he conducted them with a slow and dignified stride along another corridor. Shorter than the first, it was carpeted in the same red, and its high walls were hung with brocade.

With every step the music grew louder mingled with the confused sound of many voices. The corridor ended in an antechamber decorated in tones of pale blue and silver and lavish with delicately carved furniture.

Angel's attention was on the three broad blue-carpeted steps leading into the great ballroom. Mounting them, her knees shook slightly. She stood on the threshold listening to the babble of sound. Both sides of the room were already crowded with people, the elaborate Court costumes making a shifting rainbow of color. Here again were the glitter of crystal chandeliers and the yellow bloom of many candles. But in the center an aisle of black marble floor gleamed like an icy lake, and at the far end the King sat in a chair on a dais draped in red velvet and fringed in gold.

"Nicholas!" Angel's fingers tightened on his arm. Nicholas frowned at her. He indicated a portly individual wearing red livery, the collar and cuffs braided with gold. His tall beribboned staff in his hand, he gave them a stiff bow. His face was expressionless. He struck the floor three times with the staff and announced their names in a hoarse booming voice.

Charles saw her coming toward him, her hand on Benbrook's arm. A swaying lily of a girl, he thought her, and as delicately beautiful as a bubble of blown glass.

Nicholas bowed before the King. Drawing Angel forward, he made the presentation in a low clear voice. Charles flashed him a friendly smile and gave him his hand to kiss, but he was scarcely aware of him, and the smile and gesture were both mechanical. His attention was on the girl who now knelt gracefully before him.

The press of people about the dais had noticed the King's bemusement, and a small silence fell. Smiles were exchanged, some sympathetic, some malicious. Perhaps it was as well the Queen was indisposed, for rarely before had they seen the King pause and stare so long. Eyes turned to Barbara Castlemaine, whose face was a mask of fury. No, not even for the Castlemaine had he shown such emotion.

Charles' hand tingled as Angel touched it lightly. The soft kiss she pressed upon his ringed fingers burned like fire.

"Rise, Mistress Angel," Charles said. " 'Tis not fitting that beauty should kneel, even before a king."

Startled, she looked up into his dark amorous eyes; eyes that showed no memory at all of a half-starved girl who had with great impudence and daring managed to hold up a Royal Parade.

"Thank you, sire." Angel rose to her feet. About to move to one side, she was restrained by the King's hand.

"Nay," Charles said. "Stay beside me, Mistress Dawson." He glanced quickly at Nicholas. "You also, my friend."

Angel bowed her head. Standing at the King's left, Nicholas beside her, she did not notice the curiosity in the eyes that watched her. She saw their brilliant, though guarded smiles. Pleased, she smiled back and wondered why she had thought these people to be so far above her. They were not, after all, so very different from the simple people.

In the buzz of conversation unheard by Angel, the ambitious wagered among themselves that the charms of Mistress Dawson would very quickly oust the detested Castlemaine from the King's bed.

Benbrook's cousin, eh? Laughter mumbled. They were not deceived. By gad! The stories they'd heard! She was Benbrook's fancy piece, no doubt about it. Cousin, bah! She might not be the uneducated gutter brat of current rumor, but she was no simple country maiden either. The laughter grew louder. Even had she been, they said, 'twere certain she'd not stay simple for long.

The women were inclined to hostility. But those among them who were greedy for positions of power in the Court allowed no trace of it to show. The hand of friendship extended now to the new favorite—and they did not doubt that she would shortly become so—could bring many rewards.

The men thought of estates lost to Cromwell. Charles,

though tardy in restoring them, could doubtless be persuaded with a word or two from Mistress Dawson. They would handle her with tact and sympathy, and so induce her to plead their cause. Perhaps they would regain more than their estates. Many a fortune had been built on the power of a woman's wheedling smile, a soft bed, and a compliant king.

Angel listened to the gay music of the musicians hidden behind the flower-decked gallery. She watched the stream of people coming toward the King, and suddenly she felt overpowered by the warm perfumed atmosphere of the Palace. It stifled her, and she had a sudden longing to leave. She was ungrateful, of course, if on this, the night of her triumph, her excitement could so easily evaporate. Perhaps she had clung to the dream for too long and endowed the reality with a magic it did not possess. Or could it be that her strange reaction was natural in one of her low birth? Nicholas, she felt sure, would be certain of it.

Angel intercepted another ardent glance from the King, and she smiled at him fleetingly and turned her head away. Why must he look at her so? His too obvious interest flattered her but embarrassed her too, for it made her inevitably the cynosure of all eyes.

A man with a thin, vicious face, his meager person clad in gray satin glittering with jewels, paused before the dais. He directed a low bow to the King and another to Angel, smiled coldly, and moved on. Nicholas had pointed out Lord Rochdale to her earlier. He was a man greatly to be feared, Nicholas warned her. He had a malicious tongue that could make the truth sound like a lie and could twist the most innocent statement into a trap for the unwary. Consequently he had few friends.

Another man strolled past. He bowed, straightened, and stood unmoving, his round blue eyes fixed on Angel's face. Indignant, she looked back at him haughtily and found herself instantly disarmed by a beaming smile. He was garbed in puce satin, the jacket plainly cut, the broad lapels sewn with rubies. The breeches, heavily trimmed with frills of white lace, were so tightly strained across his immense limbs that the seams looked to be in imminent danger of bursting asunder. He had a big florid face, framed in the black curls of his wig, a wide mouth, and a straight fleshy nose. His expression was gentle, and he looked, Angel thought, like a fat baby. She grinned at him, unresentful now of the innocent curiosity in his candid blue stare.

Nicholas finished his conversation with Lady Heatherton and turned to address a remark to Angel. Noticing her interest in the big man, he said smilingly. "I see you've attracted the attention of Gentle George."

"Gentle George?"

"Aye, he is called so." Nicholas bowed to the man, who, after returning the bow, turned reluctantly away. "That was Sir George Etheridge," Nicholas continued. "I will present you to him later."

"Why does he stare at one so openly? 'Twas most embarrassing, but I vow I could not resist his smile."

Nicholas laughed. "Few can. As for his staring, doubtless he wished to impress you on his mind. The heroine of his next play will resemble you greatly, I am sure."

"I have never met a person who writes plays," Angel said in an awed voice. "Do you really think his heroine will resemble me?"

"I am sure of it. But it may be a long time in the writing. Gentle George is as lazy as he is talented. His last play, *The Comical Revenge,* was written some time ago. It is still popular."

"Oh." Angel's interest deepened. "I wonder it does not inspire him to begin a new play."

Nicholas shrugged. "He has begun, but when it will

be completed is quite another matter. He even has a title, but it may be years before we have the pleasure of seeing it performed. He calls it, so I am informed, 'The Man of Mode.' "

"But if—" Angel broke off as the music coming from the gallery grew louder. She glanced questioningly at Nicholas.

Nicholas took her hand and drew her aside. "The presentations are over," he said. "The King is about to start the dance."

The other guests also moved back. They formed a ring about the glistening space of floor, and faces were turned expectantly toward the King.

Charles rose to his feet, a tall, imposing figure in his spectacular Court dress. His coat and breeches of heavy satin were a vivid green. Wide cuffs, heavily embroidered with gold thread, flared into fantastic points; the lace frills falling from the cuffs all but hid his hands. Rubies glowed from the white satin and lace of his waterfall cravat, and a three-tiered frill of gold lace edged the knees of his breeches, secured by narrow jeweled bands. When he moved his hands they seemed to blaze, so weighted down were they with rings, one for each finger. On his right thumb he wore a heavy gold ring set with emeralds and on his left thumb a similar ring, this one set with rubies.

Angel looked from the King to Nicholas. The King was the peacock, and Nicholas in contrast a black hawk. She was awed by the glitter of the King's person, and it surprised her to find that she much preferred Nicholas' severe elegance.

The music softened into the notes of a minuet. Lady Castlemaine, her lovely face expectant, took two steps toward the dais and looked up at the King. Charles did not notice her; he was already turning to Angel. A concerted gasp came from the onlookers as the King bowed low before her. They saw his smile as he offered his hand.

The honor of opening the ball was to go to the mysterious much gossiped about Mistress Dawson, then. Could it be that she was really Benbrook's cousin, after all? And how would the fiery-tempered Castlemaine take this snub? She was so sure of her power over the King, so outrageous in the demands she made upon him, that it was time she was put in her place, high time! But it was unlikely that she would allow herself to be so slighted without exacting vengeance.

Angel rose from her curtsy. With an uncertain smile, she put her hand in the King's. Nicholas was angry, she knew. The anger was not in his expression, which was much as usual; nevertheless she could almost feel the force of it. But why should he be angry? Did it not please him that in the absence of the Queen the King had chosen to honor her above all other ladies present? This moment of triumph belonged to them both.

The King did not appear to be in a hurry to open the ball. He had chosen the minuet, and this desire had been conveyed to the musicians. They would continue to play until it pleased him to lead Mistress Dawson onto the floor. Holding Angel's hand in his, Charles smiled at Nicholas. "Were I not a lenient king, friend Nicholas," he said lightly, "I would deem it treason on your part to keep such a beautiful treasure as Mistress Dawson so long hidden."

Nicholas' answering smile was tight. "Then I must crave your pardon, Sire."

Charles suffered a slight shock at the expression in Nicholas' eyes. Damn it, it was almost hostile! Did he think he was about to seize the girl and bed her as he would any common tavern wench? He loved Benbrook well and he owed him much, but there was no denying that he could be cursed difficult at times. It was devoutly to be hoped that he had not taken upon himself the guardianship of the wench's morals. He said absently, "So you should crave my pardon. We are not often privileged to look upon such beauty." He smiled at Angel. "Come," he said, pressing her hand, "honor your King with the first dance."

"The honor is mine, Sire," she answered softly.

Nicholas bowed as they departed. Anger, and another emotion that he obstinately refused to recognize as jealousy, burned inside him. Damn Charles, damn him! His desire was plainly to be read. But King though he was, he'd not get Angel to his bed! Charles was his friend, and he cherished the friendship. In the old days of peril they'd taken whatever pleasure they could find, even shared their women. But he'd not share Angel. It was not that he loved the wench, he would have to be in his dotage before he would permit himself to love or trust any woman. No, his feeling for her was one of lust and nothing more. But no matter, Charles should not have her!

Angel's red-gold ringlets bobbed lightly on her shoulder as she followed Charles through the stately measures of the dance. His fingers were uncomfortably tight about her own, and she could feel the pressure of the rings against her flesh. They moved apart, turned and came close again. On the last turn he pulled her closer than the etiquette of the dance permitted. Confused, her step faltered, and his free arm instantly circled her waist. "The floor can be treacherous to the unwary," he spoke loudly, and she supposed it to be for the benefit of the observers. "Had I not caught you, Mistress Dawson," he went on, pressing her close to his body, "you might well have fallen."

She felt uncomfortable as she looked up into his eyes. "Indeed, Sire," she said, pulling gently away, "then I thank you."

He released her at once, but she was relieved to see that other dancers had begun to take their places on the floor. The King was attractive, she admitted, perhaps too attractive for one's peace of mind. Nevertheless, if she had read the look in his eyes correctly, he desired something that she was not prepared to give.

Standing beside her cousin, the Duke of Buckingham, Barbara Castlemaine's face was stormy. She watched the King lead Mistress Dawson onto the floor, and her rage was such that she trembled visibly. How dare Charles offer her such an insult, how dare he show his infatuation so plainly! God's teeth, but he'd pay for it!

The Duke's faint smile was malicious. He was enjoying Barbara's too obvious jealousy. But that she should show it so plainly confirmed his belief that she was unforgivably stupid. The Duke shook out the ruffles edging the cuffs of his gold-embroidered black satin jacket. Stupidity in one connected to him by blood offended him and stung his pride. He could have forgiven her her temper, her shrewishness, even the fact that she was, in his opinion, a shocking bore, but he could not forgive her stupidity, which he felt was a reflection upon himself.

Nonetheless she was a beautiful bore. She was striking in her gown of smoky blue satin, the bodice of which was cut so daringly low that most of her firm white bosom was exposed. The sleeves, slashed with silver, were fastened with minute jeweled clips; the skirt, caught up in front, showed a frothy whirl of rainbow-hued, lace petticoats. Her loosened hair was held back from her face by a wide diamond band, and about her white neck was a collar of diamonds and sapphires.

"Bab, sweet cousin," the Duke drawled. "Do you fear competition so much that you must let the whole world see it?"

She turned on him, scowling. "I had forgotten you were here," she snapped. "But now I am so unpleasantly reminded, I will tell you that I can do well without your company!"

"Dear Bab," he smiled at her. "Your voice is as the cooing of doves." He smoothed the long, blond curls of his wig with a languid hand. "Ah, how sweetly does its soft melody strike upon the ear."

She stared into his cold light blue eyes. "You fool!" she cried, stamping her foot. "Go away! I have much on my mind!"

"Do you so?" He took her hand in his, crushing her fingers cruelly. "Have you not learned, little cousin, that it is not wise to call me names? I vow and declare, it makes me quite angry."

"Damn you, Buck!" Her eyes blazed into his. "I'll call you whatever I wish!"

"You will undoubtedly." He released her fingers. "It is difficult to teach a fool wisdom, damnably fatiguing too. But tell me, would it be the angelic Mistress Dawson and the King's undeniable infatuation that weighs on your little mind?"

"Angelic!" Barbara flared. "But I have seen angelic faces on whores, you know."

"Indeed you have," he agreed, "each time you gaze into your mirror. However, you are forgetting that Mistress Dawson is cousin to the so estimable Earl of Benbrook and will doubtless prove fully as worthy."

Barbara caught the sneer in his voice. "You hate my Lord Benbrook, do you not, Buck?" Her eyes glinted in sudden amusement. "Mayhap you think he influences the King against you?"

The Duke shrugged. He spoke with a mildness that belied the cold anger in his eyes, "I hate no one, Bab. I have ever thought it a cursed waste of energy."

Barbara laughed. "You forget to whom you speak. You should remember, Buck, I know you well."

"And I you. Therefore you may count yourself fortunate that I am ever loyal to my sweet coz." He smiled. "For instance," he said softly, "were I of a mind,

I could whisper to His Majesty of your continuing affair with Chesterfield. He would take it ill, Bab. Why, 'tis even possible that he might cast you off."

"Are you threatening me?" she spoke harshly, but she could not quite disguise the tremble in her voice; for Barbara, so far as she was capable of loving, loved Philip, Earl of Chesterfield.

The Duke regarded her with indulgent amusement. "Threaten you, Bab? Never! You and I must never have a falling out. We need each other, do we not?"

She stared at him with hard challenging eyes. But she knew there was much in what he had said. They did need each other, for they thought much alike. Both of them were sly and devious, and oddly, despite their continual baiting of each other, there existed between them a genuine fondness.

Hoping to goad him into a display of temper, she inquired spitefully, "And how is dear Mary, your charming wife?"

"Well, thank you," he answered lightly, refusing to be drawn. "And your husband, the noble Roger?"

Furious color stained Barbara's cheeks. "Speak to me not of that fool!" she snapped.

"Control yourself, dear one," the Duke drawled. He shook his head reprovingly. "You have shocked me deeply, Bab, deeply! Indeed, 'twould seem to me that your words are scarcely those of a loyal and loving wife. After all, who knows when you may have need of Roger's stalwart arms. I would remind you, coz, a husband, even though he be but in the background of your life, can prove to be of great comfort when a lady is sore distressed."

"You devil!" Her eyes narrowed, and she tapped her foot impatiently. "What means you? Explain yourself, sir."

"But is it not clear? The King is obviously smitten

with the charms of Mistress Dawson. It is possible, therefore, that she will take your place in the—er—royal heart."

"Damn you, Buck! Damn you!" Barbara lifted her ringed hand. But the Duke, anticipating the blow, caught her hand and held it fast.

"Must you behave like a fishwife?" he said in a low voice. "Have a care, coz. The King has ceased his cavorting and he glances this way." He smiled. "It grieves me to report, Bab, that he retains his lovely new fancy by his side."

"I have eyes, have I not?" Barbara took a deep, shaken breath. "Lovely new fancy, bah! You have said that he glances my way. So will he ever do, I swear it to you, Buck. I am first in his life, and so will I remain. I know Charles, I tell you. He will tire easily of Mistress Dawson's insipid charms."

"Insipid?" He considered, his head on one side. "Nay," he said after a moment, "I would not say insipid. I would say ravishing, delectable, and radiantly beautiful! But never, my love, never would I say insipid!"

"I care not for your opinions!" Barbara snatched her hand away. "I say she is a milk and water miss. Depend upon it, she will bore the King to distraction."

The Duke did not answer at once. He watched the dancers forming for the gavotte. "Now there is a sight," he said, his voice touched with amusement. "Our Lord Benbrook, looking remarkably like a thundercloud, is leading little Prudence Sanford into the dance. See how he frowns upon her. Poor Prudence appears to be quite overcome."

Barbara shrugged. " 'Tis his usual expression. I have ever thought him to be a sour and disagreeable man."

The Duke's eyes left the dancers. "Doubtless my memory is at fault, Bab, but I seem to remember your finding Benbrook quite devastating. You did your best to lure him into your bed, as I recall. 'Twas distressing, was it not when the genial Lord Benbrook met your every effort with an icy rebuff?"

"Will you be silent! I will have you banished from Court! I will—I will have you clapped in the Tower! I need but drop a word or two in the King's ear!"

"I tremble." He raised a mocking eyebrow. "Before I was so amusingly diverted, you were saying, I believe, that the King would very soon become bored with the charming Mistress Dawson?"

"She is not for the King," Barbara replied in a sullen voice. "He has ever liked fire in his women. And, if I mistake not, Mistress Dawson would freeze him to his very marrow."

"Ah!" The Duke tapped his lip thoughtfully. "But then you are a very poor judge of character. I would say there is a great deal of fire in the little Dawson. It needs but the touch of the right man's hand to set her ablaze."

Barbara tossed her head. "You have my leave to warm yourself at her fire, Buck, if you think you can kindle it. But let her not get in my way, else will she regret it!"

"The Queen is a considerable obstacle to your ambition. What are your plans for her? Will she, too, live to regret?"

"The Portuguese nun?" Barbara was recovering her temper. "I heed her not," she said laughing. "Were it not that I despise her, I vow I would be quite sorry for her. She sighs with love for him, her eyes follow him whenever he is near, and the expression in her eyes is not unlike that of a sick cow. Poor ugly little Queen, she believes Charles will see the error of his ways and be to her a faithful and loving husband. Charles! Imagine!"

"Lud!" He joined in her laughter. "But I believe you

are too hard on Her Majesty. To me she has a certain shy charm. Aye, a delicate appeal."

"Then you are easily pleased." Barbara regarded him haughtily for a moment, and her lips quivered into a smile. "Buck, you fool, how easily we strike sparks from each other." She laid her hand on his arm. "Will you do something for me, dear Buck?" she said softly.

He eyed her suspiciously. "What would you wish me to do?"

" 'Tis but a small thing and easy." She smiled winningly. " 'Tis rumored that my lord Duke has his spies everywhere. Therefore would I wish you to employ those spies on my behalf. There are many tales about Mistress Dawson. There is a mystery about her, and I believe that mystery to be rooted in her past." She frowned thoughtfully. "I would give much to know the details of her past life."

"Hmm! The idea is intriguing. It may be that I will do it. But Buckingham requires payment for his services."

"You will be well rewarded," Barbara assured him eagerly. "You have my word on it."

"Have I so?" Slowly, the Duke shook his head. "It grieves me to inform you, dear Bab, but I do not trust your word."

"What! Why, you—you—" She stared at him in outrage. "Damn you, Buck, you're a cursed knave!" She gave a sudden reluctant laugh. "But why do we argue? Well do I know your methods, and you have ever known how to enforce payment."

"Very true," he agreed. "Ah, the dance has drawn to its tedious end, I see." He extended his arm. "Allow me to escort you to your royal lover. 'Twill not do, you know, to neglect your interests."

Barbara placed her hand on his arm. "You need have no fear on that score," she said coldly.

197

They strolled slowly forward. "I understand His Majesty honors George Lawford this night," he said. His nose wrinkled scornfully. "I would not employ the man to shine my boots. He is a crude oaf and the devil's own bore. 'Tis a sad pass we have come to when such as he be thus honored."

"What of Jane Twyford?" Barbara spat the name viciously. "Night and day the simpering fool prates of the time she hid Charles from Cromwell's men. Yet she is to receive not only title, but Marshfield Manor and the income from the estate."

" 'Tis sad, dear Bab. But few there are as worthy of honors as our charming selves. How enchantingly simple is Mistress Dawson's gown," he remarked, changing the subject abruptly.

" 'Tis modest indeed," Barbara answered acidly. "But methinks 'tis a deliberately contrived effect. The assumed modesty of a cheap brat! What think you, Buck?"

"How vehement you are, cousin!" The Duke paused to bow to a woman in a bright pink gown.

"Atrocious," he said, when the woman had passed on. "Her taste is so vile that were the King to banish her from Court, I vow 'twould be a boon to our sorely afflicted eyes." He patted Barbara's hand. "You seem to believe that Mistress Dawson is naught but a cheap brat, but it would seem that the King likes her so. Therefore, Bab, shall I christen her 'the King's brat.' "

"The King's brat?" Barbara repeated slowly. "Aye, Buck, 'tis a good title. So too will I call her."

"Not in the King's hearing, I trust."

Barbara was about to answer, but the Duke, stopping once more, bowed low over the hand of a vivacious brunette. He kissed the plump white hand lingeringly, and Barbara listened impatiently to the fulsome compliments he paid to the dimpling lady.

When she once more had the Duke's full attention,

Barbara said with a burst of renewed fury, "I tell you, Buck, if the King invites his brat to reside at Court, she'll rue the day. I vow it!"

"Be silent!" The Duke's fingers gripped her arm warningly. Then, smiling affably, he led her to the King.

The King greeted them with every sign of pleasure. "My Lord Duke. Lady Castlemaine," he said smiling. "We are rejoiced to see you in such radiant looks."

Barbara sank gracefully to her knee. Lifting her blue eyes to the King's face, she said in a husky appeal, "I vow, sire, your poor Bab's heart is quite broken, so shamefully has my royal master neglected me." Her eyes flicked to Angel's face. "But in truth it would seem that I cannot compete with the novel appeal of Mistress Dawson."

The Duke of Buckingham stared at the King's suddenly cold face. You fool, Bab, he thought in some dismay. Will you never learn to guard your cursed rash tongue!

"I pray you rise, Lady Castlemaine," Charles said, his voice icy with rebuke. "We would not have you kneel at our feet while so many of our young gallants impatiently await your favor."

Charles turned deliberately to Angel. Taking her hand in his, he drew her nearer to his side.

Barbara was startled for a moment at the lowering look Lord Benbrook turned on the King. Then her heart began to hammer with such fury that she felt nauseated. *How dare Charles treat her so!* Her color high, her eyes furious, she rose swiftly to her feet.

She? Barbara Castlemaine! To be so humiliated before that—that damned slut with her sly smiling face! By Christ's Body, she'd not stand for it! Did he think to dismiss her as he would a paid whore? Dismiss her, who had born him in pain and suffering, his two fine children!

Without looking at the King, Barbara placed a shaking hand on the Duke's arm. She allowed herself to be led into the dance.

"I'll not stand for it, Buck!" she muttered savagely. "I am not a paid whore to be treated thus. How dare he dismiss me in such peremptory fashion!" The Duke was laughing. Barbara stared at him in outraged astonishment. "Dear Bab," he said, the laughter still quivering in his voice, "I vow and declare, you will be the death of me! For you are exactly that, Bab, a paid whore."

"How dare you!"

" 'Tis true." The Duke drew her closer. " 'Tis indeed an honor to be the King's whore, coz. But be you paid by king or commoner, the principle remains the same."

In her desire to punish him for his audacity, Barbara was oblivious to the interested onlookers. Her hand jerked up, her fingers already crooked to claw at his face. "So I'll be the death of you, will I, you cold-hearted swine? No man calls me whore! No man!"

He caught her hand and held it tightly. "Dear Bab," he said softly, "whore though you be, you are quite the sweetest example of your fair sex."

She kicked at his leg, laughing as he gave a gasp of pain. "Dear, Buck," she sneered. "Dost remember when the King stood up at the dining table? He was so delighted with the loin of beef, he borrowed your sword and knighted it 'Sir Loin of Beef.' I would to God he had taken that same sword and cut off your pig's head!"

"Charming!" the Duke said, his light-blue eyes dangerous. "Quite, quite charming!"

The dancers circled, and Charles saw Barbara's set angry face. He was coldly offended with her. Did she think her beauty gave her the right to dictate to her King? A pox on the bad-tempered, grasping shrew!

Barbara tripped gracefully toward Buckingham. Candlelight gleamed on her fiery hair, and against his will Charles felt himself softening toward her. True, she was an avaricious bitch, but she knew how to pleasure a man. Of all his mistresses she had thus far proved the most satisfying. Nevertheless, he thought, hardening again, her insolence was becoming past bearing. Damn! Did Bab rule this realm, or did he? Plague take all women! Even his meek agreeable little Queen had taken to defying him of late. Doubtless this too he could indirectly lay at Bab's door. Catherine was offended at his interest in Lady Castlemaine, and depend upon it, Bab, in her own way, would take care to fan the fire of her jealousy.

His eyes left Barbara and sought out Mistress Dawson. She was dancing with Benbrook. Charles stroked his mustache, smiling a little. Neither of them looked to be enjoying the dance. Friend Nicholas, as usual, was looking stern and unapproachable, and Mistress Dawson looked faintly mutinous. Doubtless he was lecturing the wench for some trivial fault. Charles sighed. He was genuinely fond of his friend, but the tragedy of Lady Marianne's death had in no wise softened him, it seemed.

"Your Majesty."

Charles turned his head and smiled at Anne, the Duchess of York, and nodded agreeably to James, his brother. Charles could never look at Anne, who was the daughter of his chancellor, Edward Hyde, without remembering the storm her marriage to James had evoked. Though Charles had been inclined to take this marriage to a commoner lightly, his mother had been outraged. Henrietta Maria's anger had been so violent and bitter that its effect was felt by every member of the royal family.

Plump Anne, since her marriage, had lost her fresh, rosy look. Never good-looking, she was particularly plain in her gown of purple satin. The color cast a sickly hue over her pale skin, and her headdress of white and purple ostrich plumes, set squarely upon her limp, light-brown hair, was unbecoming. There was something forlorn about her tonight that touched Charles' heart. He said gently, "I hope you mean to honor me with the next dance, Anne?"

She flashed him a quick smiling glance. Next to James, she loved Charles, who had always treated her with kindness and consideration. "The honor is mine," she answered in her soft voice.

Over her head Charles directed a frown at James. His brother had imbibed a little too much wine. He was swaying on his heels, smiling vaguely. He was watching the dancers, and Mistress Dawson in particular, Charles noticed.

The dance ended. Nicholas led Angel back. He made his bow before the Duke and Duchess of York, and presented Angel in a low grave voice.

Anne smiled at the lovely girl curtsying before her. "Mistress Dawson," she acknowledged. Angel looked into the small kindly blue eyes and took an immediate liking to the plain little woman. Of the Duke she was not quite sure. His greeting was courteous, but she did not care for the look in his eyes.

The indefatigable dancers were already forming for the Roger de Coverly. Charles offered his arm to Anne and led her onto the floor. Angel was startled when James said in his abrupt, rather gruff voice, "Pray do me the honor, Mistress Dawson."

"Your Highness," Angel murmured. She placed her hand lightly upon the Duke's arm. From the corner of her eye she saw Nicholas' sudden stiffening. She smiled brilliantly upon her partner, and James, encouraged, returned her smile fatuously.

Once during the dance Angel came face to face with Barbara. She did not notice the angry gleam in Barbara's narrowed eyes or the blandly smiling face of the Duke of Buckingham when, in his turn, he took her hand and danced her back to her original partner. Her thoughts were with Nicholas, and suddenly she was assailed by the strangest emotion. She wanted to wrench her hand from her partner's, to run through the dancers and find some place where she might be alone. She must be insane! Why else would she entertain such thoughts of Nicholas? Nicholas! Perhaps, like the heavily breathing Duke of York, she had taken too much wine.

The Duke swung her round, and she looked straight into Nicholas' face. Nicholas looked back at her, and then she knew. It was true then. She was in love with him. In love with my Lord Benbrook, who despised her!

CLAD IN A THIN GREEN NEGLIGEE, HER HAIR loose about her shoulders, Angel sat huddled in a chair, her eyes fixed unseeingly on the fading embers of the dead fire.

Shivering in the pre-dawn chill, she glanced toward her invitingly turned-down bed. But although her eyes were heavy, her mind was as yet too active, too troubled to permit sleep, and she did not move from her cramped position.

In the distance she could hear the thin tinkling of the Watchman's bell, his hoarse, loud voice calling out cheerfully, "It's four o' the clock and all's well."

"All's well," Angel whispered. Well, perhaps it was for some, but not for her. Angel Dawson, you fool! How could you allow yourself to fall in love with Nicholas?

Tears sprang into her eyes. It had not been a question of allow. It had just happened, and there was nothing she could do about it.

But how had it happened? When had her love for him begun? Had it been there all the time, lying latent inside her? Had the realization come to her at the very moment the King had taken her hands in his? She had looked up into the King's ardent dark eyes, but she hadn't really seen him at all. She had seen Nicholas instead.

Nicholas, smiling his too rare smile, Nicholas, frowning—angry with her—Nicholas in all his moods. Had she known then, known, and yet not understood? He filled her whole horizon; Nicholas, her harsh, impatient mentor. He received her rage, her screams and her loudly expressed hatred with his usual cold indifference for the most part, but at other times he would turn the searing violent flame of his anger upon her. But he was also the man she would love—and him only—for the rest of her life.

The Earl and the guttersnipe, she thought bitterly. Even had they been born of the same class, it would have been hopeless. She had indeed reached the height of stupidity if she must yearn for such a one as he—a man who made no secret of his loathing of all women. Women he had in plenty, but he used them only when the demands of his body dictated; there was no tenderness in him.

Women! She had seen them come and she had seen them go. Nicholas drew women; he presented an almost unbearable challenge, so that each must seek for vanity's sake to conquer him. Angel had seen them hanging on his arm, and there had been an expression in their eyes as they looked at him that had made her flush with shame for them.

She had hated them—those women with their moist red mouths, the desire in their eyes—but she had never known until now the reason for that hatred.

She moved restlessly in the chair. Her thoughts turned to a tale related to her by the Duke of York. The Duke had taken her hand and led her to a quiet little alcove just beyond the ballroom. She had gone with him warily but indeed she had no choice. The Duke, though prepared to be amorous, had at first contented himself with talking. With wine-induced tears filling his eyes, he had spoken of the double tragedy that had occurred before the first

205

glorious year of the Restoration had drawn to its close. First Henry, Charles' favorite brother, had died of the smallpox, and the eldest sister, Mary, had followed him quickly to the grave, stricken by the same disease. He told her of Charles' wish to have his remaining sister Minette under his protection—for of them all, Charles loved her the best. But Minette, in France, was preparing for her marriage to the Duke of Orleans. And few indeed had been her visits to the Court of her brother.

"The separation is a great grief to my brother and to Minette," the Duke confided, "for the devotion between them is great."

Angel had listened and had genuinely sympathized. The King's love for his young sister and hers for him was well known to all. But the Duke's hands had begun to explore. She pushed his hands quickly away and rose to her feet. She curtsyed to him and walked swiftly away, ignoring his drunken protests. Just beyond the alcove, she had encountered Nicholas. He had said nothing, but there was a look in his eyes that caused her to blush vivdly. Still in silence, he had extended his arm to her and led her back to the ballroom.

Had he thought—had he imagined that she had allowed the Duke to—? Her thoughts broke off abruptly. Nicholas again? It always came back to him, to the cold-eyed, reserved, unsmiling man whom she, most unfortunately, loved.

Sitting in her chair, the dawn's light painting the room with a rosy glow, it might have given her some small consolation to know how infinitely she had disturbed Nicholas' peace of mind. But she didn't know, and she was consumed with misery.

With her debut behind her, the part of her life that contained Nicholas was over. He had fulfilled all of his promises to her, indeed, he had done more than she had a right to expect. That she had grown to love him, strange and difficult as he was, was scarcely his fault. He hadn't asked or expected her to love him. To him she was a child, nothing more. And since she no longer had an excuse to linger, she must soon leave his house. Would she ever see him again? From a distance, perhaps. Nicholas, she felt sure, would never seek her out. And what then? She had been lifted from her proper station in life, and now she was neither of one world nor the other. What was to become of her—where was she to go?

She closed her eyes and saw once again the red and gold splendor of the Palace; the King standing beside her, smiling upon her, making her feel that she was the most beautiful woman in the room. The King hadn't thought her a child, for surely you did not whisper to a child the things he had whispered to her. The Duke of York, though handsomer than his brother, had not Charles' magnetic personality, and so one was apt to discount his looks, but Angel had liked the Duchess of York. Lady Castlemaine and her cousin Buckingham she had detested. There was something about both Barbara and Buckingham, something dark and devious. It would not be wise to incur the enmity of those two, for she felt sure they would be not only dangerous and relentless but vindictive too.

In the carriage, on the short drive home from Whitehall Palace, Angel had hoped that Nicholas might praise her—only a very little, of course, for he was ever sparing of his praise. But Nicholas had seemed to be unaware of her. More distant than ever before, he had sat stiffly erect, his face turned away.

Angel had never seen Nicholas intoxicated; but when the carriage turned into St. Bernard's Square and drew up before the house, she thought he surely must be.

The coachman came forward to open the door

and to assist them to alight. Nicholas waved him away with an impatient gesture. The startled man backed off to a safe distance. Nicholas was staring at Angel in such a way that he might have been seeking to impress her every feature upon his memory.

"Nicholas—" she began. He hardly heard and with a sound that was oddly like a groan seized her hand and held it tightly in his. Dumb with surprise, she had sat through that tense moment. In the dim light shed by the carriage lamp, his eyes had glowed feverishly bright. She could not flatter herself that she had moved him to tenderness, for indeed there was nothing tender in his bruising grip, and she could hardly believe that he was really aware of her.

As abruptly as it had begun, the moment passed. Nicholas released her. With a startling return to his normal manner, he helped her politely from the carriage and escorted her into the house.

Outside her bedroom door he had paused for a moment to compliment her on her elegance of manner, had told her that he was proud of her. Saying his goodnight, he had touched her cheek lightly with his finger—always Nicholas' mark of approval—and after bestowing one of his rare smiles, he had bowed to her and departed for his own room.

Shivering in her chair, half-dozing, Angel suddenly started up. Firm footsteps, sounding unusually loud in the sleeping house, were coming along the corridor.

She listened intently. It could not be the servants; they slept in the other wing of the house, and in any case they would not stir from their beds for at least another thirty minutes. It could only be Nicholas. Perhaps he, like herself, had found himself unable to sleep. Could he have made an appointment for this early hour, she wondered?

Consumed with curiosity, Angel rose from her chair

and flew over to the window. She leaned out, her hair falling about her, expecting to see his tall figure emerge from the door below.

"Angel!" Nicholas' voice coming from behind her caused her to start violently. She drew in her head slowly, feeling the blood rise in her face.

"Nicholas!" She swung round to face him. "You—you startled me."

"My apologies," he answered. "I did knock, you know."

He lit a candle from the dying embers of the fire and set it back in its sconce. He walked over to the couch and seated himself. "I wanted to talk to you. Come, Angel, sit beside me, if you please."

She went to him slowly. He didn't look like himself at all, she thought. He was still in his Court dress; and his ruffled hair curled in damp tendrils upon his forehead. That earlier strange mood, she now saw, was with him again, for his eyes were over-bright, his hands trembling violently, and his face flushed.

Alarmed, she sat down beside him. "Nicholas, what is it? Are you ill?"

"Indeed not, I am perfectly well."

"But, Nicholas," she persisted. "Are you quite sure?"

"Naturally I am sure. Pray do not concern yourself."

The familiar note of coldness had crept into his voice, but for once she welcomed it; it was at least normal. "I'm sorry, Nicholas," she said. "You can best judge your own state of health, of course. But it did seem to me that you are not quite yourself."

He looked away from her. "Nonsense! Your imagination runs away with you. I came b—because I—I have s—something to say to y—you."

His slight stammer filled her with fresh alarm. Nicholas, except for those times when she provoked his rage, was always in complete control of himself.

"I'm listening, Nicholas," she said quickly. "Pray go on."

He did not turn his head. "You have borne me great h—hatred in the past, Mistress Dawson. You have informed me of this on a great m—many occasions. I would—would wish to know if your aversion is as g—great as it ever was?"

She stared at his averted profile. Nicholas! Cool-touch-me-not-Nicholas to ask her such a thing! Hate him! If he only knew!

"I am waiting for your answer," he said, "and be so obliging as to answer me truthfully, if you please."

She swallowed. "I don't hate you, Nicholas. No, indeed I do not!"

"If you speak truth, then I may assume that I am not d—distasteful to you?"

She didn't understand him, but she felt a desperate need to touch him. Her heart pounding, Angel laid her hand on his arm.

"No, my lord," she said softly. "You could never be that."

He looked down at her hand. "You are very k—kind," he said unsteadily. "But I would remind you that it is not necessary to spare my—my feelings."

"I speak truth." She leaned yet closer, her shoulder brushing his. "Has my past behavior made it so hard for you to believe, my lord?"

"Nay." He hesitated for a moment, then went on swiftly. "But I have ofttimes been over-harsh with you, though I cannot but think that you deserved the rebukes I administered, for you were ever an insolent jade. I had —had expected your hatred, for I know well that I am not a lovable man."

Not lovable? She stared at him. Nicholas, whose women were forever hanging around him!

"I believe, my lord," Angel said, and she tried to

school her voice to calmness, "that you must surely be one of the most loved of men. You forget, do you not, that I have seen these females who clamor for your attention? I have seen the way they look at you."

"The most loved of men!" he repeated. He laughed bitterly. "Think you that they would look upon me with favor, or spare one thought for me were I minus my not inconsiderable fortune?"

"You underrate yourself, my lord." Angel's fingers tightened on his arm. "Mistresses you would have, no matter the state of your finances. You are—are most attractive to women. Why, the King himself told me of the many women who have loved you."

"Love! Love!" Nicholas burst out violently. "How you do prate on about it! But I know it by another name—greed, lust, oh, call it what you will. But I have never encountered love!"

She did not answer him, and the disturbing thought came into Nicholas' mind, as it had so often of late. How would it sound, what would be his reaction if Angel said, "I love you!"

It was almost as if Angel had read his thoughts, for she said huskily, "And if I were to say to you—'I love you! I love you, Nicholas!' Would you then brand me a liar?"

There was a choking feeling in his throat. Damn her! Damn the baggage! He had not come to talk of love! "I love you, Nicholas!" Ah! But how tenderly the meaningless words had fallen from her lips.

Love! He remembered his mother, the candlelight gleaming on her naked body—the ever different faces of the men whose heads had rested upon the pillows of her bed—"I love you," his mother had said. "I love you, George—Henry—Robert—" Change only the name, the inflection in his mother's voice had been the same.

Nicholas had forgotten Angel for the moment. He

put a shaking hand to his mouth and strove to control the nausea that his memories provoked.

"Nicholas," Angel said again. "Would you brand me a liar?"

He swallowed hard and felt the nausea recede. "I know not how I would judge you," he said curtly, "and I care not." He was silent for a moment, then he went on slowly. "Your place shall be in this house, with me—that is what I came to say to you. You w—will not leave this house, for I have g—grown used to your presence. I am—am responsible for you, and I m—must forbid you to th—think of leaving."

"Nicholas!" She could not believe he had said it. To stay with him! To see him every day! She could ask nothing more of life! But she could not allow him to command her. She said deliberately, "Are you perchance asking me to be your mistress?"

She heard the swift intake of his breath. "Nay. I ask nothing that you are not prepared to give."

"And if I say to you that I will not stay? What then, Nicholas?"

"You will stay!"

"Because you command it?"

"Yes! If you will have it in plain words. Yes! Yes!"

"Why, Nicholas? You must tell me why!"

He was silent for so long that she thought he would not answer. Then he said, "Because I ask it of you, Angel."

She saw his hands clench until the knuckles showed white. There was a controlled violence in his tone as he added, "Nay, Angel, I do not command you, I ask it of you. And I have never before asked anything of a woman."

"And why do you now ask it of me?" she persisted.

"Oh, damn you!" He buried his face in his hands. "How do I know?" he said in a muffled voice. "What do I want with you, damned insolent brat that you are! What do I want with a cheeky-faced guttersnipe who has ever defied me?

"Plague take you, Angel! Have you not forced me into ungovernable rages? Have you not caused me to strike you cruelly and to wish to God that I had never seen you?

"There were times when I longed to strangle you for your insolence and times when I longed to throw you back into the gutter from whence you came! You have ruined my peace of mind, you have made of me a bad-tempered wreck! But—oh devil take you, wench! I need you, I suppose."

"You do, Nicholas?" This was happiness, she thought. "Do you really?"

"Yes, curse you!" He laughed somewhat shakily. "I know not why. 'Tis a mystery to me."

"Nicholas, I'll stay." She put her arm about his shoulders. "I want to stay with you."

His hands dropped. "You want to stay?" He turned his head and looked at her directly. "Oh, Angel, you ever surprise me. I had thought that you could not wait to be free of me."

She smiled at him, wondering if his unhappy childhood experience had so blinded him that he was unable to recognize a basic truth? Did he not realize that his words had been all but a declaration of love? Oh surely she could not be wrong?

"Nicholas, thank you for all that you have done for me." On a sudden impulse, she held out her arms to him. "I will be ever grateful to you."

"Let there be no talk of gratitude, silly chit!"

She thought at first that he meant to reject her, then, with a half-smile, he leaned rather stiffly toward her.

It was all the encouragement she needed. She slid her arms about him and held him close to her.

For a moment he resisted, then, with a deep sigh,

he relaxed. But even now he must seek to excuse what he believed to be a weakness in himself.

"Seek not to take advantage of me, wench," he said huskily. "That which I have denied to you in the past, I will still deny."

"Have you denied me, my lord?"

"Aye, many things. But always—or so did I believe —the denial was in your own interest. I am too cursed tired to think, therefore have I let you cajole me." He hesitated, then added sternly, "A woman's breast has ever made a fine pillow for a weary head."

"Yes, my lord," she answered, stroking his hair tenderly. "I know well 'tis your weariness that causes you to so indulge me. I promise that I will remember your words."

"See that you do," he said, settling himself more comfortably. "Aye, see that you do."

"But Nicholas," she said hopefully, "should we not seal our newly declared friendship with a kiss?"

There was a silence. " 'Tis not necessary, wench," he said, and the harshness was back in his voice.

"But 'tis a pleasant custom, is it not?"

He put her arms from him and sat up. "So you wish to be kissed, Mistress Dawson?"

With a sinking heart Angel saw the cynicism in his eyes. She should have remembered that confused by his need of her he was yet a stranger to tenderness. He would doubtless believe her to be motivated by feelings far removed from tenderness.

" 'Twas but a thought," she said hastily. "Why do you look at me so?"

"I'll kiss you," he said savagely, but her ears caught the underlying note of weariness, "aye, and I'll bed you too. What then? When shall we go shopping for those pretty baubles to adorn your person?"

"You flatter yourself, my lord," Angel said sharply. "Think you that I would allow you to bed me?"

"Flatter myself?" He laughed mirthlessly. "I know well that the willing surrender of my pretty bedmates is to the god of anticipation and not to my so charming self."

"I know nothing of your women," she said coldly, "or of their motivations. But for myself, I asked only a kiss."

He looked at her long and searchingly, and she saw his eyes soften. "I see that I have misjudged little Mistress Dawson." He touched her cheek lightly, caressingly. "Think you that she will forgive me?"

She could not help smiling. "I believe that Mistress Dawson will—will give the matter serious thought."

"'Tis a great deal more than I deserve," he answered gravely. "But doubtless she will now expect me to forego the kiss which I would very much like to give. Think you that this will be her verdict?"

Angel considered him, her head on one side. She did not know him in this mood, but she responded to the gentle note in his voice. "It is Mistress Dawson's belief," she said demurely, "that the successful pupil merits a kiss from the tutor."

"Is it indeed?" he said softly, taking her into his arms. "The lady is wise, and the tutor is grateful."

His mouth on hers was cool and firm at first, then the kiss deepened and warmed to hungry urgency.

"Nicholas!" Angel whispered, when his mouth left her. "Dear Nicholas!"

His eyes smiled into hers. "Can it be, then, that you have learned to tolerate the ogre?"

"Nay, call yourself not so. 'Tis true you are severe, often intolerant, and sometimes, when angered, you can be cruel. But you are not an ogre, dear m'lord." She leaned

215

forward and kissed his cheek. Half afraid of her own daring, she added quickly, "There! Your pupil salutes a wise and dear mentor."

"Oh, Angel!" He swept her suddenly into his arms and held her very tightly. "Are you a witch, that you create such disturbance in my mind? Thoughts come into my head, thoughts such as I have never had before. It would seem," he said, his voice dropping to a whisper, "that there is no extent to my folly, for while I hold you in my arms I could almost—almost believe—" He broke off.

"Nicholas," Angel began. "Tell me—"

"Nay," he interrupted, putting her from him. "I will leave you to your rest. Pray excuse me."

She clung to his arm as he made to rise. "Don't go, please, Nicholas. I would hear what you were about to say."

"Would you so? But 'twould be wiser not to inquire too deeply."

"You have said many times that I am not wise. Therefore, Nicholas, I pray you to tell me."

"For your amusement doubtless?" he said, his face hardening. "If you will know all of my insanity, then I will tell you. It is, that holding you in my arms I could almost believe in this continual prating of love." He looked away from her. "There, I've said it! Make of it what you will!"

Angel took a deep breath, hoping to steady her racing heart. "Dearest Nicholas," she answered huskily, "I would that you were certain, rather than almost certain."

He turned to her so swiftly that she shrank back. "Do you know what you are saying, Angel? Did I not know it to be impossible, your words would suggest that you were in love with me. Have I not lectured you on

216

the correct use of words? You see now, do you not, how easily they may be misunderstood?"

"But you have not misunderstood me, Nicholas. Forgive me if my words are not pleasing, but I love you! Oh, my dear, m'lord, I love you so very, very much!"

He was staring at her incredulously. "Nonsense!" he said at last, his dark brows meeting in a forbidding frown. "You cannot know what you are saying! It would be best, I think, if we forget this conversation."

Angel shook her head. "No," she said, her voice trembling, "you may forget, my lord, if it please you to do so. I shall not."

"You must!" Nicholas said almost desperately. "I will not have it, Angel! Do you hear me? Think you that I would be fool enough to place my life in a wench's careless hands? I forbid you to say more. I—I will not allow you to indulge in such stupidity!"

"Oh, Nicholas, you cannot forbid me. Think you that if you command me not to love you, it will be so?"

She laid her hand over his clenched fist. "Nay, my lord, seek not to cloak your fear with words. For 'tis fear, is it not? Yes, you fear love."

"You go too far," he said coldly. "Let this discussion end, if you please."

She had indeed gone far, Angel thought wryly, but not yet too far. His frown was intimidating, but she would not retreat. If, as she believed, he loved her, then she fought for his happiness as well as her own.

Deliberately she prodded at the angry, painful confusion she sensed in him. " 'Tis strange indeed that the powerful Earl of Benbrook should find himself thus defeated," she said lightly, almost mockingly, "and by so sweet and natural an emotion."

"Be silent, you insolent jade!" he thundered, grabbing

217

her by the shoulders. "Devil take you!" He shook her furiously. "How dare you speak so! How dare you!"

"Why should I not?" she shouted. "If you will not face the truth, then I must force you! I love you. I believe that you love me!"

"What?" He released her suddenly. "You are mistaken."

"I am not!"

"You will not raise your voice to me!" Then, the anger draining away from him, he said wearily, "I know not what I feel. I cannot expect you to understand, but I pray you not to bedevil me, not to persist."

He was silent for a moment, then he went on slowly, "This feeling I have for you, Angel, constantly plagues me, and freely do I admit it. But it is as yet new to me, for in truth I have never felt it before. Be not impatient, Angel. Give me time to think."

"I will, darling, I will! I promise that I will not say another word until you give me leave to do so."

"You will not call me darling," he said, but he smiled at her almost tenderly. "I will tell you when and if 'tis time to call me so."

"Yes, my lord." She looked at him with shining eyes.

"And you will not look at me in such a way—'tis most distracting."

He took her hand and held it gently. "I have decided to pay a long overdue visit to Benbrook Manor. I will be gone four—perhaps five weeks."

"Nicholas! When did you decide?"

"A moment ago," he answered calmly. "I am a neglectful landlord, and I fear me that my tenants will have many just complaints. I had meant to journey into Worcestershire long before this."

"Don't go," Angel cried. "I will keep my word, I promise!"

"There is no need for hysteria," he said curtly. "I am going. I wish to hear nothing more on the subject."

He rose to his feet, drawing her with him. "Nevertheless," he said, smiling at her, "'tis pleasant knowing that Mistress Dawson is reluctant to part with me. I had not thought to hear such a confession from her."

"You have heard a great deal this night, my lord," Angel answered. "And all of it surprising, I'll vow."

"Nay, say rather that it was unsuspected," he said.

He took her face between his hands and looked deeply into her eyes. "It may well be love that I feel for you, Angel." He hesitated, then went on softly. "I think, if I found it to be so, I would give my life and my hope of happiness willingly into your keeping. But mark me well, if I should ever find that you had betrayed me, I think—yes, I really think—that I would be tempted to kill you!"

She knew he was remembering the father he had adored, one weakened by his love for his wife, knowing himself to be less than a man when he allowed her to laugh at him and to betray him over and over again.

"Darling!" Angel said gently, "and forbid me not the endearment—for you will ever be my darling—I shall never betray you, therefore shall I live out my full time."

"What shall I do with you, my little guttersnipe? For I know not if I should punish you or kiss you, you who have dared to turn my life upside down!"

She looked into his face. The harsh lines about his mouth had softened, and the expression in his eyes was almost gentle. "I choose the kiss, dearest Nicholas."

"Aye, for you are a shameless baggage, are you not?" He kissed the tip of her nose. "I wish for a clear head; therefore must that suffice." His smile faded. He said somberly, "And will you be waiting here for my return? You—you will not depart?"

"Yes, dear m'lord, I will be here. Doubt me not, please."

"Then shall I be happy in that knowledge." His finger touched her cheek in his familiar gesture. "Yes," he said thoughtfully, as if he answered an inner question. "Yes."

Long after he had gone, Angel wandered restlessly about the room. She was torn alternately by hope and fear, for now that he was no longer with her she found herself wondering if it had really happened. Had it been she, Angel Dawson, actually confessing her love to the aloof and awesome Earl of Benbrook? He who was named England's foremost hero and known affectionately by the people—because of his daring escapes under the very nose of the enemy—as 'the vanishing Earl'?"

She was wrong to think such a man could love her, Angel thought in anguish. Why should he love her? She was a child of the gutters and had once been known as "Newgate bait!" An Earl who had known the caresses of so many beautiful women would scarcely give his love to such as her.

She had mistaken the meaning of his words, she told herself despairingly, and doubtless had greatly embarrassed him. Love her? What a pitiful dolt she was! And how high had been her aspirations when it came to this question of love!

Angel threw herself on the bed and wept for her foolishness and for the pain and humiliation she must inevitably suffer upon his return from Worcestershire. She was convinced now that his journey was but an excuse. He needed time to think of suitable words that, while gently rejecting her, would not crush her pride.

Suddenly, in the midst of her misery, Angel began to laugh. Nicholas, who had snubbed her—ofttimes severely—who had shriveled her with scorn, had lectured her, scolded her, called her imbecile! He had turned upon her invariably an icy, half-contemptuous disapproval, and he had—yes, he had even beaten her! This Nicholas must seek for a gentle way to reject her? Nay, he would be cold—he would be cruel to be kind. But gentle? Never! Only love could make him gentle.

Angel sat up on the bed with a jerk. Love? Well then, had he not been gentle with her?

"Oh, Nicholas, my darling! My dear, m'lord!" she murmured softly, her eyes brooding and tender. "Surely you, who are so proud, so arrogantly sure, so fearless in danger, surely you will not be afraid to love?"

IN THE DAYS BEFORE CHARLES' JOYFUL RES-toration to the throne of England, Nicholas, Earl of Benbrook, and his prince had fought many a battle side by side and had sealed a lasting friendship with the blood of their enemies. Charles was brave, but on one occasion he was foolhardy, and had it not been for Nicholas he might well have lost both life and throne.

Determined to rescue his father from grim Carisbrooke Castle, where he had been so long imprisoned, Charles and a small band of followers left Holland secretly in the dead of night. A fishing vessel manned by a Captain Moodey and his two sons, all loyal to the Stuart cause, set them ashore on the fog-shrouded Sussex coast. They knew Cromwell's spies were everywhere, and the Protector of England was not renowned for generosity to a fallen enemy, especially not the son of his mortal foe, the King of England.

Nonetheless their spirits were high as they set foot on the English soil. Captain Moodey wished them Godspeed and promised to return to the same spot on the following night. Taking a circuitous route, they began to make their way to Carisbrooke Castle. Charles had pored for many hours over a roughly drawn map of the castle; he knew every entry, every unguarded spot. They would enter the castle undetected, and tomorrow, if a merciful God smiled upon them, he would kneel at the feet of King Charles I and render to him once more his allegiance and his love.

But the luck that had sustained them fast ran out. In a dense forest near Chichester they were sighted by a band of Roundheads. In the fierce battle that followed, Charles' small force was routed and the Prince was wounded. Only Nicholas still fought by his side. Taking advantage of a temporary diversion, they managed to escape. The enemy was close behind them, and it would not be long before they were captured. They found the deep ditch by accident, for the branches of a fallen tree had spread a thick leafy screen over the top.

It seemed an ideal hiding place. Lying there together for hours—horseless, weaponless, cut off from their men and their pursuers all about them, they spoke of casual things and tried to ignore the danger. It was then that the idea of the ring had been born. Charles remembered the conversation very well.

"I have given much thought to your mistresses, sir, who are many and varied," Nicholas said lightly. "So varied, that it may well be that, unknowingly, I might encroach on a lady of my Prince's choice."

"Nay," Charles answered. " 'Tis not possible, for well you know that I have ever shared my mistresses with you."

"Aye," Nicholas grinned at him affectionately, "save only those ladies who are untouchable to all but your royal self. Might I suggest to you, sir, that these special ladies wear the Prince's mark?"

Charles was in pain; he was beginning to tremble, and he knew that Benbrook did but indulge in idle talk to distract him from his misery. Nevertheless his interest was caught. "My mark?" he inquired. "What mean you?"

"A ring perhaps," Nicholas said. "To be worn upon the finger of the lady who is the exclusive property of the Prince."

Charles smothered a cough, avoiding Nicholas' anxious eyes. "Aye, a ring," he said huskily. " 'Tis a good idea, friend. How think you we should design it?"

"I did but jest." Nicholas' hand touched Charles' burning forehead. "You burn with fever, sir!" he exclaimed. "We must make our way from here!"

"Let not your anxiety for my welfare lead you into folly, my lord," Charles said in a tone of sharp command.

Seeing Nicholas' eyes upon him, he said in a milder voice, "Cromwell's men, though tireless in their pursuit of the Stuart, are but human; or so they would have us believe. They have tramped these woods for many hours, but they have not yet abandoned the search. It would grieve me sore, Nicholas, were you to fall into the hands of Cromwell."

"But, sir—"

"Nay," Charles held up his hand. "Say no more, my lord, for well do I know that it was your intention to go alone."

"Aye," Nicholas said. "You are scarce fit for the effort, sir. But I will bring help, and that right speedily."

Charles shook his head. "Your Prince to lie sheltered, while my lord Earl exposes himself to Cromwell's louts? Nay, we stay or go together."

"You cannot go, sir," Nicholas said impatiently.

" 'Tis true, for I fear me that my legs would shake beneath me. But if this cursed cough of mine leads them not to our little palace, then I think that soon they will depart."

Charles was rarely stubborn, but Nicholas recognized the determined set of his mouth. He deemed it best to give in.

"Come, friend," Charles said. "Let us think on your

idea of the ring, for I like it well. What—" Another spasm of coughing caught him, and he smothered the sound against his arm.

"Now, my lord," Charles went on with some difficulty. "What think you of the initial *C?* It shall be in diamonds, of course."

"But what else, sir?"

Nicholas took off his cloak. It was damp, but it would be better than nothing at all. Ignoring Charles' protests, he tucked it about him. "It will help to keep out the wind," he said firmly.

"Thank you." Charles grinned at him, adding softly, "Your Majesty."

"Sir, I meant not—"

"Ah, Nicholas, Nicholas, 'twas but my feeble joke. Now wilt thou get thy cursed mind on the ring? Like you the idea of the diamond initial *C?*"

Nicholas could not take him seriously; nevertheless he considered the idea. "For myself, sir, I would prefer another design."

"Think well, then, for I am set on this notion. When I have regained my kingdom and am no more a pauper prince, I shall cause many of these rings to be made. But mark me well, friend, the lady wearing the ring shall be sacrosanct to the King. So seek not to tempt her from my side."

"A strange lady would she be," Nicholas said dryly, "if Benbrook could tempt her from the King."

"Think you so?" Charles' wry smile appeared. "'Twould doubtless be my handsome looks that attract her and not my regained kingdom, eh?"

Nicholas returned the smile, "And what of the pauper prince, sir, what attracts them to him? Think you it is his kingdom or his empty purse?"

"Plague take you, Nicholas! Remind me not of the state of my purse!"

It seemed to Nicholas that they lay there for an interminable time. He was consumed with anxiety for the Prince, for as the shadows lengthened, the chill in the air increased and Charles' condition grew steadily more grave.

His conversation was rational enough, but occasionally he lost the thread and began to ramble. He seemed to have forgotten that he must smother his cough; it was Nicholas, who, fearing to betray their position, placed his hand firmly over the Prince's mouth.

"Forgive me, sir," he said the first time, " 'twas necessary."

Charles' dark eyes were vague, but he seemed to understand. His burning fingers patted Nicholas' hand reassuringly. For a while he seemed to rally. He began talking interestedly of the ring, but his mind wandered again, and he talked of people long since dead, addressing his remarks to them.

Nicholas was only half listening. His ears were alert for sounds from above which now and again came uncomfortably near to their hiding place.

Much later, when Charles was firmly established on the throne of England, Nicholas told Charles of his desperate decision. Rather than surrender the Stuart into enemy hands, which would be to condemn him to the block, he had determined that he would kill his prince with his own hands.

Charles had laughed, pulling a wry face. "I understand, my lord. But thankful am I," he had answered, the ready laughter trembling in his voice, "that I avoided such a dismal fate."

But lying in the muddy ditch, in the rain with the Prince now unconscious beside him, Nicholas could not know that death was far from claiming Charles Stuart. He would not meet it from his enemies nor from Nicholas' compassionate hands. The Stuart's destiny to recover the throne was certain, though he knew it not.

At that moment Nicholas only knew the situation was desperate. He could never afterward remember, though Charles claimed that the idea was his, how they came, in their most perilous moments to decide the trivial matter of the ring. When Charles later informed him that the ring was to be of gold, and mounted upon it a ruby heart, pierced through with a diamond arrow, he still remembered but vaguely.

Cromwell's men, Nicholas thought grimly, were more tenacious than he had given them credit for. Only a short time before, he had heard their voices. It was full dark now, and a rising wind had swept the rain away. He dared delay no longer, for upon his action now he was convinced the Prince's life depended.

Charles came to as he lifted him. "Wh—what means this, m—my lord?" he muttered thickly. "Place me upon my—my feet. For I w—would surrender to my enemy as a—a man. Is the Stuart a ch—child th—that must be carried to his fate?"

"Nay, sir," Nicholas said gently. "We are not yet taken."

"Place me upon my feet!"

"You are ill, sir," Nicholas insisted. "I pray you to accept my assistance."

In the pale light of the moon, Nicholas saw Charles' faint smile. "You were ev—ever a cursed obstinate fellow," Charles said faintly. "But re—remind me not of this moment, else w—will I charge you with t—treason."

"My memory of this moment is henceforth lost," Nicholas promised gravely.

Charles did not answer. His head fell back, and he once more lost consciousness.

It seemed that luck had not entirely deserted them;

for on that long, weary walk, Nicholas, carrying the Prince across his shoulder, was only once forced into hiding.

They took refuge in the cottage of a Mistress Elizabeth Mallow, who was known to be active in the King's cause and had several times been arrested on a suspicion of harboring Royalist supporters. Nothing, however, had been proved against her. The enemies of Charles Stuart had ultimately come to the conclusion that she was a crazy but harmless old woman. Mistress Mallow fostered this idea, and thus her cottage became a welcome resting place for many a weary fugitive.

Tears ran down the old woman's face when she saw the Prince, and loud were her lamentations. But for all that, her actions were eminently practical. "Don't stand there gawking," she commanded Nicholas sharply. She pointed to a straw-filled pallet. " 'Tis the best I can offer." She watched Nicholas critically. "Gently now! Lay the lad down with care. 'Tis not a sack of logs you're handling!"

A termagant, this one, Nicholas thought. He straightened up. "His condition is grave, I fear," he said, looking down at the unconscious Prince.

"I don't need you to tell me that," the old woman said, sniffing. "But serious or not, Liz Mallow's not the one to admit defeat. I'll pull him through, never fear."

Nicholas turned his head and smiled at her. Termagant she might be, but instinctively he trusted her. "I'm sure you will," he said gently.

"Move aside, then, and let me tend him. Get you outside to the barn, you'll find a good stock of firewood there. The fire must be kept going through the night. Another thing," she snapped, as Nicholas went to the door. "I'll not have a great clumsy man getting in my way. So if you want to sleep warm, lad, you'll do your chores

228

without argument. When you're done, find yourself a corner and stay there."

"Yes, ma'am," Nicholas said humbly. He went outside and closed the door behind him.

Charles had recovered consciousness, but he did not open his eyes; the small effort required seemed to be beyond him. Dimly, he heard a woman's voice issuing rough-voiced commands, and a deep voice answering her. Where was he? Had Cromwell's men taken them? He must think, he must! Benbrook! What of him? Was he captured—dead? Charles moaned and tried to move his legs. Immediately he felt restraining hands upon him.

"Be still, lad," a woman's voice said.

He wanted to say something, but he could not. He felt so ill, so terribly ill! He lay there in his half-conscious state and tried to force his burning brain to think.

Nicholas came back with a great stack of logs in his arms. He built up the fire and piled the remainder of the logs on the stone hearth. He made four trips before the old woman declared herself to be satisfied.

Seated in his corner, Nicholas watched the woman, his eyes uneasy. Bundles of dried herbs hung from the wooden rafters. She cut a large sprig from each, chopped them finely, and tossed them into the small cauldron of boiling water suspended above the roaring fire. It was stiflingly hot in the room, and the only sound was Charles' heavy breathing and the bubbling of water. Nicholas' uneasiness increased. The odor of the herbs was nauseating. What the devil was the old crone about?

The woman removed the cauldron and poured some of the mixture into a cracked cup. Only then did she look at Nicholas. " 'Twill do him good," she said shortly.

Nicholas was on his feet at once. "Do you intend to feed that—that vile mixture to the Prince?"

·She nodded. "Aye, I do. Sit you down. I'll not have you interfering."

"But I cannot allow—"

"If you think 'tis poison I have in this cup," she said, glaring at him, "you are much mistaken." She looked at him for a long moment, and her eyes slowly softened. "Rest easy in your mind," she said gently. "Liz Mallow's cures are well known. 'Tis my prince that lies there, and I'd die before I'd hurt one hair of his head."

Nicholas hesitated. "I believe you mean well."

"And you'll trust me?"

Nicholas sat down slowly. "I must," he said unhappily. "I have no other choice."

"You'll not regret it, lad." She smiled at him for the first time.

Nicholas fought off an overpowering desire to sleep. He continued to watch the woman, but he was easier in his mind, and the first instinctive trust he had felt returned to give him further comfort.

All through that long night she tended the Prince. She bathed his fevered skin and talked to him in a soft soothing voice.

"There, there, my bonny laddie!" she crooned, her hands tender in their ministration. "There, my laddie, my prince! I'll see old Noll burn in hell before he'll lay his dirty murdering hands on my bonny Charlie!"

Through the feverish mist that held him fast, Charles felt her cool hands upon his brow. He drank obediently when she demanded it of him, and he listened to her soothing voice and was oddly comforted. He thought he was back with his old nurse who had often taken the small Charles upon her capacious lap, murmuring, "My little prince. My bonny Charlie."

His hand came out gropingly, and Elizabeth Mallow took it in hers and held it firmly. Charles smiled and slipped into a deep sleep.

The morning found him much improved, though still very weak. His brilliant black eyes had regained their old sparkling mockery; though when they looked upon the woman, they softened to a remarkable tenderness.

"Your name, my Lord Benbrook tells me," Charles said, "is Elizabeth Mallow. I am greatly indebted to you, Mistress Mallow."

Seeing him in his full senses, she grew flustered. "Aye, sir," she answered, bobbing him an agitated curtsy.

"Pray come closer," Charles said, holding out his hand.

Encouraged by his smile, she went to his side.

"Sir," she mumbled. "It rejoices me to see you thus improved."

Charles took her hand and raised it to his lips. "Ah!" he said softly. "Then it would seem that I am no longer your bonny laddie?"

She looked up, startled, her face blushing scarlet. "Pray forgive me, sir. I meant no disrespect."

"Dear mistress!" Charles squeezed her hand. "If that be disrespect then will I ever cherish the memory. Methought 'twas love I heard in your voice."

"Aye, sir. That it was!" she said in a stronger voice.

"Then am I content to remain your bonny Charlie," Charles assured her gently.

Old as she was, she seemed bemused by him. The color mounted in her cheeks again, making her look years younger. "I'd die for you, sir!" Fervently the woman responded to the Stuart magic.

"Nay," Charles said. "Say rather, gentle mistress, that you will live for me."

It was at the cottage that Harry Forbes finally found them. With a small troop of men he had searched all through the night. The home of the Royalist sympathizer was known to Forbes; and it had been his last forlorn hope.

Forbes entered the room briskly. His face lit up when he saw the Prince lying upon the rough pallet.

"Sire!" Forbes sank to his knees. He raised Charles' hand to his lips. The tears were bright in his eyes. "Your Majesty!" Forbes exclaimed. "May God be ever with you!"

Charles caught his breath. "My—my father?"

"The King is dead," Forbes said brokenly. "Long live the King!"

Charles closed his eyes for a moment; when he opened them, he said with some difficulty, "I pray you, Sir Harry, and you, my Lord Benbrook, to leave me. I would be alone."

The woman began to follow after the men, but the King's voice halted her, "Stay with me, mistress, for I have need of comfort."

"Your Majesty!" she faltered. She ran to him, stooping over him in an agony of pity. "Dear Majesty!"

"Oh, my father!" Charles exclaimed, his voice breaking on the words. "My father!" Elizabeth Mallow knelt beside him, and Charles turned to her blindly. She saw the tears on his face, and she put her arms about him and held him close. He clung to her, weeping. To her in that moment he was not the King of England but only a young man whose heart was broken over his father's untimely and tragic death.

"Weep, my laddie," she soothed. " 'Twill ease your heart. Aye, that's right, old Elizabeth has you fast!"

Later Charles tried to reward Elizabeth Mallow for her kindness, but she would accept nothing. She asked only the privilege of occasionally seeing her king, and Charles had visited her often. She lived to see him crowned, but shortly after that she died.

Frowning, BARBARA CASTLEMAINE LIFTED her head from the pillow. From beyond her closed door there was a low murmur of voices. She had told her woman to admit no one, she had a headache, and she wished to rest. What was the fool about? Had she dared to smuggle in that bucolic lover of hers? Damn her! She'd pay for disregarding orders.

Barbara pressed her hands to her throbbing temples. No, Brownlow was afraid of her. It was more likely Buckingham, refusing to be dismissed, come to taunt her again. If so, he'd get very short shrift. She was tired of his sneering remarks, his constant references to her loss of power and the King's neglect of her. Loss of power! A pox on Buck!

She moved restlessly. Of course, she had played into Buck's hands when, with her usual indiscretion, she had boasted of her absolute power over the King. How Buck had laughed at that boast, and what pleasure it gave him now to draw her attention to the gossip about her. They were sneering over her downfall, but she'd show Buck. He'd laugh on the other side of his face when she was once more installed as the King's favorite mistress—they all would! Power? Yes, she had power over Charles. She held him by virtue of her beauty. She was recognized, even by her enemies, as the most beautiful woman at Court. In the whole of England, some said. There were others who claimed that Mistress Dawson had the greater beauty of the two, but they were the sly ones, the toadies who sought a favor from the King. Angel Dawson? That slut! Did she think to usurp Barbara Castlemaine's place? Let her but try and she'd make her sorry to the last day of her life!

Barbara's eyes narrowed in sudden thought. Dawson and her determined virtue! She had the King running after her like a lovesick boy. The Earl of Benbrook with his chronic suspicion of women, had arranged for the slut to be chaperoned by the Duchess of Alverstane while he journeyed to Worcestershire. Barbara bit her lip angrily. Grim guardian though the Duchess was, she had not been able to resist the King. She looked the other way when he sought the company of Mistress Dawson.

Barbara started as a giggle came from without. She sat up abruptly on the bed. That fool! That dolt of a woman! How dare she disturb her peace with her damnable giggling! She'd dismiss her, and she'd see that she did not get another place. Barbara rose and strode to the door.

"Oh, Your Majesty!" The woman's voice had risen to an audible pitch. She sounded flustered.

Barbara stopped dead. Charles? So he could not stay away after all! Her lips tightened. Almost she smiled. But he'd pay for his weeks of neglect. He'd not get off lightly. King though he be, he must be taught to respect her. She was beautiful; she could have any man she desired; she had borne his children. Buck was constantly calling her an indiscreet fool, but she'd show him that Barbara Castlemaine was well able to take care of herself. She'd manage Charles. She smiled grimly. Charles could not bear her tantrums—he would give her anything she demanded at such times, and she intended to demand a great deal. Later, of course, she would succumb, and their reconciliation would be the sweeter for the quarreling that had gone before. A fool? No, not she. Let Buck look to himself. Some of his own past actions had not been exactly wise.

Barbara frowned. There was silence outside. What were they doing? The silence was broken by another giggle from Brownlow, and Barbara's lips curled slightly. Of course—she might have guessed. Charles, and his weakness for women. Not that Mary Brownlow was a woman. She was a nonentity, a pair of hands to serve, but she had a certain buxom charm that had doubtless caught Charles' roving eye. Nevertheless, when a king fondled a serving-wench, it gave them a false idea of their own importance.

How like Charles to descend upon her unexpectedly, Barbara thought, suddenly remembering her appearance. She flew across the room to her mirror. He might at least have sent word of his coming. Her anxious eyes could find no fault in her appearance and, reassured, she smiled. It was true that her hair was disheveled, but attractively so; her eyes were bright and her cheeks touched with a faint color. Her white velvet gown was slightly creased; but it was scarcely noticeable. Against the white velvet her hair was vivid flame. It would do, she decided. It would do very well.

Without a preliminary knock, the door opened, and Charles strolled into the room. "Why, Bab," he said, looking about him, " 'tis infernally dark in here. What ails you, wench, that you must shut out the sunlight?"

She looked at him unsmilingly; then she swept him the briefest of curtsys. "I am in mourning, Your Majesty," she said in a hard voice. " 'Tis overlong since you have thus honored me."

"It is indeed." He smiled at her, but she saw with a shock of dismay that his eyes had a bored expression.

Fury flamed in her as Charles seated himself on a satin-draped couch. How dare he treat her in such cavalier fashion!

"Well, Bab," he said, leaning back comfortably, "and is all well with you?"

"Does Your Majesty care?"

He shrugged. "Let this be a pleasant visit, I pray you. I have much on my mind."

Barbara stared at him and, quite suddenly changed her tactics. "Oh, Charles," she said, her voice quivering, "Dear Charles!" She ran to him, her hands stretched out appealingly. "I've missed you so much."

"Have you so, Bab?" he said. He caught one of her hands and drew her down beside him. " 'Twould seem to me you have distracted yourself tolerably well." She did not hear the note of cynicism in his voice. "Nay," she said, snuggling close to him and resting her head against his shoulder. "Naught could heal the grief of the thought that you no longer loved your Bab." She sat up straight and looked at him. "You love me still, do you not?"

"I have brought you a gift," he said. "I believe it will please you well."

"A gift?" she cried, not noticing his evasion of her question. "What is it, Charles? Oh, do let me see!"

"Impatient wench!" he said good-naturedly. He fumbled in his pocket. " 'Twas ever so with you, Bab. Here." He held out a small velvet-covered box.

Barbara stretched out her hand to take it. She did not open it at once. "Is this not the box presented to you by your ambassador to France?" she queried. "I seem to remember this peculiar scrolled pattern on the sides."

"Aye." He nodded. " 'Tis most unusual, is it not?"

Her lip curled slightly. "Unusual indeed," she agreed. "But 'twas most poor-spirited of the ambassador to present so paltry a gift to his king."

"There are more to some gifts than at first apparent."

"What mean you?"

He did not answer at once. He saw the frown between her brows, and he guessed at her thoughts. He would enjoy seeing the expression on her face when she opened the box, the greedy baggage.

"Why do you not open it?" he demanded impatiently. " 'Tis something you have long plagued me for."

"Oh!" Her face lit up. Charles grinned boyishly as she opened it eagerly.

"But—" She looked up at him with an expression of blank surprise. "But it's empty, Charles."

"Aye, Bab, so it is."

"Then—then 'tis a joke?" She looked at his smiling face, and her rage exploded. "You—you w—would do th—this to me?" she stammered. "You would p—present me with an e—empty box?"

"But that is the joke, you see. 'Tis not—"

"I'll not stand for it!" Barbara shrieked. She forgot that she spoke to the King. She glared at him, longing to strike the smile from his face. "I'll not be thrust aside while you pursue Benbrook's whore!"

"Be silent!" Charles thundered. He rose to his feet. "You know well that Mistress Dawson is Benbrook's cousin."

"Do I?" Barbara stood up and faced him, her eyes blazing. "Have you heard the whispers? Some there are who say she is not what she seems!"

Charles thought she looked quite mad. He was outraged, yet he could not help feeling a slight admiration. Who else but Bab would dare to speak so? Plague take the jealous, bad-tempered jade! He should send her away, he knew. Her presence made the Queen miserable. Poor little Catherine would be delighted if he sent Bab away; so would Edward Hyde, his chancellor. Barbara was too

237

arrogant, too sure of herself. She was fast becoming impossible. She created scenes and disrupted the Court with her indiscreetly babbling tongue.

Yes, he should send her away, but he was reluctant to do so. Even in his determined pursuit of Angel, he had been aware that he missed Bab. She had a way of making the act of love ever new, ever more exciting. And damn it, now he came to think of it, he'd missed that. Annoyed by his weakness, he said sharply, "Have a care, Bab, your insolence goes beyond all bounds! 'Twould take but little to persuade me to banish you from this Court."

"As you did once before, I suppose?" she panted. "Aye, but you soon recalled me, did you not?" Her sneer faded, and she felt a twinge of alarm. There was a look in Charles' eyes, a coldly arrogant look. He was no longer Charles, her lover. He was the King. Oh God! Her cursed tongue would bring her to ruin. "Charles!" she gave a wailing cry and cast herself into his arms. "Forgive me! Please forgive me!"

Not for a moment did he believe in her show of repentance, but he put his arms about her. " 'Tis well you beg my forgiveness," he said severely. "You have greatly misjudged me, and you have created a scene most displeasing to me." He put her from him. Stooping, he picked up the box from the couch. " 'Tis a trick box." Despite himself, a note of enthusiasm crept into his voice. "Watch carefully." He pressed his finger to the scrolled side. "There is a spring hidden in the pattern," he explained. "Is it not ingenious?"

But Barbara was speechless. She was staring at the emerald ring in the released secret compartment. "Oh!" she said after a moment. " 'Tis beautiful!" She took the ring from its satin nest and fitted it upon her finger. " 'Tis beautiful!" she said again.

Charles put the little box into his pocket. The secret

compartment would contain another ring tonight, a ring he intended to present to Mistress Dawson. Angel still contrived to evade him. Yet she was attracted to him, he knew, both as a king and as a man. Unfortunately, he thought, with a touch of melancholy, it was as yet but a surface attraction. He wished to inspire a deeper feeling in her, and this, so far, he had failed to do. And if he could not have Angel tonight, he could still bed the Castlemaine.

Barbara was crooning over the ring, turning her hand this way and that. Yes, Charles thought, Angel would wear the other ring. It was a ruby heart pierced through with a diamond arrow, but he would present it to her in such a way that she would be pleased and proud to wear it.

"Charles." Barbara put her hand on his shoulder. "Pray sit down. Will you take a glass of wine with me?"

"Thank you." Charles sat down on the couch again. Vaguely, he was aware of Barbara in the background. He was sure that he had fallen in love with Angel. His passion for her was deep and sincere. This time he was sure. An insidious notion tried to intrude, telling him that he had felt this way many times before and for many different women. Charles thrust the thought from him. Angel was the one and only love. His true love. Why then, had he sensed hostility in Nicholas at the Honors Ball? A hostility that had never been there before? He smiled slightly, but there was affection in the smile. Nicholas would make of his cousin a paragon of the virtues but desire her not. But I would make her the delight of my heart and desire her ever.

Nicholas would recognize the significance of the ring once he saw it upon Angel's finger. Charles' thoughts roamed on. He would recognize it, and he would know that whatever objections he now entertained, he must withdraw them.

He accepted a glass of wine from Barbara, and replied to her remarks absentmindedly. Barbara was annoyed, but she guarded her sharp tongue. Let him dream. The night was ahead of them and, in the privacy of her bedroom, she planned to make him very aware of her.

Barbara said suddenly, startling him, "I beg your leave to retire, Your Majesty. I have a new gown, and I wish your opinion on the color and the texture of the material, 'tis Italian silk, but very unusual in design, as you will see." She smiled at him, her eyes bright.

"Go then, Bab. I shall be interested to see this marvelous new gown."

"You will be enchanted, I vow," Barbara cried. She picked up her skirts and ran to the big carved screen in the corner of her big bedroom. Disappearing behind it, she called, "I will attend upon myself. I do not wish Brownlow to intrude upon our moments together."

Charles did not answer. Barbara and her whims! He smiled cynically. He was a man who desired peace above all things, and for the sake of that peace, he had given in to her in the past. He had done so again today. Even if Angel came willingly to his arms, he knew he could not put Bab entirely out of his life. Not yet, at least. Nevertheless, he must not allow himself to give in to her every demand, else would the jade bankrupt him.

Charles' thoughts returned to Nicholas, and he forgot Barbara again. Why, he wondered, should he feel relief at Nicholas' absence. He sighed. Why, he loved Benbrook like a brother, and there was nothing he would not do for him.

Who should know better the humor in him, the sensitivity? He had witnessed Nicholas' deep compassion for the wounded men. That compassion reached out to them and touched them. Devil take it, he had seen them rally and turn to fight again! And if they were fervent in their prince's cause, they were also fervent in their determination to fight under Benbrook's banner.

Charles sighed again. Danger and war brought out that side in Nicholas, but now 'twas hidden again. Why was he so unapproachable, so sternly demanding? Charles supposed that he would demand from Angel, as he had from Marianne, an unsullied reputation and a cold and inviolate chastity.

Charles shook his head. Women are but human. 'Twould be as well if Nicholas learned that. Aye, they are indeed human, as are the sacred women of one's own family.

He thought of the ruby and diamond ring that would shortly adorn Angel's finger, and he smiled with a quiet satisfaction. "You would deny me the pleasure of making Mistress Dawson my own, I feel sure," Charles murmured softly. "So, Nicholas, must I use my own means to defeat your puritanism. 'Tis plain to me that Mistress Dawson's beauty moves you not, so 'twould be selfishness to deny her to your King."

ANGEL FINISHED BRUSHING HER HAIR. SHE set the brush down, admiring the long, intricately carved handle and the ornate back studded with small diamonds.

She cherished the brush, not so much for its value, but because it had been a gift from the Queen.

Angel was pleased and flattered that the Queen should single her out. She well knew that Queen Catherine was not noted for her friendly attitude toward the ladies of Charles' Court. But she, of course, was not of the Court, and perhaps the Queen had sensed that she was not interested in becoming the King's mistress.

Poor Catherine, Angel thought. How she loved her fascinating rogue of a husband! She suffered such agonies of jealousy. There was hunger in the very way she touched him; and her dark expressive eyes seemed always to be pleading with him to love her—to be kind.

Charles, of course, was kind; it was not in his nature to be otherwise. But this kindness was not specially reserved for Catherine. He was kind to the mistresses he had discarded, giving them generous pensions and visiting them often. He was kind even to those who annoyed him, to his dogs, to the lowliest crossing-sweeper. But Catherine wanted more; she wanted his love, and this

Charles could not give her. He had an affection for her, and he would never willingly see her slighted or hurt; but it was not enough for Catherine, who wanted to be his life, as he was hers.

Thinking of the King, Angel smiled. He was attractive—much too attractive—and had she not been so much in love with Nicholas, she might, despite her pity for the Queen, have willingly shared his bed. But she did love Nicholas, and the strength of that love excluded all other men, even the King.

Angel thought of the ring the King had given her. It was a valuable ring, and she had not been quite certain if she should accept it. But he was, after all, the King. It was but a token of his friendship, he assured her. And who was she, Angel thought, allowing him to place it upon her finger, to turn aside from the friendship of her sovereign?

That his plans for her included more than friendship, Angel well knew, for the look in his eyes was unmistakable. But the King had never been known to force his attentions upon an unwilling woman. There were too many who were more than willing. And she had not been swayed.

Outside, she heard the clop of hooves, the impatient snorting of a horse and the jingle of harness.

Angel sighed. The daily round of pleasure—at first so delightful—had palled quickly. But perhaps Nicholas' prolonged absence had something to do with it. He had been gone six weeks now. How could she give her mind to pleasure or anything else for that matter while she was forced to live in this state of miserable uncertainty? She frowned; the unwelcome thought came to her, as it had often done after the fourth week of his absence, that if Nicholas needed so much time to make up his mind, then he quite obviously did not love her.

The very thought caused her heart to thud painfully. The horse snorted again, and Angel glared across at the window. It was undoubtedly John Beaufort come a-calling. Yesterday, meeting him quite by chance, he had asked if he might do so.

Her answer had been purposely vague, and she had hoped that he might take the hint. It was not that she disliked him; he was comfortable to be with, and his outrageous jokes made her laugh. But these days she had so little time to herself.

"Mind you rub him down well, John," a deep, imperious voice said. "And give him some extra feed. We've had a damn difficult journey, haven't we, Jupiter?"

Angel heard the responsive whinny of the horse, and the stableboy's, "Aye, me lord, I'll look a'ter him."

"Nicholas!" Angel rose from her chair and ran to the door. Nicholas was back! He was back!

Nicholas entered the hall with his long stride. Mrs. Sampson waited to greet him. "Welcome home, Master Nickey," she said, her blue eyes bright with pleasure.

" 'Tis good to be home," Nicholas answered. Stooping, he kissed her quickly on the cheek. "I trust I see you well, Sampson?"

She was startled and touched by his rare gesture. "I am well enough, Master Nickey, thank you. What of yourself?"

"I am v——" Nicholas broke off as the sound of running footsteps came to his ears.

Mrs. Sampson smiled to herself as Nicholas took two strides toward the stairs. He stopped, waiting, his hands clenched at his sides. "Oh, lad," she thought fondly. "You never could deceive your old Sampson. I've known this long time past that you were in love with Angel."

"Nicholas!" Angel stood at the head of the short flight of stairs. "Nicholas," she said again, unable to move.

He said nothing. His eyes held a curious expression. She was so young! The little lass was but nineteen, and he almost fourteen years her senior. Why, in her morning gown of primrose-yellow silk, her bright hair tumbling about her shoulders, she looked naught but a child. Ah, but he loved her, his little guttersnipe! Damn her for disrupting his world, and God bless her for having the courage to do so!

He saw her eyes, wide and frightened in her pale face. He swallowed against the constriction in his throat, but still he could not speak. He lifted his arms and held them out to her.

Her face flushed with color, and her eyes shone. She ran down the stairs, paused on the last two, then, laughing, she launched herself into his arms.

He caught her, held her for a moment, then, stooping, he swept her off her feet. "Hello, my brat," he said huskily.

"Darling!" Her arms went round his neck. "My darling, darling Nicholas!"

Mrs. Sampson cleared her throat loudly. "You'll be wanting some refreshment after your long journey, my lord," she said primly. "If you'll excuse me, I'll see to it."

Nicholas, who had started at the sound of her voice, flung back his head and laughed aloud. "What, Sampson," he said. "No surprise?"

The housekeeper shook her head. "No indeed, Master Nickey. 'Tis only what I've been expecting to happen. Even an idiot, which I am not, would have known you two were in love with each other."

Nicholas looked down at Angel. "And I, I suppose," he said softly, "am less intelligent than an idiot, eh Sampson?"

Mrs. Sampson shook her head. "No, my lord," she answered calmly, "stupid you've never been. Stubborn,

245

that's the word I'd choose. You always were, even as a tiny little lad."

Nicholas looked at her affectionately. "Have I ever told you, Sampson, that you have a cursed loose tongue?"

"Frequently, my lord."

"Very well." Nicholas' arms tightened about Angel. "Then might I suggest you hold your tongue? After you have wished us happy, of course."

"'Tis my dearest dream for you, Master Nickey." She turned to Angel. "I wish you very happy, Ang—Mistress Dawson."

"Thank you," Angel said quietly. "But I pray you not to call me Mistress Dawson."

"What then?" Nicholas teased. "Shall it be my Lady Benbrook?"

Angel shook her head. "Nay. I shall ever be Angel to you, shall I not, Mrs. Sampson?"

"If it be your wish, child." She turned away. "God bless you both."

Nicholas waited until the door closed behind her, then he set Angel on her feet. He took her into his arms again and kissed her, a long, hard, hungry kiss.

"Angel!" he said, his lips leaving hers. "Do you know how much I love you?"

Her hands touched his face caressingly. "Nay, dear m'lord," she whispered. "But if it be more than mine for you, then will you not survive. For my love is bigger than the world."

"Bah! What is one world? Mine is the bigger," he went on firmly. "Mark me well, baggage, compared to my love, yours is but a pale and puny thing. And that, wench, is my final word!"

"Ah, yes," she grinned at him. "You have ever told me that you are not accustomed to being defied by 'a damned insolent guttersnipe.' Have you not, my lord?"

"I?" He stared at her, a frown between his brows. "Nonsense! I would not say such a thing."

"Would you not?" She laughed suddenly. "But I care not what you call me as long as there is love in your voice."

He was silent for a moment, then he said uncertainly, "And will you always love me, my little one?" He took her face between his hands and looked searchingly into her eyes. "Think well, Angel, before you answer."

"I shall always love you, dear m'lord," she answered steadily. Sensing his need, she added, "For me there shall never be another. Never, my darling!"

"You are very young," he said tenderly. "And I—well I am almost thirty-three years of age. You—you would not deceive such a venerable old gentleman, would you?"

There were tears in his eyes and seeing them she wanted to cry herself. "Aye, I would," she whispered, "did I but know this venerable old gentleman to whom you refer. But I am in the arms of my Lord Benbrook, and well do I know him for a tyrant. Therefore would I tremble to deceive him."

He held her to him, hiding his face against her hair. " 'Tis well you know me for what I am," he said. "For I will have you know, wench, that I intend to be master."

"I pray you, my lord, teach me not a lesson already well learned. You have shouted at me, called me names, even beaten me, therefore have I learned." She felt his sudden start, and she knew he was thinking of that savage moment when he had used the lash upon her. "Nay, love," she comforted him, " 'tis forgotten."

"You have forgiven me, Angel?"

"Aye," she said. She pulled away from him gently and looked up at him. "One must forgive the formidable Lord Benbrook, else would he be sore displeased."

"You know," he said gravely, "though I remember not calling you so. You really are a damned insolent little guttersnipe."

She saw the smile in his dark eyes, and she stood on tiptoe to kiss his lips. "Aye, I am," she agreed. "But I am your guttersnipe, so forget it not, my lord."

He lifted her in his arms again. "I doubt not that you will remind me," he said, turning toward the stairs. "Cursed nagging female that you are."

"Where are you taking me, my lord?"

"To your room. I can no longer endure the sight of you. However," he added, depositing her before her door, "if you are not with me before an hour has past, I shall break down the door; and so I warn you, Mistress Dawson."

For THIS VERY SPECIAL DINNER WITH NICHolas, Angel had spent much time and thought on her appearance. She had consulted with Mrs. Sampson, who had chosen a simple white gown with touches of silver embroidery. Angel had considered this, and had finally rejected it as not being good enough. She had changed her mind a dozen times and had so tried the housekeeper's patience that the woman had finally departed, shaking her head.

"Whatever I suggest," was Mrs. Sampson's parting shot, "it will be your choice in the end. I know you, Angel."

Still doubtful, Angel had finally chosen a gown of sea-green satin. The peaked bodice was sewn with pearls, the full, slashed sleeves held together with pearl clasps. The rich material, molded tightly to her waist, flowed out into a huge skirt, the front of which was caught up, showing white lace petticoats, threaded with green and silver ribbons. Her hair, held back from her face by a wide silver ribbon, fell loosely about her shoulders, and a diamond star on a thin silver chain—Nicholas' gift—adorned her slim white throat.

She was pleased with her appearance; the clear color emphasized the whiteness of her skin and made deeper

249

and richer the red-gold of her hair. As a final touch, she slid the King's ring upon her finger. It would please Nicholas, she thought, that his future bride, far from disgracing him, was, like himself, a friend of the King. Nicholas loved her; he was not, she knew, unduly concerned with her humble birth; but she herself was very conscious of it, and she longed to shine in his eyes. She was what he had made her, and now on her own initiative she had climbed yet higher; the ring was her proof. She hesitated a moment, thinking, then she twisted the ring so that only the plain gold band showed. Later, she would surprise Nicholas. She would turn the ring again and hold out her hand quite casually. The King had assured her that Nicholas would recognize the ring for what it was, for they were designed especially for the women whom he considered to be his trusted friends.

She was glad she had chosen to wear the sea-green gown, for the look in Nicholas' eyes, when she entered the room, told her that she was beautiful.

Seated before the fire of crackling logs, she watched him. He was pouring a ruby-red wine into fragile gold-rimmed goblets—a very special wine, he had told her. He looked so different, she thought, that she scarcely knew him for the same man. His air of cold arrogance was not evident now. His dark eyes glowed, and his smile erased the deeply grooved lines of bitterness over his mouth. He was happy, she realized, and it was that happiness that had made a startling difference. The old Nicholas must never reappear. She would keep him away, she vowed. She would make him so happy! So very happy!

She smiled. Nicholas, it seemed, had given a great deal of thought to his own toilette. He had discarded his usual severe black. Tonight his coat and breeches were of a thick midnight-blue satin; the ruffles of lace at his wrists—for one of his conservative taste—were unusually extravagant. His white satin cravat, edged with lace, was held by a sapphire clasp. He wore his hair in the usual way, but since he had not brushed it back in the severe way customary to him, it curled over his forehead, and gave him, Angel thought, a youthful look.

After dinner, which Nicholas had insisted upon serving himself, startling the servants, he led Angel back to the library.

The fire had been built up, and the flames sent little flickering shadows across the walls. The fire was the only illumination in the room, but neither of them felt the need for more light. They sat together on the little sofa, very close together, not speaking, but content with the silence.

It was Nicholas who spoke first. "Angel," he said abruptly. "You know, do you not, that I am bound to make mistakes? I—I mean, this love business is so new to me."

He sat up straighter, turning his face away as if embarrassed—for surely, Angel thought tenderly, my Lord Benbrook could not be shy?—and when he spoke again, it was with something of his old imperiousness. "I shall expect you to be tolerant of my mistakes. I will not have hysterical scenes if I should unwittingly hurt you. That, I trust, is understood?"

"Yes, Nicholas."

She wanted to laugh, but he was so much in earnest. Who else but Nicholas could issue something that sounded like an ultimatum or, some might call it, a threat, to the girl he loved. Ah, but he could not change at once; she did not want him to. It was only his unhappiness she wished to banish.

"I will not share you, Angel," he went on, his hands clenching on his knees. "I am, unfortunately, of a—" he hesitated. "That is to say, that I am somewhat inclined to jealousy. Regrettable, but true. It would seem to be the aim of a great many women to arouse just this side in their husbands. It would be unwise of you to attempt this with me, and I ask you to bear this in mind."

"Yes, Nicholas," she said again.

Struck by something in her voice, he turned his head and looked at her with sudden sharp suspicion. When he saw her expression, he laughed ruefully. "Oh, Angel," he said, "am I making a complete fool of myself?"

"No, love." She put her arms about him. "But if my lord sees fit to dictate, then so too shall I."

"Oh?" He turned to her, resting his head against her shoulder. "And what would Mistress Dawson wish to say?"

"First," Angel said firmly, "that you will not have to share me. Secondly, I, too, am of a jealous disposition, and, if I may borrow some of your words, it would be unwise of you to arouse this side of me."

He sat up straight, looking at her with what appeared to be genuine astonishment. "You? To say that to me!"

"Yes, I." She looked at him with wide-open eyes. "And with far more cause, my lord," she added.

"What do you mean?" he said, frowning at her ominously.

"I refer to your women, of course. Your ever-present women. Do you think that I was not jealous? I would have liked to have killed them! You too!"

A slow smile spread over his face. "Were you really jealous, my little one?"

"Indeed I was," she answered sharply. "Especially of the fat dark one, Mistress Elizabeth Wallace. I can hear her now—'Oh, Nicholas! Oh, don't, I pray you, look at me in such fashion. You send shivers down my spine!' It was dreadful, and I hated her!"

"Mistress Elizabeth Wallace, I would have you know," Nicholas said, raising his dark brows quizzically, "was not in the least fat. Perhaps nature was—er—a little lavish in the endowment of Mistress Elizabeth, but she was definitely not fat."

"She was!" Angel cried. "She was fat! Fat! Fat! Oh, Nicholas, are you not ashamed? All those women! How could you!"

"Never mind," Nicholas said hastily. "We will not discuss them."

She looked at him, a little frown between her brows.

"Nicholas, you will not see them again, will you? I could not bear it!"

"Never again," he assured her.

"Did you—" She touched his face lightly, apologetically. "Did you care for any of them?" She rushed on before he could speak. "Not love. You told me you had never loved a woman. But did you care for them?"

"My darling, no." He took her into his arms and kissed her flushed face. "Those women, they were a convenience, nothing more. A man must have— But never mind about that. There will be no other women." He paused, looking at her sternly. "The matter is closed, my little one."

"I know what a man must have," Angel's voice trembled with laughter. "I know, my darling discreet Nicholas."

"Angel!"

He sounded so shocked, that she sobered at once. "I'm sorry. But darling, I'm not a child, and you must not treat me as one. Nicholas, will I—will I satisfy y—you?"

"What a question!" He made an impatient gesture, and his hand touched her soft breast. It lingered there, his fingers tightening slightly. "I love you, Angel!" his voice deepened. "My one and only love! It will be only you! Only you!"

She pressed closer to him, her hands drawing down

his head. "Nicholas," she said against his lips. "We—we do not have to wait." Her body was hot and quivering, aching with desire. "D—do we, my darling? Do we?"

"We are to be married," he said jerkily. "Why should we wait?" His hands pushed her down gently. " 'Tis only a few mumbled words that will unite us."

He rose to his feet, then knelt beside her. "Only a few mumbled words. But we are already one, and I want you now, Angel! I want you now!"

His hands fumbled awkwardly at her bodice. "Damn the cursed thing!" he muttered. "Why will you women wear—" He broke off, seeing her quick glance toward the door. "Nay, my darling," he reassured her. "There will be naught to disturb us. I gave instructions to that effect."

"What of visitors?"

"No visitors. They are to say we are not at home." His eyes sobered suddenly. "Are you sure, my brat? I—I would not force you."

"I'm very sure. I love you, Nicholas! I want you!" Her hand fluttered out, and he caught it in his and pressed his lips against it.

Her eyes were closed. She did not see the flash of the firelight on the ruby heart of the King's ring. Overlarge for her slim finger, it had twisted to the front again.

"Nicholas?" she said queryingly, wondering at his stillness. She opened her eyes and looked at him. "What is it? Nicholas! Look at me!"

He dropped her hand, but still he did not move. She stared at him, her heart beginning to beat in agitation. There was something terrifying about his absolute immobility.

"Nicholas!" her voice rose. "I pray you to look at me!"

254

"You slut!" His eyes lifted, and she saw the bleak coldness of them. "You filthy little whore!"

Anger boiled inside her. What was wrong with him? Was he insane? Hot words rose to her lips, but before she could utter them she found herself remembering Nicholas' mother. Was it possible that Nicholas imagined that she—in offering herself to him—was just such another as Lady Catherine?

But he had been willing, she thought, her head spinning in bewilderment. He had wanted her as much as she had wanted him! Then what—? Had he been testing her, was that the answer? What, then, did he demand in the woman he had decided to marry? But she was human, and she wanted him! Surely he did not think that she would behave so with other men?

"Nicholas, we will wait." She moistened her dry lips. "I did not really intend to—to—" her voice faltered on the lie. She shook her head helplessly, unable to go on.

Nicholas rose to his feet. "You did not intend to what?" he asked tonelessly.

"You know," she said, her face flushing hotly.

"No. Tell me?"

"Very well, if you will have it so. I did not intend you to make love to me."

He began to laugh, and the sound made him shiver. "How charmingly you lie. But a slut is a slut!" his voice took on violence. " 'Tis well known that they are ever generous of their favors." He stopped speaking, staring at her with eyes that narrowed slowly in speculation.

"But perhaps, after all, you speak truth," he went on. "You would not be the first King's whore to consider herself sacrosanct to her royal master."

"Are you mad?" Angel's eyes blazed with anger. "How dare you speak so to me? How dare you call me the King's whore!"

255

He shrugged. "I will leave you now." He turned toward the door.

Something broke inside her. She leaped from the couch.

"And is this to be the end of it?" she shouted. "You insult me! you call me King's whore. Then, just like that, you walk out of my life?"

"Just like that," he agreed levelly. He smiled. "I regret if I have spoiled your little game. But you must not be greedy, my dear. You cannot have it both ways."

She saw his smile, but she was blind to the pain in his eyes. She thought she knew the reason for the change in him. He was afraid. Yes, that was it, he was still afraid to put his trust in love. But he was a man! He could not go on being a frightened trembling boy all his life. If he could not bury the past, then he was no use to himself or to any woman. But why must he hide his own cowardice behind insults?

"Move aside from the door, if you please," he said.

"Coward!" Her hand seemed to move of its own accord, lashing against his face. She lost her head completely then.

"Coward! Coward!" she screamed, her hand striking again and again. "Damn you! You pitiful excuse for a man!"

He had not moved. It was as though he did not even feel her blows. When she stopped exhausted, he said politely.

"I beg you to excuse me."

She did not move. He could not leave her like this! Surely he could not! She saw the marks of her fingers across his face, and she began to tremble. Coward, he might be, but she loved him. No, when it came right down to it, he wouldn't be able to leave her.

But it seemed that he could. His hands came out and grasped her shoulders, lifted her and set her aside.

"Goodbye, Mistress Dawson," he said politely. "May you surpass the Castlemaine."

He was gone. She heard his footsteps crossing the hall, the sound of a door opening. Then his raised voice calling.

She could not distinguish his words. Goodbye! He had said goodbye.

"Nicholas! Nicholas!"

She ran into the hall. Her foot tangled in a rug, and she fell headlong. Sobbing, she lay there, her fists beating at the floor. "Damn you, then!" she shouted. "Damn you to hell!"

THE LATE AFTERNOON SUNLIGHT, FILTERing through the wind-tossed branches of the trees, cast shifting patterns of light over the Queen's head and over the soft blue of her gown. Catherine, setting her minute stitches with care, appered to be intent on her embroidery, but her thoughts were, as always, with her husband. Charles, dear Charles! Why could she not give him the one thing he desired, an heir?

Her eyes misted with tears, and she blinked them quickly away before setting her next stitch. When she had lost the baby she had been fearful of Charles' anger; instead, he had consoled her and wiped her tears away.

"Why, Catherine," he had said, "look not so sad. 'Tis a grief that we share equally. A lost child will ever leave a scar upon the heart; but I would have you know, madam, that your husband is a very potent man. We will have sons, my small one. Strong sons."

He had stayed with her many days, neglecting his mistresses to do so. Lying in her bed, her hand on his warm relaxed body, Catherine would struggle against sleep. He was here, and she wanted to savor his presence to the full. Sometimes she would put her arms about the sleeping Charles and hold him passionately close. But when the rhythm of his sleep was disturbed, he would turn restlessly away. Sometimes though, her passion would awaken him, and he would rekindle the candles. Slowly, almost teasingly, he would divest himself of his nightclothes. Pulling off her clothes, his fingers would touch her body. His eyes would be understanding, for Catherine would tremble so violently that the bed shook beneath her. With his lean brown body welded to her own, his experienced hands seeking out her vulnerable places and sending white-hot shocks of screaming delight through her throbbing body, Catherine could almost believe that he loved her, that he was hers alone. Barbara Castlemaine, that insolent woman! She simply did not exist. Nor did the many other women who constantly took Charles' light fancy.

On one occasion Charles, his hand caressing her body, had said, "You constantly surprise me, Catherine. You explode into such passion that 'tis a rare delight to explore you. Methinks 'tis folly to stray so often from your bed."

Catherine sighed. How hopeful she had been, hearing those words. But of course he hadn't meant them. No one woman could long satisfy him. He had meant them at the time, she knew, for Charles was always sincere, but other faces, other willing bodies, would very soon erase her memory. Catherine sighed again. If he but loved her, her alone, she would ask nothing more of life.

Angel, seated near the Queen, was also lost in thought. Her head was bent industriously over her embroidery frame, but her hand had not moved for several minutes. She had heard the Queen's sigh. Poor little Queen. Her unhappiness, her longing for her husband, seemed but a reflection of her own misery, her own ceaseless longing for Nicholas. Though Catherine was the Queen of England and she but a make-believe lady, it created a bond between them.

Nicholas! Where was he now? When he had walked

out of the house he had walked out of her life, vanishing as though the earth had opened and swallowed him up. After the Restoration and Angel's presentation he had had little to do with Court life. His sword would always be at the King's service, he had declared. He did not wish a place at Court, but rather a private life. The King had been pleased to grant this wish. It was for this reason that the King had made no attempt to find him. He would say, with his charming smile that turned aside all inquiries, "Friend Nicholas wished for a private life. He will return when he wishes to return."

There were times when Angel wished quite desperately for the King to have need of Nicholas' services; perhaps then, he would send his couriers in search of him. After all, he had been gone almost a year, and she knew not if he were alive or dead.

It had been the King's wish that she should reside at the Palace and, as Nicholas' cousin, take her proper place at Court. She had agreed listlessly, for she had been too heartbroken and bewildered to find excitement in the prospect. Even her fear that she would in some way betray her humble origin failed to disturb her. Without Nicholas she was incomplete, and she cared not if she be discovered in her impersonation.

Mrs. Sampson had promised to send word at once if she heard aught from Nicholas. She had not sent. Angel visited the housekeeper at least once a week and found her equally distressed at the lack of news. To Mrs. Sampson, Nicholas was the son she had never had.

Barbara Castlemaine's enmity and the spiteful whispers she circulated might have made Angel's position difficult if it had not been for the friendship of the Queen. There had been a time—and not so long ago—when she had been tempted to yield to the King's persuasions. He attracted her, and his openly expressed desire was balm to her lacerated feelings. But Angel had grown very fond of the Queen. Catherine trusted her—poor lady, who trusted few females—and she could not bring herself to betray this trust. Nevertheless, she had all but made up her mind to take a lover. If Nicholas did not want her, he must be made to see, if she ever saw him again, of course, that other men desired her even if he did not.

Catherine noticed Angel's heightened color, and she wondered of what—or whom—the girl was thinking. Charles was attracted to Angel, Catherine knew, and the possession of this knowledge had ofttimes inclined her to a slight coldness of manner toward Mistress Dawson. It was not that she did not trust the girl; it was simply that she could not imagine anyone being able to resist Charles. Remembering that occasional coldness, Catherine felt remorseful.

She smiled warmly. "Allow me to inspect your work, Angel," she said, stretching out her hand. "I would see if there has been improvement."

"Yes, madam." Angel rose. She grimaced slightly as the Queen took the embroidery frame from her hands. "I fear you will be displeased, madam."

Catherine shook her head as she inspected the clumsy stitches. Angel was too impatient, too restless, she thought. She did not like to sew; her boredom showed in her stitches.

"Oh, Angel," the Queen laughed softly, "you do well to fear. But there, mayhap your talents lie in another direction, for this work is truly disgraceful."

" 'Tis the peace of the Queen's Retreat," Angel said, her voice unrepentant. "It induces sleepiness, and I grow careless, madam."

Catherine smiled. The Queen's Retreat. Charles had planned this little walled garden for her enjoyment; she dispensed with Court etiquette whenever possible and would invariably retreat to her garden. The King had christened it the "Queen's Retreat."

As though her thoughts had conjured him up, the King's deep, lazy voice said from behind them, "And how fare you, ladies, on this gusty day?"

"Charles!" Catherine's eyes brightened. "I hoped you might join us."

Charles strolled forward, his dogs frisking about him. He patted Catherine's shoulder. "Blue becomes you, Catherine," he said. "Wear it more often."

Angel curtsied before him. " 'Tis a pleasant afternoon, sire," she murmured.

"Aye," Charles said, seating himself beside Catherine, "but windy."

"Charles," Catherine broke in before Angel could answer. "Does this color really become me?"

"Have I not said so?" Charles answered.

Poor Catherine, the King thought. How easy 'tis to please her. I would that I could be to her all that she desires me to be. But I am a graceless unfaithful fellow, and 'tis hard for me to play the saint.

"I will plan an entire new wardrobe," Catherine was saying, "and all of my gowns shall be of this same blue."

"Nay," Charles protested. " 'Twill grow monotonous. Some variation there must be."

"Oh." Catherine looked crestfallen. "I had but thought to please you, Charles."

Charles sighed inwardly. "I am well pleased with you, madam," he said gently.

"Would that it were true." Catherine spoke so mournfully, that Charles realized that she had forgotten Angel's presence. So he was not surprised when Angel, curtsying again, said, "I beg your leave to retire, sire—madam."

262

Charles smiled at her, and Angel saw his dark eyes glow with an added warmth. "You have our leave, Mistress Dawson," he said.

He watched her until she was out of sight, then he turned to Catherine. "I come bearing gifts, small one," Charles said softly, his smile caressing her.

Small one, Catherine thought. How she loved him to call her that! It made her feel that her battle was not yet lost. That even now—by the strength of her love alone—her beloved sinner would discover that he had for her a like love.

" 'Tis gift enough that you are here by my side, dear husband." Shyly, Catherine laid her face against his shoulder. "But that you think of me does but rejoice me the more."

Charles put his arm about her and dropped a kiss on her hair. "Be not so humble, Catherine," he said, an edge of irritation in his voice. "You shame me."

"Nay. 'Twas not my intention." Catherine stroked the dark-red velvet of his jacket with a loving hand. "Forgive me, Charles."

"Make me not apologies," Charles said, and he sounded so annoyed that Catherine sat up, startled.

"Charles," she faltered. "How have I offended you?"

Charles bit back the hot words that clamored to be uttered. He was amiable by nature, but sometimes Catherine drove him too far. It was guilt, he supposed, because he could not love her, and because he knew that her heart broke afresh at every new evidence of his unfaithfulness.

"You have not offended, Catherine," he said, forcing himself to speak gently. "If offense there be, then must it always be on my side. For well do I know that I am a most unsatisfactory husband."

"You shall not say so!" She touched his cheek lovingly, "You are the most wonderful man in the world!"

"Catherine! Catherine!" There was a rare note of pleading in his voice. "Do not love me so much, I beg of you."

She looked at him, her dark eyes luminous. "As well ask the sun not to shine," she said, her voice trembling. "For love you I do, Charles, and will until I die." Her head drooped. "And even after death, dearest love," she added in a low voice, "I shall go on loving you."

He put his fingers under her chin, raising her face to his. " 'Tis too intense, this conversation, small one." He smiled. "I like it not, for I am a very shallow fellow."

He saw that she was about to make a further protest and spoke quickly, coaxingly, "Come, Catherine, do you not wish to see your gift?" His finger tickled her under the chin, making her smile. "Are you not just a little curious?"

He was looking at her expectantly. He wanted her to be curious, so she would be, to please him. "Do show it to me," she said eagerly.

He put his hand in his pocket. "Madam," he said, "the daughter of Yvette begs to be presented to you." He drew out his hand and held a small black wriggling bundle toward her.

"Charles!" Catherine took the puppy from him. "Then Yvette is delivered?"

"Aye," Charles grinned wryly. "Yvette, the hussy, is quite shameless. 'Twill be her fourth litter, and though I have threatened to cast her into outer darkness, still she adamantly refuses to tell me the name of her seducer."

Catherine laughed uncertainly. " 'Tis a pity that she cannot speak."

The puppy licked her cheek with a soft pink tongue, and Catherine exclaimed delightedly, "He is beautiful!"

"You wrong the little one," Charles said gravely.

" 'Tis a wench. I have given her a name, but if you like it not, you may change it."

"What is it?"

Charles gave a little bow. "The Lady Charlotte Stuart most earnestly begs Madam, the Queen, to find for her a place in her household."

"It shall be granted." Catherine kissed the top of the puppy's head. "Charlotte?" she said softly. "You knew I would love the name, Charles, did you not? For it is like unto yours."

"Aye, I hoped 'twould please you."

"It does. For now I have Charles Stuart to love—and Charlotte Stuart."

Charles stroked Charlotte's floppy ear. " 'Tis so. But Charlotte, you will find, is the more worthy of your love."

An hour later, after having left the Queen in her apartments with Charlotte, both surrounded by a group of admiring ladies, the King went in search of Angel.

He found her, as he had supposed he would, still in the walled garden—for she had the Queen's permission to use the Retreat as her own. She was seated, her hands folded in her lap, a faraway expression in her eyes.

Angel made to rise, but the King's gesture stayed her.

"Mistress Dawson," Charles said abruptly. "I would talk with you."

He seated himself beside her. "I do not often embrace lost causes," he went on, "but in my pursuit of you I have done so. I have been patient, I think you will agree?"

Angel flushed. "Indeed," she said. "But Your Majesty does me too much honor."

"Honor! Bah!" Charles reached for her hand and held it firmly. "Play not with words," he said, his smile faintly sardonic. " 'Tis rare that I hear truth from the flattering silken tongues about me. 'Twould be refreshing were I to hear it from you."

His fingers tightened about her hand. "I would be your lover, Angel, this you know well. But you have ever eluded me. I ask you now, if I am to accept defeat at your hands?"

She was silent. After a moment, Charles said softly, "Am I then physically unattractive to you?"

"Oh, no!" Angel said, startled. "You must know that you are not." Seeing his expression, she added quickly, " 'Tis truth I speak."

Charles sighed. "Then 'tis still Benbrook?"

She turned her head. "What mean you, Your Majesty?" she said. "I do not recall expressing an interest in my Lord Benbrook."

"Nay, you did not." He smiled at her. "But I am experienced in the follies of women."

"Follies?"

"Aye." He raised her hand to his lips and kissed it lingeringly. "To fix your heart on the unobtainable is folly, is it not?"

"Your Majesty means that my Lord Benbrook is the unobtainable object?" Angel said stiffly.

"You must know it." Charles put his arm about her shoulders. "Friend Nicholas places great value on family ties, as do I. As his cousin, he would give you loyalty, mayhap some small affection."

"Your Majesty, I—"

"Nay," Charles interrupted, "let me continue in my frankness; 'tis for your own good. Nicholas has only one use for women; they afford him physical release and are to him no more than a convenience."

"I had thought, Your Majesty," Angel said indignantly, "that my lord was your friend."

"But naturally he is my friend." Charles frowned.

"Benbrook is to me as my own brother. But I would not have you hurt, Angel. Think you he will talk to you of love? Do not delude yourself, my poor child. The woman does not exist who will hear those words from his lips."

"Yet I have heard them." The words were out before she could stop them.

Charles stared at her. "Do you speak truth, Angel?" he said in a stifled voice. "Benbrook has—has told you that he loves you?"

Angel's lip curled bitterly. "Aye, Your Majesty, he told me; and in the telling was, for a while, a different man."

Charles removed his arm. "For a while? What mean you?"

"Would that I knew," Angel's voice trembled. "He —he said we would be m—married. He said many things. Oh, Your Majesty, gladly would I have wagered my life on the belief that he loved me!"

"Plague take it, Angel, do not cry," Charles said rather desperately.

He drew her close. "There, little one," he soothed. "There, there!" Her sobs increased. "I pray you to desist," he urged, "for well do you know that a woman's tears destroy me."

"I—I am s—sorry," she said, her voice muffled against his jacket. "Forgive me, Your Majesty, but he —he changed so. He said things to me—unforgivable things. He called m—me—" she broke off, gasping.

Charles stiffened. "What did he call you?"

"I cannot tell you."

"You will tell me. Come, Angel, I command it."

She was silent for a moment, then, her voice breaking, she said, "He called me—the K—King's whore!"

She heard Charles's sharply indrawn breath and felt the sudden tightening of his arms. He seemed distressed, and Angel was moved. But it was like him to care, she thought. He was so good, so kind! Would that Nicholas had been more like him!

But he thrust her away from him and turned his back. The ring, the cursed ring! It must be that. And he who desired Nicholas' happiness had done this to him. He had destroyed him and incidentally this poor child. But how could he have known, he thought defensively. Who would have thought that Benbrook, of all people, would fall in love? And with his own cousin! But cousins did fall in love. Why not? But Benbrook! Od's Fish! He'd not have thought it of him.

Angel's sobs had ceased, but Charles scarcely noticed. A vision of the ring seemed to dance before his eyes. Damn it! What a cursed coil he had created! Benbrook off, only God knew where, so how was he to make amends? He could explain to Angel—but—Charles shuddered away from the thought. He was a peaceable man, and the ladies, God bless them, were prone to hysteria. But perhaps the trouble had not been caused by the ring —typically, the thought relieved him. Of course, it need not be the ring. Of a certainty he'd been castigating himself for nothing. But the King's whore? Damn it, it must be the ring, else why call her that.

"I beg Your Majesty's pardon." Angel's voice was low. "I had no right to burden you with my troubles."

"No right?" Charles exclaimed. "Of course you had a right! I have heard rumors that Benbrook wanders through Spain. I will ascertain if this be so. Should it be, I will command his return to our shores."

"I beg that Your Majesty will not," Angel said quickly.

"My mind is made up." Where before he had been remorseful, Charles now felt thoroughly incensed with Benbrook. It eased him to feel so.

"Your Majesty is angered?" Angel asked.

Charles' frown lifted. "Aye," he said ruefully. "But

my anger is not directed against yourself nor my Lord Benbrook."

He leaned forward and dropped a light kiss on Angel's cheek. "Worry not, Mistress Dawson," he said softly. "I'll pursue you no more." He smiled at her warmly. "Henceforth you shall be known as 'the Stuart's lost cause.'"

Long after Angel had curtsied and retired, Charles sat there, his brow furrowed. 'Twould not be easy to explain to Benbrook, for the rogue stood not in awe of him. But explain he must and would.

His spirits considerably lightened, Charles rose. After all, he thought, strolling casually toward the Palace, the fellow would have to forgive him. Damn it, it would be treason else, for was he not the King?

Charles whistled to his dogs. "Aye," he said, stooping to fondle the excited creatures, "and a miserable blackguard King, if I do not soon untangle this coil."

Yvette responded by leaping into his arms. "Ah, Yvette," Charles stroked her soft fur. "Would that you were human, my canine beauty. Od's Fish! What a mistress you'd make!"

BARBARA CASTLEMAINE LOUNGED ON THE sofa, her skirts spread about her. She smiled at her cousin, who sat nearby. "I vow, Buck, I had not expected you to unearth such incredible news!"

The Duke of Buckingham smiled sleepily. He did not believe in going over a subject already exhausted, and he did not trouble to reply.

Barbara cast him an impatient look, then she relaxed against her cushions. Why plague him? He had done well. Angel Dawson, a gutter wench! A one-time inmate of Newgate Prison! Oh, it was famous! Famous! The King should hear of it, she'd see to that. Her brow wrinkled. Charles and his damnably soft heart! How would he receive the news? But surely he would be angry when he thought of a wench who was after all little better than a prostitute associating with his queen and the ladies of the Court.

The Duke was familiar with Barbara's mental processes and followed her thoughts with amusement. It wasn't too difficult since in the last hour she had referred to Mistress Dawson as "that whore" at least six times. Barbara, of course, would not think of herself as a whore. The word thus applied would have shocked and angered her. She was of the mighty Villiers family who could do no wrong.

He eyed her critically, but he could find no fault with her appearance. Barbara was always lovely, but today she was ravishing. Her white silk gown, a recent import from France, was a gift from her latest lover, Lord Denbigh; the square neckline was edged with minute jeweled flowers, the wide skirt, banded at the hemline with alternate rows of emeralds and pearls, was caught up in front to reveal fluffy green petticoats. Diamonds gleamed about her white throat, and the Duke, recognizing them, wondered how long it would be before Lady Denbigh missed them or, alternatively, saw Barbara wearing them.

He grinned to himself. There would be the devil to pay, he had no doubt. For Lady Denbigh was notoriously hot-tempered. Perhaps it would be amusing to pay a call on that lady. A few well chosen words here, a few there. A wish expressed to be shown once again the fabulous Denbigh diamonds. Yes, he would give himself that pleasure. Barbara needed to be taught a lesson, for she had been more than usually annoying.

"Buck," Barbara said suddenly. "I have a plan. I have long meant to visit the Carlson Fair, so tomorrow or the next day we will plan a little expedition, shall we?" She smiled. " 'Twould be a pity to miss it, would it not?"

"And?" The Duke's fair brows rose.

"And then," she said slowly, "I will suggest that we make a tour of Newgate. Mistress Dawson, of course, will be one of the party. The other ladies will be enthusiastic, for those who have never known squalor and misery are fascinated when they see it being suffered by others."

"Perhaps I am unusually dense," the Duke drawled. "But think you that Mistress Dawson will consent to make one of our party?"

Barbara nodded. "Aye, for I shall apologize for my

past misdeeds, and I shall be so charming that she will be quite unable to resist me." She paused, then added triumphantly, "Also, I have something she desires."

"And that is?"

"The King's latest gift to me. My black page. She cannot bear to see me jerk the chain about his neck; it wounds her tender heart. She would take him willingly, were I to offer him."

"My dear Bab, I have never known you to voluntarily give something away." His eyes gleamed mockingly. "Am I then to assume that you are not pleased with your latest acquisition?"

Barbara shuddered. "No indeed. The little black beast is revolting to me."

"Then it is as well to consign him to Mistress Dawson's tender hands." The Duke yawned. " 'Twould have been very careless of you, Bab, had you allowed the King to glimpse the chain about the boy's neck. His Gracious Majesty, as you know, is notoriously tenderhearted and easygoing to the extreme. Cruelty has a way of driving him berserk. He simply cannot bear it, which I think is very tiresome of him. But the point is, coz, had he seen the chain, he would doubtless have freed the boy and then banished you."

The Duke caught sight of Barbara's scowl and laughed. "You do not know our Charles in a fury, Bab. I have seen him knock down a man almost twice his weight, and merely because the poor devil was administering a well-deserved thrashing to his dog; 'twas awe-inspiring, I don't mind telling you. There lay this great hulk of a man unconscious; and there was our prince, the heir to the throne of England, holding a flea-ridden cur in his arms and crooning over the damned thing as if it were a precious treasure."

"Most interesting," Barbara said coldly, "but I believe we were discussing our gutter brat, were we not?"

The Duke laughed softly. "You have changed her name, Bab. Does the title of King's brat no longer please you?"

There was spite in Barbara's smile. "It matters little. I expect that after our little expedition, she will quietly disappear."

"And if she does not?"

"She must," Barbara said fiercely. "I care not where she goes; but I like her not, and I intend to rid the Palace of her presence."

"Her very disturbing and beautiful presence," the Duke said maliciously. "But though you may dispose of Mistress Dawson, Bab, you cannot do likewise with all your rivals. The King is a man of varied tastes, and already he begins to look languishingly on the maiden from France."

Barbara snorted. "That chit! I can deal with her."

"And the others, Bab?"

"If I have to." Barbara smiled. "Do not underestimate my influence, Buck. The King is still strongly attracted to me."

"I doubt not your influence, Bab. How could I, when you prate of it so often?" The Duke's voice had a faintly bored edge. "But your influence is waning. The King turns ever colder, for he likes not your disagreeable temper and your incessant demands."

"The King must put up with it," Barbara's voice rose. "Have I not borne him children, have I not—"

"Not the old refrain, I pray you," the Duke interrupted. "Seek not to work off your tantrums on me, for I quite simply will not put up with them."

Barbara glared at him. He was quite capable of striking her, she knew; he had done so often enough in the past. Even so she might have retorted hotly had a thought not struck her.

"Buck," she said slowly, "I had forgotten my Lord

273

Benbrook's concern in the matter. Why think you he consented to this masquerade?"

The Duke shrugged. " 'Tis hard to believe, I know, but doubtless he was enamored of the wench and allowed her to persuade him."

"Icicle Benbrook!" Barbara's eyes opened wide. "Think you it could be so?"

"I would have wagered against it. I have ever believed the man to be inhuman." The Duke frowned thoughtfully. " 'Tis strange though, the attraction he held for females; they all but clamored to be bedded."

"And did he oblige them?"

"Aye, with a will." The Duke laughed ruefully. "I detest the man, but I am forced to admit that, though he took little note of the female, he performed quite brilliantly."

"Undoubtedly that would excite your admiration," Barbara said scornfully. "As for myself, Benbrook repels me."

"Naturally. But since you pursued him quite shamelessly, and he rejected you so brutally, what else can you say?"

"How dare you! I hate him, I tell you!"

"Bah! Even now Benbrook has but to crook his finger, Bab, and you'd go running like a bitch in heat."

Again Barbara swallowed an angry retort. "Think what you please," she said sweetly. "I care not. Buck, will you accompany us to the Carlson Fair?"

The Duke considered. "Hmm! As a general rule I avoid the haunts of the plebeian. However, if you can successfully cajole the charming Angel, I will be happy to lend my support. I have, as you know, a taste for drama, and I have every anticipation that it might lend itself to just that."

Barbara laughed. "What a cold-blooded swine you are, Buck!"

" 'Tis a Villiers trait that we share, my dear," he answered, rising to his feet. "I will now take my leave of you." He raised her hand to his lips. "Farewell, my beautiful cold-blooded sow."

"Oh, Buck!" she exclaimed, snatching her hand away pettishly. "It seems that you must always have the last word. But I had thought you would wait to greet our Newgate doxy."

"She is coming here?"

"Aye. At the moment she is out riding with our dear royal Jamie." Barbara's lip curled scornfully. "But my message will be delivered to her in due course."

"Jamie, eh?" said the Duke thoughtfully. "Doubtless she has realized that 'tis as well to keep on the good side of the King's favorite bastard."

"She wastes her wiles. He is but a child."

"Aye. But forget not, Bab, that children grow up. And Jamie, as you know, is extraordinarily precocious."

"It matters little," Barbara said lightly. "She will not be here to see Jamie's flowering. Well, Buck, will you stay?"

He shook his head. "Nay. The Angel appears to have developed an aversion to my so charming self. My added presence might have the unfortunate effect of provoking her hasty refusal, and, sweet coz, I would not for the world ruin your pretty scheme."

"You forget, do you not, that I still have my little black beast?"

"Nevertheless," he said, strolling toward the door. "I wish you a good day."

Even as he put out his hand to the latch, the door opened, and Angel was ushered in.

The Duke's eyes traveled over her swiftly and appreciatively, for she was exquisite in her sapphire-blue riding habit with a little flat hat of the same color. Her loosened hair against the blue of her habit seemed to have taken on extra vitality and richness of color.

"A merry good day to you, Mistress Dawson," the Duke drawled, bowing. "I was about to take my leave; therefore may I beg that you will hold me excused?"

"Yes indeed, my lord Duke," Angel answered coldly. She curtsied. "Pray do not let me detain you."

She moved toward Barbara, and the Duke said softly, "I fear me, Bab, that we grow old in that we see Jamie as still a child."

He opened the door. "Nay, Bab," he went on, pausing. "Our Jamie, after all, is not so very young."

THE LITTLE BLACK BOY SAT CROUCHED IN A corner of the room. His wide frightened eyes were fixed upon Angel. He looked strange and somehow pathetic in his bright scarlet breeches and vivid yellow silk jacket; an unhappy little boy, self-conscious and ridiculously dressed. An enormous scarlet turban sat low over his brow, the draped front decorated with a limp white ostrich feather. A gold collar held his neck as if in a vise, and from the collar there dangled a length of chain.

Drucilla Waterman, Angel's maid, stood beside Angel's chair, regarding him with openmouthed astonishment.

"Whatever is it, mistress?" she asked.

"Do not say 'it,'" Angel said sharply. "He is a little boy."

Angel held out her hand to him. "Come," she said. "Don't be afraid."

He got slowly to his feet, hesitated, then moved reluctantly toward her. In front of her he stopped, standing with eyes lowered, his small body trembling.

"Will you tell me your name?" Angel said softly.

"I am called Pip," he answered, enunciating each word clearly. Picking up the dangling chain, he proffered it to her. "Here is my chain, mistress."

When she made no move to take it, he added, "If I go too far away and you have need of me, you pull on the chain."

Angel shuddered, remembering herself chained and helpless.

"No, Pip," she said, "if you are to stay with me, you will not wear a collar and chain."

"You—you do not wish me to wear the c—collar?"

With a quick movement Angel unbuckled it. "There," she said, throwing it aside. "That's the end of that. You are a little boy, not an animal."

The boy stared at her, slow tears welling in his eyes. "I am a b—boy," he repeated. His head lifted proudly. "I am a boy, not an animal."

Angel eyed his bright clothing, her nose wrinkling in distaste. "I think," she said, "that we must dress you like a boy. Do you agree?"

His trembling grew more violent. "I need not wear these clothes?" his voice rose on a note of wild hope. "Oh mistress, is it true? You will not make me wear them? I can—I can dress like a man?"

She smiled. "Like a boy, Pip. You are not yet a man."

"But I have fifteen years, mistress."

"Fifteen!" She stared at him in astonishment. "I would not have thought it."

"I am small for my age." He hesitated, then added shyly. "I am almost a man, mistress."

"You are indeed," Angel agreed.

The tears glistening in his eyes brimmed over and spilled down his cheeks. "You do not hate me because my skin is black?" he asked wonderingly. "You do not call me beast like the other lady did?"

Unable to speak, Angel shook her head.

"You are kind t—to m—me," Pip went on in a

breaking voice. "You are l—like unto the man. He, too, w—was kind."

"The man?" Angel asked. "To whom do you refer?"

"He of the tall slenderness and the gentle eyes. He whom you call Majesty."

"The King?"

Pip nodded. "Yes. Majesty feeds me many sweet-meats, and he knows that I am almost a man, because he talks to me of many things and many places. I thought Majesty meant to keep me with him, but instead he gave me to the lady. The lady is kind to me only when Majesty visits, but when he is gone she is no longer kind."

Suddenly, his movement so abrupt that it took her by surprise, he cast himself at Angel's feet. "Don't send me back to the l—lady," he implored, his hands clutching at a fold of her gown. "Let me stay, mistress! Let me stay! I will be your friend and your servant. No harm shall come to you while Pip watches over you. Oh, let me stay! Please!"

Drucilla's eyes met Angel's. "Poor boy!" she said.

Angel could feel his hot tears soaking through the thin material of her gown. "Hush!" she said. Lifting the heavy turban from his head, she handed it to Drucilla.

"Don't cry, Pip, please don't cry." Her hand stroked his short hair. "Of course you shall stay with me. The lady has given you to me."

He looked up at her, and she saw a light in his eyes. "Thank you," he said simply. "I am happy to be your slave."

"Not slave, Pip," Angel shook her head decisively. "You are free to stay with me or free to go. But if you stay, it shall be as you said, as my servant and my friend."

"Yes, mistress, I shall be your very sincere friend." He smiled. "Friends must speak only the truth, so I will

279

tell you that my real name is M'Zeli. I am the son of M'Hali, who was chief of the M'Pbezi tribe."

"And your father?" Angel asked. "What of him?"

"He is dead. The white men came to our land and they made war upon us. They killed my father, but I remember that he died proudly."

"I'm sorry," Angel said softly. "So sorry!"

As though he gave consolation to her, Pip patted her hand. "The white men bound many of us with ropes, and they took us away from our tribe. I was very young when they took me away, but I vowed always to remember my name, my father's name, and that of the tribe to which I belong."

"Perhaps you will go back some day, M'Z—M'Zeli," Angel's tongue stumbled over the difficult name.

Pip's eyes glinted with merriment. "It is a hard name to say, mistress. I am used to the name Pip. I have been so called since first I came to this country, so why do you not use it?"

"Well," Angel admitted, smiling at him, "It would be easier."

"Then so be it." Pip said. "But all the same, mistress, I am happy that you know my true name." He was silent for a moment, then he said hesitantly, "Is it permitted that I know your name?"

"Of course. My name is Angel Dawson."

"Ah, yes, and you are like the pictures of angels." He sat up straight. "I think, Mistress Angel, that I shall be your friend forever."

Impulsively, she bent and kissed his cheek. "And I yours, Pip," she said softly. "I yours."

Only later, turning restlessly in her bed, did Angel attempt to examine Barbara's true motives for giving her the black page and issuing that cordial invitation. But the more she thought, the more puzzled she became.

Barbara had been friendly and charming, too much

so. Not for one moment had she believed in Barbara's repentance for past unkindnesses or in her earnestly expressed wish that they, from now on, should be friends.

At first Angel had been adamant in her refusal to join the expedition. But the sight of Pip's mournful face made her change her mind. Barbara was not to be trusted, she was sure of that. Was something supposed to happen tomorrow? Angel wondered. Something that might possibly discomfit her?

She sat up in the bed, her heart beating very fast. Quite suddenly she felt terribly afraid. She tried to laugh herself out of it, but the smothering fear remained. Was it a premonition? Did Barbara intend her harm? It was almost dawn before she dropped into an uneasy sleep. When she rose in the morning, heavy-eyed and yawning, the fear was still with her.

B ARBARA CASTLEMAINE, TOURING THE FAIR with her little party, attracted more attention than the freak shows, the Italian acrobats, or the penny shies. Followed by an attentive and awed little crowd, Barbara could not resist performing for them. She stopped before a wooden building. The rough walls had been painted all over with bright whorls of color, birds, and deformed-looking animals. A printed sign advertised "The wild woman. This creature was smuggled from the heart of the African jungle. Do not touch or feed." Standing before the door was a small, bright-eyed man, his hat held out expectantly.

"But how intriguing," Barbara cried, clapping her hands together. "A wild woman, imagine! I simply must see her."

Beaming ingratiatingly, the man stepped away from the door. "Worth seein' 'n' all, she is. You ain't never seen nothin' like her before. Jus' don' get too near her," he warned. "Bite your han' clean orf if you give her half a chance."

The Duke of Buckingham shrugged. Tossing some money into the man's hat, he strolled languidly after Barbara, who had already darted inside. The rest of the party followed. The crowd, unwilling to lose sight of the notorious Lady Castlemaine and the great Duke of Buckingham, paid their pennies and filed in silently.

It was hot inside the wooden building and dark. An unpleasant odor pervaded the place. Barbara wrinkled her nose distastefully.

"Where is she, Buck?" she demanded petulantly. "Where is the wild woman?"

The Duke looked about him. "Beneath that heap of rather foul-looking straw, I would imagine," he said, pointing with the small cane he carried.

"Can the creature be sleeping? Do rouse it, Buck."

" 'Twill be my pleasure." The Duke stepped over to the pile of straw. "Come, come," he said, prodding with the cane. "Show yourself, my wild jungle maiden."

A snarl answered him, and a head shot through the straw.

Barbara gasped. "Buck!" she breathed, stepping back hastily. "Is it dangerous?"

"Oh, excessively so," he answered. Amused, he stared calmly at the wildly rolling eyes in the ebony face, the great thatch of woolly black hair, and the skinned lips, showing yellowed teeth, filed into sharp points.

"Come away, Buck," Barbara said sharply. "It's getting up!"

"So it is," the Duke drawled, his eyes on the rising apparition. "But I am in no danger, I assure you."

Fully revealed, the wild woman was short, almost dwarf-like in stature. Her scrawny sweating black body was naked; her breasts, hanging like empty bags, had been painted in vivid stripes of red and green. The chain about her waist, the end secured to the wall, had rubbed her flesh raw. She stood before them, hissing behind her pointed teeth, making wild gestures with her hands, and lunging forward threateningly.

Lady Melford, standing behind Barbara, gave a little

shriek. "Oh dear, what an appalling creature! Do let's go."

Barbara ignored her. "Mistress Dawson is looking quite pale, Buck." She shot a sly look at Angel, who was standing just inside the door. "Methinks she does not care to see a creature chained."

"No." Angel answered. "I do not."

"Heavens!" Barbara gave an amused laugh. "How serious you are! One would think you had felt the weight of chains upon your own limbs."

Angel did not reply. The crowd looked at her curiously, but their eyes almost immediately returned to Barbara. Oh, the scandals this woman created, the tales they had heard! She fascinated them, this perfumed and arrogant whore who, if the tales be true, was so dear to the King's heart.

"Come, Buck," Barbara turned to the door. Her head high, she swept out into the sunshine. The Duke lingered for a moment. " 'Tis only fair to warn you," he said, touching the wild woman's sweating body with the end of his cane, "that your paint is running."

Startled, the woman looked down. The Duke laughed, and his laughter enraged her. "Think you're bleedin' clever, don' you!" she snapped. "Get out o' here, you lousy swine, or I'll have me man teach you somethin' what you won' forget."

"Ah," the Duke raised his fair brows. "A genuine wild woman, I see. 'Tis doubtless easier work than spreading your legs for any man with a penny in his pocket."

The woman gave a scream of rage. "Penny? Me! Never took nothin' off my gen'lemen but silver. I wasn' no penny whore, an' no bleedin' toff's a-goin' ter say I was!"

"Interesting." The Duke turned and strolled to the

door. "You may restore your paint now. Good day to you, beautiful wild one."

His boredom slightly alleviated by the little exchange, the Duke rejoined Barbara. Followed by the ladies of the Court and her admiring audience, she was indefatigable.

Sullenly he allowed himself to be steered past heaped-up stalls of vegetables, sweetmeats, and little flat cakes. He waited while the ladies turned over great bolts of muslin, exclaiming over the color and texture and finally to the disgust of the owner of the stall walking away leaving unfurled and crumpled bolts of cloth behind them. Only Angel, the Duke noticed, stood apart, her page standing quietly beside her.

Barbara exclaimed over the pig-faced boy, the half-man, half-reptile, the fat woman, and the two-headed dog. She screamed with excitement over the tumbling twins, whose bodies were joined together from shoulder to knee; she had her fortune told, and she bought hot mutton pies and ate them with every sign of enjoyment.

"Enough," the Duke said at last. "You play the innocent country maiden badly, Bab. 'Tis becoming cursed tedious."

She gave him a black look, but she did not protest when he led her firmly past a stall bright with ribbons and laces.

The crowd still followed. Lady Castlemaine was more fun than the fair. Whore, she might be, but she was very beautiful in a gown of gauzy yellow, the skirt embroidered with bright butterflies. Her cheeks were rose-flushed, her blue eyes sparkling, her red hair a flame in the sunlight. But beautiful as she was, eyes turned more frequently to the girl who walked slightly behind her, and who wore a simple gown of lime-green silk. For beauty, the crowd decided, this girl had their vote.

285

The black page, keeping close to the side of the girl in green, roused some good-natured mirth, so proudly did he strut.

Though Pip still cast an occasional fearful glance in Barbara's direction, he was indeed proud and happy to be in attendance upon his Mistress Angel. She had restored his manhood he felt, and for that alone he would have adored her. In the dark-blue uniform that Drucilla had managed to procure from sources unknown save only to herself, Pip stood tall and felt that he had left boyhood behind. Mistress Angel might look upon him as a boy if she so desired, but he was a man, and if she were in need of protection, as a man he would protect her.

Pip looked down at the lime-green cloak he carried over his arm. Mistress Angel had not wanted to bring her cloak on such a hot day; but Pip had insisted, knowing how easily an English summer day could turn chill. So, in a sense, he could tell himself that he was already protecting her.

Pip glanced up at Angel. She was smiling at a remark made by one of the Court ladies. She seemed happy and carefree, and yet, the boy decided, she was not happy. Something was troubling her, he could sense it. Was it something to do with the Lady Castlemaine and the tall man with the light hair, him they called the Duke of Buckingham?

Casting a lowering suspicious look at them, Pip moved nearer to Angel, his shoulder brushing her arm.

"Are you enjoying yourself, Pip?" Angel asked.

"Yes, mistress," he said, returning her smile.

Angel opened her small embroidered purse. "Here," she said, taking out some coins. "You have seen none of the shows as yet. 'Tis not often the fair comes to London; therefore would it please me if you would enjoy some of the attractions."

Pip looked at the coins she was extending to him. "I thank you, mistress," he said politely, "but I prefer to stay with you."

Angel looked at him doubtfully, but seeing the determined set of his mouth, she said mildly, "Very well, but take the money anyway. You must buy yourself some sweetmeats at least, must you not?"

She pressed the money into his palm, and he took it protestingly. "Yes, mistress," he said soberly. Aware that he might be lacking in courtesy, he smiled at her, adding, "I thank you."

Barbara had overheard and remarked loudly, "Come now, Angel, you must not spoil the creature. They are apt to take grievous advantage of our weaknesses, I fear."

"I am sure that my Lady Castlemaine would not under any circumstances show weakness," Angel answered demurely. "But I do thank you for your concern."

Hearing the Duke's soft laugh, Barbara flung him an angry glance. But determined not to allow him to upset her, she turned her head and smiled winningly at Angel. "Will you not call me Barbara?" she asked. "For I mean us to be the greatest of friends, you know."

Angel hesitated. "If you wish it, of course," she answered almost reluctantly, "then I will call you so."

Lady Melford threw a startled glance at her sister. The Countess of Danford-Haven, returning the glance, said softly, "'Tis not like the Castlemaine to be so friendly. What think you, Anne, can be behind it?" Lady Melford shrugged. "Anything is possible with that woman, Margaret, as well you know. All the same, I would not like to be the object of her tender attention."

Barbara, stopping short suddenly, swung round to face them. "Buckingham is bored, good people," she declared. "We must banish his gloom, must we not? How

287

say you all, shall we on to the next attraction in this most pleasant day?"

Lady Melford, whose feet were hurting her, hurriedly agreed. The others—with the exception of Angel —followed suit.

Ignoring Angel, Barbara cried out merrily, " 'Tis a famous surprise I have. Not only is it a novel idea, but we will at the same time be doing our bounden duty to the wretched and the poor."

A murmur greeted this, and Barbara went on in her loud voice. "For only if we be knowledgeable may we hope to improve their lot."

Blank faces looked back at her. The Duke smiled. "I pray you, Bab," he said softly, "no noble speeches. I have ever found them cursed boring, to say nothing of the fact, sweet coz, that you are not suited to make them."

"Will you not put us out of our suspense, Lady Castlemaine?" the Countess asked. "Pray tell us your plan."

" 'Tis a tour of Newgate that I have planned," Barbara said triumphantly. "There, is that not thrilling?"

"Indeed!" Lady Melford cried, forgetting her aching feet. "I have oft wanted to go there."

"And I," the Countess said. " 'Tis a clever idea." She gave an anticipatory shudder. "Is it safe, think you?"

A fat woman standing near to the Countess cried out truculently, "Don' you worry none, me lady! The poor swines ain't goin' ter spoil your pretty face none. Locked away they are an' can' get ter you."

"Aye," a man shouted. "You can trus' 'em ter act pretty for the bleedin' King's whore!"

"Bab, dear heart," the Duke murmured, "the crowd grows ugly. They like not your noble act."

Barbara had not even heard them. Her eyes, narrowed and malicious, were on Angel's white face. "You look so pale, Angel," she said. "Is anything wrong?"

"Nothing." Angel looked straight into her eyes contemptuously.

Barbara flushed. "Then you approve?" she demanded, prepared to argue.

She knows! Angel thought. This, then, is the reason for her show of friendship. Newgate! Dear God! She could not! She could not! Even were she to fall in with the plan it would avail her nothing, Barbara would spread the news far and wide. Why should she subject herself to this added torture then?

"Do you approve?" Barbara persisted. "Of course, if you're afraid, I shall understand."

So that was it? My Lady Castlemaine wanted her full satisfaction. She wanted her to grovel at her feet, to beg, to plead. Damn her! She'd not give her that too. Besides, what had she to fear? Newgate could not engulf her again. She was a free subject.

"Afraid?" Angel heard herself say calmly. "But why should I be? The tour is, in my opinion, in poor taste, but I am willing to accompany you."

The flash of Barbara's eyes told Angel that she was right. Barbara had not so much wanted to tour Newgate as she had wanted to see the complete disintegration of her victim.

"Then shall we go?" Barbara snapped.

"A wise decision," the Duke said, his eyes on the stone clenched in the hand of a little wizened man. "Though I cherish you dearly, Bab, I have a strong objection to spilling my blood in your cause."

For the first time Barbara became aware of the temper of the crowd. But she was not without courage. "Out of the way, you!" she shouted, pushing the man nearest to her. "How dare you bar my way!"

"Ain't she a gran' lady?" A jeering voice cried.

"Me Lady Castlemaine don' like for you ter put them dirty han's o' yours on her!"

"We'll show her! Hang the bleedin' whore up by her heels!"

"Hang 'em all up, says I! The whole perishin' lot o' 'em!"

Pip pressed close to Angel. "I will not let them harm you," he said, trying to speak confidently. He patted her arm with trembling fingers. "I will not!" he repeated.

"I know." Angel tried to smile at him. "It—it will be all right."

The crowd swirled in upon them, faces menacing, hands clenched. Then, as if in answer to a prayer, a woman's shrill voice cried excitedly, "Look! Look! 'Tis Nellie Gwynne!"

"Aye. Pretty Nellie's come to dance us a merry jig."

Somebody raised a cheer, and the crowd took it up. "Nellie! Nellie! Bless her sweet face!"

"Nellie's raising her petticoats for a jig. Where's the fiddler? One o' you start the bleedin' music for our Nellie."

Like magic, the crowd melted away and surged toward the new attraction.

Angel saw her then, little Nell Gwynne of the King's Theater. With her skirts raised to her knees, her honey-gold curls tumbled about her flushed piquant face, her blue eyes flashing, Nell danced her jig.

Angel tried to push forward, but the crowd, increasing with every second, were packing themselves tightly about the little figure.

" 'Tis the gutter actress," Barbara said scornfully.

"They say the King casts his eyes her way," Lady Melford cooed, her eyes on Barbara's face.

The Duke did not hear Barbara's retort. He followed thoughtfully after them. If the King was indeed interested in the little orange vendor turned actress, then who better than Buckingham to fan that interest to a stronger flame? Charles was at all times generous, and how much more so would he be with pretty Nellie to fondle? It had been said that Charles had already enjoyed the charms of Mistress Gwynne, but Buckingham was not inclined to believe it. The wench was a tempting piece, very tempting indeed, and 'twould not be like Charles to let her slip away.

NEWGATE, GRAY AND UGLY, WAS ABOUT TO swallow her again! The Duke, with Barbara on one arm, politely extended the other to Angel. She laid the tips of her cold fingers on his sleeve. Moving forward like someone in the grip of a feverish nightmare, she could not rid herself of the impression that Newgate had won. It had reached out for her and found her, but this time it would not let her go.

"Show us the Common Side first, fellow," Barbara commanded the guard.

The stench hit them like a blow; only Angel, moving through her nightmare, seemed unaware of it. Voices came to her, but faint and far off. She saw lacy kerchiefs pressed to fastidious noses. She heard Pip's whimper, the Duke's curse, and the ladies' horrified shrieks, but they were the visitors in her nightmare; only for her was it reality.

Stony-faced, she traversed the endless corridors, descended once more the steeply winding staircases, and in the dark bowels of the prison, halted before that same door that had enclosed her into terror and despair.

The guard, fitting the key in the lock, hesitated and looked inquiringly at Buckingham. "It ain't a sight for ladies what's del'cate bred," he ventured.

"Open that door, you fool!" Barbara snapped, "And be quick about it."

The guard shrugged, but he obeyed.

Angel stood there, hands folded in front of her, and not a muscle of her face moved as the shrieking prisoners made a forward rush. Those gaunt frames, those yellowed diseased faces, the wild hopeless eyes, the savagery of them—they were real to her. She could feel their hatred as they glared at the finely dressed visitors; it leaped out at them like a lightning flash, and to Angel it was like a violent physical blow.

She could feel herself changing, coming alive again, but alive to a terrible hatred of the beautiful arrogant woman who had brought her back to this thing. She turned her eyes toward Barbara, and the Duke too suffered a shock as he met their savage glare.

"Back!" the guard bellowed, as the prisoners surged forward. Snatching his whip from his belt, he lashed out at them. "Back, you whores! Back you stinkin' animals!"

Pip watched. He did not like this place, and he felt that he could not breathe in the darkness and the horror. He stood like a small black statue, his eyes darting from one to the other but always coming back to his mistress. He would not run, as every instinct urged him to do; he would stay with her and lead her safely back to a bright sane world. His eyes sharpened as he saw Barbara Castlemaine's furtive backward step. Another step she took, then another. Now she was standing behind his mistress, and she slowly lifted her hands.

"Mistress!" Pip screamed. "Turn, Mistress! Turn!"

Angel whirled. In a second she saw the trick and her rage and hatred exploded. She caught Barbara's extended hands. "So you'd throw me to them, would you, you scented whore?" Her grip tightened like iron bands. "Well, see how you like it, my Lady!"

293

"Buck!" Barbara shrieked, as Angel dragged her to the door. "Help me, Buck!"

Angel's laugh was loud and harsh. "Too late!" she panted.

Barbara felt her feet slipping beneath her. "Let me go, you gutter scum! Buck! Buck!"

With a strong thrust, Angel sent her hurtling into the midst of the prisoners. The shrieks of the other ladies mingled with Barbara's.

The Duke had not moved. His face was a little paler than usual as he watched the screaming women swarm over Barbara's sprawled body, their fingers tearing, gouging, as each fought for a share of the spoils.

"Your Grace!" the guard shouted. He stared at the Duke, waiting for his command. It did not come. "Y—your grace. They'll kill her!"

It was Angel who sickened first. "Get her out," she commanded the guard. "Now! At once!"

Sobbing, Barbara was forcibly dragged from the women. Her gown had been ripped from her body, and there were long, angry gouges across her breasts. Her face was bruised and bleeding, and one corner of her mouth was torn.

"Buck! You swine!" She collapsed on the floor. "I'll make you pay! I'll kill you!"

The Duke, his nostrils flaring in distaste, stepped back. Taking his cloak from his shoulders, he handed it to the guard.

"Cover the lady," he said. "The stench she gives off turns my stomach."

"Yes, your grace." The guard took the cloak. Hesitantly he draped it about Barbara's shoulders. "There, me lady," he muttered. "Now you'll be all right."

Barbara clutched the cloak about her and rose shakily to her feet. Her eyes searched wildly for Angel and discovered her in the midst of the ladies.

"As for you," she shouted, spitting out her words venomously, "you'll be sorry for this day's work!" She began to tremble. "Thief! Dirty whore! I'll have you back in there with your true class!"

Angel suddenly felt very tired. "I do not doubt it, Lady Castlemaine," she said. The words came out in a strange slurred sound.

"And now you will pretend it was an accident, Dawson, I suppose?" Barbara sneered. "Your class has ever thought that tears and groveling serve them well."

Her voice pricked Angel back to life. "Lie to you, Lady Castlemaine? Grovel? Never! I would do it again! My place was in there once, as you have said. You deserve to know what it is like too! Perfume and paint and fine gowns, the luxury of the King's bed—do you think these things disguise what you are?"

She took a step nearer to Barbara, her eyes blazing, "You are what I have called you—a scented whore! A bitch in heat! You are lower than a gutter drab, for they, at least, are honest. They seek not to call their profession by another name as you do!"

"You are insolent, Dawson!"

"Am I so?" Angel lifted her hand and smacked Barbara's face. "Add that to my account, Lady Castlemaine!" Barbara reeled from the blow.

"I will," she said. Her hand went to her throbbing cheek. "Oh, I will, Dawson, you need have no doubt!"

The guard looked from one to the other, his eyes worried. If aught went wrong with these fine ladies, then it would be he that would be blamed. Fine ladies! he sneered inwardly. Shouting, calling each other names! Bah! They were all the same when they lost their tempers. The grand Lady Castlemaine, now, she was no better than his Meg, for Meg, when she was in one of her furies, carried on the same way. There wasn't a happorth of difference between the classes, not when females lost their tempers. As for that Lady Castlemaine, though she gave herself such grand airs, it wouldn't surprise him to learn that the other lady was right. He glanced at Angel. She was different from Castlemaine, he grudgingly admitted. She was highborn all right, you could see that with half an eye. And that being so, it just made it the more shameful. She oughtn't to have acted the way she did; she'd been brought up to know better.

The Duke shrugged his satin-clad shoulders and began strolling away. The guard's alarm increased when the other ladies followed the Duke's lead, casting frightened glances behind them.

"My lady," the guard cut ruthlessly across Barbara's continuing tirade. "His grace is leavin'. I don' wan' ter be respons'ble for you, not when it's me what'd be called ter account if harm come ter you."

"Wait for me, Buck!" Barbara cried imperiously. "Oh!" her voice rose as she hurried after him. "How dare you leave me!"

Holding his lamp high, the guard peered at Angel. "Best foller me close," he said gruffly. "People has been known ter get 'emselves los' down here." Grumbling under his breath, he followed after the party. The swells always made trouble, he thought. Likely he'd not get a penny for his trouble either. The Duke, now, he was a mean one; he'd seen his type before. And with Lady Castlemaine in such a fury, it wouldn't surprise him if she gave him a smack on his nose instead of a tip. It wasn't his fault, of course, but it was no use expecting females to be reasonable. The lady in the green gown might hand him something, but he wasn't too hopeful. It had been a bad day, a very bad day.

He looked over his shoulder. There was no sign of the other lady or the black boy. Oh well, he'd see this lot off the premises, then he'd come back for her. Frowning, he obeyed Barbara's sharp command. "Hold the lamp higher, you fool!"

Angel watched the light disappearing; yet she could not make herself move. Pip crept closer to her. He would not have thought that the feeble light of the lamp would have made such a difference, but the creeping darkness was terrifying. His mistress was only a vague outline to him now. He wanted to urge her to move, to beg her if necessary. He couldn't understand her terrible stillness which quite suddenly he found more frightening than the darkness. He fought the sob rising in his throat; he was a man, he must remember that, and it was for him to protect her.

Trapped! Trapped! The words echoed in Angel's head. She was not even aware that Pip was standing so stiffly at her side. The silence was complete, except for the dripping of the water from the perpetually oozing walls. No sound penetrated from beyond those thick doors. The darkness was like a thick, enveloping cloak dropped over her head, shutting off her breath, her life!

Pip fought another sob and lost, and the sound broke the spell which bound her. With a wild cry, she picked up her skirts and fled along the corridor.

"Mistress! Mistress!" Pip screamed.

She didn't hear him. Terror-stricken, she blundered along one corridor and down the next. It seemed to her that the walls were closing in upon her, and she flung her arms wide as if she would push them farther apart. Often, losing her balance, she went reeling against the damp walls, bruising her flesh and catching her gown on sharply projecting points; ripping the bodice so badly that the two halves hung down over her arms. By luck rather than judgment, she found the first staircase and fought her way upward with the breath laboring harshly in her lungs, her hands clawing at the iron rail.

"Light!" she moaned. "Oh, God, let me but see the blessed light!" She must climb out of this dark pit! She must find the light once more!

Pip managed to keep up with her, and now, though Angel did not know it, his hand clutched a fold of her skirt. Stumbling behind her, his feet slipping on the stairs, he noticed the darkness graying. Another tortuous flight, then another, and all the time the light grew stronger. Pip released her skirt. They had found their way out. There was the first corridor along which they had come before starting the downward descent. There at the end the door which led into the grimy office.

"Mistress," Pip called, running after her.

Angel whirled. "Pip!" she cried, as though surprised to see him there. She recovered quickly. "Come, Pip," she said urgently. "Come now!"

She began to run again. Reaching the door, she tore it open and fled past the startled guard, who was on his way back. Snatching up his keys, he went after her to the next door.

"Wait, ma'am, I got ter unlock the door."

Angel saw the keys in his hand. Freedom lay just beyond that last great scarred door. Her legs began a violent trembling. Sighing, she sank to her knees and covered her face with her hands.

The guard made no move to assist her. "Your frien's is waitin' outside for you, ma'am," he said.

His eyes narrowed as they flickered over her torn bodice, the low-cut white green-ribboned shift beneath, the firm white breasts which were almost entirely revealed.

"God's teeth!" he muttered low, "but ain't she a little beauty!" Ah! What wouldn't he give to have her in his bed!

The black boy ran to her side. Encountering the

boy's fierce scowl, the guard grinned. The way the black imp glared at him, you'd think he'd raped her. He should give him a smack on the ear for looking at him like that, but it was too much trouble.

Raped her! The guard smiled rather wistfully. Just give him the chance! He leaned against the door, his keys jangling in his hand. He didn't mind waiting until she'd pulled herself together. He liked looking at her. He craned his neck a little to see past the boy. Most of all, he liked looking at her luscious breasts.

Pip bent over Angel protectively, trying to hide her from that man with his greedy eyes. "Mistress," he began, "shall I—?" he stopped short, his eyes widening as he saw the scars on her bowed back.

He bore similar scars on his own back. He understood her frantic flight now. She had been in bondage, even as he, and once again had felt herself to be trapped and helpless. He took the cloak from his arm and shook it out. Gently, he laid it over her shoulders.

Angel looked up. "Thank you." She hesitated. "I must have seemed strange to you. If I frightened you, then I ask you to forgive me. There was a reason—for the way I behaved, I mean—but I have no need to explain, it will be clear to you ere long."

"It is clear now," Pip answered. Kneeling before her, he smoothed the cloak over her shoulders, tied the ribbons in a neat bow under her chin, and drew the hood forward to hide her tangled hair. He smiled at her. "I have seen the mark of the slave," he said, touching her back, "and it does but make the bond between us stronger. You are my mistress and my friend, and now, through the union of our suffering, you have become to me as my mother and my sister."

Rising to his feet, he extended his hand. "You must walk with pride and dignity, for that is every man's right.

And one man may not humble his brother in another's eyes without he bear the smudge of shame upon his soul."

She placed her hand in his, and he said gravely, "Pull the hood a little more forward, mistress, for in its shadow much may be hidden from prying eyes."

He drew her to her feet. How strange he was, she thought, and how gentle his personality. Sometimes he seemed—as indeed he was—a child. But at other times almost terrifyingly mature.

"My shoulder is strong, mistress," Pip said, looking up at her. "If you will rest your hand upon it, you will find it to be an aid to your weakness."

Smiling at last, Angel shook her head. "I thank you for the offer, but I have no need of support. You have aided me, little friend, far more than you can possibly know."

"But I do know, mistress." He gave her a wide, sparkling grin. With that grin, the maturity dropped from him. He was no longer M'Zeli, son of a chief, he was Pip, her page.

Angel nodded to the guard. "Open the door, please."

"Yes, ma'am," the guard said and hastened to obey.

"Thank you." Angel opened her purse. Selecting two gold coins, she placed them in his ready palm. "You have been most patient."

The guard looked down at the money. "I ain't got no complaints," he assured her with a beaming smile. "Thank you kin'ly, ma'am. You're what I call a real lady, you are, 'cause you knows how ter treat a workin' feller decen'."

SURROUNDED BY HER LADIES, THE QUEEN sewed on her tapestry, and listened to the sweet singing of Elizabeth Holt. A faint smile lifted her lips.

The blue room was tiny and compact—a rarity in that palace of great, echoing chambers—it was peaceful too, and secluded. Next to her walled garden, the Queen thought contentedly, she liked to retire to this room.

Part of her contentment, of course, she admitted honestly, was due to the continuing absence of Lady Castlemaine. Catherine's soft mouth hardened as she thought of her. How brazen the woman was, how arrogantly sure of herself! She hated her! Catherine could never forget the time when Charles had requested—though later, when she proved stubborn, he had ordered—that she take the brazen creature into her household. She had all but cried herself blind, but Charles was not to be moved from the stand he had taken. And so she, his wife, no longer able to bear his displeasure, had been forced to take in his mistress.

Charles was always so kind to her, so sweet-tempered—except in that one distressing instance—and she hoped, in view of the story circulating, that he would be charitable to little Mistress Dawson.

The smile grew almost malicious. Lady Castlemaine's condition when she returned from that ill-fated trip to Newgate Prison had been quite deplorable. Guiltily Catherine straightened her lips. It was wicked to smile—wicked to feel pleased over another's misfortunes—and when she made her confession, the good Father would undoubtedly tell her so. Nevertheless she had been pleased, and when the full story was made known to her she had secretly applauded Angel's action.

She had sent for Angel and had heard from her lips the true tale of the great deception. She was a queen and the daughter of a queen; yet she had understood Angel's desire to lift herself from her sordid life. She tried to picture herself in the girl's position. Given such an opportunity as the one held out by Lord Benbrook, she too would have grasped it eagerly.

Angel's concern had been for Lord Benbrook. She feared that the King, angry at the deception practiced upon him, might not find it easy to forgive his old friend. Catherine had softened still further—for her passionate and hopeless love for Charles enabled her to recognize love in the mere uttering of a name—and there had been love in Angel's voice when she spoke of "my Lord Benbrook." But she could not soothe the girl with easy assurances of the King's understanding; for gentle and easygoing as he was, a deceived Charles was a different man.

Charles had not yet heard of the incident. He had joined the Duke of Reading's hunting party, but the riders he had sent on ahead had brought the news that the King would return today. Catherine hoped that he might be sympathetic, and she had promised Angel that she would intervene on Lord Benbrook's behalf.

Catherine glanced out of the window. It would be pleasant in her garden, but perhaps she should stay here. Charles knew well her habits, and it was here that he invariably sought her after a prolonged absence. He, who was careless in many respects, was punctilious in presenting himself to his wife and inquiring after her health. She could wish, though, she thought wistfully, that it was love rather than duty that brought him so immediately to her side.

Elizabeth Holt was requesting to render them another song and was about to do so, but a tapping on the door interrupted.

"Enter," Catherine called.

The door opened, and Lady Ashley came into the room. Her face was flushed, her hair slightly disheveled. "Madam," she said rather breathlessly. "The King comes this way."

Catherine's lips tightened. Lady Mary Ashley was one of Barbara Castlemaine's few intimate women friends, and she could not believe it to be mere chance that Lady Ashley should chance to be sauntering in the little-used corridor leading to the blue room. Had she been set to intercept the King? Her blush, the untidiness of her usually neat hair, seemed to be proof that she had encountered him.

"Thank you," Catherine said calmly.

Lady Ashley looked as if she would say more, but meeting Catherine's eyes, she wilted. Curtsying, she left the room.

Catherine folded her work. Dismissing her ladies with a pleasant smile, she sat back in her chair, her eyes on the door.

She had not long to wait. It opened abruptly and Charles entered. Her heart leaped, as it always did at her first sight of him. "Charles," she said, the quiver in her voice betraying her emotion. " 'Tis good to see you."

He went to her side. "You are well, Catherine?" he inquired, stooping to kiss her cheek.

"Thank you, yes."

"I am glad to hear it. 'Tis reassuring to find someone who has not a tale of woe to impart."

She saw the frown between his brows, and her heart sank. So he had heard. He was not only angry but abstracted too, and because he was so rarely angry—with her at least—she did not speak. He would tell her what was in his mind in good time.

Lovingly she watched him wander over to the window. The part of her mind that was entirely divorced from the problems that beset her admired his tall, elegant figure clad in his favorite wine-red jacket and breeches. Catherine smiled to herself as she thought of Charles' extensive wardrobe. No matter how many additions he might make, he obstinately refused to part with that jacket or the breeches. His Master of Wardrobe complained bitterly of the threadbare condition of the garments, but to all his complaints Charles would smile and say lightly, "Are you king or am I? 'Tis strange that you would deny your King the comfort of his old clothes."

Charles stared unseeingly out of the window. It would seem that an ill star hovered over him, he thought, tapping moodily on the window frame with his fingertips. First there had been the news that his sister, Minette, had been forced to delay her sailing date—on that last visit Minette had seemed tense. And it appeared to him that she had lost much weight. Plague take it, he was worried about her! If that were not enough, he had learned that Barbara was once more pregnant. His child, she insisted—though he doubted it—nevertheless his conscience, if not his belief, would force him to provide for it.

His frown deepened. He had thought Lady Ashley to be wandering in her mind when first she had poured out her extraordinary story of Benbrook's deception. And then she had rattled on about the visit to Newgate Prison where, it appeared, Mistress Dawson unappreciative of Barbara's offer of friendship, had pushed her in among the prisoners.

He had been inclined to dismiss the whole thing as nonsense, but Mary Ashley was a pretty wench; and after one or two kisses he had consented to visit the injured Barbara.

"Charles?" Catherine ventured at last. "You—you seem disturbed."

He turned to face her. "Disturbed, Catherine?" he said, with a fine edge of sarcasm to his voice. "I wonder why you should think so?"

He moved toward her. "Am I to understand," he said, seating himself beside her, "that you know nothing of the adventures of Mistress Dawson or of her sponsor, Lord Benbrook?"

"I know, Charles. It is on this matter that I wish to speak."

"Indeed?" He raised his dark brows. "Then why did you not speak?"

"Because," Catherine answered with a touch of indignation, "you seemed to wish to be alone with your thoughts."

Charles considered this. " 'Tis true," he said. He looked at her, and she saw a faint twinkle in his dark eyes. "Tactful Catherine, who seeks the right moment to put her case for Mistress Dawson."

"And my Lord Benbrook," Catherine said quickly.

" 'Pon my soul!" Charles exclaimed. "I'd not have thought it of Benbrook!" He brooded darkly for a moment. "It ill becomes him to practice such deception upon his King and friend!"

"Charles!" Catherine said, distressed. " 'Twas not a harmful deception. If you would but allow me to tell you

305

the story as Mistress Dawson recounted it to me, then I believe you will readily forgive them."

He had already made up his mind to do so. He valued Benbrook's friendship; and as for Mistress Dawson, how could he be angry with the beautiful minx? However, experience had taught him that it did not do to relent too easily.

"And what of Lady Castlemaine's grievous injuries?" he inquired coldly.

"I care not!" Catherine cried, her hatred and jealousy overwhelming her. "I hope her injuries are proving to be painful! 'Tis doubtless wicked of me, but I do hope that! I do!"

Charles could not have been more astonished at her fiery defiance. "Madam!" he said, trying to speak harshly. "I cannot believe you to be so lacking in Christian sympathy."

"Where Lady Castlemaine is concerned, I have none at all."

"Well!" Charles said weakly. "Well!"

He thought of Barbara's battered appearance, the ludicrous black eye and the swollen nose, crimson at the tip.

"M—madam," his voice quivered. "You sh—should be ashamed. I tell you to your f—face that you, madam, are a v—vixen."

"Charles?" She peered at him doubtfully. "Charles, are you laughing?"

"Aye." His shoulders shook. "For I h—have ever been a cursed c—c—cold-hearted man."

"Oh, Charles!" Catherine laid her hand on his arm, laughing at last. "We are both very wicked, are we not? But her appearance was—was most comical. Oh, Charles, I pray you, stop laughing! 'Tis giving me a pain in my side."

A tap came on the door, and Charles tried to sober. " 'Tis doubtless Mistress Dawson," he said. "I bade her present herself." He looked at Catherine, his eyes still full of laughter. "You are wicked, madam, and I'll have naught to do with you. Bid the wench enter."

Angel came in quickly. Her manner, when she knelt to kiss the King's hand, was faintly defiant. It was obvious that she meant to plead her case, or at least, Charles thought with a twinge of jealousy my Lord Benbrook's.

"Your Majesty," Angel began. "Have I your permission to speak?"

He had meant to adopt a tone of dignified rebuke, but the wench, gazing at him with those great violet eyes, was just too beautiful. Dignified rebuke was not for Charles Stuart, not if he must apply it to beauty in distress. Smiling, he rose to his feet. "All is forgiven," he said, holding out his hand. Assisting her to rise he added, "Though doubtless I shall have much to say to my Lord Benbrook upon his return, the nature of which, I trust, will blister his ears. I doubt if 'twill seriously discomfit him, the insolent rogue!"

Angel returned his smile. "Your Majesty is not angry?"

"Aye," Charles said. "Angry that Benbrook did not allow me to share in the molding of such beauty."

Catherine smiled at her. "You see, my dear, all is well."

Angel drew a deep breath of relief. "Your Majesties are indeed gracious."

"Aye, 'tis so," Charles answered. He laughed, and with that distressing lack of attention to Court etiquette or to the King's dignity that so often appalled his ministers, he winked merrily, adding, "Why, damn it, where is the Sovereign to compare with the perfection of the

Stuart?" He turned to his wife. "'Tis true, is it not, Catherine?" he said, catching her hand in his. "Say 'tis true," he commanded, squeezing her hand tightly and frowning fiercely.

Catherine laughed happily. "Indeed it is. There is no one like you! No one!"

At the fervent note in her voice, Charles bit his lip. He released her hand. "'Tis well you agree."

Angel caught the faint note of impatience in his voice, and was sympathetic. She loved the Queen; but she knew that Charles, who believed himself to be the exact opposite of perfection, would have preferred the lighter tone, for he loved to laugh. If Catherine would but learn to harness her passionate response to his every statement—reserving that passion for the bedchamber—if she would but laugh with him; then perhaps she would win for herself—not his fidelity—but the lasting and tender love of Charles Stuart.

Angel shrugged mentally. She was so wise where the Queen was concerned, she thought bitterly, but far from wise when it came to managing her own affairs.

"You seem pensive, Mistress Dawson," Charles said.

Angel started, "I ask Your Majesty's pardon," she said hastily, wondering if in her preoccupation she had missed a remark put to her. "Did Your Majesty address me?"

Charles shook his head. "Nay, but I am about to do so. I think, Mistress Dawson, that 'tis best if you absent yourself from the Court for a while."

Catherine gave a soft cry of sorrow, and Charles said quickly, "Nay, Catherine, 'tis not a punishment. I have ever loved daring and novelty; therefore am I in sympathy with Mistress Dawson, if not entirely with my Lord Benbrook. But you misunderstand me, my lack of sympathy is due in part to pique. Benbrook should have trusted me."

"But, sire," Angel said impulsively, "you are the King. You could not have countenanced such a deception."

"Not openly perhaps," he answered. "But may not a king have a secret enjoyment?"

Angel saw the twinkle in his eyes, and she understood him well. "Indeed, sire," Angel said softly. " 'Tis inexcusable that 'twas denied you."

She smiled upon him. Seeing the tenderness in his eyes, Charles was gratified. Angel was thinking that next to Nicholas she dearly loved this fascinating man with his lean, clever face and his dark, smiling eyes. To follow the Stuart was to be caught up in that special aura that radiated from him, an aura that excited undying loyalty from men and love and devotion from women. Yes, had she not known Nicholas, she could have loved him; and doubtless like poor Catherine would have been torn with jealousy because she could not possess him entirely.

"There are certain ladies," Charles said, "who will endeavor to make Mistress Dawson's position untenable, Catherine. You understand?"

The Queen nodded. "Yes, Charles. You are right, as usual."

"Then we are in agreement," he answered with a wry smile. "I deem it best, therefore, that you return for a while to the home of your—er—cousin."

Angel flushed. "Yes, sire."

Charles held out his hand. "You have our leave to go. I imagine there is much you must do."

Angel knelt before him once more, her skirt rustling. "Thank you, Your Majesty," she said, kissing his hand. "You are most kind."

Charles withdrew his hand. "You know, do you not, Mistress Dawson, that you may rely upon my support?"

"I do, Your Majesty." Angel lifted her eyes to his. "And I will take comfort in the thought."

For the first time, Charles looked faintly uncomfortable. He said earnestly, "Upon my Lord Benbrook's return, I desire to have immediate speech with him. Request him, please, to present himself without delay."

Angel felt a pang. "I—I do not expect to see him, Your Majesty."

"He cannot wander forever. Of course you will see him." Charles' brows drew together in a frown. "Lord Benbrook had my permission to retire from Court, but now his absence pleases me not. He is friend to me as well as subject, but should his wanderings be much more prolonged, he will incur my grave displeasure."

Angel bowed her head. She looked at the Queen, who was smiling at her sympathetically. "Madam," she said, taking Catherine's small, ringed hand and kissing it. "Be assured that I will remember your kindness."

She rose to her feet. "Thank you." She curtsied before them.

When the door had closed behind her, Charles turned to his wife. Meeting his eyes, she blushed.

Charles could not think of the remark he had been about to make, for it had occurred to him now that he looked more closely, that she was looking remarkably pretty.

Perhaps it was because Charles had laughed with her and held her hand, or because, as now, his eyes lingered on her warmly, but Catherine's small, plain face had indeed taken on a transient prettiness.

Charming, Charles thought. Quite charming. There was a flush in her cheeks, and her large brown eyes—her one real beauty—held a bright glow. He eyed the gown she was wearing approvingly—it was one he had not seen before—the rose-colored silk suited her coloring he decided. The neckline was, for her, cut unusually low and gave him an enticing glimpse of her breast; and the clinging bodice, the wide skirt, embroidered with a design of silver bees and purple and white clover flowers, made the most of her tiny, graceful figure.

The desire he felt for her was as transient as her prettiness, but he did not think of that. Gripped by an unusual excitement he rose slowly to his feet and held both hands toward her. "Come here, Catherine," he said unsteadily. "Come, my small one."

"Charles!" She stared at him unbelievingly, then, swift as the flight of a bird, she was out of her chair and running into his outstretched arms.

"Charles! Oh, my darling! My dearest darling!"

She looked up into his dark face. His eyes were tender, and his smile, softening the cynical mouth, made him look young and eager.

"Catherine!" His long dark hair fell forward as he pressed his lips to hers in a long, seeking kiss; and she responded with all of her pent-up longing, all of her starved passion.

He kissed her face, her hair, the cleavage between her breasts; he unhooked her bodice and laid his face against her soft, quivering whiteness.

"Your breasts are beautiful," he said thickly. "Catherine, my little Portuguese savage, is there a welcome for Charles Stuart in your bed?"

"You know, Charles! Oh, you know!" she half-sobbed, pressing his hot face against her bosom. "Always! Always!"

She trembled violently at the touch of his seeking experienced mouth. "Charles, dearest Charles! T—Take me now!"

"What!" He tried to sound shocked, but his laughing eyes betrayed him. "And shall the King of England take his wife as he would a tavern wench?"

"Yes!" she urged him feverishly. "Yes! Yes! Yes!"

A delighted smile spread across his face. " 'Tis a novel idea." He pointed to the blue and gold carpet. "There is your couch, my little queen. Take off those plaguey garments and let us to our pleasant work."

THE SUMMER WAS MERGING INTO AUTUMN when Angel finally left the Palace. Accompanied by Pip —who had stubbornly refused to leave her—her departure was not the shameful event that Lady Castlemaine would have wished. The King and Queen were there to speed her on her way, their attitude making it plain that she was a dear and honored friend.

The King helped her into his own private carriage and raised her hand to his lips. His brilliant smile flashed. "I trust you will not desert us overlong, Mistress Dawson. 'Tis a sad thing to say farewell to so charming a friend. Therefore let it be soon that I may say, 'greetings, Mistress Dawson, and a hearty welcome.' "

"Your Majesty is kind," Angel answered huskily. Tears came to her eyes when the Queen came forward and kissed her on the cheek.

" 'Tis a dismal day," Catherine said, patting Angel's trembling hand. "You must keep well wrapped up you know, for 'twould not do for you to take a chill."

Angel had looked from one to the other, the little Queen and the tall elegant King, and she felt a surge of love and pride. It would be a sad day for England, she thought, when the reign of Charles Stuart drew to an end.

Angel caught a glimpse of the Duke of Buckingham's face. He was smiling his cold smile, seemingly unperturbed by the warmth of the royal farewell. Angel wondered what went on behind that calm smiling mask.

Standing beside the Duke, Barbara Castlemaine's expression was in complete contrast. Her face flushed with fury, she scowled blackly at Angel.

Her hatred was so evident and the look she now turned upon the King so full of smoldering rage that it was remarked by all. Some of the ladies standing behind her tittered. Barbara swung round on them, her fists clenched. "How dare you laugh at me, you—you fools!"

The Duke sighed and, still smiling, moved away. The King, on the other hand, was coldly offended.

"My Lady Castlemaine," Charles said, sharp rebuke in his voice. "I fear you are overwrought. The Queen and I give you permission to retire."

When amiable Charles Stuart used that tone, one did not disobey. For a challenging moment, Barbara stared into his implacable eyes, but hers were the first to drop. Her mouth sullen, she curtsied before him, imbuing the act with as little courtesy as possible. With her head high, she had gone on her way.

Wrapped warmly in her furs, Angel was glad of the luxury of the King's carriage. Pip was seated opposite her. The wheels swept over cobbles that were a sea of mud. A howling wind blew drifts of leaves before it; and the gutters, swollen with rain, overflowed their boundaries and sent streams of filth to wash over the feet of passersby.

Angel's mood was in accord with the day. She had no doubt that the housekeeper would welcome her, but Mrs. Sampson was, after all, an employee of Nicholas'; it was not for her to open the house to any waif and stray.

Angel's soft lips tightened with resolution. She had no claim on the Earl of Benbrook. He had made that abundantly clear; therefore she would make no claim. If she could prevail upon Mrs. Sampson to allow her to stay for a few days until she obtained a position, it would be all she would ask.

An excited shriek from Pip recalled her to her immediate surroundings. "What is it, Pip?" she said sharply. "You startled me."

He had drawn the leather curtain aside and was leaning half out of the window. "Look, Mistress! Look! A rat. A great rat!"

"Nonsense, Pip!" Angel smiled at him indulgently. "Rats have more sense than to come out in broad daylight and especially in a busy street where people are passing all the time."

"I tell you, Mistress, it is a rat!"

The carriage swayed, throwing Angel into the corner. She heard the snorting of the horses as they drew to an abrupt halt.

"God's blood!" she heard the driver exclaim. "Will you look at that!"

There was a babble of voices, and a woman's shrill voice said indignantly, "What's the country coming to, that's what I'd like to know? Rats in our street, bold as you please!"

Fearfully, Angel edged along the seat to the other window, her hands were trembling as she pushed the leather curtain to one side. Rats! She had always hated and feared them.

"Oh!" She pressed a gloved hand to her mouth. The size of the creature! It was almost as large as a good-sized cat!

The rat foraged calmly among the decaying rubbish that had been swept from the gutter; its flat ugly head darted from side to side, the yellow eyes glowing, but other than that it seemed to be quite undisturbed by the gathering of excited people.

Angel saw one man step forward. He was carrying a stout stick, he raised it above his head and prepared to strike but even as he did so, the rat crouched defensively, its fur bristling and its mouth set in a snarl that showed long, dangerous teeth.

"Don't, William," a woman cried, catching at the man's arm. "Oh Jesus God! Get back before it goes for your throat!"

The man, visibly shaken, turned away. "We can't have this!" he shouted. "Something'll have to be done!"

"My boy plays in the street all the time," a woman's voice yelled. She began to weep hysterically. "I'll be afraid to let him out now!"

"Don't you worry," another voice soothed. "We'll send for the catchers; they'll get rid of 'em in no time."

Angel could not drag her eyes away from the creature. Near to it she saw the quick dart of other furtive dark shapes. More rats! They were gathering.

With a little cry, she dropped the curtain. "Pip! Pip! Bid the driver go on."

Pip turned his head and looked at her pleadingly. "May we not stay a little longer, mistress?" He smiled. "Mayhap," he added cajolingly, "the catchers will soon arrive. I would like to see them at their work."

Angel shuddered. "No," she said firmly. "You will convey my message, if you please."

"Yes, mistress," Pip said. Scowling with disappointment, he put his head out of the window and called to the driver.

"Ain't that the King's carriage?" a man demanded.

"Yes. See there? That's his coat of arms painted on the side."

"The King! The King!"

Angel felt hands on the carriage, making it sway from side to side.

"Nay," the driver cried. " 'Tis the King's carriage, but I carry a lady, not His Majesty!"

"The King's whore! Rats in our streets, and the King's whore rides in a fine carriage!"

"There ain't no rats in the Palace, I'll wager!"

"Who says so? There's lots of 'em. Human ones, though."

"We want our streets cleaned up!"

"A fine King, he is! His harlots have the rich life, wallow in luxury, and what does he care if our children are bitten by rats?"

Angel's breath came fast, but she sat erect her hands clenched inside her fur muff. She smiled tremulously as Pip laid a protective hand on her arm.

"Get back!" the driver shouted.

Angel heard the crack of his whip; it was followed by shrieks and curses, but then to her infinite relief the carriage lurched forward. For a moment it seemed that the crowd would bar its way. But the whip cracked ominously left and right, and the carriage bowled smartly forward.

Angel went limp, and Pip, sitting back opposite, looked at her with big eyes. "There is no more need to worry, mistress," he ventured. "We have left the people behind."

"I know." She gave him an apologetic smile. " 'Tis a coward you have for a mistress, I fear. Though 'twas not so much the people I feared."

"Not the people? What then, mistress?"

"I have fought people before," Angel said, "and I well know how to defend myself. 'Twas the rats I feared."

"Oh." Pip looked faintly scornful. "I have caught many rats. 'Tis good sport." Looking at her white face, his scorn for her feminine weakness vanished. He said gently, "I will look after you, mistress; you need have no fear."

It was a relief to arrive at the house. Mrs. Sampson's brisk kindly greeting seemed blessedly normal. The housekeeper, it seemed from her lack of surprise, had been expecting them.

"Your room is all ready for you, Angel."

"Thank you." Angel brought the black boy forward. "This is Pip, Mrs. Sampson. He—he wanted to stay with me. Is it—is it all right?"

Mrs. Sampson gave her a sharp look. "You have no need to ask, Angel, as you well know."

"But my Lord Benbrook? Might he not—"

"Master Nickey allows me to run the house as I see fit," Mrs. Sampson interrupted. "In any case, he'd not dream of turning anyone from his door."

"There are some that he might consider turning away," Angel said bitterly.

Mrs. Sampson did not answer this. She turned to Pip. "Come, lad," she said, laying her hand on his shoulder. "We'll all go to my sitting room. It's a chill day, and I expect you could do with a hot drink."

Following after them, Angel thought of the King with gratitude. He had doubtless guessed how hesitant and uncertain she was about returning to this house, and in his thoughtful and considerate way, he had sent a messenger ahead to Mrs. Sampson. He had done his best to smooth the way for her; and she knew, should she ever decide to return to Court, that his pleasure would be genuine.

Seated before the big fire in Mrs. Sampson's pleasant room, Angel felt so warm and relaxed that she was able to listen to Pip's recounting of their adventure with the rats with scarcely a shudder.

Mrs. Sampson listened with interest, but to Pip's

disappointment, she did not seem to be too impressed. "I'm glad you were amused, lad," she said. "But I can't see why you're making such a fuss about it. The rats have always been with us, and I dare say that they always will be."

"But if you had seen them," Angel said, leaning forward. "They were of such a size! They made me feel —" she broke off for a moment, then added in a low voice, "I can't really explain how I felt, but to me, at that moment, they seemed like creatures from a nightmare!"

"Pshaw!" Mrs. Sampson looked at her indulgently. "You're much too sensitive."

"I?" Angel's eyes opened wide. "How can you say that, knowing the life that I led?"

"What of that? I tell you, child, sensitivity can flourish in a gutter as well as a palace."

Pip had been listening with interest. "Madam, is this to be the new home of Mistress Angel and of myself?" he asked suddenly.

"No," Angel said quickly.

"Yes," Mrs. Sampson said, just as quickly.

Pip looked from one to the other. "I do not understand."

Angel ignored him. "Mrs. Sampson, I thought you understood that I would stay but a few days. I am in need of a position, and I hoped you might help me obtain one. You see—something happened, an—an incident. I will explain later."

"No need," Mrs. Sampson answered. "I know what happened."

She smiled into Angel's puzzled face. "I have friends at the Palace, you know. Two of them, in fact. They work in the kitchens; nevertheless they manage to hear everything."

"I see. I didn't know that."

"Well, you can't hope to know everything, can you?"

Angel shook her head. "I suppose not. But you do see that it is of the utmost importance that I obtain a position, don't you?"

Mrs. Sampson stared thoughtfully into the fire. "You have a position, Angel. Temporary, I admit, but nevertheless a position."

"What do you mean? What position?"

"Housekeeper. You will be taking my place for a while."

"What!"

"I need to rest," Mrs. Sampson said slowly. "I've been having a few fainting spells. It's my heart very likely." She leaned forward to poke the fire. Straightening again, she snapped, "And there's no need to look at me like that! Gracious, child, I'm a long way from dying."

"Oh," Angel sank back in her chair. "You frightened me."

Mrs. Sampson looked faintly gratified. "No need to worry; I'm too cantankerous to suit God or the devil, so likely they'll wait till the last minute before closing the book on me. But be that as it may, I am in need of a rest. With you to help out I'll be strong again in no time."

"I hope so." Angel looked down at her hands. "But it would be best if you got someone else. 'Tis out of the question for me to stay here."

"Master Nickey?"

"Yes," Angel answered, her face flushing. "He mustn't find me here."

"He won't find you here."

"Do you mean—Oh, Mrs. Sampson, have you heard from him?"

Mrs. Sampson heard the note in her voice. So she's

still in love with him, she thought. Good! Very good! Aloud, she said, "Maybe I have, and then again maybe I haven't. But you'll be safe enough, take my word for it."

"Oh!" the light died out of Angel's eyes. "I'll stay, of course," she said dully, "if you're sure you want me."

"I wouldn't ask you if I didn't," Mrs. Sampson's voice was brisk again. "Now then, you're to have your old room." She glanced at Pip. "As for you, young man, you're to have the little corner room. It's right near your mistress, so you won't be lonely."

"You are very kind," Pip said. "I shall enjoy being here."

"Gracious!" Mrs. Sampson exclaimed. "To listen to him, one would think him a prince in disguise."

Angel smiled wanly. "Well," she said, trying to speak lightly, "he is, after all, the son of a chief."

"Is he so?" Mrs. Sampson winked at Angel. "Then this poor house is honored by his presence."

Pip inclined his head. "Yes," he said gravely. "It is quite understandable that you should think so."

"Well!" Mrs. Sampson looked scandalized. "Angel, I do believe that boy is serious!"

At the look on her face, Angel broke into helpless laughter. "Yes," she assured her, "he is. Pip is very conscious of his heritage."

"Then I can only hope that he won't object to doing a few jobs about the house?" Mrs. Sampson said, snorting.

"No, indeed," Pip assured her calmly. "For you and Mistress Angel are my benefactresses, and as such you may be assured of my loyalty."

"Well!" Mrs. Samspon said again, looking at Angel rather helplessly. For once she was at a loss for words.

Recovering after a moment, she rose to her feet and briskly replenished the fire.

Angel watched her, a puzzled frown between her brows. There seemed to be nothing wrong with her, she thought. But Mrs. Sampson had ever scorned to give in to weakness—as she termed it—and it might be that she was suffering discomfort.

On this thought, Angel said, "Mrs. Sampson, should you not be in your bed?"

"In bed?" Mrs. Sampson looked at her blankly. "But why should I—" she broke off, her face changing. "Bed?" she said in a faint voice. "Yes, to be sure. I feel very weak, child, very weak indeed. Perhaps you would be good enough to assist me to my bed?"

"Yes, of course."

"Thank you, child."

Mrs. Sampson swayed. Alarmed, Angel sprang forward. A supporting arm about her, she helped her tenderly up the winding, graceful staircase. All her doubts were gone now. She should have remembered how Mrs. Sampson loathed to admit to an illness. Rather than do so she would work until she dropped. The only way she could hope to keep Mrs. Sampson in her bed was to become fully as efficient as the woman herself. And I will be efficient, Angel vowed. I shall prove to be so satisfactory that the only thing she'll have to think about is getting well.

Holding Mrs. Sampson's other arm, Pip smiled faintly to himself, his eyes enigmatic.

Outside her door, Mrs. Sampson declined further help. Her eyes lingered on Pip for a moment. "Young man," she said sharply, "be so good as to bring me a cool drink. You need not hurry; an hour from now will do."

"Yes, madam." Pip made her a small bow. "An hour from now."

Mrs. Sampson watched him descend the stairs, then

she turned to Angel. "A nice lad, that. But he gives himself too many airs."

"Not really," Angel assured her. "It's only his way."

"Hmm." She turned to her door. "I'll see you in the morning. Goodnight."

It SEEMED TO ANGEL, RUNNING UP AND down the stairs a dozen or more times a day, that any resemblance she might bear to a housekeeper was merely superficial. It was Mrs. Sampson who still commanded the household; her imperious voice that issued the orders and oiled the wheels of smooth progress.

Nevertheless, she appeared to be a genuine invalid —if an autocratic one. Propped up in her bed by a nest of pillows and looking unfamiliar in her severe white nightdress, she presented to the uncritical eye a frail, almost pathetic appearance.

Mrs. Mott, the cook, or any other servants who were constantly in and out of the sickroom had a different tale to tell. They were not deceived by the frailty of her appearance; they found that her tongue was just as sharp, her reprimands for neglected tasks fully as acid. The general consensus was that the "old devil" could see through walls and floors, and those who had been inclined to slack were forced into conscientiousness.

Angel's suspicions waxed and waned. One moment she was certain that Mrs. Sampson did but play the part of the invalid; the next moment she was uncertain. Invariably, when remonstrated with, Mrs. Sampson would apparently suffer an alarming relapse. Angel would feel miserably guilty until the invalid would brighten and send Pip—who was constantly in and out —to bring one or the other servants into her presence.

September blew itself out in a squall of rain, and October and November brought raw cold. Angel asserted herself and ignored Mrs. Sampson's biting comments on waste. She ordered that fires be kindled in every hearth. The Christmas season was carried out by Angel on a lavish scale that brought further explosions from the sickroom. But Pip was ecstatic and the servants delighted with the generosity and imagination of their gifts; even Mrs. Sampson, after her first indignation, seemed grimly content. Only Angel was unhappy, for the smiling faces about her seemed to increase her aching longing for Nicholas. It was only the hope that she might see him once again that kept her—when her suspicions of Mrs. Sampson grew into uncertainty—from forcing an explanation.

Had it not been for her unhappiness over Nicholas, her life was pleasant enough, and she was discovering in herself an increasing reluctance to move on. Pip was happy too, far happier than he had been at Court. Mrs. Sampson was even indulgent to the boy, and he was a universal favorite with the servants.

Angel found that the King and Queen had by no means forgotten her, for January of 1665 brought Lady Frances Gardiner, the Queen's favorite lady-in-waiting, to the house. She brought New Year's gifts from the King and Queen and an amusing fund of gossip. Lady Castlemaine, it seemed, had been involved in a scandalous affair with Lord Ingersoll. The King, though tiring of her, had nevertheless been enraged enough to banish Lord Ingersoll; and he had refused to acknowledge Barbara's latest child as his own. He had commanded her, with icy courtesy, to apply to Lord Ingersoll. Barbara, furious, had used all her wiles to bring the King around; nothing had availed.

Not all of Lady Frances' gossip was amusing, however. She spoke of the unhappiness of the Queen who had miscarried again. She had not quite given up hope of presenting Charles with an heir, Lady Frances confided, but she often despaired. Then the Princess Mary had been hurt—though fortunately not seriously—while taking an airing. Her carriage had been all but overturned when a rat had scampered across the road, startling the horses. Her governess had received a cut on the forehead and numerous bruises.

This news had brought back the incident of the rats she had seen when leaving the Palace, and again Angel was touched with shuddering horror. Lady Frances was inclined to make light of Angel's fears, and beyond commenting that the rats were perhaps becoming overbold she changed the subject, remarking idly that it was unseasonably hot for January.

The unusual heat continued, and spring came, not gently, but with a blast of summer heat. The trees were still misted with the tender green of spring, and the earth, retaining its moisture, pushed up fragile shoots. Blossoms unfolded, but their delicate perfume was lost in the all-pervading stench of overflowing gutters. It was like a poisonous miasma over London. Great clouds of flies swarmed over the piles of accumulated filth piled beside the choked gutters, sometimes settling on the heated flesh of passersby.

Occasional stories were heard of rats attacking children at play. One child, it seemed, had had its throat torn open. The stories were disturbing, but the London populace paid little heed. Their children played in the streets, they argued, and they were perfectly healthy and unharmed. They were amused at the alarm of the city officials, who at last became appalled by the rapidly increasing rat population and were training men to deal with the crisis.

"What crisis?" the people asked each other. Wasn't it true that over a million rodents had been killed last year? In view of this fantastic depletion, how was it possible for the rats to have increased their numbers? City officials, bah! Wouldn't you think they'd have something better to do with their time than to go around spreading false tales and alarming honest people? Life was hard enough without that.

The weather was a trial too. The sun continued to blaze from a sky of harsh blue, and tempers grew short. The crime rate rose alarmingly, and even those who were accustomed to the stench of the London gutters became nauseated as it grew increasingly virulent.

Seeking relief from their everyday tensions and the persistent rumors of an impending war between England and Holland, people crowded more and more into the theaters. At the King's Theater, they were reassured by the sight of the King smiling from the royal box and doffing his hat to the audience. On the stage, pretty Nell Gwynne, curls tossing, lithe, shapely legs flashing, her saucy smile warming them, further delighted them in the play *Thomaso*.

In March the storm broke. War between England and Holland was no longer a rumor; it was a fact.

Mrs. Sampson, abandoning the role of invalid, rose from her bed. She went about her duties with a white set face, for the times were perilous, and with Master Nickey far from home, who knew what might happen?

She quashed a possible rebellion on Angel's part by forbidding her sternly to seek another situation. She was done with play-acting, she declared, and if Angel had no thought for the master, she might consider her, a lone woman who would be quite at their mercy if the Dutch invaded.

Angel could not imagine Mrs. Sampson being at

the mercy of the Dutch or of anyone for that matter; but she needed no persuasion to stay.

War! Where was Nicholas? Angel pictured him as a captive of the Dutch, or—heart-chilling thought—dead! She grew almost as thin and as pale as Mrs. Sampson. The fiery temper she had learned to suppress came to the surface and exploded on the slightest provocation. She was impatient with Pip, who not understanding how he had offended, looked back at her with big, wounded eyes.

Every night, Angel prayed fervently for Nicholas' safety, her prayers a jumbled mixture of begging and threats. If she could but see him come through the door, it would be all that she would ask. In her heart though, she felt that Nicholas must be far from England. If he were near, she was convinced, she would know, she would feel his presence.

In view of this conviction, it was strange that she had no presentiment; for when Nicholas entered the house on the first day of May, Angel in her room had no prior warning at all.

"COME IN," ANGEL CALLED IN RESPONSE to a soft tapping on the door.

The door opened slowly, and Pip came into the room almost diffidently. He gave her a quick smile. "I do not mean to trouble you, Mistress Angel, but I wondered if there was something I might do for you?"

He looked down at the floor, shuffling his feet like one not quite sure of his welcome. "I do not mean to trouble you," he said again.

Angel felt a rush of compunction. Poor Pip! Poor boy! She'd taken out her fear on him, and of course he didn't understand the change in her. His life had been so uncertain, and just as he was beginning to be sure of something—of one particular person, she had done this to him. She was annoyed with the tears that sprang into her eyes. What was the matter with her? She was always weeping and wailing lately.

"Pip!" she cried impulsively. "Oh, Pip! I'm so sorry!"

He looked up quickly, understanding her at once. "It is because you grieve," he said. "I know this is so, mistress, though I do not know for whom."

"Yes." She nodded her head. "But 'tis no excuse for my behavior."

329

He saw the tears on her face. "No, no!" he exclaimed, running to her side. "I pray you, mistress, do not cry!"

He touched her face with a trembling finger. "I love you, mistress," he said, his voice shaking. "Tell me who has hurt you. Tell me, so that I may kill this person!"

She put her arm about him. "I believe you would!"

"Aye," he answered, his eyes flashing, "for have I not told you that you are to me as my mother and my sister."

She kissed his forehead. "Then," she said, trying to laugh, "your mother and your sister must forbid such violence." He made a sudden movement, and she went on quickly. "Nay, Pip, 'tis not a matter of killing."

"Then why do you weep?" he demanded.

"There is—is someone I love very much," she began hesitantly. "I worry for his—his safety."

His stormy face cleared instantly. "Mistress Angel!" he gave her a beaming smile. "Now I understand. You grieve for the man to whom you have given your heart?"

She stared at him, a smile touching her lips. But he was so serious! His smile disappeared as he waited for her answer, and she repressed her slight amusement. "Yes, Pip, that is so," she answered.

"If you will tell me where he may be found, Mistress Angel, then I will bring him to your side."

"Will you, Pip?" This time she could not resist a teasing note. "And if he will not be brought to my side, what then?"

"I will force him!" Pip cried. "If you love him, then he must love you!"

"Oh, Pip, you cannot force people to love you."

He looked back at her, baffled. "If he does not love you, then truly the spirits have robbed him of his reason," he said.

"I thought once that he loved me." Angel was not sure why she confided in this boy, but she went on slowly.

"Something happened, I know not what. But he—he decided that he no longer cared for me."

"Then I, M'Zeli," Pip cried, drawing himself to his full height, "say that he is not worthy of you!"

"Ah, 'tis the son of the great chief I hear," Angel said, forcing herself to speak lightly. "But M'Zeli is mistaken; it is I who am not worthy of him."

"This I will not acknowledge to be truth," Pip said heatedly. "You are as your name—you are an angel!"

She shook her head, the foolish tears filling her eyes again. "Nay, Pip, 'tis not so. But thank you."

Pip's indignation left him. He said uncertainly, "There is much weeping today. You, mistress, I have seen you weep before, and though your tears hurt me, yet I am used to them. But I had not thought to see Mistress Sampson weep." He shook his head dolefully. "There is much fear in me when such a woman crumbles."

"Mrs. Sampson?" Angel looked at him in dismay. "Pip!" she cried, beginning to tremble. "Did—did Mrs. Sampson receive a messenger? Somebody who brought her news?"

"A man comes to the house," Pip answered. He looked fearfully at her white face. "But I think, mistress, that he is not a messenger. He is tall, and he wears fine clothes. He walks like unto one who owns the earth."

Angel stared at him, a wild thought leaping into her mind. Nicholas? No! It could not be!

"He has a dark face," Pip went on. He touched his own face. "Not as dark as mine, but dark like that of majesty. When he enters the house, he looks at me, and I bow to him. He bows back, and says, 'How do you do, young master.' So I think, Mistress Angel, that despite his frowning brows, there is kindness in this man."

"Did you hear his name?" Angel whispered.

"No. But I think Mistress Sampson likes him, for

she smiles before she weeps. She does not mind that he is disrespectful to her."

"Dis—disrespectful?"

"Aye. He has courage, that man," Pip said, an admiring note in his voice. "I trembled for him when he called her Sampson. But she does not mind." A faint frown creased Pip's brow. " 'Tis strange, but I think that she liked being called so—" he broke off, looking at Angel in alarm. "Mistress! What is it?"

"Nicholas!" his name was a sob on her lips. "Nicholas has come home!" She rose swiftly to her feet and made for the door. "Where are they, Pip?"

"In the room of many books," he answered. "But, mistress, what—"

"Never mind," she cut him off swiftly; then, as he made to follow her, she said breathlessly. "Stay here, Pip, please. You may tidy my room, or, if you would prefer, help Mrs. Mott in the kitchen."

"I will stay here. But, mistress, are you sure you do not need me?"

"No, no!" She looked at him with burning, impatient eyes. "But thank you, Pip."

She left the room, closing the door behind her. Flying noiselessly along the corridor and down the winding staircase, she wondered how she could bear it if Nicholas looked at her with that same hatred. But he was home! He was safe! It was enough for the moment.

Approching the library, she heard the murmur of voices, and her steps slowed. She was afraid, now that the moment was upon her. What would he say to her? Would he question her right to be in his home?

She drew nearer. The voices coming through the half-opened door were clear to her now.

"I did not see the King," she heard Nicholas say. "The Queen granted me an audience. The King returns this afternoon. I will call upon him then."

Angel leaned against the wall. She would not go in yet. Just a few moments longer to regain her breath and find her courage.

"Well, Sampson," Nicholas said impatiently. "I have answered your questions, have I not? Now, if you will be so good, pray answer mine."

"Which one, Master Nickey?"

"Sampson, you try me too far!" Nicholas sounded as though he spoke through gritted teeth. "I have been marvelously patient with you. I have allowed you to parry my questions, but now my patience is at an end. I will put up with no more of your evasions. Where is Angel?"

Angel caught her breath sharply. Why was Mrs. Sampson evading the question? She strained forward, listening.

"The—the Queen did not tell you?"

"Sampson!" Nicholas' voice rose slightly. "I have informed you that the Queen expressed the hope that Mistress Dawson was faring well and that she would soon be back at Court. By that I gathered that Angel was here."

"It does not necessarily follow, does it, Master Nickey? She could be many places, could she not?"

Angel clenched her hands tightly together. What was wrong with Mrs. Sampson? Why didn't she tell him the truth? Was it possible that she was afraid to admit that she had taken her in?

"What are you saying, Sampson?" Nicholas said sharply. "Are you telling me that you have no knowledge of her whereabouts?"

"Why do you want to find her, Master Nickey?"

There was a short silence; then Nicholas said coldly, "My reasons are no concern of yours, Sampson."

Angel was amazed to hear Mrs. Sampson answer calmly. "Yes they are. I'm fond of the child. I'll not see her hurt again, not even by you, Master Nickey."

"You forget yourself, Sampson!" Nicholas' voice was icy.

"Very well, my lord. It will not be easy for me to forget that I nursed you and fed you and guided your first steps, or that I love you as I would my own son. But if you wish me to keep my place, my lord, I will do so."

Nicholas groaned. "Oh damn you, Sampson! You know well that I had no intention of hurting your feelings. Just tell me, do you or do you not know the whereabouts of Angel?"

"I might remember, my lord," Mrs. Sampson answered in the same calm voice. "If, of course, I knew your reasons for seeking her out, my lord."

"Will you stop calling me my lord!" Nicholas exclaimed, goaded again. "Where is Angel?"

"Why do you seek her, my lord?"

"Very well!" Nicholas shouted. "If you will have it, you interfering old busybody, it's because I love her! Now are you satisfied? Now will you tell me what I wish to know?"

Angel thrust her hand against her mouth to stifle her cry. He loved her! Nicholas loved her! Her eyes, which had begun to glow, dulled again. But he had said that before. He hadn't meant it then. Why should she think that he meant it now?

Mrs. Sampson appeared to be considering, for there was a silence. Then, almost as though Angel's thoughts had entered her brain, she said slowly, "I know nothing of what happened between you, Master Nickey. Angel told me nothing, and it was not my place to inquire. But I know she loved you, and I believed you loved her. For some reason, known only to the two of you, you changed your mind. How do I know you will not change it again? As I have told you, I learned nothing from Angel, and it was not my pl—"

"Not your place to inquire," Nicholas finished for her. He gave a short, hard laugh. "But in case you have overlooked the fact, you are inquiring now. Perhaps it would be as well if you remembered to keep your place with me."

"Yes, my lord."

"Sampson, I could very easily strangle you, you know!"

"Yes, my lord. Nevertheless, unless you are very sure, there is no point in telling you where she is. I think —" she broke off, her voice changing. "Master Nickey! Oh, my dear lad! Come now, come! I didn't mean to bedevil you!"

Her heart beating very fast, Angel nerved herself to peer into the room.

Nicholas was slumped in a chair, his head in his hands. "I've been such a fool, Sampson!" he said in a muffled voice.

He began to cough suddenly. Angel drew back, listening, and the harsh, dry, painful sound he made filled her with a curious dread.

"Master Nickey!" Mrs. Sampson said sharply. "That's a bad cough."

"I haven't been feeling well," Nicholas answered huskily. "A chill, I suppose. But your cursed stubbornness on top of it was—well, it was a little too much. I'm sorry for making a fool of myself, Sampson."

"Now, lad, you've done nothing of the sort. Master Nickey, I don't want to interfere, and you don't have to tell me anything, but I must think of Angel. Are you sure this time? Sure that you love her, I mean?"

"Yes," Nicholas answered abruptly. "You might as well know it all, Sampson. I said just now that I've been a fool. I was, for I found I couldn't forget her, and God knows I tried hard enough!"

"But why?" Mrs. Sampson said, bewildered. "Why

335

did you want to forget her? You both seemed so happy. So much in love."

"I was happy, Sampson. Happier than I've ever been in my life. I can't speak for Angel, just myself."

"But she loves you, Master Nickey. So I'll speak for her."

"I think not. But I seem to have lost all pride where Angel is concerned. I love her! I want to marry her! And damn it, I'll take her on any terms she likes to state!"

"But I—I don't understand."

"I know you don't." There was a savage note in Nicholas' voice. "I asked Angel to marry me, you know that. But when I asked her, I didn't know that she was already the King's mistress!"

The King's mistress! Angel gasped, feeling the shock of his words like a violent physical blow. What did he mean? Was he insane?

"But that's not true!" Mrs. Sampson's voice rose in protest. "I know Angel. It couldn't be true!"

Nicholas began to cough again. After a moment, he said wearily. "It is true. She was wearing the King's ring. The King has them designed especially for his mistresses. They are the King's warning that, once he has placed the ring on the lady's finger, then she is sacrosanct to him alone."

"I've never heard of such a thing!" Mrs. Sampson said, outraged. "If Angel had such a ring, Master Nickey, then I'm sure she wore it in innocence."

Angel closed her eyes, waiting for Nicholas' answer.

"No," he said. "The King, you see, has made it into a tradition. The ring is bestowed upon only his mistresses. But, Sampson, I don't care any more. I love that wench, and were she mistress to a dozen men I would still go on loving her!"

Angel was unable to bear any more. She stepped forward, pushing the door wide. Mrs. Sampson looked up sharply, but she said nothing. Nicholas did not see her, his face was turned away, one hand hiding his eyes.

"Go away, Sampson," he muttered. "Unless you want to see me make a bigger fool of myself?"

Mrs. Sampson patted his shoulder briefly, then she moved over to the door. She went out, closing it softly behind her.

Angel's gown rustled as she went to Nicholas' side. She knelt down beside the chair, touching his hand almost timidly.

"I told you to go away, Sampson," Nicholas said, an odd choking sound in his voice. "Damn you, woman! Get out!"

"Who d' you think you are then?" Angel said in a shaking voice. "Jus' 'cause you're a bleedin' lord it don' mean you c'n go slingin' orders aroun', do it?"

Nicholas was still for a moment, then his hand dropped and he turned his face toward her. "Angel!" he whispered, his eyes unbelieving. "Oh, Angel!" He leaped to his feet, pulling her up.

"Nicholas!" She hesitated only a moment, then she put her arms about him and held him close.

"Forgive me, Angel!" He laid his head on her shoulders. "Oh, darling, forgive me!"

In the past she had loved him and hated him; and when he had left her she had often thought of the revenge she would take upon him. But now, feeling the shaking of his shoulders, listening to the agonized sounds he made, she wanted nothing so much as to comfort him. Her strong, arrogant, dictatorial Nicholas crying! No! He must not, she could not bear it for him!

"Ah, don't love! Don't!" She tightened her arms about him. "Come now, my lord, else will I be joining you. 'Tis a happy day, is it not?"

There was silence between them, save only for the muffled sounds he made; then he said in a tight, controlled voice, "What must you think of me, Angel? 'Tis the first time I have cried since—since I was a child. I ask your pardon. It must have been dis—distressing for you."

" 'Twas painful," she said slowly. "But my pain was for you, my darling. Not myself."

"Will you let me try again, Angel? If you—you can love me again, I will try to make up for all that has gone before."

"Be not so humble, my Nicholas," Angel said, trying to rally him. "Indeed, my lord, it does not suit you." She hesitated for a moment. "But is it not for you to forgive me?"

"Nay!" he said. "It no longer matters. Nothing matters if we love each other!" He put his hands on her shoulders. " 'Tis an admission that I never thought to make, but I am glad the King discarded you, else would you not be here with me."

"Discarded me?"

"Aye. Had he not done so you would still be at Court."

She felt a brief flare of anger. She said coolly, "My lord, even the King cannot discard that which he never had."

He stared at her. "But the King's ring? 'Tis never given to any other than his mistress."

"Then 'twas given to me under false pretenses." She held up her hand. "See, Nicholas, I wear it still, for the King informed me that 'twas a token of his friendship."

His eyes were on the ring. "He—he said that?"

"Aye. Do you believe me?"

He raised his eyes to her face. "Yes," he said. "Yes."

She shook her head. "You lie, Nicholas, you believe me not."

"I have told you that it no longer matters," he said, a desperate note in his voice. "What else can I say, Angel, save that nothing matters if you love me?"

338

"It matters to me. There must be nothing between us." She slipped the ring from her finger. Placing it in his palm, she closed his fingers about it. "Take it to the King, he will tell you that I speak truth."

"Angel, is it not enough that I—"

"Nay," she interrupted. " 'Tis not enough for me. 'Tis important that you learn the truth." She laid her hand over his clenched fingers. "But that you want me—believing as you do—that, too, is important. I love you, Nicholas, much more than I can ever tell you. Therefore must there be truth between us. Will you take the ring? Will you ask him why he gave it to me?"

He nodded. "Aye." He shivered convulsively. " 'Tis cursed cold in this room."

"Cold? But, Nicholas, 'tis unbearably hot."

He fell back in the chair, not answering, and she saw that his face had whitened.

She bent over him anxiously. Putting her hand on his forehead, she was alarmed at the burning heat of his skin. "Nicholas, you're not well! You must go straight to bed."

"Nay, 'tis nothing. I feel a little nauseated, that's all. I have always been a bad sailor, and 'twas a damned rough crossing." He gave her a faint smile. "Even on land I find that the effect tends to linger."

"Are you sure?"

"Aye. 'Tis a nuisance, but Sampson will tell you that it has happened before. I—" The cough interrupted him.

When the spasm passed, she said quickly, "The cough, at least, needs attention."

"Mayhap. Sampson will doubtless have some mixture which she will insist on forcing down my throat." He drew his handkerchief from his sleeve and pressed it against his lips.

Angel, watching him closely, saw the startled look on his face. "Nicholas?"

"I think it best you leave me," he said faintly. "And —and quickly."

"I'll do nothing of the sort."

"Please!" Unable to say more, he bent forward, retching violently.

Angel supported him, but though he retched again and again, nothing came up.

"I'm sorry," he said, when she helped him to lie back in the chair. "Darling, I'm so sorry!"

"There's nothing to be sorry about. But you will go to bed now, will you not?"

"Nonsense! I shall do nothing of the sort. Come now, my little guttersnipe, I like not to see you with a long face. I'm feeling much better now."

"But—" she broke off, looking at him doubtfully. He did look better; there was a faint color in his cheeks now, and he had spoken in his normal tone. "Very well. But I trust not your assurances, Nicholas. Men are ever foolish with their health. I shall consult with Mrs. Sampson."

Nicholas caught the underlying threat. "Not that, my dearest, I pray you," he said, smiling ruefully. "In the past, I have suffered many times at Sampson's hands, so 'tis a cruel fate to which you condemn me."

" 'Tis for your own good."

"Nay," he shook his head firmly. "You know not Sampson's methods." He looked up at her, a smile in his dark eyes. "Angel!" he captured her hand and pressed it against his cheek. "I am happy! So happy!"

"And I." She knelt beside him again, resting her head against his arm. "But I cannot be completely happy until you have spoken with the King."

She felt his hand touching her hair. "I will do so, if it pleases you. But I want you to know that, though I doubted you but a few moments ago, I believe you speak the truth. I need not the King's word."

She looked up at him. "Nicholas! Do you really believe me?" She saw the truth in his eyes. "You do, you really do!"

He raised a whimsical brow. "You know, of course, that you will be marrying a fool?"

Smiling, she rose to her feet again. "I think not. I have called you many things in my mind but never a fool, my darling Nicholas. Never that!" She turned to the door. "I'm going to the kitchen. I must tell Mrs. Mott that her dinner tonight must be very, very special."

After she had gone, Nicholas rose cautiously to his feet. He did indeed feel better, he thought. The nausea seemed to have passed. He was conscious of a slight dizziness, but other than that he felt quite normal.

ANGEL PAID THE SHOPKEEPER FOR THE herbs and thanked him absentmindedly. Outside she paused, her back against the shop window, surveying the long row of market stalls. People jostled past her but she did not heed them. There was something she had forgotten to purchase. Was it important, she wondered. She couldn't seem to think. All she could remember was Nicholas.

Nicholas! She stared at the packet of herbs in her hand. Nicholas was ill, very ill; there was no point in deluding herself any longer. She hadn't wanted to leave him, but Mrs. Sampson believed in her herbal mixture, and she would trust nobody else to procure the herbs. Herbs! Angel's fingers clenched over the packet. She did not share Mrs. Sampson's belief in their healing power.

Last night, only last night, she had been so happy. Nicholas had seen the King, and when he had returned from the Palace he had held her in his arms for a long time—not speaking, just holding her tightly—then, when he had released her, he had said huskily, "I doubt that I can ever forgive myself, Angel, for the hurt I caused you. But that you can forgive, my dearest, is miracle enough for one man. I have not the words to tell you how very much I love you, but I'll try to show you! Darling, I will try!"

Later, at the King's insistence, they had attended a performance at the King's Theater. Nicholas seemed to be quite recovered from his earlier indisposition. He had held her hand tightly, and they had laughed freely over Nell Gwynne's spirited and amusing performance. She had never seen him so relaxed and, in his happiness, so —well, almost boyish! She marveled that she had ever thought of him as cold and arrogant, or that she had believed that she hated him. Hated him! Her Nicholas! She adored him!

He had seemed to know what she was thinking too. For he had turned to look at her, and his eyes had been so tender that she could scarcely refrain from throwing herself into his arms. Instead she had smiled, and he had touched her cheek lightly in that familiar and now beloved gesture.

On their way home, Nicholas had been very quiet, but she hadn't minded that. She had been content to sit closely beside him, her hand on his shoulder. She had felt a shudder go through his body, then another. When she sat up and looked at him, he was leaning back, his eyes closed. In the light of the carriage lamp, she saw great beads of perspiration on his forehead.

"Nicholas!" At her touch he seemed to collapse, for he had doubled over, making those painful retching sounds.

"Oh God!" he exclaimed, "I'm sorry." He almost fell toward the window, wrenching the leather curtain aside. Leaning half out of the carriage, he had vomited violently and helplessly; while she had held on to his convulsed body with both hands. Listening to his choking efforts to draw breath, she had sensed that this was no ordinary sickness; it was something grave, something terrifyingly serious.

When the attack was over, Nicholas had sunk wearily back on the seat, but he had seemed strangely reluctant to have her touch him. Nevertheless, she had put her arms about his shivering body and held him close.

John, the coachman, had helped her to assist Nicholas into the house. "It ain't the plague, is it, Mistress Dawson?" he had asked in a frightened voice. "I did hear tell that there's been an outbreak down by the docks."

"Don't be ridiculous, John!" she had answered sharply. "Of course it's not the plague!" John appeared to be reassured, and in the absence of Meadows, Nicholas' valet, whom he had not yet recalled from Benbrook Manor, he undressed Nicholas and helped him into bed.

Pacing the corridor outside Nicholas' room, John's words kept coming back to her. Plague! Oh God! Merciful God! Don't let it be that! But plague at the docks, where Nicholas had disembarked! Let it be anything else but not that! Not that!

When John left, she had gone into Nicholas' room. "Don't come too near to me, please," he had ordered curtly, turning his face away. "John could be right. I might very well have the plague."

Ignoring him, she ran to his side. "I pray not!" she said bending over him. "But if you think to keep me from your side, you, my lord, are much mistaken."

"Leave me!" he said harshly.

"No." She had caught his burning hands in hers and held them firmly. "Seek not to use that tone, it will avail you nothing, for I know you now, my darling."

"Angel!" He turned his head and looked up at her with fevered, haunted eyes. "I want you to leave London. Go to Benbrook Manor. Take—take Sampson and the rest of the household with you."

"You want me to go off and leave you here alone?"

"You must! Listen to me, Angel, I have seen cases of the plague before. I am certain that I have it. So go, go! There are nurses to be had, for a price. I'll be taken care of."

She shuddered, thinking of the women who called themselves nurses. Mostly, they were filthy raddled hags attracted by the prospect of easy pickings. They were content to ignore the danger of possible infection.

"Yes," she had answered him slowly, "there are nurses. Do you think you can sleep now, darling?"

"I know not and I care not." His head turned restlessly on the pillow. "You will go, Angel?"

"I will not," she had said, shaking her head firmly. "But I'll send Mrs. Sampson and the household to Benbrook Manor."

"No, Angel! I will not allow you to stay!" He had spoken in the old curtly commanding voice. "I ask you to understand that in this, at least, I will be obeyed!"

Her determination to stay remained unshaken, but he was becoming agitated, so she had murmured soothingly, "We'll see."

"Damn you, wench, do you take me for a fool? I mean it, do you understand? I mean it!"

"I know," she had answered, stroking his hair. "I know. But lie still, else will you be sick again."

"Go to bed," he ordered. "I don't want you here."

"I know. But you see, my dear, dear, Nicholas, you are unable to enforce your orders."

She bent to kiss him, but he turned his face away. "If you have any love for me," he muttered, "you will do as I say."

"I have love for you," she had answered. "But let us talk of my possible departure in the morning."

He had not answered, and after a moment she had gone away. But only to his dressing room. Leaving the door open, she had curled up in a chair. Sleepless, her ears alert for any sound he might make, she had stayed there all night.

It was in the early morning hours that his retching started again. Snatching up a basin, she ran to his side. The attack was, if anything, even more violent.

When it was over, she settled him gently back against the pillows. Dampening a towel, she bathed his face and hands, murmuring to him soothingly.

"Oh, Angel!" he had moaned. "Angel, my darling, in the name of God, leave me! Go, darling, and thank you for wanting to stay!"

Angel had met further trouble with Mrs. Sampson and Pip. She induced the housekeeper to leave by pointing out that Nicholas would need her when he recovered. Pip, she dealt with in another way. Cold-faced, she had threatened him, telling him that if he did not obey her in this, she would never again allow him to work for her. Looking at Mrs. Sampson, her face stained with unusual tears, and at Pip, who was frankly sobbing, she had felt brutal. But it had to be done. In this much she would obey Nicholas.

Pip had clung to her, begging her to leave with them. Mrs. Sampson had seemed to understand that she was not to be moved from her purpose, for she had said nothing. Only in one thing did the housekeeper remain obdurate. Leave she would, if the master commanded it, but not until she had tried her herbal mixture on him. "It has been known," she said, "to work miracles."

There was nothing to do, Angel knew, but to give in. Snatching up her cloak, she had fled in the direction of the marketplace.

Pip had called something after her. Something about a man who knew many secrets of healing. MaHeber, that was the name he had shouted. At least, it had sounded like that. She hadn't waited to find out; she wanted to get back to Nicholas as quickly as possible.

Again Angel looked along the market stalls. No, she couldn't remember what else she had been asked to buy. She was wasting precious time just standing here.

She started to move away but halted again, as a woman began screaming hysterically.

"Lizzie! Lizzie!" Angel heard. "Oh my God!"

Angel pushed her way through the crowd that was rapidly gathering. The screaming woman—Angel recognized her as the owner of the lace and ribbon stall—had just snatched up her child from the edge of the overflowing gutter.

Angel felt sick as she saw a large gray rat, its fangs buried deeply into tender flesh, hanging from the child's wrist.

The woman was striking frantically at the creature. "Help me! Somebody help me!" The child was shrieking.

Angel heard somebody swear; she turned her head and saw a man snatch up a thick chunk of firewood from a nearby stall. He charged toward the screaming woman and struck savagely at the dangling rat; stunned, it dropped heavily to the ground. But it had not lost its fighting spirit; a gasp of horror went up as they saw it bare bloody teeth in snarling defiance.

"Would you, then!" the man shouted. Lifting his arm, he brought the chunk of wood smashing down upon the creature's head, pulping it out of all recognition. Grunting with satisfaction, he picked up the limp body by its tail and hurled it into the gutter; tangled up in a pile of rotting fish, the body floated for a moment, then, as it was swept clear, it was sucked down beneath the green surface scum.

People began to gather about the woman, but Angel turned blindly away. Her hands felt icy cold, despite the heat of the day, and she could not drag her mind away from the gruesome sight she had witnessed.

She was almost home, when her attention was attracted by another crowd.

"Stand back from her!" a man was shouting. "I know the plague when I see it, and she's got it!"

The crowd fell back quickly, revealing a woman lying on the cobbles. She was on her back, her wide-open eyes staring up at the sky, her lower limbs jerking convulsively. She had obviously been vomiting, for her gown was soaked and smeared. Even as Angel stared, she saw the woman's chest heave; vomit sprayed from her mouth, spattering her face and hair and running along the cracks between the cobbles.

Moaning piteously, the woman turned over. The people fled in panic as she began crawling toward them. She was mouthing something that might have been a plea for help.

The man who had spoken, looked at Angel. "You'd better get on home," he said. "There ain't nothin' ter be done for her."

He began to walk on. Angel caught up with him, matching her steps to his long strides. "How do you know that woman has the plague?" she asked.

"I know, that's all," he grunted. "I seen a lot of it, I have. Ain't struck me yet, though."

"How do you care for somebody who has the plague?" Angel questioned him urgently.

Too urgently, for the man said in a voice heavy with suspicion, "If you know someone what's got the plague, you got ter report it, see? Have 'em took off to the pesthouse. It's the only way ter stop it spreadin', and even that don' always do it."

"It—it isn't that." Angel avoided looking at him. "I'd just like to know, that's all."

"Well, you look healthy enough," the man said in a

348

more normal tone. "So I'll tell you. Doctors ain't no good, see. All they knows is bleedin', and that ain't no good. Best thing for a plague patient is ter keep bathin' 'em in cold water. It helps ter keep the fever down, see? Another thing, when the plague boil swells up big, you can sometimes get it ter bust if you keep puttin' on poultices of hot bread." He shook his head gloomily. "But with all the agony what they're already sufferin', them poultices is li'ble ter drive 'em clean off their heads. Terrible, the pain is, and if that ain't enough, the poor bloody devils vomit 'emselves ter death. My whole family was took in the last epidemic. Always been a marvel ter me, it has, why it never got me."

"But is there nothing one can give them?" Angel insisted.

"Well, there's a brew what you make out of rue and sage and buttercup roots. You mix it up in wine, see, then you throws in a touch of angelica and snake foot, and a pinch of saffron." He shrugged. "Don' think it's much help though. Seems ter me as they die, no matter what you do for 'em. Listen, I got ter go."

"Yes," Angel said. "Thank you."

"Look," the man said, "if you want some good advice you'll get out of London, see. I'm goin' ter." He hesitated. "It ain't that I wan' ter worry you, ma'am, but jus' 'fore I come on that woman back there, I seen two more of 'em lyin' in the street. Same as her, they was, a-vomitin' and a-moanin'. 'Twouldn' be no su'prise ter me to find we got ourselves another epidemic, that it wouldn'."

He nodded to Angel, then went swiftly on his way. She stared after him, her eyes wide with anguish. Nicholas had the plague! She had to face it.

"But I won't let him die!" she said aloud. "I won't! I won't!" She looked up at the sky, hating the blazing blue, the stifling heat that hung over the city. "Damn it! He won't die! He can't!"

349

She began to run. Arriving at the house, panting and disheveled, she found Mrs. Sampson dressed and ready to go. Outside, two carriages waited.

Mrs. Sampson held out her hand for the package. "I'll make up my mixture," she said, "then I'll be on my way."

"No." Angel shook her head. "They're waiting for you. Tell me how to do it."

"The instructions are written out," Mrs. Sampson said reluctantly. "You'll find the paper on my table. I put it ready. I always look at it in case I leave something out."

She looked at Angel, the slow difficult tears filling her eyes again. "I don't want to leave my boy," she said in a breaking voice. "I don't care if he thinks he's got the plague. I don't believe it's that serious. He's like my own boy, and I've always nursed him before."

"There's plague in the city," Angel said quietly.

Mrs. Sampson's face went gray. "Then you think that Master Nickey has—"

"Yes," Angel interrupted. "I do think so."

"Then you'll need me. Let me stay."

Angel shook her head. "I've been very close to him, you know that. Go, please! You must keep healthy. If anything should happen to me, he'll—he'll need you."

Mrs. Sampson's mouth quivered. "You're trying to make it easy for me, aren't you, girl? You know well that I've been close too."

"I'm younger than you," Angel answered firmly, "and I'm stronger."

"Aye, 'tis true." Mrs. Sampson lifted a gloved hand and impatiently wiped her tears away. "Look at me, sniffling like a great fool!" She took a step nearer to Angel. "You'll save him, won't you, girl?" she said pleadingly. "You'll save my Master Nickey?"

Angel's eyes glowed with a fierce light. "I will!" she vowed. "I'll save him, or I'll die with him!"

"None of that!" Mrs. Sampson said sharply. "I'll listen to no talk of dying!" She turned blindly to the door. "Send for me if you need me. I'll come at once, you need have no fear of that."

"I know," Angel said softly. "Goodbye, Mrs. Sampson."

The old woman nodded. "God bless you, girl, and God bless my Master Nickey!" She went out of the big front door, closing it gently behind her.

Angel ran quickly up the stairs. Outside Nicholas' room, she paused, her heart pounding. Then she flung open the door and walked boldly into the room.

Nicholas was lying on his back, staring vacantly at the ceiling.

"Darling!" She bent over him. "It's Angel."

His head turned. "Sick!" he said, looking at her without recognition. "Feel so sick! H—help m—me!"

His hands flailed wildly. Retching, he clutched at his throat. He was choking even as Angel slid her arm beneath his shoulders. With the strength of desperation she pulled him over to the side of the bed. She was only just in time. Supporting him, her arms grew numb, but she dared not lay him down again, for no sooner was one spasm over than another began. It was as the man had told her. Nicholas—her Nicholas—was vomiting his life away.

"No!" she whispered. "Help him! Please help him!"

She noticed after a while that, though he continued to retch, the vomiting had stopped. Exerting all of her strength she raised his sagging body and laid him down again. He lay there inert, his night clothes soaked with perspiration. Little rivulets coursed down his flushed face. His swollen lips moved in ceaseless muttering.

Hearing her name, she bent over him. "I'm here," she soothed him. "I'm here, Nicholas."

He looked at her vaguely. "Angel," he said again.

"A—Angel, need you!" A frown drew his brows together. "No, no! Selfish of m—me. Go away, Angel! Go, my—my darling!"

She took his hands in hers. "I'll never leave you, Nicholas! Never!"

He looked straight at her. "I w—w—want Angel."

Weeping, she rose to her feet and stumbled out to the tall oak press where Mrs. Sampson kept the linen. Her arms loaded with sheets and towels, she hurried back expecting—she knew not what.

He was lying just as she had left him. He did not seem to notice when she wiped the perspiration from his face and gently bathed his hot body with a towel wrung out in cool water. Only when she raised his left arm did he utter a sharp cry. She saw then that there was a red swelling in his armpit. The plague boil! Shuddering, she remembered her conversation with the man in the street. Poultices of hot bread, he had advised. But she couldn't just take the man's word. She must have help. Some kind of medical advice. "Doctor's ain't no good," the man had said. Perhaps he was wrong; perhaps he had been talking for the sake of talking. Angel's lips tightened. She was remembering that some people liked to frighten others with hair-raising tales; and if they succeeded in inspiring fear, the better pleased they were.

Nicholas' body was shaken with tremors, and he had begun to moan—a low sound, like somebody who was only beginning to touch on agony; again she thought of the man. "Terrible the pain is," he had said gloomily.

Nicholas' moans stopped abruptly; he began to mumble again. His head turned restlessly on the pillow; his eyes stared wide-open but apparently unseeing for once or twice he looked straight at her without a change of expression.

Angel hesitated, wondering how she could leave him. What if—while she was seeking the doctor—he should get out of bed or injure himself in some way? Her hesitation was only momentary. It had to be done, and she remembered old Doctor Vickers lived in the Square. If she found the doctor in, she need only be gone for a few minutes, and perhaps if she tucked the sheet tightly about him, he would be safe? To think was to act. His mumbling broke off as she smoothed the sheet over him. She straightened his arms, wincing herself as he gave a shout of pain, and enclosed him beneath the tautly drawn sheet.

She was trembling as she fled along the corridor and down the stairs. At the door it was some moments before she could force her quivering hands to open it.

It was unreal, she thought, when she saw a man who had been walking just ahead of her reel, stagger forward for a few erratic paces, then fall heavily to the ground. She tried to tell herself that the man had been drinking, but passing his sprawled body at a run, she heard the choking sounds of his nausea. It was the plague! The plague!

Doctor Vickers was in. He came quickly toward her as she was ushered in, and she did not notice the apprehension in his eyes.

"I will visit when I can," the doctor said wearily, when her voice had faltered into silence. "But I cannot promise when that might be."

"What!" She stared at him in mingled fear and outrage. "But why can you not come with me now?"

"I have a never-ending list of patients asking for me," he explained. " 'Tis only fair that I take them in turn."

"Plague patients?" Angel whispered.

The doctor gave the answer with a lift of his shoulders. "There are other doctors," he said compassionately, glancing at her white face, "but I fear that they will give you the same answer." He was silent for a moment, then, his narrow, pale face flushed. Bitterly, he added, " 'Tis the fault of those in whom we were foolish enough to repose our trust. We have been deceived so that whatever skill we of medical profession may possess, 'twill be impotent now." He shook his head. " 'Tis hopeless, that is my belief. Quite hopeless!"

Angel fought the dread his words had provoked. "I don't understand. What do you mean?"

The doctor picked up his three-cornered hat. "I mean," he said grimly, clamping the hat firmly on his gray head, "that the plague is so widespread in the poorer quarters of the city that it has reached outward. There is no confining it now. Already, it has reached Drury Lane. I mean," he went on, taking her arm and leading her firmly to the door, "that the city officials, with their usual incompetence, thought that by suppressing the news, they would avert a panic. It did not occur to the thickheaded fools that, had they laid the problem before us, we might have been in a position to avert a serious epidemic."

"There—there is a man lying in the street," Angel forced the words from her dry throat. "I think he—I think he has the plague." She clasped her cold hands together. "And earlier, I saw a woman in like condition."

"I don't doubt it," the doctor said gruffly. " 'Tis but the first of many such sights. In this square alone three families have been stricken. I——"

He broke off as a bell began to toll. "The death bell," he said, averting his eyes. " 'Twill become a familiar sound."

"The death bell?" Angel queried faintly.

"Aye. 'Twill toll each time the plague claims a victim." He looked at her keenly. "Perhaps, while there is yet time, you should leave London."

"No!" Angel started back. "My Lord Benbrook needs me and I'll not leave him!"

"He would not want you to stay, you know," Doctor Vickers insisted gently. "Dorothy—my wife—is leaving today. Dorothy is a very sensible woman. Why not talk to her? Perhaps she can persuade you to follow her example."

Angel's jaw set mutinously. "You mean to be kind, I know. But I will not leave him."

The doctor sighed heavily. "Then I can only pray for you."

"You can do more than pray," Angel said urgently. "Come with me. Mayhap you can suggest something to bring his fever down, something to—to ease him."

He shook his head firmly. "As soon as it be humanly possible, I will come. 'Twill be a miracle if I am alive myself," he added bitterly. "Now, listen to me carefully—"

Angel listened numbly to his precise voice issuing instructions, and as she listened her despair grew. He was a doctor, yet he could tell her nothing that her common sense had not already dictated.

She looked at him blindly, nodding her head to show that she had understood; then she turned from him abruptly and walked quickly away. Reaching the house, she stepped into the hall. Breathlessly, as if she had been running a long way, she used both hands to close the heavy door. Bolting it securely, she went with leaden feet up the stairs.

Nicholas had managed to struggle onto his side, and Angel ran quickly to the bed. She was half expecting to find that he had vomited again, and she was relieved to see that he had not. His eyes were closed and he did not stir at her approach. How quickly the ravaging plague had altered his appearance, she thought painfully, studying his gaunt bearded face. His nose had sharpened, and his deeply tanned complexion had faded to a sickly yellow hue, leaving mottled patches of vivid color in his cheeks. He no longer looked like Nicholas. She watched him, knowing that she had never loved him as much as this moment, when she must face the prospect of losing him forever.

She laid her hand caressingly on his damp hair, and the tears she could no longer control coursed down her cheeks and splashed onto his face. Some of her agony must have penetrated the fevered half-conscious state that held him, for his eyes opened slowly and stared at her. Dark eyes that looked oddly unfocused, but they were Nicholas' eyes—unchanging in that terribly altered face.

She smiled at him. "Nicholas," she said his name softly.

She saw recognition dawn. "Nicholas," she said again. Taking his hand in hers, she held it tightly.

His fingers moved in feeble response. His throat worked painfully as though laboring to force out words. "A—Angel," he said in a thick, difficult voice.

She bent lower. "Yes, darling, it's Angel."

The breath rattled in his lungs as he tried once more. "L—l—let m—me die," he said. His eyes pleaded with her. "Leave m—m—me."

"No!" Her moment of weakness passed. "You're going to live, Nicholas! Do you hear me? You're going to live. You must!"

His eyes narrowed. "D—die," he repeated, looking at her with something that was very close to hatred. "Pain, I—I can't s—s—stand it!"

"You can! You will!" she shouted.

His brows contracted. Strong convulsive shudders began to shake his body. His body beneath the sheet was nude, but his fingers—as if unable to bear the weight—clawed frantically at the light cover.

A whimpering scream came from him, and Angel caught both his hands and held them firmly. With a strength she would not have believed possible, he tore his hands from her grasp and flung both arms above his head.

Angel gasped. The plague boil—even in that comparatively short space of time—had increased to at least three times its original size. The skin stretched over the enormous red, yellow-streaked protuberance was shiny and faintly purple.

Nicholas screamed again and again, and Angel, fearful that he would throw himself from the bed, struggled to hold him still. She felt his blows on her head, her arms, and she tasted the salt of her blood as his wildly flailing fist, pulped her lip, but she would not release him. At last, when she was on the point of screaming herself, he went limp beneath her.

Cautiously she raised herself, her hands poised in readiness to hold him if he should move again. He was conscious; she could see the glitter of his eyes between slitted lids, but the frenzy had left him. His chest heaved as he struggled for air, and his mouth, sagging open, revealed a swollen tongue that all but filled up his mouth.

He was dying! Black despair gripped Angel. Her movements became almost apathetic. She supported him when he began abruptly to vomit once more. The spasm subsiding, he lay against her with his head resting heavily on her breast. The whimpering sounds he made were like those of a sick and bewildered child. Listening to them her apathy left her. Anger took its place, a good healthy anger that roused her fighting spirit. Die! Not while she still had the strength to fight for him!

With an effort, she managed to lay him down again. He did not fight her, and when she spoke to him in a low, soothing voice, it seemed to comfort him; for he sighed once or twice and turned his head as if listening.

Angel did not delude herself; she knew that he did not hear her. He had reached a plateau of exhaustion that put him for the moment beyond pain. But the pain would return and with it the madness and violence.

Still talking, Angel rose from her crouched position beside the bed. Looking down at him, she could not help remembering some of the stories she had heard of the plague that had struck London some sixteen years before. The death toll had been dreadful, and those who were able had fled. The city became a graveyard. If a member of a family was stricken with the plague, the city officials ordered that the house be locked, and a guard was placed outside to prevent a possible escape. Because of this order many people died unnecessarily, for the healthy, in forced imprisonment with the sick, soon succumbed.

Nicholas groaned. Would it be for him, Angel wondered, as it had been for the victims of that other plague? Many of them, she had been told, had been so maddened by the incredibly shocking pain of the swelling plague boil that they had taken their own lives.

Night and day the church bells had tolled for the dead, and the death carts were overflowing with piles of corpses. There had been gruesome stories of those who, not quite dead, had been thrown into the death cart while they yet breathed. With the cold stiff corpses for companions, they were buried alive in the hastily dug pits used for communal graves.

Like a horrifying echo of her thoughts, a bell began to toll, its slow ponderous strokes filling the room. It brought a cold sweat of terror to her brow.

But Nicholas would not die, she swore! She would not let him! No one must know that there was plague in the house, for if she was to help Nicholas she must be free to come and go, she must be free to buy the things that would be needed. If a guard were to be stationed outside the house, he would do his duty as ordered. No appeal of hers would move him; he would be instructed to keep everyone within the house, and he would be unconcerned if they starved to death.

Angel thought rather uneasily of Doctor Vickers. Would he report her? She shrugged the thought of him aside; it would not do to dwell upon the possibility; all of her energy, all of her strength, must be concentrated on one goal: to save Nicholas. If he died, there would be nothing left of her world, and she would as soon join him in death as live on without him. Doubtless, she thought, with a touch of grim humor, her death would be easily arranged. The plague was known to be highly infectious, and few there were in contact with it who escaped.

Nicholas was moving restlessly again. The little broken cries escaping his lips would, when the pain claimed him fully, become screams of agony. She must bind him. It was for his own safety, and she cared not if he struck her or cursed her. There were silken cords holding back the draperies in the green drawing room, they were thin but strong; she would use them to tie his hands and feet to the bed rails. With a last look at Nicholas, Angel went swiftly to the room.

The slow-plodding desperate hours that followed brought a strength to Angel that—had she stopped to think about it—would have filled her with an amazed awe. Invincible, indefatigable, she ran up and down the stairs, heating broth, spooning it into an unwilling mouth, cleaning up after him when he vomited it back. She bathed him, changed the bed linen, her slender arms—imbued with a desperate strength—moving him as easily as if he had been a child. She shopped, sidling past suspicious-eyed guards, her hood drawn forward to hide her bruised face. Nicholas, when she untied his hands for a moment, had struck her with savage frenzy in his delirium and pain. He did not know her; he knew only

359

the pain that mounted steadily to an unbearable crescendo.

The hours passed into one day, then two, and Nicholas was still alive. But looking at his sunken face, hearing his screams of agony, seeing him choking on the impediment of his swollen tongue, she knew that she was losing the battle. It would be kinder to let him die, but she could not! No, not while she still cherished any small grain of hope! Nicholas must live! Oh, dear God, he must!

She listened to the bells tolling, tolling, forever and endlessly tolling for the dead! She heard the spine-chilling cry of the death patrol: "Bring out your dead! Bring out your dead!" And she would lift her head, her cheeks wet with tears, her heart feeling like a frozen stone in her breast, but finding in her fear and resentment and anger, a new surge of that all but miraculous strength.

In the early hours of the third day, Nicholas began vomiting blood. It gushed from his mouth and trickled in a steady stream from his nostrils. Listening to his choking efforts to breathe, Angel knew that she must let him go. The blue plague spots that denoted death's final victory had not yet appeared; nevertheless she could not let him go in such horrifying suffering.

She stood beside the bed, her eyes burning in her exhausted face. Her brain grappled with her decision and made it final. Giving in at last, she sagged to her knees beside the bed.

"My darling!" She pressed her lips to his hot, dry forehead. "My dearest love! I'll never leave you," she promised fervently. "For when—when it is over, I shall lie beside you and take you in my arms. You will be at rest then, and very soon, so too shall I."

She rose to her feet again and, very gently, she slipped the pillow from under his head. One last long yearning look she took at him, then she settled the pillow over his face.

"Mistress Angel!" a voice said from the doorway. "What is it that you would do?"

"Pip!" Angel saw the black boy through a wavering haze. "Pip, how did—how did—" she broke off, staring.

Pip started across the room. "You must not do this thing," he said, snatching the pillow from Nicholas' face.

"Oh pray do not!" Angel collapsed to the floor. She burst into anguished sobs. "I cannot b—bear him to suffer more! Oh, Pip, I cannot!"

"I knew it would be so," Pip answered. "I am sorry, Mistress Angel, that my return has been so delayed. But there were things that I needed."

"How did—did you get into th—the house?" Angel said faintly. Her brain felt thick with confusion. She hoped that he would go on talking, that she could lie where she was, listening, and never have to rise to her feet again.

"I have my ways," Pip said. "But that is not important. The thing I must do—the thing that I came here to do is to make the lord well again."

She heard him. Her hands dropped from her face. "You will make him better? You will?" Hysterical laughter shook her, and she said, between gasps, "Look at him! Can you not see that it's too late?" Her spiraling laughter was strangled by sobs. "Do you not th—think I w—would give my life to save him?" She doubled her fist and began beating at the floor, hard blows that Pip feared would surely break the delicate bones in her hand.

"Oh God!" Angel screamed. "I tried! I tried! But it's no use, it was never any use!" She turned her head, glaring at Pip through a bright glitter of tears. "Go away!" her voice rose to a new high. "Leave me to die with him! Go! Go! 'Tis the only way—'tis the kindest way!"

Pip looked back at her. His eyes were inscrutable,

but he did not move. She did not look like his beautiful Mistress Angel now. Her face was stark and pale, her hair pulled back and fastened into a tight knot. Her eyes were feverish and desperate, the flesh surrounding them swollen and discolored from much crying. She looked, the boy thought, almost plain. He felt a rush of love for her, and suddenly she seemed to him to be more beautiful than ever before. It was her love for the dying lord that had worked this havoc. Such a love was rare, it should be guarded and cherished above all other things.

"Why do you not answer?" Angel demanded. "Why do you just stand there? Go, I tell you! Leave us together!"

"Enough!" Pip said harshly. He walked toward her. "Come," he held out a hand to her. "Rise to your feet, Mistress Angel. Rest, and let your mind know ease. I will not let the lord die. I, M'Zeli, tell you this."

Angel stared at his hand almost stupidly, then, as his words penetrated, she began to cry again. "Oh, Pip, if—if you only could!"

"It can be so," he insisted, still holding out his hand.

Reluctantly Angel allowed him to draw her to her feet. Why did he mock her with false promises of a cure? Why did he not go away and leave her with her darling?

Pip settled her in a chair. "How can you do it?" she asked dully.

"There is a man living in this city," Pip answered, "a man of my own country, his name is MaHeber. Once, before MaHeber came to these shores, he lived through just such a plague. From this experience he learned many things. There are herbs, unguents, many things, and I have brought with me the fruits of his great wisdom; with these to aid me I will cure the lord."

"African magic?" Angel's lips twisted into a bitter smile. " 'Twill not work."

"The lord will live," Pip assured her calmly. "Rest, please. Trust me."

She watched with dulled hopeless eyes as Pip went quietly to work. He bathed Nicholas' fevered body with cool water, his touch so light that there was scarcely an interruption in Nicholas' disjointed mumbling. He screamed once when Pip, after securing his arm again, took a black paste from a small jar and smeared it over the great carbuncle.

Hypnotized, Angel made no protest when Pip pounded something that looked to her to be a cluster of small green berries into a bowl, whipped it into a paste, and turned out the resulting mess onto a piece of clean linen. A peculiar odor filled the room, and she stirred uneasily as Pip, working with calm, efficient movements, folded the cloth over the paste and knotted it at both ends.

"What are you going to do?" she cried, starting out of the chair.

Pip turned and looked at her, and there was something in his eyes that quelled her fear. Wearily she sank back into the chair. "What are you going to do?" she said quietly.

Pip gave her a nod of approval. "In my country," he said with a faint smile, "many things are known to us. There is, for instance, a certain tree that bears a berry that induces sleep. When crushed, its fumes bring surcease to suffering. It is this crushed berry that I have placed in the linen. I will hold it under the lord's nose and very soon he will be deep in untroubled sleep."

"But—but it might kill him."

"As you planned to do, Mistress Angel," Pip reminded her. "But have no fear; it will not kill him. He will sleep without pain, and when I tend him he will not awaken. Come to the bedside," he commanded her. "I will show you."

Kneeling beside the bed, Angel watched as Pip held the little linen bundle under Nicholas' nose. He began squeezing it gently, so that the odor grew stronger. Nicholas' head turned restlessly on the pillow, and he gave a little cry; his inflamed lids lifted, his eyes were wild, as if he protested this invasion of his senses. But within the space of a few seconds his eyes dulled, his lids drooped heavily; he gave a shuddering sigh and then was still.

Too still! Angel pressed a clenched hand to her mouth.

Pip glanced at her understandingly. "The lord is not dead, Mistress Angel. Do you not see how evenly his chest rises and falls?"

It was true. The weak tears filled Angel's eyes again. Nicholas looked peaceful. For the first time in all those agony-wracked hours, he was free of pain.

She looked up at Pip. An enormous gratitude rose within her. "Thank you," she said, her voice tear-choked. "Even if he should die, you have given him some peace, and for that I can never thank you enough!"

"But he will not die, and you need not thank me. Are you not my friend, my mother, and my sister?" He laid his hand lightly on Nicholas' shoulder. "You love the lord; therefore do I also love him."

"And you are not afraid, Pip? You do not fear the disease?"

He shook his head. "There is a greater fear, Mistress Angel, 'tis to be bereft of the company of loved ones. I know that the lord must be restored to you, else would you also die, and this, you understand, is a calamity not to be borne."

She was about to stammer forth her gratitude again, but Pip's upraised hand stemmed the words on her lips. There was a new dignity about him, she observed, and she sensed that, though lacking the years, he nonetheless had become the man he had always claimed to be. She felt a rush of genuine love for him. Pip saw it in her eyes. Gently he said, "The unguarded eyes reveal much,

364

Mistress Angel, and what I have seen in yours this night will ever be a cherished memory."

He moved away from the bed. Angel said in quick alarm, "Where are you going?"

"I go to the kitchen quarters." He gave her a reassuring smile. "My preparations must be complete against the time the lord awakens."

Pip was gone for some time; when he returned he brought with him a tall glass full of a light purple liquid. "For the vomiting," he explained.

Nicholas slept for many hours, and with each one that passed Angel felt the hope she had thought dead growing ever larger.

Pip scarcely glanced at her, his whole attention was concentrated on Nicholas. He annointed the swelling mass beneath Nicholas' arm with a bewildering array of unguents and strangely colored powders, explaining in an absent voice, "The unguents and powders cannot be mixed into one whole blending, though 'twould be easier so to do. But it does not work that way. They must be placed in layers. There is a reason for this, but it would take too long to explain."

Angel looked on with wondering eyes as Pip, ending the treatment with a further layer of brownish, sword-shaped leaves, bound the whole together with a long strip of soft linen.

"Leaves?" she said. "What purpose do they serve, Pip?"

"It is necessary to the treatment," he said in the same absent voice. "And though they bear a resemblance to leaves, they are not." He did not explain further, and Angel was suddenly so overcome with weariness that she did not ask.

Pip was indefatigable. Through the mists of sleep that she would never quite allow to claim her, she was vaguely aware of his activities. She drifted along in this pleasant haze, her mind blessedly freed of anxiety; but it came rushing back when Pip touched her lightly on the shoulder.

She sat up with a start, her eyes widening with apprehension. "Nicholas! Pip, he's not—not—"

"The lord still sleeps, but soon he will awaken. It is best therefore that you take some nourishment."

She became aware of the silver bowl in his hand. "It is kind of you," she said, her eyes sliding past him to the bed. "But I cannot eat. It would choke me, I fear."

"It is only broth," he said coaxingly.

"I would rather not." She smiled at him to soften her words.

Pip looked at her sternly. "You will eat, Mistress Angel."

He took up the spoon and dipped it in the broth. "Come now, open your mouth, please."

She wanted to refuse him, but he was insistent. She was so very tired. There was a pain starting just behind her eyes, and she felt faintly nauseated, but perhaps it was better to comply. He was holding out the spoon, obviously expecting her to open her mouth. Like a docile child, she did so.

The broth was hot and savory, but after she had swallowed it it seemed to increase her nausea. "No more, please," she said, after the fourth spoonful.

Pip sighed. "Perhaps, later, you will feel hungry."

"Perhaps," she agreed. "Pip, how is he?"

"When he awakens you will find that there is an improvement, but—" he stopped, frowning.

"But?" Angel urged. "Tell me, please."

"I did not realize the extent of the lord's illness," Pip said slowly. "I shall need more herbs, more unguents; therefore must I leave you for a while."

"No!" Angel exclaimed. "Please don't leave him, Pip."

"But I must. It is imperative that I visit MaHeber."

"I will go." Angel clutched at his arm. "Please! He needs you!"

"The guards are nervous," Pip said, looking at her with worried eyes. "I know how to slip by unobserved. If they had the faintest suspicion that you came from a house of the plague, they would imprison you in the pesthouse."

"But they will not know," she insisted. "Pip, please! I have kept the secret, have I not? You do not see a patrolling guard in front of this house, do you?"

"W—well—" he bit his lip and shot her a quick look. "Very well," he said, "but if aught happens to you, then the weight of blame will ever go with me."

"No, Pip, you must not think—" she broke off, her eyes flying in fear to the bed. "He's—he's moving."

"Yes," Pip said, moving to the bed. " 'Tis time. Come, Mistress Angel. When he is fully awake I will raise his head, you will spoon the liquid into his mouth." He nodded toward the tall glass containing the light purple liquid. "You understand?"

Nicholas' eyes, when they opened, looked hazy, but he did not appear to be in severe pain.

"The pain is deadened," Pip said, in answer to her glance of inquiry. "But I need more medicines." He hesitated. "It is possible that the plague boil will burst, of course, and in that case further medicines would be unnecessary. Once the poisons drain out, the patient has a good chance of living. However, it is as well to be prepared for all eventualities."

At a signal from Pip, Angel picked up the glass. Her hand felt numb and cold, and the spoon rattled against the glass as she prepared herself for the ordeal she felt sure was to come.

"A—A—A—" it was a dry whisper, like the rustling of dead leaves. "A—A—A—gel."

"The lord calls you, Mistress Angel," Pip said. Calmly, he slid his hands beneath Nicholas' wildly ruffled dark head. "The first spoonful, please," he instructed.

"Please, Nicholas!" Angel said entreatingly. "Try. For me."

Surprisingly the swollen lips opened obediently. At first, as the liquid trickled down his throat, Nicholas choked and fought for breath. But there was a look in his eyes, as he glanced from Angel's white strained face to Pip's dark intent one, that showed a kind of trust. Again and again his lips opened, and each time the swallowing grew easier. Once, when he groaned and retched, Pip slid one hand free and reached behind him for the basin. He placed it within convenient reach and gently raised the suffering man. But Nicholas, although his breath came in great gasps, did not vomit.

"It is well," Pip said with quiet satisfaction, laying him down again.

The tears started to Angel's eyes as she saw Nicholas rest his cheek against Pip's hand. He was trying to thank him, and somehow that weak gesture touched her unbearably.

"Just one more spoonful, darling," she coaxed, when Pip turned Nicholas' head toward her. "See, only one."

His mouth opened, but his eyes clung to her face as if he could not have enough of the sight of her.

The liquid bubbled in his throat, and Angel thought that he meant to reject it, then he gave a last convulsive swallow and it was down.

"He will sleep again," Pip said, as he took his hands away.

Nicholas gave a great sigh. "A—A—"

"Yes, dear love, it's Angel," she said softly. She put a hand to either side of his face and very gently kissed his sunken cheek. "I love you, dear m'lord! I love you so very much!" She kissed him once more, then as Pip cleared his throat meaningfully, she straightened.

Pip nodded significantly toward the door, and she knew that he was urging her to hasten.

Her mouth trembled. She did not fear the journey through the polluted streets as much as the thought that she might be looking her last upon this man who had come to represent her whole world.

It was the panic in Nicholas' eyes, as Pip draped her cloak about her shoulders, that steadied her. Did he think that she was deserting him? Leaving him to die alone?

"Nay, love!" Angel fell to her knees beside the bed. " 'Tis only for a little while that I go." She picked up his thin, twitching hand and pressed it to her lips. "I would never leave you! Never!"

Relieved, she saw that he believed her, for the expression of panic faded. "Sleep, love," she urged. "Sleep."

He made a strangled sound deep in his throat, and she saw the chords straining as he fought for words. "I— I lo—lo—you."

"You love me," she interpreted.

The faintest nod answered her. "Then we are in accord, my lord," she answered, trying to speak lightly. She stroked his hair. "One day, when we have hours to spare, I will show you how ardently I return the feeling."

To her horror, she saw a tear fall from the corner of his eye. "Don't, love!" she exclaimed, wiping the tear away with her finger. "Indeed you must not!"

Pip, attracted by something in her voice, came to lean over the bed. "Ah!" he said, and he sounded so pleased that Angel glanced at him in surprise. "Be thankful, Mistress Angel, 'tis a good sign. Moisture returns to his body." He clasped his hands together and for the first time Angel saw the flash of his old delighted grin. "All will be well now. He will need but little more of the medicine, but," he said with sober face, "that little I must have, and soon."

"I know." Angel rose to her feet. " 'Twill not be for long," she said, giving Nicholas a reassuring smile. "I will be back very soon, and in the meantime Pip will take very good care of you."

Nicholas' head turned slowly on the pillow, his lips moving as if they would form words.

"Do not speak, my lord." Pip smiled at him and patted his hand. "Later, when you are well, you may beat me for my impudence. But for now I must request you to keep silence. 'Tis better so."

Something that might almost have been a smile lightened Nicholas' eyes. "R—ro—rogue," he jerked out defiantly.

"Yes, my lord." Pip bent over him, adjusting the covers over his body. "But though you are a great lord, you speak now with the son of a mighty chief, and as such I will be obeyed." He laughed. "I hope, my lord, that we understand each other."

In the deliberate diversion created by Pip, Angel slipped out of the door. Her heart was lighter than it had been for days, and had it not been for her pounding headache and her steadily increasing nausea, she would have felt almost happy.

ANGEL HURRIED ALONG THE NARROW street, trying to ignore the burning in her lungs and the painful stabbing in her side, for she dared not slow her footsteps. It would be full dark soon, and she had yet to reach the lodging of MaHeber.

She shivered as she felt the hard, suspicious eyes of the two patrolmen she passed on the corner of Bleek Street. Suspicion! Fear! It hung over devastated London like a black smothering pall. The patrolmen had the lower half of their faces covered with vinegar-soaked cloths. They took a step or two toward her, and she was terrified that they intended to call the Watch. She nodded and gave them the most brilliant smile she could muster.

"Wha's a gran' lady the likes o' you doin' out in the streets, eh?" one of them called.

Angel halted, her heart fluttering. But suddenly inspired, she laughed shrilly. "Lady? Tha's a good 'un, that is! You ain't goin' ter catch no bleedin' lady a-walkin' her feet off, are you?"

The man hesitated; then he said gruffly, "Be off will you, then. Don' you let me catch you hangin' 'bout, see, or I'll have you taken up by the Watch."

Thankful to escape, she walked on, calling over her

shoulder, "It's nice ter meet a coupla gen'lemen for a change."

Her thin shoes were soaked through from the puddles of scummy water that had overflowed from the gutters and collected in pools between the worn cobblestones. Beneath her dark hood, pulled well forward to hide her face, she could feel her hair clinging wetly to her skull; droplets trickled down her neck, and there was a glaze of perspiration over her face.

She swallowed against a sudden surge of nausea. Oh God, she felt ill, desperately ill! She had the plague, she knew it now. But she must force herself on—she must find MaHeber's house. It was for Nicholas! Nicholas! She must keep telling herself that.

Shoreditch, at last. Angel paused to get her bearings. Yes, there was the Ale House Pip had spoken of—The Plough and Bull. It was dark and shuttered, the owners fled. The sign moved in the wind, making a dismal sound as it grated on the iron supporting arm.

Angel moved on; the rough cobblestones over which she trod seemed to shimmer, to move, so that she was afraid she might fall. She blinked her eyes hard. Not much further now; she would soon be at MaHeber's house. Surely she would find sufficient strength for the journey back to St. Bernard's Square? It was for Nicholas! For her love! If only there was a coach to be had! But no one could now ride through the deserted London streets in a coach, especially since someone had started the rumor that horses were carriers of the plague. Dizzy, she leaned back into a shop doorway.

The houses, tightly clustered and inclining forward, seemed to be trying to catch her up in dark arms; terror filled her, and she shook her head to dislodge the absurd fancy.

"A little more, Angel Dawson," she muttered. "Just a little more."

No! No! She mustn't talk to herself, she would arouse suspicion! Guards, looking half-sick themselves, were standing before the doors that were marked with the fatal red cross; in the light of their lanterns, she could see the words scrawled beneath the cross—"Lord have mercy upon us!"

"Listen," one of the lounging guards called, straightening himself. "Ain't that the death cart a-comin'?"

"Aye," another guard called in reply. "I got three in this house what's dead. Best move aside, I s'pose. I ain't handlin' none o' 'em, an' there ain't 'nough money ter make me!"

Angel's stomach lurched. She pressed her hand hard against her mouth, fighting to stem her sickness. That sound! Even in the few moments of uneasy sleep she had sometimes managed to snatch, she had dreamed of it. The tinkling bell—the heavy creak of turning wheels—the voice calling loudly its ghoulish request: "Bring out your dead! Bring out your dead!"

The bell's thin tinkling notes, sounding unnaturally loud, filled her ears. The wheels creaked and groaned protestingly as they rounded the corner, and suddenly, like something from a nightmare, the death cart was there!

Angel was unable to drag her eyes away from the grim procession. First came the bellman—there was something almost arrogant in his bearing as he plied the bell vigorously. Walking slightly behind the bellman, a man in a round hat with a heavy coat buttoned to his throat carried a flaming torch high above his head. The leaping flame lit the heavy, sullen face of the driver, and the meaty hands holding the reins negligently. A bony horse with a dulled chestnut coat dispiritedly pulled the cart, neither hurrying nor slowing its pace in response to the curses of the driver.

Angel drew in her breath with a little sobbing cry at sight of the bodies piled in the cart.

The driver pulled up the horse. Another man came from behind and stood by the side of the cart, his torch illuminating the scene to full horror.

Some of the bodies, Angel saw, were wrapped in sheets—the last pitiful service rendered to them by their grieving loved ones. But most were naked, their stiffened limbs frozen into the agonized position in which they had died. Lodged in that tangle of limbs was a child, its tiny arms flung wide as though in appeal, its face so contorted with the death agony that it looked scarcely human.

"Bring out your dead!" the driver shouted. "Come on! Them as wants their dead meat buried, bring 'em out!"

Near to Angel, a window squeaked open. She could hear the sound of loud sobbing; a body came flying through the air and landed with a sickening thud beside the cart.

"Clumsy swine!" the torchman roared, shaking a clenched fist in the direction of the window. "We gives you good service, we does, an' we ain't 'bout ter be knocked off our feet by your stinkin' dead meat!"

"Shut up," the driver growled. "Help Sam heave it up on the cart."

Still grumbling, the torchman adjusted the vinegar mask over his face. Handing his torch to the driver, he and the bellman lifted the body and threw it on top of the pile.

Angel waited for no more. Careless of being seen, she went stumblingly along the street. Her hood fell back, and her loosened, windblown hair whipped across her face as she searched frantically for MaHeber's house. There it was at last. It stood back from the row of dark, huddled houses; a squat wooden building, standing alone on a patch of stony ground. A rough path led to a splintered sagging door. Sharp stones pierced the sole of Angel's shoe as she hurried along the path, but she scarcely felt them. She was beset with a new fear. The house looked deserted. Had MaHeber fled the city? Oh merciful God, no! MaHeber must be inside! He must!

She stared at the dark narrow windows, the peeling paint that hung from the walls like strips of gray dead skin, and hysteria seized her.

She almost fell against the door. "MaHeber!" She pounded on it with clenched fists. "MaHeber!" she shouted. "MaHeber! I come with a message from M'Zeli. Let me in! Let me in!"

In that street of dark, dread silence, her pounding roused someone to an anguished plea. A voice, sounding from the house opposite cried, "Who's there? Who knocks? Help me, I'm dying! In the name of the merciful God, help me!"

Sobbing, Angel covered her ears. "Oh don't! I can do nothing for you!" she moaned. "Nothing! Nothing!"

The door in front of her opened abruptly. "Be silent!" a voice hissed.

Angel did not resist when a hand grasped her arm and pulled her through the doorway and into a narrow hall. It was dimly lighted by a lantern draped with a thin green cloth, and the air was filled with a strange fragrance.

A man picked up the lantern and guided her along the hallway and into a room to the right, frugally lit by three candles. It was small and crowded with furniture. The windows were draped with a thick black cloth which effectively kept the candlelight from showing through to the street.

Her guide released her arm. "What do you wish of me, woman?" he said in a soft sibilant voice.

Angel stared at the man before her. He was small and frail and now stood unmoving, his dark, wrinkled face politely inquiring. His thin monkeylike hands emerging from the sleeves of a red silk robe were folded before him; his hairless head caught a dull reflection from the candlelight. Despite his appearance of great age, his brown eyes, very sharp and bright, were fastened most disconcertingly upon her face.

"Are—are you MaHeber?" Angel stammered.

"I am." He made her a small, stiff bow. "I ask you again, what is it you wish of me?"

"Pip—I mean M'Zeli, he—he sent me."

The old man's expression altered. "Your name, please?" he queried, with a trace of warmth in his voice.

"Angel. Angel Dawson."

"Ah!" The bald head nodded. "Then you are M'Zeli's good angel?" A slight smile curved his lips. "I have heard much of you. And this lord, for whom the young chief showed such great concern, how is he?"

Angel stared at him vaguely. It was so hot in this room! Why was she here? Who was this odd little man standing before her? Her brain felt thick, and it was hard to think. Nicholas! Pip! Of course, of course, the little man was MaHeber.

"Herbs!" she blurted. How strange her voice sounded. "I want to—to thank you for sa—saving Nicholas—" She broke off, searching for words. "Saving him," she resumed at last.

"You need more of the herbs?" he prompted.

Pain shot through her head as she nodded. "Yes, and ung—ung—"

"Unguents," MaHeber said gently. "I understand."

There was something she wanted to ask him. She must think. "So—so many d—dead," she began. "Why do you n—not tell them of your c—c—cure?"

He laughed bitterly. "I too have seen the dead. I have seen the bodies heaped into pits and covered thinly with soil. I have seen those pathetic graves black with crows who, with their cruel ripping beaks, offer the final desecration to the sacred flesh of the dead."

376

She gave him a strained, uncomprehending smile. The pain in her head! Oh, it was becoming unendurable!

"I have offered them my cures," MaHeber went on fiercely. "I have begged them, asked them in the name of their god to try them! But they will not. Dogs have been set upon me, and there have even been accusations that I, MaHeber, am in some way responsible for the terrors of this devastating plague."

Air! She must have air! She was going to vomit. What would the strange man, moving so vaguely before her, say? He would be angry with her. But she felt so ill! So terribly, terribly ill! She could see a face floating before her, a darkly handsome face with coldly critical eyes. The lips in the face parted. "Back straight!" a commanding voice said. "Are you deformed, you little fool, that you cannot straighten your back?"

The wailing cry that broke from her caused Ma-Heber to start.

"Nicholas!" Angel panted. "The herbs! Oh, please!" She extended appealing hands toward MaHeber.

She saw his oddly broken outline moving away from her, the flicker of his shadow upon the wall. She wanted to beg him again, but she could not force out the words. She stood there dazed, tears running down her cheeks. She had no idea how long he was gone; it might have been a minute or an hour. Suddenly he was there before her. Something was placed in her hands. "Take it," his soft voice said. He closed her fingers about the something he had given her. "Return home by the shortest route, woman, for it is apparent to me that the shadow is upon you. Tell M'Zeli that you have need of my cure."

The package he had given her felt heavy in her hands. She stumbled a little as he guided her to the door. The boom of its closing was a thunderclap in her ears. She must rest, but only for a very little while. Somebody was waiting for her. It was important! Very important!

She put out a hand and felt cold stone beneath her fingers. Somewhere a dog was howling on a long, melancholy note. The dead! The dog was keening for the dead! Her fingernails scraped the stone wall, sending a violent shudder through her. She heard almost with surprise the choking sounds she made as her stomach twisted inside her. A sour flood bubbled upward, clogging her throat, forcing itself from her mouth. She bent almost double, the sounds of her retching loud in the ghostlike silence of the street.

Exhausted, she leaned against the wall. Now, in her mind's eye, she saw the same darkly handsome face, but so changed, so ravaged and wasted by disease. The swollen lips were opening; a hoarse choked voice was saying, "I—I—lo—lo—you."

"Nicholas!" Angel whispered. He was calling to her! He was pulling her back. She must get to him, though it cost her her life. "I—I'm coming."

Clutching the package tightly to her breast, she reeled drunkenly along the street.

MaHeber, sitting motionless on a cushion in the center of the room, sighed for the shadow of disaster he had seen gathering about M'Zeli's good angel. Yes, he knew well that it was death he had seen in her eyes. For himself, death would be a friend. He was done with life, and he was glad.

MaHeber smiled. It was time for him to die; he felt it in his heart.

He reflected on the peculiarities of mankind. On a people who shunned him because with his black skin he was alien to them. He had wished to pass on to them some of the accumulated knowledge and wisdom of his ancient people, but they hated him. They would accept nothing from hands that were black, for how could he, an ignorant slave with a heathen heart, possess a knowledge superior to that of their learned doctors? Their men had not the skill to save the victims of the plague, but at least they had the advantage of a white skin.

"Nay," they had whispered to each other; it was witchcraft the jungle man offered them. Black witchcraft, as black as original sin, as black as his skin!

MaHeber rose to his feet and went to his narrow bed beneath the black-draped window. He lay on his back, his limbs composed decently as long ago his mother had taught him to do. He closed his eyes, rejoicing in the knowledge that very soon he would join his wife, lovely MaHatalia; in her love, he would become once more a strong young warrior. Love was stronger than death, he had always known that; it lived in the winds, in the rains that comforted the parched earth, in a smile, a word. It lived in the hearts of men, if they would but open the locked gates and allow it to fly free.

Love! MaHatalia was love! The god who knew no boundaries of creed and color would smile upon a lonely old man; he would take him by the hand and lead him back to the arms of that one beloved woman.

Over stricken London the bells tolled mournfully for the dead. MaHeber did not hear them. Smiling, he waited. Death came, and he was carried swiftly forward to his glory and his triumph.

Lɪᴛ ʙʏ ᴛʜᴇ ꜰʟᴀʀɪɴɢ ᴛᴏʀᴄʜᴇs ᴀɴᴅ ʜᴇʀ-
alded by the tinkling bell, the death cart came rumbling
over the uneven cobblestones.

The driver called wearily, for the hour was late,
"Bring out your dead! Hey, you what's listenin'! Bring
out your dead! An' them as won't can keep 'em to warm
'emselves by!" The tired horse stumbled, and the driver,
cursing, flicked the animal's sweaty, twitching body with
the whip.

"Get up!" he shouted. He turned his head and shot
a look of alarm at the pile of precariously-swaying bodies
in the back of the cart.

"Keep an eye on the cold meat," the driver shouted
to the torchman. "We don' want 'em to go orf on their
own, do we?" He chuckled in appreciation of his little
joke.

The torchman grunted sourly, " 'S all right as long
as we don' shove no more in. You might jus' as well
stop callin', Tom. One more on top o' that lot'll topple
the bleeders."

"Ain't you even got room for a little 'un?" the bellman called. He pointed with a grimy finger. "See? Her
over there. Now there's a wench what'd 'preciate a ride."

The torchman shrugged. "Le's make her the las', then. Pull up, Tom."

"Wench, eh?" The driver tugged on the reins, bringing the horse to a slithering halt. "Don't you boys go kissin' her, now. Else it's you what'll be takin' a ride."

The torchman ignored him. Adjusting his mask, he nodded curtly to the other man. "Le's heave her, then. We ain't got all bleedin' night to waste."

Somewhat sullenly the bellman followed him. He did not care for Sam Tapper's commanding tone. "He's forgot," he thought, "that it's me what's the 'portant one. 'S my ringin' what they lis'ens for."

His sullenness vanished as he peered at the dark crumpled form of the woman. "She dead?" he asked.

"Don' know. If she ain't now, she soon will be. Looks dead, though."

"Got nice hair, ain't she?" the bellman said, eyeing the red-gold hair illumined by the flaring torch.

"I ain't got no time ter go lookin' at hair." He laid his torch on the cobbles; it spluttered fiercely, its flame leaping higher, but it did not go out. "You take her legs."

The small spark inside her that had retained a desperate hold on awareness told Angel that she was being touched. Voices came to her, faint and far off.

"Don't seem to me as she's dead," a man's deep voice said. "I thought I heard her give a moan."

Dead! Angel opened her mouth to scream a protest, but although her lips writhed, no sound came forth. But she must tell them, she must! No! No! Not dead! Oh God, please help me! Make them see!

"There," the deep voice said. "She jus' give another moan."

"Don' make no diff'rence," another man answered. "The wench'll be nice 'n' ready by the time we get ter the graves."

"If you say so. It don' make no bleedin' diff'rence ter me. Throw her on."

Someone was grasping her ankles. Hands were clutching her beneath the armpits. Hard, hurting, uncaring hands. How could this be happening? Couldn't they see that she wasn't dead—didn't they care?

Somebody laughed and said lightly, "Pity, ain't it? An' her with that nice hair 'n' all."

Nicholas! Nicholas! They were swinging her body. What were they going to do? Why couldn't she speak—tell them? Oh, please! I'm not dead! Nicholas! Help me, Nicholas!

Another swing, and she landed with a jarring thump on something that was hard and cold. Her feebly clawing fingers tangled in a soft silkiness. Hair! the word screamed in her brain. Her fingers traveled lower, encountering the shape of a nose, the flabbiness of a sagging mouth. Cold flesh! Dead flesh! The pumping of her heart shook her body, and she surrendered thankfully to the darkness that claimed her.

It was the wheels, jolting over a large obstacle, that shook her back into consciousness. She lay still, fighting the monstrous pain in her head. Where was she? Why did she feel so strange? Somewhere near to her she could hear men swearing. "It's broke the bleedin' wheel," she heard one of them say. "It'll take us hours ter mend!"

Men talking—a broken wheel? Angel's pain-shocked mind groped awkwardly. Cold flesh beneath her. Where —? The death cart! Oh God! No! They were taking her to the burial ground! She was to be thrown in with these polluted bodies—thrown in alive! Almost she could feel the earth being thrown into her face—it was clogging her lungs! It was choking her!

Terror gave her a burst of surprising strength. Her hand reached out and clutched at splintered wood. She gripped the edge of the cart and struggled, slid and fought her way over the heaped-up bodies. Reaching the end of the cart, she flung herself outward.

A shock of pain went through her body as she struck the cobblestones, but she was up in a moment and lurched along the street with a sudden burst of strength.

The driver turned from his inspection of the broken wheel. "Christ's body!" he exclaimed, staring after her. "I tol' you she was alive." He took a step forward, hesitated, then shrugging his shoulders he turned back to the wheel. "Let her go," he growled. "We got 'nough on our han's without runnin' after half-dead meat. 'Sides, sooner or later we'll be gettin' her back."

Angel stumbled on, the breath burning in her lungs. She was dying, she knew that. Out here it would come to her, in a dark, windswept street, with horror chasing hard on her heels, and that same horror forcing her on and on beyond her strength. Only, she thought, her steps slowing in exhaustion, she could not now remember the form of that horror. What was she running from? She was a little speck whirling in black space, without name, without knowledge. The one true reality was pain, the burning fever of her body, the spinning green nausea. She fell once and, lying there, her body convulsed as she vomited helplessly, she wished that she could stay where she was, undisturbed, uncaring of others who might inhabit the black space that enclosed her. But the unknown terror brought her painfully to her feet again and sent her crawling forward. She wanted something—someone— but she could not put a name to it, it lay just beyond the edge of memory.

The huge golden bell, lit by flickering lantern light, seemed to grow up out of the darkness before her. She felt cold metal beneath her hands, but she could not tell what was real and what was dream. The bell rope dangled like a long black snake, and she caught it in both hands, swinging on it, her slight weight leaving the ground. Backward and forward she went, and with each movement the great clapper struck the sides of the bell. Laughing crazily at the thunder she aroused, consumed with pain and fever, she was suddenly brushed by the feather-light touch of horrifying memory. It was gone in a moment, but her laughter was stilled. Words remained, senseless words. Whimpering, she swung slowly on the bell.

"Bring out your dead!" she muttered. "Bring out your dead!" Then louder, as she swung faster and faster, her voice pitched itself to a scream, "Bring out your dead! Bring out your dead!"

The rope was slipping from her hands. She must hold on! She must! A black bottomless void awaited her falling body. She must hold! Hold!

Grim-lipped, silent now, she clung tenaciously. With part of her mind she was aware of voices, of bolts being withdrawn. A hand touched her, a face surrounded by a white cowl loomed before her.

"My child," a soft voice said. "You must not fear. We will care for you. Have faith, as we do, and all will be well."

Angel's eyes rolled upward in her head. Without a sound, she crumpled to the ground.

Sister Agnes signaled to two other nuns. Together they lifted Angel's unconscious body and carried her through the gates of the Convent of the Angels.

PIP STOOD QUIETLY BY THE BED, HIS HANDS clasped before him. There was in his study of the sleeping Nicholas a genuine compassion, mingled with an almost dispassionate interest. It brought him a strange excitement.

Did doctors feel this way, he wondered, when they had brought a patient successfully through a crisis? Ambition stirred inside him. He would study medicine, he determined, and somehow he would achieve his goal, for he felt now that it was destined to be.

But how little they knew, these men of the medical profession. Pip frowned thoughtfully. He would be different. He would devote his life to the study of disease. He would make discoveries, big discoveries; to this end would he dedicate himself; and perhaps, in the years to come, many lives now doomed would be saved. It should not be necessary to bleed a patient excessively. Though the doctors thought highly of this practice, he did not. But who was he to judge? He was but an ignorant boy. Pip's frown deepened, but he would not remain ignorant, he vowed, and it did seem to him that bleeding depleted a patient's strength rather than aiding him.

How wonderful to have the power to eradicate disease! For instance, he thought, his eyes on Nicholas' face, this plague that took so many lives. He had defeated it this time, for he knew now that the lord would live. But it had not been his victory, it had been MaHeber's—that wise good old man—whom he revered.

Death had brushed the lord with rough wings; it had left its sullen shadow on the yellowed skull-like face, the hollowed temples, the raw look of cheekbones that looked as if they might at any moment pierce through the fragile covering of skin.

Pip became aware of an overwhelming weariness, but he forced himself to move away from the bed. The muscles in his back and his shoulders ached as he stooped to gather up the pile of bloody rags from the floor. It was as well, he thought, throwing the rags into a basin, that Mistress Angel had not witnessed the terrible battle that had raged in this room. The sight of the screaming, pain-crazed man would have been more than she could bear.

It was the sudden and unexpected bursting of the plague boil that had driven the lord into a kind of insanity. He had reared on the bed like a mad animal, and with his one free hand he had attempted to strangle himself, so great was his agony. It had taken all of Pip's strength to wrench the gripping fingers free from his throat and to fasten the hand to the bed rail. Fortunately the lord's feet and his other hand were already fastened securely. He had taken that precaution earlier, substituting his own sturdy knot for Angel's weak ones, but even so, the lord had fought so violently that he had all but burst the restraints asunder.

In order to staunch the great flowing of poisoned matter that streamed from the exploded plague boil, it had been necessary to tear up three sheets. With seeming impassivity during this operation Pip had endured the frenzied screams, the red glare of mad eyes; nevertheless, inwardly he was trembling. Only when the arm had been cleansed, and the fumes of the berry that brought sleep had sent the lord into merciful oblivion, had he turned aside and wept, sagging onto the floor and covering his face.

The bells had been tolling all day, only occasionally fading into silence; now they began again, their clangor filling the room. As if to emphasize their mournful message, there was a rumble of wheels in the street below.

"Bring out your dead!" a hoarse voice shouted. "Bring out your dead!"

Pip gripped his trembling hands tightly together. He wandered over to the window and, carefully averting his eyes from the torchlit macabre scene below, he stared ahead into the blackness of the night. He had not thought to see a great city laid low, yet so it was. London was crippled by this savage pestilence. Ships stood idle, drifting at anchor like imprisoned white-winged birds. Shops were dark and shuttered, their owners fled—for only a few hardy souls had the courage to remain—and in the deserted streets the fast-growing grass was already thrusting its way between the cobblestones. The intense heat continued unabated. It even melted the pitch in the seams of the houses, sending it dripping like black tears over the cracking surfaces.

Pip pressed his forehead against the window, thankful that the glow from the torches surrounding the death cart was already in the distance. MaHeber had told him that the disease would weaken with the coming of winter. Pip thought that then the people might begin to return, and life would go on as before. There would be puppet shows at Moorfields, and on the Bankside the Bear Gardens would open their doors for the bear baitings. Yes, once more the people would laugh and love and dance. They still would dance in the shadow of death, and they knew it but they would forget it.

The bells ceased suddenly, and somewhere in the

distance Pip heard the mournful howling of a dog. The sound chilled him, and the fear he had been suppressing leaped up again. Where was Mistress Angel—where? The hour was well advanced and she should have returned long since. It seemed to him, now that he thought of it, that her flesh had been fevered. He remembered her eyes, so shadowed and heavy, and his sense of foreboding increased. He had allowed her to walk unaccompanied through the plague-stricken streets. She was the only one except the lord who had shown him kindness and understanding. Had he sent her to her death?

A faint rustle behind him caused him to turn sharply. The lord was awake, and the eyes staring at him from the pitifully wasted face were asking an urgent question.

"You are much better, my lord," Pip said. Smiling, he walked to the side of the bed.

Nicholas' head moved from side to side in weak impatience. Seeing his cracked lips open, Pip said quickly, "Nay, my lord, 'tis better if you do not talk. Very soon the swelling of your tongue will go down and you will be able to converse easily."

Nicholas made a stifled sound. Pip laid a hand over the twitching fingers on the coverlet. "I know of whom you would speak, my lord. Mistress Angel has not yet returned."

"F—f—find h—her," came Nicholas' anguished whisper, and there was appeal in his eyes fixed on the boy's face. Pip had recognized the pride of this man when first he had laid eyes on him. It was hard for him to make an appeal, but he had done so. Pip's shoulders straightened, and the look he returned to Nicholas was full of confidence. "I will find her, my lord. But you must make me a promise."

Again the eyes looked a question. "You must stay in bed," Pip answered, interpreting correctly. "Mistress

388

Angel is weakened with the strain of anxiety. She will need your strength."

Nicholas stared at him, and Pip saw the fear in his eyes. "You must not fear, for I will bring her safely to your side."

The fingers beneath Pip's hand twisted, curled, and clung in a weak pressure, the gesture saying as loudly as if he had spoken, "Thank you."

"I love Mistress Angel," Pip said. "We are not of the same color or race, but she is to me as my family. Therefore may you trust me, is it not so?"

Nicholas' eyes seemed to smile, and he felt the faint pressure of fingers again.

Pride swelled in Pip. "I, Pip," he said clearly, "am happy in your trust."

Nicholas' head moved in a negative motion. "M— M'Z—M—M'Z—Zeli."

Tears filled Pip's eyes. He understood that to this lord he was no longer Pip, the black page. He was M'Zeli, the young warrior, the son of the proud chief M'Hali. He went down on his knees beside the bed and took Nicholas' thin hand in his. "As you have honored me, great lord," he said huskily, pressing a kiss on the hand, "so do I, M'Zeli, render unto you my homage."

Their eyes met in mutual trust, then Pip rose slowly to his feet. "You must eat, lord, else will you not regain your strength. Then, if you will swallow as much of the good soup as I deem advisable, I will feel free to go in search of Mistress Angel. It is understood?"

Nicholas nodded. Pip bowed before him. "It is well," he said. He picked up the basin of bloody rags. "I will return shortly, lord," he added, and went swiftly to the door.

THE QUEEN STARED AT HER EMBROIDERY without really seeing it. Her eyes were misted, but she continued to set her stitches, though haphazardly and without regard to the design. Despite her determined control, a tear dropped on the linen, making a dark star-shaped splotch, and was followed quickly by another.

The Queen darted a quick look at Charles. He was still standing by the window, his brows drawn together in a frown. He seemed to be completely absorbed in the view, but, Catherine thought, dabbing furtively at her wet cheeks, his thoughts were doubtless with this question of divorce. Would he give in to the demands of his advisers —and if he did, could she blame him? He was the King, he owed a duty to his country, and that duty was to marry a woman who could produce a healthy boy—an heir to the throne of England.

Bitterness welled up inside her, twisting her lips into a mirthless smile. How strange that she, who would give her life for Charles, could not give him a child. Why did her pregnancies always end in misfortune, when Barbara Castlemaine—wicked, selfish Barbara—produced one healthy child after another? Although Charles did not deny paternity of Barbara's children—possibly because it was easier to claim them than to put up with the woman's screaming tantrums if he did not—Catherine was sure, as was Charles, that he had not fathered them all.

She stole another glance at him. He had not moved from his position. Her eyes lingered on him with longing and love. There was no one like him, no one! Even though he had visited her with the express intention of casting her off, he would do it gently, of course. Charles was always tender with a woman's feelings; but he would do it; he had an obligation to his country. Even so, she thought wistfully, she would remember him as he was today. So tall and elegant, so splendid in his black velvet tunic and breeches; white lace falling over his jeweled hands, his dark hair blowing in the February wind that swept through the open window.

Charles, though deeply thoughtful, was not concerned with the question of divorce. He had returned to his stricken city in January, for he could no longer reconcile his absence with that perpetually uneasy thing, his conscience. The plague, he found, was on the wane. The death toll was staggering; but for some, the King thought, remembering Benbrook, there were worse things than death.

It was of Nicholas and his lost Angel that he was thinking now. He could not remember them without guilt, for by his action he had parted them. If he had not done so, they might have known some happiness together. True, he had not known of the love between them when he had presented Angel with the ring; but the feeling of guilt was there, and ofttimes he found it difficult to bear.

Angel! What had happened to the wench? Seven months ago she had disappeared from sight; and for seven months Nicholas and his page, Pip, had searched for her. She was dead, of course. Why could they not admit it? Recently, he fancied, Nicholas had shown signs of abandoning his hopeless search. Perhaps, though, it would be better if he continued to search; for he sometimes had the uneasy feeling that Nicholas would not live very long if he once lost hope. He was barely alive now if one were to judge by his painfully thin frame or the expressionless eyes in his thin sharpened face. Nicholas, who had despised women! It was incredible! Love had altered him out of all recognition, and now his grief was consuming him!

Angel had succumbed to the plague. It was inevitable. How could it be otherwise when she had nursed Nicholas so untiringly and without regard to her own health? In her weakened condition she had probably died quickly. The King shivered. It was unbearable to think of bright-haired Angel, her huge violet-blue eyes closed in death, her delicately formed body thrown into a communal grave. For undoubtedly, if she had died in the street, she would have been taken up in the death cart. And if the thought was intolerable to him, who had only desired her, what must it be for Nicholas?

The King turned abruptly from the window. He looked at Catherine, and smiled a little. She was an antidote to troubled thought, sitting there so serenely, her dark head bent over her embroidery.

"Your pardon, Catherine," he said. "I am poor company today, but I have much on my mind."

He settled himself in the chair opposite her, waiting expectantly for her quick disclaimer, her shy smile.

Catherine's head bent lower over her work. "I will make it easy for Your Majesty," she said in a choked voice. "I am aware, you see, of the purpose of your visit."

Charles' black brows drew together in a puzzled frown. "The devil you are, Cat! Oblige me, then, I pray you, by explaining it to me."

Cat! The little fond name he had used on their honeymoon. Tears filled her eyes again and flowed down her cheeks. He seldom used that name; why must he do so now, when he had come to tell her that their life together was over?

"Od's Fish!" Charles exclaimed in exasperation. "Women and their unexplainable tears! What is it now?"

He got up from his chair and went to her side. "Come now, Cat," he said gently, putting an arm about her shoulders. "Cease this infernal crying, else will I be much displeased." He accompanied the words with a squeeze of her shoulder.

Catherine abandoned all pretense. Throwing her embroidery to one side, she covered her face with her hands and wept bitterly.

"Oh, Charles! Charles!" she wailed. "You do but prolong the agony, for well do I know that you have made up your mind to divorce me!"

"What!" Charles thundered. "What maggot have you got in your brain now?"

She looked up at him. "They urge divorce upon you—you cannot deny it, my husband." Her mouth quivered. "'Tis right that you should divorce a barren wife—right for England."

His eyes softened. With her tear-stained face, the pain that looked out at him from her large soft eyes, she looked infinitely pathetic.

"Nay, Catherine," he said softly, taking her hand, "I'll not deny that divorce has been spoken of. But fear not, my little one, for I have told them that I'll have none of it."

The relief was so great that she thought for a moment that she would faint. "But—but they will force you, Charles," she faltered. "'Tis for the good of England. There must b—be an heir."

"I am the King," Charles said, his head lifting proudly. "They cannot force me to do that which is against my conscience and my will."

Catherine's face lit up. "I am so happy, Charles, so

relieved! For truly I could not bear the thought that I might never more look upon you." She laid her face against his sleeve, "I love you, Charles! I care not if I be Queen of England or farmwife, for my heart is bound up in you. If I may remain at your side for the rest of my life, then shall I be the happiest of women!"

A shadow crossed his face. "You shame me, Cat. I know well that I am a cursed unsatisfactory husband."

"Nay." She caught his hand and carried it to her lips. "You are all that I desire."

"Then shall I call upon your sympathy," he said, striving for a lighter note.

"Why?" She sat up straight, looking at him in alarm. "What has happened?"

Charles patted her shoulder. Returning to his chair, he seated himself. " 'Tis naught that need cause you concern," he answered, smiling at her lazily, " 'tis only that I have been called upon to do my duty. Though it shames me to admit it, I like not these occasions, for I find them cursed boring."

"What occasion is it, Charles?"

" 'Tis a nun whom I am told cured many plague victims. John Tenford tells me that she claims that the cure was given to her by an old man—a black man, I believe Tenford said. I would like well to reward her handsomely, for she has done much good. But she will have none of worldly rewards. She desires instead that I visit the convent and plant a tree. This tree, she informed Tenford, is to be in memory of the old man who gave her the cure."

Catherine looked thoughtful. "I have heard of this nun. Sister Agnes, that is her name. 'Tis hard to believe in this cure, for I hear that the doctors discredit it. Yet even so, if half the stories I have heard be true, then do I think that the question of this cure should be investigated. Do you not think so?"

"I do not believe in it," Charles said, smiling at her. "If cure there be, then would the doctors have found it long since. But even so, she did much to calm the panic of the people, and perhaps that is why these stories have arisen. Cure or not, I am grateful to her. Therefore shall I plant this infernal tree. But though I like not the task, my expressed gratitude at least shall be sincere."

He rose to his feet. "I will take my leave of you, madam." He took her hand and raised it to his lips. "Tenford awaits me." His eyes were warm and soft on her face. He bent closer. "Tonight, mayhap, we will conceive our heir, what say you?"

She blushed. "I—I pray so. I will await you, my husband."

"So I should think." He released her hand and chucked her lightly under the chin. "Remember this, madam, I will like it not should I find one of your lovers skulking in your bedroom."

"Charles!" The color flamed in her cheeks.

"Aye, madam," he said, laughing. "You may well look shocked, for if I catch the knave I will run him through."

"Oh, Charles! Oh, I see. You do but joke."

Charles sighed, the merriment leaving his face. "Aye, Catherine," he said patiently, "I do but joke."

He took his leave of her. Catherine was dismayed. He had looked faintly displeased when he left. Almost—almost as if he was disappointed in her. Why? What had she said? How strange that she seemed so often to displease him, when she loved him beyond all other men.

IT WAS THE FIRST DAY OF MARCH. A VERY important day, Sister Agnes thought. Today the King was to honor the convent with his presence. He would turn the first spadeful of earth, and he would bless the ground wherein the tree was to be planted—the tree that would honor her dead friend MaHeber, of blessed memory.

Soon the peaceful flower-scented bird-haunted courtyard would be full of the sounds of men's voices and the trampling of horses' hooves, but for now she would allow herself these few moments of relaxation.

Sister Agnes folded her hands on her black-clad lap. She sat on a bench beneath her favorite tree, and the thin sunlight filtering through the branches touched her tired face with light and shadow. She felt a great contentment. She sniffed, delighting in the smell of the rain-soaked earth and the scent of growing things—the perfume of spring all about her. There were tight new buds on the lilac tree; and in the flower beds the hardy crocus thrust pale shoots through the damp earth. Beside her, in the round bed, the daffodils were preparing to unfurl their bright-yellow skirts. They stood tall and graceful, surrounded by clumps of delicate white snowdrops.

Some of Sister Agnes' contentment faded as the memory of the ravaged city beyond the convent walls intruded. She thrust the thought quickly from her. Tonight she would pray for all who had suffered and were still suffering, but not now. Today was MaHeber's day, though he knew it not—or did he? Sister Agnes felt ashamed of her lack of faith. But of course MaHeber knew, she chided herself severely.

Her eyes fell on the slim, gray-clad figure of a girl kneeling beside the long flower bed. The girl was working quietly and methodically, her thin fingers packing earth tightly about the bulbs she was planting.

The gray veil that covered her head had fallen back, and the sunlight playing over her red-gold hair turned it to flame.

Watching her, Sister Agnes' eyes softened. She was very fond of Mary—for that was the name they had given her, since she could not remember her own. Mary had been the first patient to benefit from MaHeber's treatment. At that time, Sister Agnes had not been sure of the results of MaHeber's strange potions, and she had been almost afraid to try them on the girl. They had found her outside the convent walls, her hands clinging to the bell rope, swinging backward and forward and making the great bell thunder. She had been delirious and so near to death that Sister Agnes, after kneeling for a moment in prayer, had decided to use MaHeber's treatment.

Sister Agnes smiled. How glad she was that her prayers had instilled her with the courage to proceed. For Mary, once recovered, had become like a daughter to her—the daughter she might have had, she amended hastily, had she not decided to devote her life to the service of God. All the same, Mary was such a comfort to her that there were times when she almost wished that the girl would never recover her memory. It was wicked of her, she knew—for somewhere perhaps the girl had parents, maybe a sweetheart—but she did not want Mary to leave the convent. She sighed heavily; she was constantly asking God to forgive her the sin of possessive joy. Since it seemed she could not relinquish the sin, tonight she would ask Him again. When the time came to send Mary back into the world—as come it surely must—she must let her go cheerfully, rejoicing that God in His great mercy had made her whole again. But for the moment, she thought wistfully, might she not enjoy the girl's company?

"Mary," she called. "Will you not sit in the shade for a while?"

The girl turned her head, nodded, and rose gracefully to her feet. She clapped her hands together to loosen the clinging earth, and then walked swiftly toward the sister.

"How are your dreams, Mary?" Sister Agnes inquired, when the girl had seated herself. "Do they still trouble you?"

Mary smiled faintly, and turned her blank violet-blue eyes on the other woman. They were always blank, those beautiful eyes, the sister thought, rather like the eyes of a sleepwalker.

"Yes, sister," she answered quietly. "But 'tis just the one dream now."

"The dream of the man?"

"Aye," Mary said. She laced her fingers nervously together. "He comes to me every night, but never do I see his face, for always his back is toward me. I hear his voice calling me—if you will forgive the expressions, sister—'whore! guttersnipe!' Then he calls to his angel. 'Angel, angel, come back to me, angel.' "

" 'Tis strange, this preoccupation the dream man has with angels," Sister Agnes said thoughtfully. "Perhaps he calls to his guardian angel." She laughed. "But how foolish of me. 'Tis your dream, and doubtless we are making too much of him. Endowing him with an existence he does not possess—outside of your dream, that is."

"I know not," Mary answered, and for once there was a faint flicker of expression in her eyes. "But sometimes I think—were he to face me—that I would know him."

"Do you wish to see his face, Mary?"

"Sometimes I think that I do. But at other times I am terrified that he will turn." She was silent for a moment. "I think," she went on, "that he is connected to both love and hate, but I am afraid to find out. I am afraid that if I once see his face I shall be destroyed."

"Or healed," Sister Agnes said quietly.

Mary bowed her head. "Or, as you say, healed. But, sister, which will it be?"

"I cannot tell you." The sister looked at her sadly. "God will arrange all. You must not fear, child."

"Will He?" Mary said with a tinge of bitterness. "I am often afraid, but perhaps it is better to be afraid than to be as I am—a nothing—a nobody!"

Silence fell between them, but before it could lengthen, Sister Agnes forced a light note into her voice and said quickly, "You have not forgotten, Mary, that we are to be honored by the King today?"

"No." Mary half rose, as if anxious to escape, but at a touch of sister's hand she sank back again.

"You are not looking forward to the ceremony, Mary?"

"'Tis true, sister." The girl gave her a quick, apologetic look. "'Tis peaceful here, and I—I shrink from crowds."

"Why?"

"How do I know?" Mary shivered, and the faint color in her cheeks faded.

"Well, never mind," the sister said soothingly. "'Twill be but a short time you must endure before our life returns to normal paths. They tell me, though, that the King, though an excessively ugly man, is most gracious."

"Ugly?" Mary exclaimed. "One could never consider the King truly ugly, for he has such warmth and charm. Indeed, when he smiles one is apt to consider him the handsomest of men."

"I see." The sister's eyes rested on the girl speculatively. "You have met the King?" she shot the question quickly, so quickly that Mary shrank back in alarm.

"I?" The blank eyes widened. "But of course not."

"Perhaps, then, you have seen him in person?"

"It is not unlikely, I suppose." Mary laughed nervously. "But why do you ask?"

Sister Agnes shrugged. "I was interested, that's all. I understand," she added, changing the subject, "that you have been assigned to help Sister Theresa in the kitchen."

"Yes." A faint frown drew Mary's brows together. "I had rather have helped in the dining hall. I—I do not care for kitchen work."

"Perhaps," the Sister suggested softly, "it is Sister Theresa for whom you do not care?"

"No." Mary shook her head in denial. "I like Sister Theresa. It—it is just that her hands are always so—so cold."

"And that bothers you? Why?"

"I know not," Mary said, her eyes avoiding the keen gaze bent upon her. "But the touch of cold flesh fills me with such horror that I—" she broke off for a moment. "You will think me insane, sister," she added awkwardly.

"No," Sister Agnes said gently. "You are a sleepwalker, Mary, moving through a long, strange dream. But you are sane enough, I assure you. Doubtless this horror you have is connected in some way with your past. Something you have buried in your mind and refuse to take out and examine."

"Perhaps." The girl turned her head and gave the sister a steady look. "Do you think I shall ever awaken from the dream?"

"I hope so. I pray so."

"And if there is horror in the awakening?"

"If there is, Mary," Sister Agnes said, her eyes warmly compassionate, "then it may be that there will be compensations enough to erase the horror."

The girl did not answer. After a moment, she rose to her feet. "I pray you to excuse me, sister; my work awaits me."

"Of course, of course."

Mary smiled, and went on her way. How gracefully she walked, Sister Agnes thought, beaming fondly after her. Her carriage was always so erect, her shoulders straight and held well back; so well back indeed, that it almost gave one the impression that she walked with a board under her habit.

MARY STOOD BETWEEN SISTER AGNES AND
Sister Margaret, the latter chattering incessantly in a low
excited voice.

"Oh, Mary," Sister Margaret sighed, blissfully unconscious of Sister Agnes' severe glance, "is not our King
the most romantic figure you ever saw?"

Mary nodded. During the bustle of the royal arrival,
she had stolen one quick glance at the King and then
averted her eyes; but that glance had been all encom-
passing. She retained the impression of his magnificence.
He wore a tunic and breeches of black velvet, the tunic
heavily embroidered with silver thread. His lace cravat
foamed like a waterfall; it was pierced through with a
ruby pin. More lace edged his wide cuffs, and his long
fingers were laden with brilliantly jeweled rings. No less
brilliant had been his smile when first he had arrived.
He was indeed a figure of romance, and Mary, though
she could not explain her reluctance to look fully at him,
was secretly in sympathy with little Sister Margaret. A
faint echo in her mind said that the Stuart charm had
proved the undoing of many a woman. But what did
she know of the Stuart charm?

All through the long ceremony she had kept her
eyes lowered. But the King's voice, the warm, lazy timbre

of it had stirred uneasy feelings. With each word that he spoke she seemed to hear a door straining to open, and then, as she flinched away, closing firmly.

"Come." Sister Agnes whispered in Mary's ear. "The King will soon depart, and you have not yet been presented to him."

Mary stiffened. " 'Tis not necessary that I be presented. I am unimportant."

"We all have our importance in God's universal scheme," the sister rebuked her. " 'Tis evident that our King thinks so, for he desires that all here be presented to him."

"Then I will take myself away," Mary said desperately. "Then in all truth I shall not be here."

"Nonsense!" Sister Agnes laid her hand on Mary's arm and tightened her fingers about it. "He is particularly interested in you, for you were my first cure."

"No!" Mary hung back. "Please! I would rather not! I—I can't explain why. I would just rather not."

"His Majesty is easy to talk to, Mary," she soothed. "He has a manner which puts you instantly at your ease. Please, Mary, would you shame me? I have promised the King that you shall be presented."

Mary closed her eyes for a moment, conscious of that door that strained to open. Then, her heart beating high in her throat, she allowed herself to be led forward.

The King was surrounded by his small company of gentlemen, all of whom were lavishly dressed, their long intricately curled wigs falling to their shoulders. Several of the sisters had joined the group about the King, their black-clad figures punctuating the bright costumes of the gentlemen. Mary could not explain her curious reluctance as Sister Agnes urged her forward. There was something she did not care to remember—dared not remember! But surely it could have nothing to do with the elegant smiling King. But he was part of it, she felt sure, a figure from her foggy past; and if she remembered the whole, might not that unknown terror catch up with her?

As the crowd parted to let them through, Mary's ears seemed to be filled with the rumbling thunder of turning cart wheels, and somewhere in the distance a hoarse voice was crying out, "Br——"

"No!" Mary's inner voice shrieked. "No! Don't let me hear it!"

"This is Mary, Your Majesty." Sister Agnes' quiet voice dispelled the rumble in her ears.

"Mary," the King's warm voice said. " 'Tis a pretty name."

His jewel-laden fingers were under her chin, forcing her to look up. She stared into dark amorous eyes, saw them widen, go blank with shock.

"Od's Fish!" the King exclaimed. " 'Tis Angel!"

Angel! Angel! Angel! The name—if name it be—beat like a hammer in her brain. The King! Was he the man in the dream?

Vaguely she was aware of the startled faces turned in her direction, of the pressure of the King's hands on her shoulders.

" 'Tis a miracle!" the King said, his teeth flashing in a delighted smile. "Nicholas' Angel! By God!"

Nicholas! The rumbling wheels sounded in her ears again. Nicholas! Her Nicholas! He was dying! Help him, Pip! Help him! The herbs! MaHeber's herbs. She must get home with them! She must! Plague! She had the plague! The wheels, they were coming closer—closer! "Bring out your dead! Bring out your dead!"

"No!" Angel screamed. "Nicholas! Save me, Nicholas!"

"She's going to faint!" somebody said.

Darkness descended upon Angel, and in the center of the darkness was a beloved face, but so thin, so wasted! A thick, difficult voice sounding like a clap of thunder in her ears said, "I—I—lo—lo—you."

"Nicholas!" Angel gasped. She crumpled at the King's feet, and the darkness was complete.

The King brushed aside his attendants. "Nay, gentlemen, your King claims the privilege." Stooping, he gathered the unconscious figure into his arms, lifting her easily. " 'Tis a miracle!" He said again. "And I myself will bear this miracle to my Lord Benbrook."

Sister Margaret watched, innocently thrilled at the sight of the tall fascinating King holding Mary in his arms. She sighed a little, remembering arms that had once held her.

Sister Agnes watched, too. So she was to lose her Mary after all? Well, it was better so. Bright-haired beautiful Mary belonged to the world; she was not meant to be confined behind gray convent walls. Sister Agnes touched her crucifix with thin, trembling fingers. It was the will of God, she thought, bowing her head. So be it!

NICHOLAS STUDIED THE CANVAS INTENTLY, his black brows drawn together in a fierce frown.

He had failed, he thought. Bitter despair swamped him. He would never now capture the essential spark that was Angel—that lovely glowing quality that caused her to live and breathe and move through all of his haunted dreams.

She looked back at him from the canvas; her flesh pearly-tinted, red lips curving into a smile, beautiful hair tumbling loosely about her bare white shoulders. Angel? No, it was not Angel! She was gone, irrevocably gone! The portrait could not live because now, at last, he had accepted her death, and he had painted that final defeat into the shadows about her beautiful eyes. In life, she had slipped away from him, vanished into a moment of time where he could not follow. And now, in this—the last portrait he would ever paint—she had escaped him again.

In all those long months of searching he had managed to keep his frail hope alive—for how could she be dead? She seemed very near at times, as though, if he turned a corner, he would see her coming toward him with her skimming graceful walk. Then there were those other times when she had receded far from him. Sometimes lying sleepless in his bed, he would imagine he heard her voice calling to him, "Nicholas! Nicholas! Nicholas!" There was such terror in her reiteration of his name, that he would start up in the bed, his forehead beaded with perspiration.

Together he and M'Zeli had turned London upside down. They had searched every street, asked questions, demanded to see the death records, only to find that they hardly existed for the plague victims, and had found not the slightest clue. She might never have lived, so completely had she disappeared. And still he would not believe her dead—dared not believe it!

M'Zeli! The tight, bitter line of Nicholas' mouth softened. How stubbornly he clung to the belief that Mistress Angel was still alive! It was the lad who had inspired him to fresh efforts when he would have given up.

Acceptance! He stared at the portrait with something like horror. With his brush he had set the final seal on the death of his little guttersnipe.

"No!" he whispered, his eyes burning. "No, Angel! No!"

Savagely, he tore the canvas from the easel and sent it spinning across the room.

He was tired, he thought, sinking down onto a stool. So terribly, so devastatingly tired! There was no point in life if she did not share it! No point in anything! He covered his face with his hands. Love! It had not come easily to him, and even when he realized that Angel had invaded every corner of his life, still he had fought it. He could see her now—her eyes defying him, hating him. A thousand pictures of her, her face tearstained, her voice telling him that he was a "bleedin' swine!" Angel, in his arms at last, her voice saying, "I love you, Nicholas! I love you so much!" Angel, as he remembered her through the fevered frenzy of the plague, her hands gentle as she supported him, her voice soothing; and later still, violet eyes, burning and fanatical in the strained white mask of her face—holding him to life, refusing to let him slip away. So often, in the pain-muddled recesses of his brain, he had prayed for death, but she would not let him go. And because he loved her he had—without knowing he did so—fought back. He had won through with the help of M.'Zeli—but to what purpose? He had cheated death, and now death had cheated him.

The throbbing silence of the room was broken by a sudden burst of activity from below. He heard the creak and the jingle of harness, the snorting of horses, and many voices that seemed to be all talking at once, mingled with laughter.

Somebody cried out words in a high, excited voice— it sounded like Sampson—but he could not make out the words.

The babble of voices rose to a new pitch. Nicholas frowned, hearing footsteps coming along the corridor. He had given Sampson orders that he was not to be disturbed. He cared not if the King himself was below; he would see no one.

Nicholas stiffened as the door opened. "Sampson," he said, without turning. "I gave you orders that I was not to be disturbed. You may go downstairs again and tell whoever is below, that I am indisposed. Do you understand?"

"Aye, dear m'lord," a soft voice said. "Right well do I understand."

Nicholas froze. Angel? Angel's voice? He stood there, his trembling hands clenched at his sides. He was afraid to turn, afraid that he would find the room empty and her voice but a figment of his imagination.

Footsteps again, quick, light footsteps crossing to his side. A hand was laid on his arm. He looked down, gazing fixedly at the slender fingers resting against his dark sleeve. On the thumb, just below the nail, was a little crescent-shaped scar. Angel's hand? Angel's!

"Will you not look at me, my lord! My darling!"

"Angel!" The breath choked in his throat as he spun round, staring at her incredulously.

"Y—you—you!" His hand came out, touching her gropingly, as a blind man would; touching her hair, the tears shining on her cheeks, her tremulous mouth. "Angel! Oh, Angel!"

He swept her into his arms, holding her fiercely close. "I don't believe it!" he said in a shaken voice. "My darling! My beloved little guttersnipe! I can't believe it!"

She was beyond words. She felt his kisses on her hair, the hands that put her gently from him. She saw his eyes, intent and glowing, fixed in wonderment upon her face, and she closed her own against tears. His mouth touched hers, softly at first, then hard and possessive and hungry.

"It's true!" he said, raising his head to look at her again. He took her back into his arms, and she felt the hard beating of his heart beneath her cheek.

"The—the King is below," Angel said.

"The King?" Nicholas repeated blankly.

"Yes. He f—found me. He will tell you about it." She stirred in his arms. "We must go down. He is awaiting us."

"Later," Nicholas said, his arms tightening. "Just let me hold you for a little longer."

She relaxed happily against him, wishing that the moment might go on forever. Then she felt him stiffen. "What the devil do you mean by it?" he said, his arms falling away. "How dare you put me through this torment?"

"What!" She stared into his frowning face. "But—but, Nicholas, I—"

"You deserve a beating, and damned if I haven't a mind to do it!"

"Nicholas," she began. She stopped short, seeing the laughter in his eyes. "You fraud! I thought you meant it."

"I did." Laughing, Nicholas seized her hand. "Come, brat, the King awaits us."

Charles looked up, hearing footsteps on the stairs. He smiled at the housekeeper, who stood by his side, then he turned and beckoned to Pip.

"Our host comes," he said, his ringed hand resting lightly on the boy's shoulder.

"Forgive me, sire," Nicholas said breathlessly, stopping before the King. He bowed, his hand still holding Angel's tightly. "I did not mean to keep you waiting."

"Did you not?" Charles drawled. "What a cursed strange fellow you are, then. Had I been you, my King's wait would have been considerably longer." His amused eyes rested on Nicholas' smiling face. "Ah, my friend," he said softly. "It rejoices my heart to see the return of the Benbrook I once knew. I am happy for you."

"Thank you, sire, But how did it happen that—"

The King raised a hand, cutting him off. "Explanations later," he said firmly. He put out a hand to Angel. "Come here, Mistress Dawson."

She put her hand in his. "I claim a privilege," Charles said, stooping to kiss her cheek. Over her head, he grinned at Nicholas. "You cannot blame me, friend Nicholas, for 'tis an uncommonly handsome wench, is it not?"

" 'Twill do," Nicholas answered in the same vein. " 'Twill do very well." He sobered, looking at Charles almost wonderingly.

"And you found her, sire. I still cannot believe it."

"Aye," Charles said, his eyes twinkling. "Why could

you not find her for yourself? Plague take you for a lazy hound! Must your King do your work for you?"

In the laughter that followed, Nicholas' eyes fell on Pip. "M'Zeli," he cried, an awed note creeping into his voice again. "Come forward and greet your mistress. She's home, M'Zeli! She's home!"

The boy ran forward. "Mistress Angel!" Taking her hand, he raised it to his lips. "I shall forever bless this day!"

"Thank you," Angel said, stooping to kiss his cheek. "Thank you, dear P—M'Zeli."

"Sampson," Nicholas turned to the housekeeper. Putting his arms about her, he embraced her. "Tell them to bring wine, Sampson; we must all drink to this occasion. For Angel is home again! She's home!"

Charles' smiling eyes met the housekeeper's, "Gad!" he murmured, "what exuberance. I vow that it quite exhausts me."

Mrs. Sampson dropped him a flustered curtsy. "I'll get the wine, sire."

"Do," Charles said, flashing his charming smile, "and, madam, before you depart on your errand, I would inform you of something you might not know."

"Sire?" Mrs. Sampson looked at him inquiringly.

"It is that Angel is home." Charles winked at her. "Yes indeed, the troublesome brat has returned."

ROMANCE...ADVENTURE...DANGER...

DUCHESS IN DISGUISE
by Caroline Courtney   (94-050, $1.75)
The Duke of Westhampton had a wife in the country and
a mistress in town. This suited the Duke, but his young
wife, whom he'd wed and tucked away on his estate
was not pleased. So, being as audacious as she was
innocent, she undertook to win his attention by mas-
querading as a lady he did not know — herself.

WAGER FOR LOVE
by Caroline Courtney   (94-051, $1.75)
The Earl of Saltaire had a reputation as a rakehell, an
abductor and ravisher of women, a dandy and demon
on horseback. Then what lady of means would consider
marrying him — especially if she knew the reason for
the match was primarily to win a bet? When he won a
wager by marrying her, he never gambled on loosing
his heart!

SWEET BRAVADO
by Alicia Meadowes   (89-936, $1.95)
Aunt Sophie's will was her last attempt to reunite the
two feuding branches of the Harcourt family. Either the
Viscount of Ardsmore marry Nicole, the daughter of his
disgraced uncle, or their aunt's inheritance would be
lost to the entire family! And wed, they did. But theirs
was not a marriage made in heaven!

PHILIPPA
by Katherine Talbot   (84-664, $1.75)
If she had to marry for money and Philippa knew she
must — then it was fortunate that such a very respectable
member of The House of Lords was courting her. It
would be difficult, though, to forget that the man she
loves would be her brother-in-law. . . . . A delightful
Regency Romance of a lady with her hand promised to
one man and her heart lost to another!

LILLIE
by David Butler   (82-775, $2.25)
This novel, upon which the stunning television series
of the same name is based, takes Lillie Langtry's story
from her girlhood, through the glamour and the triumphs,
the scandals and the tragedies, to 1902 and Edward
VII's accession to the throne.

ROMANCE...ADVENTURE...DANGER...

GLENDRACO
by Laura Black (81-528, $2.50)
Within the walls of the great castle of GLENDRACO in Scotland, no one will tell beautiful Kirstie Drummond of her grandfather, once lord of the castle. Rumours abound that Kirstie had bad blood and will give her body to any man who wants her. Then danger strikes, driving Kirstie to the slums of Glasgow, and the climax is unnerving. A novel of scandal and passion!

GARNET
by Petra Leigh (82-788, $2.25)
For the love of a man, she sheared her long hair and bound her curving body into the uniform of a British ensign. No war would keep Garnet Mallory from the man she wanted. Disguised, she searched for him across Europe, only to discover that hers was not the only charade; that love itself often wears a mask!

DUCHESS
by Josephine Edgar (82-423, $2.25)
The intriguing adventures of the shopgirl so captivating, beautiful and daring they called her DUCHESS. She came to London to work in an elegant Victorian department store, but no one could keep the magnificent Viola from a love affair that could bring only tragedy to a girl of her class!

THIS TOWERING PASSION
by Valerie Sherwood (81-486, $2.50)
500 pages of sweet romance and savage adventure set against the violent tapestry of Cromwellian England, with a magnificent heroine whose beauty and ingenuity captivates every man who sees her, from the king of the land to the dashing young rakehell whose destiny is love!

A LOVE SO BOLD
by Annelise Kamada (81-638, $2.50)
Gillian was the wife of a brutal, sadistic noble who was an intimate of the King. And James was bound by memories and guilt to another woman. In 14th Century England, such a love was doomed, but this was a love that would not surrender, A LOVE SO BOLD it obeyed no law but its own!

YOUR WARNER LIBRARY OF
REGENCY ROMANCE...

THE FIVE-MINUTE MARRIAGE
by Joan Aiken   (84-682, $1.75)

When Delphie Carteret's cousin Garth asks her to marry him, it is in a make-believe ceremony so that Delphie might receive a small portion of her rightful inheritance. But an error has been made. The marriage is binding! Oh my! Fun and suspense abounds, and there's not a dull moment in this delightful Regency novel brimming with laughter, surprise and true love!

LADY BLUE
by Zabrina Faire   (94-056, $1.75)

Meriel is the beautiful governess to an impossible little body who pours blue ink on her long blonde hair. When she punishes the boy, she is dismissed from her post. But all is not lost — the handsome young Lord Farr has another job in mind for her. Meriel's new position: Resident "ghost" in a castle owned by Farr's rival. Her new name: LADY BLUE!

AGENT OF LOVE
by Jillian Kearny   (94-003, $1.75)

Was Alicia the innocent she seemed, delighting in her first London season? Was Rob the dashing young blade he appeared to be as he escorted her to routs and ridottos? They played the conventional games of love — but were hearts or empires at stake?

ACCESSORY TO LOVE
by Maureen Wakefield   (84-790, $1.75)

A love child is an embarrassment to her unwed mother, to her wealthy father and to a society that doesn't like to have its conscience troubled. But when the child becomes a woman as enchanting as Saranne, she can't be hidden forever! Saranne was surrounded by love — surely some of it someday could be hers.

THE MIDNIGHT MATCH
by Zabrina Faire   (94-057, $1.75)

He saved her honor. She saved his life. Was what they felt for each other love or gratitude? What had she done? Carola trembled at the thought — she was married to a perfect stranger. . . . She was so happy!

ROMANCE...ADVENTURE... DANGER...

LOVE'S TENDER FURY
by Jennifer Wilde   **(81-909, $2.50)**

The turbulent story of an English beauty sold at auction like a slave who scandalized the New World by enslaving her masters. She would conquer them all — only if she could subdue the hot unruly passions of the heart! The 2 million copy bestseller that brought fame to the author of DARE TO LOVE.

AURIELLE
by Annable Erwin   **(91-126, $2.50)**

The tempestuous new historical romance 4 million Annabel Erwin fans have been waiting for. Join AURIELLE, the scullery maid with the pride of a Queen, as she escapes to America to make her dreams of nobility come true.

THIS LOVING TORMENT
by Valerie Sherwood   **(82-649, $2.50)**

Born in poverty in the aftermath of the Great London Fire, Charity Woodstock grew up to set the men of three continents ablaze with passion! A bestselling sensation, this loving torment is the fastest-selling historical romance in Warner Books history!

A PASSIONATE GIRL
by Thomas Fleming   **(81-654, $2.50)**

The author of the enormously successful LIBERTY TAVERN is back with this gutsy and adventurous novel of a young woman fighting in the battle for Ireland's freedom and persecuted for her passionate love of a man.

LIBERTY TAVERN
by Thomas Fleming   **(91-220, $2.50)**

A rich, full-blooded saga of the American Revolution and its scorching effect on the men and women of Liberty Tavern who lived by their wits, their fists and their love for the country they were helping to conceive.

side nail. When he had finished he composed
utiful song:

Pye, pye, kapembe kangu
Kali Kamuyadzi ng'wale
Kapembe – yatovage nu lulele kapembe
Kukyanya nde kulilikoko valume
Pye pye kapembe kangu

Pye, pye, my whistle
From a lost francolin
Whistle – the one who was soft
Whistle – the one who was soft
Is there a beast up there?
Pye, pye, my whistle

phant was also taking a walk nearby when he sudden
rd Mr Hare's song. He listened for a few moments an
d it very much so he went over to where Mr Hare wa
ng.
'hat's a beautiful song you are singing,' he remarked
'es, it is,' agreed the hare proudly.
Vho gave you the whistle?' Elephant went on
iring it.
made it myself – come, take it and have a go,' Mr
e offered. He seemed to have forgotten his problems
he moment.
r Hare's problems had begun three days before when
had started stealing groundnuts from a nearby
er. On the first day that he had gone to the farm the
of the owners had been keeping watch over the crop.
Hare had gone up to the boy and had asked for a dim
at he could roast some hashish. When it was ready
ad given some to the boy and it had made him fall
p. This had given Mr Hare the chance to dig up as
y groundnuts as he wanted.

my goat harmed any of the cattle?' He looked from one
villager to another as they stood at the gate of the kraal.
The cattle were making their usual morning noises.
Musugu looked over the gate and marvelled at the
nearest bull which was making its way to the centre of the
herd. His goat lay in pain close by the gate.

'I see,' he said as his eyes moved from the bull to the
goat, 'that the goat cannot stand. Something is wrong
with it.'

A villager explained how they had found the goat with
one of its legs broken. They all agreed that one of the
bulls must have done the damage.

'Well, kill and eat it,' Musugu said to them quite
simply, showing very little anger.

'You will surely share the food with us won't you? the
villagers implored him.

'I never eat goat meat, only cattle meat,' Musugu said
smugly, then he went back to his room to prepare for his
departure. As he walked away from the kraal he glanced
back and noticed that the bull which had caught his
attention earlier had made it to the centre of the herd
and was causing trouble in there. He smiled to himself
and went on.

As the villagers busied themselves with preparing the
goat they discussed how kind the stranger was. They all
agreed that they had never met a nicer man. He did not
complain, he showed no anger, and now they were about
to have a good piece of meat from the stranger's goat.

Musugu remained out of sight until the goat had been
eaten and the bones were being chewed by the guard
dogs. Then he made his presence known by coughing and
rubbing his hands together in a gesture of politeness and
warmth. The head of the village coughed in reply, giving
Musugu permission to speak his mind.

'I think it is time for me to continue my journey,'
he said rubbing his hands together again. 'Except that it

would be unusual if—er—er I were to go back home without—er—you know.'

Then truth dawned in the headman's mind. How silly they had been. How could they expect to be let off that easily after *causing* damage to the goat and then swallowing it up so comfortably? He looked at the *polite* stranger and their eyes met.

'Well,' said the headman at last, 'in that case you had better take one of our precious bulls in payment. Although it is a pity that we have to part with it.'

Musugu glanced about him and from where he stood he was able to see into the kraal since the villagers were preparing to take the cattle to graze. The chaos in the centre had calmed a bit but he could still locate *his* bull. He had already decided that that was the one he would take away and he managed to do it.

Back in his own village Musugu explained to his fellow villagers how he had accomplished his amazing feat. He told them how he had exchanged his food for clay, clay for wood, wood for a cock, a cock for a he-goat and finally a he-goat for a bull. The bull was of excellent breed and in no time Musugu's kraal, which had originally contained only two cows, became too small for all his animals—he had to build a bigger one.

This was one coup out of many for Musugu and this and his many other exploits provided endless stories and entertainment for his fellow villagers.

The Hare and the Elephant

Mr Hare was taking an afternoon walk wh[en he] found a large grassfire barring his way. [He was] angry because he wanted to go straight [on and it] prevented him. While he stood there won[dering how he] could get past the fire a francolin came a[long. It looked] at the pensive Hare and wondered wha[t troubled] him.

'Why are you so pensive?' the francolin [asked] at Mr Hare with curiosity.

'Oh,' Mr Hare pretended to have bee[n startled, 'oh,] it's you my friend. In a few moments I sha[ll be on] the other side of the grassfire but becau[se of some] problems on my mind I suddenly found [myself] here lost in thought.'

'I am going on too—but—can I help [with your] problem?' asked the francolin.

'No, thanks all the same,' said the [Hare. He] added, 'Perhaps you would like to go thr[ough since] you are in such a hurry?'

The francolin took up Mr Hare's offer [and flew] to get through the fire but he was immed[iately caught by the] high flames. As soon as the fire on that sp[ot died down] little Mr Hare grabbed one of francoli[n's legs] and pulled it from the ashes then he made[...]

'You lazy and stupid boy,' the father had raged next morning. 'So you slept deliberately to let your friend Mr Hare eat all our groundnuts. Your mother will keep watch from now on.'

But the next night, when the boy's mother was on watch, Mr Hare had done exactly the same thing. The farmer himself had guarded his crop on the third night but Mr Hare had outwitted him yet again.

Then the farmer had thought of a plan. He had made a statue of wax, dressed it and had sat it down close to the groundnuts, placing a bowl of stiff porridge with meat beside it. When Mr Hare had come back that night he had found the statue and had greeted it three times without getting any answer.

'Well,' he had muttered, 'if you aren't going to speak to me, I'll eat your porridge.' Still there had been no answer, so he had eaten a lump of ugali.

'I'll eat your meat as well unless you greet me back,' he had threatened the statue and when no reply came he had eaten all the porridge and the meat.

'Now I am going to hit you,' Mr Hare had said, seeing the statue's hat moving a little in the wind, and he had given it a blow with his right paw which to his amazement had stuck there. He tried again with his left paw, but the same thing had happened. In desperation he had used his head and legs which had also got stuck and there he had remained a funny figure sticking to the statue, until the following morning when the owner of the farm had come with his friends to collect him.

'I have got you at last!' the man had said happily as he held up the hare for his friends to see.

'You surely have,' Mr Hare had replied, 'and now that I've been caught I will tell you the easiest way to kill me.'

'What is that?' the farmer had asked eagerly.

'All you have to do is collect some grass and then drop me *hard* on to it. That will be the end of me.'

87

The farmer and his friends had obeyed the crafty hare and had dropped him onto a heap of grass whereupon Mr Hare had got up and run away. The men had tried to follow but they had lost him and in the end they had set fire to the grass hoping to kill him. It was at this point that Mr. Hare had tricked the francolin.

As Elephant blew the whistle he found himself playing the same beautiful song that Mr Hare had played and he decided that he wanted to keep the whistle for himself. Then suddenly they heard some shouts and Mr Hare knew that the men were still after him because of the groundnuts.

'Elephant,' he said, 'give me my whistle, those people are after me.'

'No, I want to keep it for myself,' Elephant replied.

The Hare became very agitated for he knew that the men were nearby and could hear their voices cursing him. His only way of escape lay through the fire and that was still burning far too fiercely. What could he do now?

'Come on, Elephant, hide me then,' Mr Hare pleaded after some thought.

'All right. Get inside me from behind and keep still.'

A few moments later Mr. Hare was safe inside Elephant's stomach. Then the men arrived and found Elephant all on his own. They asked him who he had been talking to and he told them that it had been Mr Hare but now he had disappeared. The men rushed away again and when he could no longer hear them Elephant asked Mr Hare to come out.

'No, I won't', came Mr Hare's muffled reply.

'Why not?'

'You refused to give back my whistle so I am going to stay in here.'

'Do please come out and I will give it back to you,' the Elephant promised.

'I would have come out as soon as the men went away if

you had not tried to keep the whistle, but now I am very weak,' said the Hare from the depths of the Elephant's stomach.

'Why?' Elephant asked, puzzled.

'Hungry, man. I am terribly hungry. May I have a piece of your liver to give me a bit of strength?' Mr Hare asked very politely.

The Elephant thought for a while then replied, 'Take only a little.'

At this Mr Hare gobbled up the whole liver.

'I am still hungry,' he complained again when he had finished.

'But surely you aren't only feeding on me today, are you?' Elephant shouted, getting very angry. 'Do come out, then I will give you back your whistle.'

'I will come out, surely, but for more strength may I have a bit of your intestines — then you'll be free of me.'

Elephant gave Hare permission to eat a little but once more he quickly gobbled up all the intestines and then Elephant dropped down dead.

The men, who were still searching for Mr Hare, came back to the place where they had met Elephant and found his lifeless body lying on the ground. Pleased with their find they gathered to collect some elephant meat then they saw Mr Hare dash out of the elephant's body. They gave chase but finally he ran into a shallow hole in the side of a bank where he might have been safe had one of his legs not been sticking out of it. One of the men grabbed the exposed leg and held on to it but then Hare called out:

'How silly you are. You are leaving my leg free in order to hold on to a root! What is wrong with you?' While he spoke he was busily digging deeper into the hole so as to come out on the other side of the bank. The man who was holding the leg let go of it and grabbed a root instead and this was Mr Hare's chance to escape. With a final

89

effort he managed to burrow through to the other side of the bank while the men stood around waiting for one of them to fetch a hoe in order to dig the hare out. As the Hare raced away one of the men caught sight of him.

'There is the Hare,' he shouted then, facing the one who was supposed to be holding the Hare's leg he raged, 'And what are you holding on to?'

It was at this point that the men gave up running after the crafty Hare and decided to make a trap for him instead.

The Forbidden Love

Once there was a woman who had three daughters with whom she was always very strict. She made sure that the girls were close by her all the time except for when they were assigned special duties. Yet nobody in the village could understand why she acted like this.

Each day her eldest daughter, Tumalye, took the cattle to graze on the moors and because she went alone her mother was even more worried about her than about her other daughters and would often send Tumalye's youngest sister to spy on her. The little girl always brought home a good report, however, and this satisfied the woman while it lasted.

Then one day the youngest daughter came running back to her mother after one of her trips to the moors.

'What is it daughter?' the woman asked immediately.

'I don't know, mother, but Tumalye was playing with a boy.'

'Are you sure?' her mother demanded.

'But I saw her, mother; it was a game I don't know,' the girl reported.

On the following day the woman sent her second daughter to spy on her elder sister and she too reported the same thing. When Tumalye returned from the moors that evening her mother told her quite simply that she was not to take their animals to graze any more.

'But why not?' Tumalye demanded.

'I am your mother and I order you to leave things in the hands of your sisters,' was her mother's reply.

From that day on Tumalye stopped going to the moors. She also stopped talking. Whenever her mother spoke to her she just remained silent and shed tears. She never ate — at least they never saw her eat anything — she only did her work about the house, weeping often. She did all the pounding and grinding at home, she drew water and fetched wood but in all these activities, especially those which took her out of the house, her younger sister was assigned to watch her.

One evening two women were drawing water at the river and as they did so they discussed the strange family.

'Why is the mother doing this?' asked the stout one, pulling her pot from the river.

'I have no idea,' her companion replied, 'she is being too hard on those daughters of hers. Who is going to marry them when she hides them away like she does?' This woman was tall and although she was the younger of the two she was well known in the village for her wisdom. 'Tumalye is the saddest girl I have ever known. Since the death of her father she has been denied three husbands and I think that is very bad for her.'

The shorter woman laughed rather oddly and whispered, 'But something is going to happen, you wait.'

The two women picked up their pots and left the river. As soon as they were out of sight Tumalye left the bush in which she had been hiding and began to draw water alone. Since her mother's reprimand she had been avoiding everyone but from the bush she had heard all the talk between the two women.

'So they know about me,' she murmured to herself.

She filled her pot with water then went to a dark corner of the river to wash. She had just removed her clothes when a boy appeared and spoke to her quickly and quietly.

'I don't want to be seen here because of your mother but I must know if you are going to have my baby.' Tumalye nodded her head and the boy continued, 'Please, when it is born, let me see it . . . I very much want to see it.'

Tumalye nodded again and the boy ran off. When she had finished washing she dressed again then picked up her pot and walked back to the house. As she put down the pot her mother watched her sternly and finally she spoke.

'You are very big nowadays. What is wrong with you?'

Tumalye did not reply.

'Aren't you going to tell me why?' her mother persisted, 'I know what you did and I know why you are so big. As soon as I catch that monkey-faced young man I shall strangle him to death.' The woman emphasized each word she spoke and Tumalye listened with tears in her eyes. She was only big on the breasts and stomach — the rest of her was very thin, since she ate nothing but wild fruits which she gathered whilst collecting firewood. Her mother's attitude caused Tumalye a great deal of misery but she found that her younger sisters were beginning to sympathize with her.

'Mother,' the youngest daughter asked one day, 'do you want to kill our sister? She is going to die if you keep on being cruel to her. From now on don't ask me to spy on her because I won't do it anymore.'

The woman looked to her second daughter for support but she too had defiance written all over her face.

A short time later Tumalye collected together her few belongings and in a moment she was out of the house. Her mother tried to call her back but she refused to listen; nor would her sisters follow her when their mother asked them to.

'We can't,' they told her, 'You are responsible for whatever happens to our sister.'

Tumalye felt quite alone once she had left the house. She could not go to the boy's mother because she had never been to his home before and they might refuse to accept her. She wondered where else she could go. In the end she decided to visit the wise young woman whom she had seen at the river but as she began to walk in that direction her strength began to leave her. Suddenly her knees buckled and gave way and soon she found her body labouring in the middle of the path which led to the wise woman's house. A short time later Tumalye's son was born then suddenly, out of nowhere, the child's father appeared to help her.

'I'll find someone,' he called as he rushed to the wise woman's house to ask for help. Fortunately the woman was at home and she helped them to wash the baby and wrap him in the special skin Tumalye had with her. Then she prepared some food for them and Tumalye ate heartily feeling strength creep back into her body with every mouthful, she also felt a warmth that she had never felt before in her life.

'Could we name the baby please?' Tumalye asked the boy after a while.

'It is usually the grandmother who names it,' he replied, 'however, since the poor boy does not seem to have proper grandparents I shall name him myself.'

He asked the wise woman for a cloth and tied it round the child's wrist. 'We will call him Musule, the unwanted,' he said softly.

They stayed with the wise woman for the night and in the morning the child's father told them that he had to leave, although he could not take his wife and child with him yet. Before he went away, however, he asked the wise woman to give shelter to his son and his wife until he was ready to collect them.

'Tumalye's mother will be searching every house for her,' the woman said thoughtfully. 'I cannot keep them here but I can tell you where they can hide from her for a while. You must take your wife to the rocks on the east side of the village,' she went on, 'there you will find a strange rock which I do not need to describe. Hide your child there and Tumalye can stay with him during the day; after she has fed him for the night she can come back here to eat.'

The two young people left with Musule to find the rocks the woman had mentioned. When they reached the place they saw that one rock was red in colour and quite different from the others. Tumalye knew that it must be the one the woman had mentioned so she sang:

> Kaganga badu badu
> Ndivikumwana vangu
> Musule kwa pape.

> Open rock
> So that I can put in my child
> Whose grandmother doesn't want him.

Almost immediately the rock opened and inside they discovered a beautiful hollow exactly the same size as Musule. They laid him down in it lovingly and Tumalye sang to make the rock close. Then the baby's father prepared to leave, promising to return for them as soon as he could.

'But where are you going?' Tumalye asked.

'I don't know, but I must find a place for the three of us,' he told her, 'we cannot stay here. My mother has refused to let me take you home because of your mother's strange ways and everyone in the village says I should not take you for a wife, except for the kind woman who understands; she thinks I should,' he finished, his eyes fixed on Tumalye.

'What is wrong with me?' Tumalye asked quietly.

'Haven't I given you a son?' She could not understand the attitude of the villagers. 'Is there anything else I should do besides keeping your house and giving you children?' Now she was getting angry; she could not understand the gossip.

'It is not that,' the young man replied quickly, 'you are everything a man wants. It is your mother whom they hate and that is why your sisters will never marry. Your mother wants to keep all of you at home.' He paused, 'I am going now but I will come back; take care of our little Musule.' With that he left and Tumalye watched him go. She loved and admired this young man for his behaviour and he was certainly the best of the few she had met. She was going to take great care of his son until he came back.

Later on that evening Tumalye sang to the rock again so that she could feed her baby for the night.

> Kaganga badu badu
> Nditolelumwana vangu
> Musule kwa pape.

> Open rock
> So that I may take my child
> Whose grandmother doesn't want him.

The rock opened and she found Musule safe and happy and while she fed him she hummed a tune. She held the baby for a while after he had finished then, as darkness approached, she put him back inside the rock and went to visit the wise woman.

'How is Musule?' the woman asked enthusiastically when Tumalye arrived.

'He is fine and thank you very much for all you have done for us,' Tumalye said gratefully as the woman handed her some food.

'Your mother has combed every corner of the village in search of you and the boy,' the wise woman told Tumalye

96

as she ate. 'She says she'll kill both of you, together with the baby.'

'But she can't do that,' Tumalye protested. 'Anyway she won't find me, nor will she find our precious Musule. I am only afraid for Musule's father; I don't even know where he has gone,' her voice was a little shaky as she said this.

'That one is the nicest young man in the village, Tumalye,' the wise woman said reassuringly, 'he loves you and the baby as a man should. But I also fear for him; your mother is a very cruel woman. I hope he takes good care of himself.'

'Do you know where he has gone?'

'Honestly, no,' the woman replied.

For the following month things went according to plan. Tumalye arrived at the rocks early each morning to feed her child, then she would collect a bundle of wood. She fed him in the afternoon and then waited until evening to feed him again. While the baby was asleep she made baskets to exchange for food. Each night she would pick up her bundle of wood and go home to the kind and wise woman.

One morning Tumalye asked the woman to accompany her to the rocks.

'Today Musule is one month old and I would like you to see how big he has grown. I also have a lot of wood and the baskets to bring home, so perhaps you could help me.'

The two women left for the rocks very early in the morning so that they would not be seen by the other villagers. Because they talked as they went along the distance seemed very short.

'We are already here,' exclaimed the wise woman suddenly and at the same moment Tumalye felt a thud in her breast and she almost fell down.

'What is is?' the older woman asked.

'I don't know, my body feels heavy and limp. I am sure that something has happened to the child!' she said tearfully.

The two women walked on, hesitating at every step then Tumalye, who was a little ahead, gave a sharp cry. The other woman drew near. The red stone was now quite close to them and there, at the foot of the nearest rock, lay a child's arm. It had been amputated with a very sharp knife. A little further away they saw a child's leg, then an ear and on top of one of the rocks was half of the child's head. Tumalye was trembling all over. She did not need to sing to make the red rock open for the lid was off and inside it lay one half of the dead child.

'This is my mother's doing!' cried Tumalye bitterly. She could scarcely believe her eyes although she knew that her mother was capable of doing great harm to the child.

'But how did she find out?' she gasped in the midst of her sobs.

The kind woman did not reply. Silently she collected the scattered pieces of the child and wrapped them in her own cloth.

'We must leave this place,' she said harshly when she had finished, 'The child has only just been killed and your mother might still be around; she must not catch us here.'

'But what do I tell his father? He will think I did not take care of Musule, the son he named, the son he loved . . .' the girl began to weep afresh:

> 'Vakomilumwana vangu he.
> Vavomilu Musule vangu he.
> Ndivemba ulutalamu.
> Ve dade Musule twinalukomi,
> Nde Muyago si yune.'

> They've killed my son.

They've killed my Musule.
I am crying bitterly.
We are in trouble, Musule's father,
But it isn't me.

The wise woman led Tumalye away from the scene in silence. When they were a good distance away from the rocks they stopped for a few moments and the wise woman advised Tumalye to go away with her dead child. 'You will not survive if we go home together,' she explained.

'I know. If the boy comes tell him what happened because we might never see each other again,' Tumalye whispered. Then, with the dead child on her back, she turned and walked away from her companion.

Tumalye walked for days stopping only occasionally to rest and weep for all that had happened. At night she slept under trees nursing her dead son but as soon as morning came she would leave her shelter and move on. Sometimes she wandered a little in search of water and wild fruits but she always avoided buildings, which were very few anyway. One day, however, when she felt she could walk no more, she decided to stop at the first hut she came to.

'Hodi!' she called when a hut came into view.

'Who are you?' came the reply.

'I am a lost traveller,' she called back.

After a few moments the door of the hut opened and an old woman came out. As soon as she saw Tumalye she invited her in then she asked abruptly, 'What brings you here with a dead body?' Tumalye was taken aback by the question and she wondered how the old woman could know that there was a dead child in her bundle, she kept her face calm, however.

'Aren't you surprised that I know you have a dead child?' the old woman persisted.

'No, I am not. You are old and you know everything,'
Tumalye told her. The old woman was very pleased with
this answer and after a short while she gave Tumalye
some food and a mat to sleep on.

Early the next morning Tumalye got up and lit the fire
then she picked up the gourd the old woman had placed
at the door in order to go and draw some water. As she
was leaving the old woman got up and called, 'Leave
your child with me.' Then she showed Tumalye where
she should go to draw the water.

Tumalye followed the old woman's instructions but she
walked fearfully for the path was very thick. It was
obvious that nobody else drew water from this place. At
last she reached what appeared to be the well and then
she almost cried out in horror at what she saw. There
were the heads of people, blood, and all sorts of dirty
things strewn around the water and the water itself was
very dirty. Nevertheless she filled the gourd and carried it
back to the old woman's hut.

'Did you find it?' the old woman asked as she went in.
'Yes.'

'Is it all right?'

'Yes,' Tumalye lied. At this the old woman laughed
then told her where she could draw clean water.

When Tumalye got back the second time she told the
old woman that she would like to continue her journey.

'No, you can't go today. I need firewood from the
forest. Can you bring it to me? I'll take care of your dead
baby.'

Tumalye went to the part of the forest which the old
woman had indicated to search for firewood but all she
found when she arrived were the bones of people lying
everywhere; there was not a single piece of dry wood in
sight. Then great fear overtook her. She wanted to run
away as fast as possible for she was now sure that this was
the land of man-eating witches. How could she leave the

place alive? And why did the old woman insist on keeping her dead son's body? Tumalye did not know what she could do. She looked around carefully but could not find any wood to take back and in the end she decided to return without it.

As soon as she reached the hut the old woman asked why she had brought no wood back with her.

'I sprained my foot and I had to come back to treat it before collecting any wood,' Tumalye lied. The old woman again appeared to be pleased with her answer then she showed Tumalye the correct place to go. This time Tumalye found plenty of good firewood to bring back to the old woman. By now Tumalye had made up her mind to leave in spite of not knowing where to go. When she told the old woman, however, she still refused to permit it.

'You must tell me all about your strange journey with the dead child,' she insisted. So Tumalye recounted her story and at the end the old woman sighed bitterly.

'You will be the first person to leave my hands,' she muttered. 'From the time you came I noticed that you were different. All the others have ended their lives here after collecting water and fire for their own flesh. In a moment my friends will be arriving, for they know about your presence here but I will hide you in my inner room. Do not stir, do not cough while you are there or else they will search you out and kill you. Instead I will give them the body of your baby.'

'No,' Tumalye shouted, 'not that. I have to find his father first so that we can bury him together.'

At that moment there was a lot of noise outside the hut and the old woman quickly hid Tumalye and her baby in the inner room. Almost immediately a number of old women walked into the hut and straight away made a big fire with the wood Tumalye had brought. When they had put a pot of water on the fire they asked for the victim but the old lady told them that Tumalye had gone out some time ago and had not returned.

'Has she run away?' one of them asked.

'I think so,' lied the old woman.

'If you have let her go with her dead child then you shall be our victim,' one of them added and immediately they began to search the house. Tumalye could hear the women poking about the corners of the hut but she remained safely hidden in the tiny inner room.

After a long search the women gave up and left one by one, promising to come back as soon as they had consulted their oracles as to where the victim was. When the last one had gone the old woman went to Tumalye's hiding place and told her that she must leave straightaway.

'Do not go to the west; keep going to the east all the time,' the old woman advised her as she set off with her bundle.

Tumalye walked along as quickly as she could for she dreaded being caught by the old women whose oracles might direct them towards her. Days and nights went by, however and she met no one, nor did she see any houses.

Several days later, when her feet were sore and tired, Tumalye stopped by a brook to drink its water and wash her clothes. Then she stepped into the water herself to get cool and clean. Her dead child rested on the bank still wrapped in the cloth the wise woman had placed around him. Just as she was about to finish washing Tumalye heard a man's voice:

'Pamwandi wakalavaga
Wali ni lileme
Umwana vangu alikwiya?'

The last time you washed
You were pregnant.
Where is my child?

102

Tumalye was startled; she looked about her and saw no one but still she gave her reply:

> Iliyuva likomile Umusule.
> Linondadzile tumusile
> Nyuve muyangu umusile.'

> My cruel mother killed Musule.
> Now I've come — we bury him and you too comrade
> Should bury him.

Tumalye then left the water and put on her clothes. When she had finished dressing she picked up the bundle containing her dead child and sat down on a stone, waiting. Her feet were swollen from walking and she was very weak from hunger. A few minutes passed then suddenly the boy appeared and took the dead child from her. He undid the bundle and looked at the pieces and at the other half then a tear dropped from his eyes. Without a word he went and buried the child in the sand by the brook. When he came back he had some leaves in his hand which he pounded on a stone, squeezing the liquid into the sores of Tumalye's feet.

'Now tell me what happened,' he spoke for the first time since his appearance but his voice was gentle and Tumalye poured out the whole story up until the time she had reached the brook.

'Your mother is dead,' the boy said very simply when she had finished. 'I killed her.' He waited for Tumalye to burst out in anger but she remained silent. 'I came back a week after you had left and the wise woman told me everything so I went in search of your mother who was still out to kill us. I found her one afternoon and shot her with my arrow. Nobody wept for her, not even your sisters, and they are now in my home which is very near here. Would you like to come and cook for me?'

Tumalye took his *nyengo*[1] and followed him home. He had built a very nice house near the brook and had already started a farm around it. Tumalye's sisters were overjoyed to see her again and then, together at last, they mourned for Musule.

[1] an instrument for cutting trees and grass, but also a symbol of male strength.

The Ordeal

There was once a girl who got married away from home but after giving birth to her first son she went back to show the child to her parents. This was the custom in her husband's country.

'You will stay with them for seven days and then you must bring back my son,' her husband told her on their last day together before she went away. 'Remember that he had some taboos which must be observed,' he added.

When the young woman arrived at her parents' home they were very happy to see her again and to see that her son was big and strong.

'My grandson is very healthy,' the girl's mother remarked as she held the little boy in her arms, and she felt proud as he wrestled to free himself in order to go back to his mother.

Everybody who saw the child admired him and felt happy that the young woman had brought him on a visit to her people, even though the young woman made it known to all her relatives that in her husband's country it was the custom that no one, apart from the mother, should wash the child or shave him. All her family accepted the girl's warning and promised not to try and help in those particular duties.

On the sixth day of her stay the young woman announced that she must get ready to leave since she would have to be home on the seventh day.

'Surely you will bring me some wood before you go, won't you?' her mother asked as soon as she heard the news.

'Of course I will, if you will take care of my son. He should never go into the woods,' the daughter replied.

Then the young woman went to collect wood in the forest, leaving her son with his grandmother. As soon as she had gone the girl's family were overcome by their curiosity; they had never known a child with so many taboos. It had never happened that any child in their village should only be washed and shaved by his mother! In most cases the elder sisters, aunts, sister's-in-law, grandmothers and cousins all co-operated in taking care of an infant. They could not believe their ears. This was the young woman's sixth day and since her arrival she had never left her son in anyone else's care. They had been allowed to hold the child but nothing more and now they could restrain themselves no longer. They wanted to prove that nothing would happen if they followed their own customs which included washing the child and shaving him, for he badly needed a hair cut.

Water was heated by an anxious woman and a razor was brought in readiness. The child was sleeping but his grandmother woke him up and put him into the warm water. Nothing happened. Then she washed him and still nothing happened, although in the course of washing him she discovered a large louse on his head.

'How could he escape keeping lice with so much hair?' she exclaimed, becoming very excited.

'But you've seen only one louse, there aren't any others,' corrected an aunt who was among the many spectators that had gathered around.

Without delay the child's grandmother killed the louse then she shaved the baby's head and immediately the child stopped breathing.

'He's dead!' hissed one of the onlookers.

'No, he's all right. He's sleeping,' muttered the grandmother who was now very nervous.

'But he is dead; you've killed him mother,' one of her daughters cried out accusingly. The woman was very much disturbed by this. She shook a finger at the daughter and repeated that the child was only sleeping, then she put the baby into bed and destroyed all evidence of the baby's bath and shave. All the visitors went away quickly and silently wishing that they had not been part of the tragic event.

After a while the young woman came back with her bundle of wood and dropped it down in the yard before rushing in to see if her son had been unhappy while she was away.

'May I have my child again?' she asked her mother as she hurried into the hut.

'He's still sleeping,' her mother lied in a weak voice, pretending to be cheerful.

'You have killed him, I know it,' the young woman suddenly shouted glaring at her mother who denied the accusation. The girl's sisters who were also in the house huddled together in a corner and waited; in a moment the young woman was screaming at the sight of her son. He was dead as she had feared and this was because of the louse her mother had killed. As she collected her things together ready to go home she wept bitterly then she was gone, taking her child with her. Even from a distance her family could hear her crying:

'What will my husband say?
He will think I came here to kill his son.'

She was still sobbing when she arrived home, the dead child in her arms. As she approached the house her husband came out and looked at his wife. He could tell from her face that she had done all she could to prevent her people from harming their son. He moved towards her and looked at the child then he shook his head and bit his lower lip. After a moment he asked, 'Who did it?'

'I think it was my mother,' she replied.

'Did she say so?'

'No, she denied it.' The young woman was trembling from head to toe, not knowing what her husband would do. She had never seen him get angry before but now his eyes were ablaze with anger. Foam was coming out of the sides of his mouth and his eyes were very red. He took the child from his wife and went back into the house; when he came out again he had his walking stick in his hand. His wife cowered in a corner of the yard.

'You stay here and make me some food. I'll be back very late,' he told her and with that he went away. The young woman crept into the house and looked for the corpse of her son. It was on the bed. She did not touch it anymore, only began to prepare some food for her husband. When it was ready she put it near the fire and waited.

The sun had long gone down and it was very dark but still her husband did not return. Midnight came and she was beginning to think that he must have left her completely when she heard him at the door. When he came into the room she asked him if he would eat something straight away.

'Not now,' he told her. 'There are many people out there who must pass through the ordeal before we bury our son and we don't have much time. You must come with me as well,' he added.

They went out together and the young woman was surprised to see a crowd of people from her own village; even her mother was there. Then the girl's husband led everyone to the site of the ordeal where a large fire was burning in a hole. Each person was expected to jump across the fire — those who managed to get across were

108

presumed innocent whilst those who fell into the hole were judged to be the guilty ones who had had a hand in the killing of the child.

First the husband jumped across, then his wife then followed a number of people collected by the young woman's sisters and aunts who had witnessed the death of the child. One woman crossed, another one followed and then another. But when the next one jumped she fell into the fire.

'Oh,' the people exclaimed, 'she's the one who held the child when he was shaved.'

There were cries and shouts from all around but the father of the dead child paid no attention. He only urged the people to hurry since day-break was coming and the ordeal must only take place under cover of night. When the turn of the child's grandmother came she also fell into the fire and the people looked at one another, grunting and whispering. At last everybody had crossed the flames and the two women were dead then the girl's husband told everyone to go back to their homes. As they slowly walked away he faced his wife and asked, 'Are you coming with me?'

'Yes,' she answered gratefully.

When they were alone again they buried their son quietly and mourned for him.

Some years passed and the couple had three other children, a boy and two girls. This time the woman refused to allow her children to go anywhere that was far away; either they remained at home or they went with her to the farms.

One day, when she went to visit the place where her mother had died, the woman discovered that a pumpkin was growing there. It was very big and of the type she liked, so she took it home sliced it, and put it in a pot to cook. Her husband was out hunting and she was pleased to have found something good to eat with the meat he would bring back with him. While the pumpkin was cooking the woman worked outside and after a while she asked her son to go in and add wood to the fire. The boy did not come back immediately so she sent her elder daughter to check that he had done as he was told, thinking that the boy must have gone off to play, but the girl did not come back either and this time the woman was worried.

'Let me go,' offered her last daughter.

'No, I'll go myself,' she said and walked into the kitchen. She sat down to blow the fire but stopped when she heard the pumpkin speak to her from the pot:

> 'Yuve ye wangungumye,
> Nayune ndihigungumila,
> Milu!'

> You ate me up,
> I'll eat you too,
> Swallowed!

Now she knew where the children had gone: the pumpkin had swallowed them. This time the woman did not wait to see her husband; instead she collected her own and her daughter's belongings and quickly they left the hut to seek refuge in another country. She knew that her own people would not receive her again; she also knew that if she stayed at home the ordeal would not be for her people this time, only for herself.

The Hare and the Hyena

The Hare and the Hyena were once great friends, such great friends in fact that they hunted and ate together each day. This state of affairs did not last for long, however, and their friendship came to an abrupt end when Mr Hare began his tricks.

One day the two friends caught a rabbit which they decided to roast for their dinner. Together they skinned it and prepared it for roasting on the big fire which was glowing in readiness.

Just as Hyena was placing the rabbit on the logs Hare began to pant and said, 'I am very thirsty. I do need a drink of water very badly.'

'Me too,' replied his friend.

'Do you know where to get it?' Hare asked.

'Oh, yes. The river is on that side.'

'In that case you had better go first while I watch over the meat then, when you come back, I'll be able to follow your footmarks.' As he spoke Hare watched Hyena's face closely. The Hyena immediately agreed to this plan and hurried away to the river. As soon as he was out of sight Hare quickly ate all the roasted meat, collected the bones and put them back on the fire. He then went to sleep a little distance away.

When Hyena came back he found the bones on the fire

and presumed that the meat had been burnt. He looked around for Hare and found him sleeping.

'Friend,' he shouted, 'how could you sleep while all the meat burned?'

'Oh, has it? What a pity—I was sleeping to keep off my thirst,' said Hare, yawning. He curled up again and went back to sleep so the Hyena left Hare alone and went hungry for the rest of the day.

When darkness came each animal went to sleep on his mat but in the middle of the night Hare was restless and decided to punish Hyena for not being quite satisfied about the meat. He got up quietly and taking his mat he covered the Hyena with it and beat him hard, then he ran back to his place to sleep. In the morning Hyena told Hare about the beatings during the night.

'It is strange that you do not know who did it,' said Hare with a smile.

'It was dark so I couldn't see. Was it you?' Hyena asked suspiciously.

Of course Hare denied it, but as the day went on he grew bolder and began to sing about what had happened. Then Hyena knew for certain that Hare was the source of all the evil that had taken place. At that moment he started running after the Hare and he does; so to this day. If the Hyena catches the Hare he will eat him.